DARK CORNERS
A PETER BLACK THRILLER

DAVID ARCHER

VINCE VOGEL

RIGHTHOUSE

ISBN-13: 978-1-63696-331-0

ISBN-10: 1-63696-331-5

Cover design by: Damonza

Printed in the United States of America

www.righthouse.com

www.instagram.com/righthousebooks

www.facebook.com/righthousebooks

twitter.com/righthousebooks

PRAISE FOR THE PETER BLACK SERIES

"A Twisting Tale of Murder, Revenge and Love."

AMAZON REVIEW

"I read the Orphan X series, the Reacher series, the Gray Man series, and many others. It's rare to find authors whose books grab you like this one did."

AMAZON REVIEW

"...the action is almost nonstop and you're not prepared for what happens on any given moment."

AMAZON REVIEW

"Ranks with the best of the genre: Flynn, Thor, Ludlum, Hagberg, etc..."

AMAZON REVIEW

PETER BLACK THRILLERS

Burden of the Assassin (Book 1)
The Man Without A Face (Book 2)
Unpunished Deeds (Book 3)
Hunter Killer (Book 4)
Silent Shadows (Book 5)
The Last Run (Book 6)
Dark Corners (Book 7)
Ghost Operative (Book 8)

PROLOGUE

AFGHANISTAN, 2007

A REMOTE VALLEY STRETCHES OUT, FLANKED BY imposing mountains. As the wind travels over the land, it carries whispers of conversations and unsettled dust, adding an eerie aura to the scene.

Three figures, distinguishable only as men from their size and posture, kneel on the valley floor, their hands cruelly tied behind their backs. The rough ropes bite into their skin and black hoods cover their heads, rendering them faceless. Every short, sharp breath they take rustles the fabric, the world outside muffled.

Six shadowy figures, members of the local Taliban, stand sentinel around the prisoners. Among them, a teenage boy, Ali, stands out starkly. The weight of what's to come makes him appear more like a child lost among wolves than a warrior in the making.

One of the men is fussing with a video camera. He

meticulously checks every setting, ensuring the focus is just right and the view is capturing the entire grim tableau. "Right," he commands in crisp Arabic, his voice reverberating eerily in the vast valley. "Make sure your masks are up."

The men dutifully raise their face veils, revealing eyes that show a mix of resolve, fervor, and—in some—a glimmer of doubt. The father of the teenage boy helps him, lifting his veil and making sure it stays in place. Their eyes meet, and the father offers a gentle, reassuring smile.

"Are you ready to witness the work of God, Ali?" he asks, his voice tender yet laced with an undeniable fervor.

Ali nods, trying to mask his apprehension. "Yes, Papa."

His father's gaze hardens, and he continues with gravity, "It is a gruesome, brutal task. But it is essential for our people's future. For the foundation of the caliphate."

A tense silence stretches, only to be broken by the camera operator. "We're rolling."

As the red recording light blinks to life, Ali's father steps forward, standing ominously behind the three prisoners, assuming the grim stance of an executioner. The wind picks up, a mournful howl that seems to sense the looming tragedy.

"These kuffur," Ali's father proclaims in English with a voice that reverberates across the expanse of the valley, "have trespassed on our holy land." With a swift motion, he rips the hoods off the prisoners one by one. Each face that is revealed reflects a cocktail of emotions: fear, defiance, resignation. "They infiltrated our sacred places, spreading their venomous deceit," he continues. "They masquerade as saviors, as bearers of charity. Yet their true intent is clear—to obliterate our faith, to render us weak and dependent."

Every word he speaks is imbued with conviction, the echoes of his voice underscoring the gravity of the situation. Ali watches on from the sidelines, torn between admiration for his father's command and a burgeoning dread for what is about to transpire.

Addressing not just those present but the unseen viewers of the recording, Ali's father issues a stern warning. "To anyone contemplating alliance with these foreign aid agencies that dare tread on our soil—" he declares, lifting a machete high. The polished blade catches the sun, gleaming menacingly. "You are unwelcome. Your presence is a declaration of war against our faith."

As the machete arcs downwards, intent on delivering its grim message, a sudden, sharp report pierces the tense air of the valley. Before the blade can find its mark, Ali's father is struck in the chest by a .50 caliber round shot from a Barrett M82. The shock is instant. The machete clatters to the ground, the sun now reflecting off a growing dark stain spreading across the gray fabric of his kameez.

Time seems to slow. Birds take flight, their wings flapping in an abrupt and disjointed rhythm. Ali's scream, a mixture of disbelief and anguish, fills the void left in the aftermath of the gunshot. The scene devolves into chaos. The members of the Taliban scramble, searching for the source of the shot, their earlier assurance replaced by panic. The fate of the prisoners, momentarily reprieved from imminent death, hangs uncertainly in the balance of a valley now reverberating with turmoil.

The abrupt gunfire has set the scene alight with frenzy. Men scuttle like cornered animals, their calm veneer shattered in an instant. The dust, previously still, now swirls violently, mirroring the bedlam on the ground. The sun, once a neutral observer, casts long shadows that dance menacingly from the panicked men.

Kalashnikovs, which moments ago lay idle by their sides, are now clutched desperately by trembling hands and everywhere there's movement: men shouting, trying to form a defensive perimeter, their voices a cacophony of confusion and fear. But even as they rally, their invisible assailant begins picking them off. Each shot is precise, calculated—a sharp, resonating report followed by the thud of a body hitting the ground. Dust clouds puff upward with each fallen fighter, making it seem as if the earth itself is gasping in horror.

Amidst it all, Ali, the teenage boy, is paralyzed. His eyes, wide with terror, dart around, processing the unfolding massacre. Close by, one of the Taliban, perhaps only a few years older than Ali, desperately tries to return fire on the unseen force taking them out one by one. But it's clear he doesn't know where to aim. Each burst from his rifle seems more an act of desperation than defense. And then, like those before him, he too crumples to the ground, a red stain blossoming on his chest.

Another, thinking he's found the sniper's location, fires off a full magazine in the general direction of a distant ridge. But his hope is short-lived; he's cut down mid-reload, the magazine falling to the ground, reflecting brief glints of sunlight before being swallowed up by dust.

The camera, forgotten in the melee, continues to record, its lens now smeared with dust and blood splatter, capturing a scene of unbridled mayhem.

Ali, though young, is not without survival instincts. Using the gathering dust as cover, he drops to the ground, pressing his body flat against the earth, as if willing it to swallow him whole. His heart pounds loudly in his ears, each beat a frantic drum of survival. The fallen machete, the instrument meant to execute the captives, now seems to offer a glimmer of hope. Crawling slowly, Ali reaches out and grips its handle, the cool metal instilling a small sense of purpose amidst the chaos.

As the last of the Taliban fighters is gunned down, the valley descends into a haunting silence, broken only by the rapid breaths of Ali and the distant cawing of a bird. The prisoners, still bound but alive, shift uncomfortably, their previous dread now replaced with cautious hope.

From a nearby ridge, a silhouette appears—tall, armed, and daunting. His approach is slow and methodical, a stark contrast to the disarray of the men he's just dispatched.

Ali, clutching the machete, contemplates his slim chances. Does he flee, confront the approaching figure, or continue to hide, hoping the stranger will overlook a lone, terrified boy?

The weight of his decision, combined with the trauma of the past few minutes, threatens to overwhelm him. But one thing is clear: Ali is the last man standing, the sole survivor of a violent interruption to what was meant to be a display of power. Now, with the tables turned, he must decide his next move in this deadly game of survival.

The dust-laden air of the valley churns, giving life to the emerging silhouette, a specter of death, advancing with deliberate intent. Ali's eyes, clouded with a mix of despair and defiance, dart to his fallen father's Kalashnikov. In a last-ditch effort, he throws down the machete, lunges, fingers outstretched, grasping for the weapon that could buy him a chance.

But even as hope ignites, it's snuffed out. A bullet, precision-guided, strikes the rifle, sending it spinning away from Ali's desperate grip, rendering him once more defenseless.

It is then, as he contemplates throwing his body after the gun, that something stops him. From the ground nearby, a feeble voice struggles through labored breaths. "Ali..." his father rasps. Despite his weakened state, he is vehemently shaking his head, the message clear: to grab the rifle will be to die.

So instead, Ali rushes to his father's side, cradling the dying man's head. Hot tears course down the teenager's cheeks, blurring his vision. "Dad, what do I do?" he chokes out, every ounce of his being crying out for guidance.

His father's eyes, clouded with pain but sharp with resolve, lock onto Ali's. "Surrender, my son," he whispers, each word a labor. "Surrender now... and fight to die another day."

Before Ali can process the heavy counsel, his father's life force ebbs away, leaving the boy all alone amidst the carnage.

The sun, now beginning its descent, casts the approaching figure in an almost ethereal glow. As he nears, details emerge: devilish eyes masked behind dark shades, a swathe of pale skin peeking through the dust and grime of the battlefield, and what to Ali seems to be a cruel smirk playing on his lips.

Ali's gaze drops to his father's side, spotting the handgun in its holster. Maybe his father is wrong. Maybe now is as good a time to fight as any. In a blur of motion, he snatches up the pistol, turning on the looming assassin with trembling hands. But his adversary is faster, more experienced. In a swift move, the man has ahold of Ali and disarms the boy, the handgun clattering uselessly to the side. Rough hands then twist Ali around, zip-tying his wrists with brutal efficiency.

Defeated, Ali is pushed to the ground, his face pressed against the dusty earth. The weight of loss and helplessness bears down on him, and he weeps, his tears mixing with the soil.

The assassin, seemingly unfazed by the turmoil around him, activates a cell phone. His voice, cold and emotionless, slices through the valley's mournful silence. "This is Azrael. I've secured the aid workers. Only one survivor among the targets. Some kid."

Through his grief, Ali's mind latches on to that name: Azrael. The Angel of Death. In that heart-wrenching moment, a young boy's sorrow hardens into resolve. He now knows the name of his father's killer, a name he vows never to forget.

ONE

BEIRUT, FIFTEEN YEARS LATER - TRINITY SUNDAY

THE STREETS OF BEIRUT, BATHED IN A SILVERY nocturnal glow, hum with a quiet intensity. Yet beneath the tranquility of the night, old vendettas silently pulse.

A van, a mere silhouette against the dimly lit streets, speeds through downtown Beirut. Its engine growls, mirroring the urgency of the night. Every twist and turn it takes intertwines with the rhythm of a ticking clock.

Inside, five men sit, their faces obscured by the scant light. Eyes, sharp and unyielding, give away nothing. The air within is dense, pregnant with anticipation.

Amidst the night-time hum of Beirut, an auditorium stands, illuminated by the moon's soft glow. The sound of a congregation in harmonious chorus flows from the arched windows of the building. The age-old hymn "Holy, Holy, Holy! Lord God Almighty!" rises, a beacon of faith in the deep of night, its purity oblivious to the shadows gathering outside.

The first van slides into the auditorium's parking lot, its tires crunching gravel. Almost simultaneously, two more vans emerge from the night, converging from different directions. The doors of all three swing open in a choreographed cadence.

Figures emerge, their count reaching fifteen. The minimal light paints them in shades of gray, but their collective intent is clear. The juxtaposition of the sacred hymn resonating from within and the gathering assembly outside amplifies the tension, making the weight of the impending moment all the more profound.

The clock, indifferent to the drama unfolding, continues its march, and as the hymn reaches its crescendo, it becomes evident that Beirut's midnight hour holds a destiny yet to be unveiled.

The silver glow of the moonlight paints a deceptive serenity over the old buildings of the city. But in the shadows, chaos unfurls with ruthless precision.

The fifteen men move in concert like a dark tide. As one, they descend upon the security guards at the main entrance with brutal efficiency. Flashes from their AK47s briefly illuminate the night. The unsuspecting guards crumple, the grim harbingers of what's to come.

Three teams splinter off, each heading to a different entrance to the main concert hall. With ruthless efficiency, chains are produced, and they begin sealing the fire doors. Their intent is clear: to ensure there is no escape.

Inside, the sprawling building reverberates with the powerful chorus of "Holy, holy, holy!" The notes rise and twist, creating a cocoon of sound that masks the sinister preparations taking place just beyond.

The doors fastened, the operatives disperse, their movements swift and purposeful. The grand concert hall beckons. Inside, the crowd remains engrossed in their spiritual connection, their unified voices creating a beautiful yet tragically deceptive bubble of security. Four cameramen, their focus on capturing the event, are startled as dark-clad figures appear behind them. The cold steel of a gun barrel pressed against their backs delivers a chilling message.

"Keep filming the stage," a voice, raspy and demanding, hisses in Arabic. The gravity of the situation sinks in, and the camera crew, paralyzed by fear but guided by instinct, comply.

As the gunmen infiltrate deeper into the hall, the veil of safety begins to fray. The once harmonious singing falters, replaced by a rising tide of murmurs and anxious glances. The transition is stark: The spiritual haven is rapidly morphing into a chamber of angst.

Faces, once lit by joy and devotion, now reflect dawning realization and fear. As the clock's relentless ticking merges with the quickening heartbeats of the gathered masses, the grim theater set by the assailants reaches its crescendo. The night, once a refuge, now holds them hostage in its cold embrace, the audience breathless as they anticipate the next phase.

It soon arrives.

The soft glow of the stage lights casts long, menacing shadows as the leader of the group strides onto it and makes his way toward a priest who had been conducting the singing only moments ago. The ambiance, once filled with harmony and devotion, is now tainted with an oppressive dread.

Without hesitation, the leader strikes the priest, a resounding slap that echoes the cold brutality of the moment. The priest's microphone, once a conduit of love and spiritual guidance, is wrenched away.

With a guttural roar, the leader screams into it: "Allahu akbar!" The words, charged with a jarring aggression, reverberate through the auditorium. His gunmen raise their voices in unison, their refrain of "Allahu akbar!" amplifying the chilling proclamation.

Before the terror-stricken audience can fully process the sudden, horrifying shift, the menacing rattle of assault rifles fills the air. A torrent of bullets begins sweeping through the rows, each shot snuffing out a life, a dream, a prayer. The pews, which moments ago held families, friends, and lovers, become monuments to horror.

A panic ensues, raw and primal. The instinct to survive overtakes the crowd, and a frenzied stampede erupts. Bodies press against bodies, the weak trampled by the strong, as terror renders humanity's better angels mute. The cries of the fallen, the pleas of the trapped, form a heart-wrenching counterpoint to the relentless gunfire.

Through this macabre dance, the cameramen, trapped in their own nightmare, continue to roll. The gunmen guarding them, ever watchful, ensure that each horrifying moment is captured, orchestrating a symphony of fear for the world to witness. "Keep filming," they growl like dogs. Directing them with cold precision, they ensure that the lenses focus on the faces of the terror-stricken, the fallen, making certain that the world won't forget this night.

As the clock continues its unforgiving march, the concert hall, once a beacon of hope and unity, is drowned in darkness and despair. The chilling harmony of the gunmen's cries of "Allahu akbar!" the deafening roar of their weapons, and the heart-rending screams of the innocent converge, crafting a nightmare from which Beirut may never awaken.

———

OUTSIDE THE BELEAGUERED CONCERT HALL, a cacophony of sirens wails into the night, their blue and red lights painting the Beirut streets in urgent, strobing patterns. The very fabric of the city seems to tremble beneath the weight of the unfolding catastrophe.

First to arrive are the ambulances, their drivers wide-eyed, the tires screeching to a halt, leaving trails of rubber on the asphalt. From another direction, police and Special Forces approach, their armored vehicles storming in with tactical precision. Soldiers, dressed in full tactical gear, disembark swiftly, rifles at the ready, surveying the scene with trained eyes, their every movement broadcasting disciplined urgency.

Yet just as they are setting up a perimeter, the roar of military trucks signifies the army's arrival. Troops pour out, their camouflaged forms blending into the night but their intent clear—to take charge and control the situation.

The chaos outside mirrors the devastation within. The multitude of emergency services, each vital in its own right, now seems to hinder more than help. Radios crackle with overlapping transmissions, the myriad of languages and codes only intensifying the bedlam. Leaders from each outfit, chests puffed up with importance, shout orders, often contradicting one another. Hand gestures fly. Arguments ignite. Egos clash.

And in the meantime, in the heart of it all, the auditorium stands silent and wounded, waiting for someone, anyone, to take the definitive lead in its rescue.

INSIDE THE CONCERT HALL, an eerie silence begins to settle, punctuated only by sporadic, heart-wrenching screams that echo throughout the vast space. It's a chilling aftermath, the air heavy with the acrid smell of gun residue, blood, and fear. The once grand hall, which had reverberated with melodies of faith and unity only minutes ago, is now a mausoleum of the innocent.

The harsh overhead lights cast a grotesque luminescence over the scene, revealing piles upon piles of bodies, thrown together in a macabre tableau of tragedy. Shoes, belongings, and shattered glass litter the floor. Here a child's toy, there a fallen crucifix.

The terrorists move methodically, their actions cold and calculated. Every step they take, every movement, is deliberate. No rush, no haste, just a mechanical progression through the hall to ensure no survivors remain.

One of them, his boots crunching over shattered remnants, spots a woman's foot peeking out from under the seating. With cold detachment, he aims and fires, the report of his gun echoing loudly. The foot jerks once and then falls limp.

Elsewhere, a faint cough pierces the quiet. It's a fragile,

desperate sound. Another terrorist, attuned to any sign of life, immediately zeroes in on its source. He listens closely, head tilted slightly, narrowing his focus to a wing of seats. Beneath them, the faint, raspy breathing of a survivor is audible.

A man, bloodied and terrified, looks out from his hiding spot, his eyes wide with dread. "No! No!" he pleads, hands raised in a futile gesture of surrender. But mercy isn't on the agenda tonight. The gunshot is swift, its finality ringing in the vast emptiness of the auditorium.

As these final murmurs of life are extinguished, the grim dance of death continues, every corner of the hall a testament to the horrors of this most fateful night, the bodies scattered everywhere.

The remaining cameramen, their faces pallid and slick with sweat, are shadows of their former selves. Trembling violently, they're trapped in a nightmarish scenario that none could have imagined when they arrived earlier to film the joyous occasion. Their equipment, meant to capture moments of faith and unity, is now a tool of terror in the hands of these invaders.

One of the gunmen approaches, his movements deliberate and predatory. "Point it on him," he orders venomously, nodding toward the central figure on the stage.

With shaking hands, the cameramen redirect their lenses, framing the imposing leader on the stage. The sharp glare of the stage lights casts dramatic shadows over him, making his features seem even more menacing.

He takes a deep breath, standing tall and defiant against the backdrop of devastation. "Allahu akbar," he declares with conviction, his voice trembling across the hall like a wave hitting the shoreline.

Before the gravity of his proclamation has a moment to sink in, shots ring out again. The gunmen have turned their weapons on the cameramen, executing the final witnesses with ruthless precision. One by one, they slump to the ground, their bodies joining the grim tapestry of the fallen.

Another gunman approaches the equipment. With a swift movement, he reaches down, switching off each camera.

In the stillness that then settles over the scene, the terrorists exchange glances, nodding almost imperceptibly. They know what comes next. Each man moves to one of three large duffels that they have brought with them. With swift, practiced movements, they unzip the bags.

From inside, they retrieve small, unassuming devices, no larger than a finger. Wrapped securely in condoms for waterproofing and ease of insertion, they glisten ominously under the overhead lights. The true purpose of these devices is not immediately clear, but the methodical manner with which the gunmen handle them indicates their sinister intent.

Two gunmen work together for each victim. One holds open the mouth of the deceased while the other, with a detached efficiency, forces the device down the throat. There's no gentleness in their actions. It's a brutal process, made even more chilling by the lack of resistance from the lifeless victims. The muffled sounds of latex against flesh and the occasional grunt from the gunmen as they ensure the placement are the only sounds that pierce the eerie silence of the hall.

As they move from body to body, there's a palpable

tension in the air. Each insertion, each step, brings them closer to the realization of a plan that remains shrouded in mystery, but its malevolence is clear. Whatever the next phase is, it promises to be as terrifying, if not more so, than what has already transpired.

———

As the clock strikes midnight, the atmosphere outside the building is churning with tension. The hour marks a tangible transition from hope to desperate action. Shadows move surreptitiously, the dim lights reflecting off helmets and visors. On one side of the concert hall, the special forces are assembled, instruments of penetration at the ready, every breath syncing with the heartbeat of the operation.

Hushed whispers intertwine with covert hand gestures, commands traveling swiftly through a cadre of unyielding gazes. Expert hands place explosive charges with precision along the formidable wall of the concert hall.

The night is shattered as the explosives detonate, a symphony of concussive blasts rendering the wall vulnerable. With engineered precision, a breach forms, a wave of debris and dust mushrooming into the midnight air, heralding the onset of the next phase of the operation.

The muted hum intensifies, climaxing with the sharp sizzle of gas canisters launched inward, hurtling through the breach. They skitter across the hall's floor, spinning and releasing their contents, filling the air with thick, white clouds designed to incapacitate. The special forces are finally ready to breach the building, the newly created opening serving as their gateway amidst the clouds of incapacitating gas.

The fight is instantaneous.

As soon as the special forces move in, their progression is immediately halted by the terrorists, equipped with gas masks, prepared for this exact scenario. The hall, filled with an eerie, foggy glow, becomes an arena of fierce combat as gunfire erupts, reverberating through the vastness of the building.

Bullets ricochet off walls, bright muzzle flashes punctuate the smoky darkness, and shouts of commands intertwine with the screams of the wounded. The battle is intense but brief, the superior training and tactics of the special forces quickly overcoming the terrorists.

As the smoke begins to clear, the magnitude of the operation starts to take shape. While scouring the fallen terrorists they discover high-tech comms earpieces, still warm from the terrorists' ears.

One of the men places an earpiece into his own ear. Muffled static comes back and something else: a man's breathing. Then it goes dead.

The revelation sends a chilling ripple through the unit. They've managed to secure the building and neutralize the immediate threat, but a lingering unease remains. The puppeteer, the one orchestrating this horrific act from the shadows, is still out there.

TWO

BEIRUT, THE NEXT DAY

The sun rises over Beirut, casting a muted orange hue over the city. The normally bustling streets are eerily quiet, weighed down by the grief of the previous night's horror. Birds that usually serenade the dawn seem stifled, as if even they sense the city's latest sorrow.

Throughout the day, the grim task of accounting for the deceased has ensued. The once-vibrant auditorium now resembles a war zone, scarred by violence and filled with the remnants of chaos. Emergency workers clad in white overalls move with a somber precision.

The sheer number of victims is staggering. Body bags line up row upon row along the auditorium's parking lot, each one a life, a story, a family shattered. The sight is gut-wrenching, even for the most seasoned first responders, some of whom take occasional breaks, stepping outside the broken building to catch their breath, wipe away tears, or simply stare into the distance.

The city's morgues are woefully ill-equipped to handle such a mass casualty event. As a result, vans and trucks are dispatched, shuttling between the auditorium and multiple morgues throughout Beirut. It's a haunting caravan of death, winding its way through Beirut's narrow streets, an unending procession that seems to go on for hours.

At each morgue, grim-faced workers receive the bodies, their facilities quickly overwhelmed. Refrigeration units fill up rapidly, forcing some to make use of makeshift cold storage solutions, while others have to turn to neighboring cities for assistance.

As for the populace, throughout Beirut, there's an undercurrent of tension. Rumors circulate, some born of genuine concern, others the product of fear and speculation. Whispers of other potential threats keep everyone on edge, and security checkpoints mushroom throughout the city. Beirut, a city that has known its fair share of violence, finds itself in the throes of a nightmare once again, a chilling reminder of the fragility of peace.

In a corner of a discreet rooftop café, one man, however, sits among the city's trepidation with an air of nonchalance.

The warm aroma of his freshly brewed tea mixes with the faint scent of jasmine from the nearby trellises. The wrought-iron chairs and tables around him are mostly empty, an unusual sight for a place that is generally abuzz with patrons this time of the day.

Given last night's horror, though, it's not surprising.

The man's eyes flit to the screen of a sleek smartphone. On it, a sophisticated app displays several pulsating dots, scattered strategically across a map of Beirut. Each dot is connected to a GPS signal. And each signal is nestled deep within a victim, who now lays motionless on a gurney in the basements of seven hospitals scattered across the city and its neighboring towns.

Yet it isn't only GPS tags inside the bodies of those poor people. Something else is nestled deep inside. Something that the world will soon find about.

The man's lips curl into a slight, self-satisfied smirk. While the city is consumed by grief and chaos, he finds himself in the eye of the storm, quietly orchestrating what comes next.

He leans back in his chair, taking one last look at the wounded city unfurling all around him. The final phase of his plan is about to begin—the cherry on the cake, if you will —and Beirut, still reeling from last night's terror, has no idea of the further devastation that awaits it in just a few seconds.

His fingers move swiftly across the screen, typing a six-digit code with precision: 40—the age of the Prophet Muhammad when he received his first revelation—99—for the ninety-nine names of Allah—and 37—the age his father was when he died.

He barely has time to set the phone down when the first blast shatters the relative calm. It is followed by another, and another. Each explosion is a thunderous testament to his meticulous planning. The sound waves bounce off build-ings, creating an ominous chorus of destruction that rever-berates throughout Beirut's neighborhoods.

Columns of smoke rise rapidly, merging into a thick, ashy veil that begins to obscure the once-clear evening sky. The familiar chaotic soundtrack of the city transforms.

Honking horns and yelling street vendors are replaced with the shrill of a million car alarms, screams of panic, and the relentless wailing of emergency sirens.

At the café, the man remains unmoved. There is grim satisfaction evident in the taut lines of his face and the glint in his eyes. From his central location, he has a panoramic view of the devastation unfolding. Fire, smoke, and the cries of the city erupt all around him. A waiter, initially frozen in shock, approaches hesitantly, his face a mask of fear and confusion. "Sir, we need to evacuate. It's not safe here."

The man doesn't respond immediately. Instead, he takes one last, sweeping look at the city, as if imprinting this moment forever in his memory. Then, standing up, he nods at the waiter. "Of course," he says, his voice betraying no emotion. Leaving a few bills on the table, he moves with purpose, descending a set of stone steps into the street and disappearing into the tapestry of Beirut's bustling labyrinth.

Without hurry, he walks past the frightened bystanders, not one of them acknowledging him in any way, their focus elsewhere, on the plume of smoke and dust rising from the direction of the nearest hospital, on the cries and sirens echoing up to the heavens. The man fades into the streets, another faceless figure in a city that has just been irrevocably changed.

He pulls out his phone once more and dials a number he knows by heart. Almost immediately, as if the person on the other end has been eagerly awaiting his call, the line connects. Without preamble, he speaks. "It is done."

A brief pause ensues, filled with the ambient noises of sirens, distant screams, and the inescapable noise of devastation. Then a voice, chilling in its calmness, responds, "Allahu akbar."

There's a tangible satisfaction in that voice, a pleasure derived from chaos. It continues, reveling in the moment, "Today is a great day for the caliphate."

The man takes a deep breath. "But tomorrow will be greater. Now make sure Hezbollah pay the rest of the money into the account."

"Of course. I'll get on the phone now, get them to release the funds." The voice on the line, as if sensing his thoughts, delivers a final statement. "Now it is time for you to come home, Musa."

"Yes," Musa replies as he drifts past the stunned people. "It is time for us to paint our masterpiece, Ali."

THREE

NEW YORK, USA

IN THE HEART OF A WARM, INVITING WASHINGTON Heights apartment, the aroma of a home-cooked meal fills the air. Peter Black, his rugged appearance contrasting the elegant surroundings, is seated at a dining table. Across from him, his son Michael and Michael's girlfriend, Mayu. Both students at Columbia, their youthful energy brings a vibrant contrast to Peter's experienced, weathered demeanor.

As Michael carves a roast beef, Peter can't help but marvel at the young man's maturity. He's proud of him, especially after the life he's had, losing his mother at fourteen, then the next years as a fugitive alongside Peter. Those years were tough. But now he's at college, living with his fiancé in this nice place, the owner of a good life. It's a testament to the kid's resolve.

Mayu, noticing Peter's silent observation, smiles.

"Michael's become quite the chef," she says, pride evident in her voice.

Peter nods appreciatively, taking a bite of the potato dauphinoise. "It's delicious," he praises, genuinely impressed.

The conversation flows easily, traversing a wide range of topics. They discuss Mayu's studies at Columbia, Michael's plans for the future, and current affairs. Michael hesitates for a moment before adding, "Did you hear about the recent stuff in Beirut, Dad? It's been all over the news."

Peter nods gravely, recognizing the gravity of the situation but choosing not to delve deeper, preferring instead to introduce lighter topics to the conversation.

The evening, filled with laughter and heartfelt moments, is a testament to the bond they share. Amidst the backdrop of Washington Heights, within the four walls of Michael and Mayu's cozy little apartment, they find comfort and warmth in each other's company.

As the evening reaches its end, however, Peter, realizing there's never going to be the perfect moment, becomes all serious. The lights above seem to dim ever so slightly as if sensing the change in mood. Taking a deep breath and struggling momentarily to maintain eye contact, he says, his voice shaking, "I've decided recently that I need to be honest with you both. I don't want any secrets between us. That's why I need to tell you that..."

"You're not really working on oil tankers," Michael finishes for him. "You've rejoined the CIA."

Peter is a little taken aback. "You knew?"

Both Michael and Mayu nod.

"Yes, Dad," Michael says. "We knew."

"It's been pretty clear you've not been going away to sea," Mayu adds. "Not once has any of your clothing returned smelling of the ocean or of oil. I'd expect after two months on an oil tanker to at least smell one or the other."

"And the last two trips," Michael interjects, "you've come back with wounds you claimed were caused by welding accidents, but they looked remarkably like bullet wounds."

Peter offers a sheepish smile. "I guess I underestimated both of you. Thought I was getting better at covering things up."

Michael leans forward, earnestly looking at Peter. "Look, Dad, did you really think you could hide that type of stuff from us?"

Peter sighs, running his hand through his graying hair. "I was hoping to keep you both out of it."

Mayu takes Peter's hand. "We're not asking for details, Peter. But you should be honest with us."

Michael nods, adding, "We're grown adults now. And while we'll always worry about you, it's important for us to be on the same page. No more stories, Dad. Just the truth."

Peter looks from Michael to Mayu, feeling a mix of gratitude and regret. "I promise," he says firmly. "From now on, only the truth."

———

PETER STEPS out of the apartment building. The streets of Washington Heights come alive around him—the chatter of the people, the distant siren of an ambulance, the soft hum of city life. He takes a moment, allowing the weight of the recent conversation to sink in, feeling both lighter and yet burdened by the knowledge that his family knows he's back with the agency, knowing that they will worry about him.

As he navigates the bustling streets, pulling up his coat collar against the gathering wind, his phone vibrates. Peter pulls it from his pocket, glances at the screen, then answers.

The voice on the other end is familiar, gravelly, and bears a touch of impatience. "Peter, it's Knight."

Peter stiffens. "I wasn't expecting to hear from you so soon."

A pause. Then, "You ready to go back to work?"

Peter hesitates, glancing back at the apartment building where his son resides. The weight of responsibility tugs at him. Yet the call of duty, a force he's known and grappled with for most of his life, beckons.

Taking a deep breath, he responds, "When do we start?"

There's a momentary silence on the other end, then Knight says, "Pack your bags. I'll brief you en route."

As Peter ends the call, the city's ambient noise seems to amplify. It's as if life itself is pulsating around him, reminding him of the dual path he treads—family and duty, a balance he must maintain.

FOUR

NEW YORK

AMBER STREETLIGHTS CAST A DIM GLOW THROUGH the rain-soaked windows of a Williamsburg apartment. The city's relentless energy seems somewhat subdued, giving way to the silent hum of a million souls preparing to rest. But inside one particular apartment, activity persists into the early hours.

The living room is a fusion of organized chaos and just plain old chaos. Articles, photographs, and scribbled notes cover the walls. At a desk, amidst a collection of fast-food cartons and cold coffee cups, sits Kara Tate. With her raven-black hair tied in a messy bun, eyes squinting against the glare of a laptop screen, and fingers racing across the keyboard, she epitomizes the rabid determination of the investigative journalist. The kind of determination that comes with knowing you are close to a story that could shake the foundations of the city's powerful. Open some eyes to the iniquity happening around them.

The piece she's writing is the culmination of months of work. It is titled: "Shadows in the Gallery: The Arts District Financial Fraud." She writes:

THE ARTS DISTRICT in the city has always been a bustling hub of creativity, where avant-garde artists, vintage stores, and quirky cafes abound. However, beneath the sheen of paint and the vibrant performances, there's a darker side, one of financial deception.

Through my elaborate network of sources and a little undercover work, I have discovered four main branches of fraud that is rampant in our city's art scene.

KARA LEAVES it there for the moment, taking a break to review her work critically. Engrossed in her thoughts on structuring the next part of her article, she barely registers the soft glow of her phone. The silhouette of New York City sprawls outside her tenth-floor window, but it's the incoming email notification that captures her attention. It's from a confidential source in one of the galleries.

The email has no subject or words. It is blank, except for an attachment. Kara's heart rate accelerates as she clicks on the video file. The scene that unfolds is raw and unfiltered. In the dim lighting, the shaky cameraphone captures a loading bay, bathed in darkness, with only the intermittent glow of external lights. The muffled sounds of the city in the background provide an eerie soundtrack.

The footage is jumpy, as if taken hastily, from a concealed vantage point. As Kara strains her eyes to make out the details, a dump truck enters the scene, backing up towards the camera. It comes to a stop and its trailer begins to tip, dropping its load. The cascade of white powder catches Kara's attention. What is it? Drugs? Chemicals? The ambiguity gnaws at her.

In rapid succession, shadowy, out-of-focus figures move with well-practiced efficiency, transferring the powder into barrels using shovels. The sealing of each barrel seems methodical, almost ritualistic. The hum of a forklift breaks the monotonous sounds of the loading bay as it moves the barrels seamlessly into four waiting vans.

Suddenly, Kara's heart is in her throat as one of the figures turns, his face catching a glint of light, revealing a neatly trimmed black beard. His eyes seem to pierce through the dim light straight into the lens of the camera. He yells, the words indistinct but the tone alarmingly authoritative.

A rush of movement blurs the scene. The video becomes more erratic as the source seems to scramble for safety. And just as abruptly as it began, the video cuts off.

Kara sits back, the afterimage of the footage burnt into her retinas. The risk her source had taken was palpable. She could almost feel the panic, the desperate bid for escape. She grips the edge of her desk, processing the gravity of the situation. What was that they were barreling up? Something they were desperate not to have filmed.

The video's abrupt end leaves a weighty silence in its wake. Kara's initial shock gives way to a profound concern for Amy, her source. She snatches the phone back up, her fingers moving with urgency as she dials Amy's number. The monotonous tone of the unanswered call grates on her nerves.

Voicemail.

Kara curses under her breath, disconnecting the call and trying again, hoping for a different result. But again, voicemail.

A storm of scenarios whirls in her mind. What if Amy's been caught gathering evidence for Kara's story? What if she's in danger? Or worse?

Kara rakes a hand through her hair, biting her lip in worry.

After a few tense moments of contemplation, her resolve hardens. She can't just sit here and do nothing. Every second counts.

She stands up, pulling on her jacket. With swift steps, she crosses the wooden floor of her apartment to the door, snatching up her car keys on the way.

FIVE

Somewhere over the Atlantic Ocean, a Gulfstream G650 soars through the skies. The aircraft, with its sleek furnishings and state-of-the-art equipment, is no ordinary private jet; it serves as an airborne base for the agency's most crucial operations.

"You like the plane?" Ben Knight had asked when Peter had met him in the hangar at Kennedy. "It used to belong to the godfather of Putin's youngest daughter. Not anymore. Now it belongs to the CIA."

A few minutes into the flight, Peter, his athletic frame swathed in a bespoke suit, reclines on a luxury leather seat. He grips an iPad, fingers scrolling rapidly, posture rigid. The device illuminates the harrowing evidence of the recent atrocities in Beirut: aerial views of decimated hospitals, pillars of smoke snaking upward where they once stood.

To his left sits Ben Knight, a white-haired, stick-thin figure whose gangly height, perched forward on the edge of his seat, makes him seem almost otherworldly. Despite his frail appearance, Knight's voice carries a resonance that demands attention. "Only a year after the port explosion, and now this," he says, gesturing toward the screen. "A city of two million people, and in a single act of terror, they lose seven hospitals. Five of those were their only oncology units."

Peter's jaw tightens. "It's always the innocent who suffer most." The imagery keeps coming. Disturbing clips from various angles, survivors pulling others from the debris, moments of terror frozen in time.

Then a particularly graphic segment begins—the slaying at the auditorium. The footage is a little out of focus, the cameramen trying to spare the victims in any way they could, yet the heinous act is unmistakable. "Thank God the Lebanese authorities cut the transmission just seconds into the massacre," Knight says, his voice a mix of relief and disgust. The screen changes again, showing media clips of victims being carried away in body bags. Then the frantic, heart-wrenching scenes of relatives filling hospital lobbies.

Knight continues, "Many rushed to the hospitals where their loved ones were taken. When the bombs detonated, those hospitals were packed. We're looking at a death toll that's potentially over a thousand."

A heavy silence follows, only interrupted by the soft whirring of the plane's engines. Both men know the weight of their mission, the necessity of justice. Peter finally breaks the quiet. "We know who was behind it?"

Knight nods, determination gleaming in his eyes. "Yes."

"Who?"

"A terrorist collective known as the Wolf Pack."

"I've heard of them."

"And what do you know?"

"Not much. That they're made up of Westerners who have converted. That they have associations with ISIL, al-Qaeda, the Taliban, Hezbollah, Hamas, and anyone else willing to fund their agenda of a global caliphate."

"Cue up the next file, will you?"

Peter looks down at the screen, finds the file, and plays a covertly recorded video. The angle suggests a body camera discreetly tucked into clothing, capturing a seemingly mundane setting—an Internet café. The glow from the booths, each housing a computer, lights the room's periphery in a neon haze. Dominating the foreground, three men sprawl across leather couches, their attire reminiscent of the ISIL militia—beards, combat fatigues, and the unmistakable presence of Kalashnikovs propped beside them.

"You're looking at footage from half a decade ago," Knight begins, "captured in Raqqa just before ISIL's fall."

Pausing the video, Knight leans in, pointing out each individual in turn, laying out their histories as if presenting a deck of most-wanted cards.

"Here," he says, indicating a stout man with a round head and wispy beard, "is Zachariah Thompson. After his conversion to Islam, he adopted the name Abu Umar al-Britani. He was once a promising computer science prodigy from London. But his trajectory took a dark turn." Knight's voice drops, the weight of the man's actions evident. "Before being radicalized and heading to Syria, he hacked into military databases, exposing identities and coordinates of Western operatives. Some say he fell with Raqqa. Others believe he's still at large, living among the general population."

"That's nice," Peter remarks dryly.

Knight, trying to maintain his balance against a slight rumble of turbulence, shifts in his seat, pointing to the next image. His finger moves to the man sitting next to al-Britani. "This here is one of our own," he says, his voice slightly raised to be heard over the hum of the engines. "Straight from the bustling streets of New York comes Daniel Foster, known in extremist circles as Abu Ayoub al-Amriki. This former Army recruit, turned radical after a prison stretch, orchestrated bombings against Western-backed forces in Iraq. Though it's thought that a drone strike claimed him, his body remains elusive."

Peter looks up from the screen. "So what's our official stance on where he might be?"

Looking him dead in the eyes, Knight replies, "Beirut has his fingerprints all over it. The placing of the explosives inside the victims is very similar to al-Amriki's habit of implanting IEDs in the bodies of children while ISIL was being chased out of Syria."

Peter's attention returns to the iPad.

Knight's finger hovers over the images as the camera pans across the room, then pauses it. "Lastly," he says, his voice resonant in the confined space, "we have the man I believe is the mastermind behind the whole collective."

Unlike the others, he is wearing a balaclava, only his eyes showing. The Gulfstream's ambient lighting casts elongated shadows, making the masked man appear even more ominous on the screen.

Peter narrows his eyes, scrutinizing the image. "His face is covered. Do you have a photograph with him uncovered?"

"I don't even have a name, Peter," Knight replies. "All I have is this. His face is a mystery. He's shown it only to a select inner circle within ISIL."

"I take it he spends most of his time in the West," Peter deduces.

"He does," Knight acknowledges. "His anonymity is his strength. Along with his cunning. Beirut is only the tip, Peter. The latest piece of carnage. Our intel suggests it's nothing compared to what is coming next. We've heard from very reliable sources that he's coming stateside. America."

The light in the cabin appears to dim. Knight leans back, the weight of their mission heavy in the air between them. "Stopping the Wolf Pack isn't just about justice anymore, Peter. It's about survival. We have to get ahead of him, anticipate his next move, or the carnage will continue."

Peter leans forward slightly, the leather of the seat squeaking in protest. "So that's who we're hunting, then?"

"It is."

"And our first clue?"

"The al-Hawl refugee camp."

Peter's gaze deepens. "Oh, joy," he remarks dryly.

"Joy indeed."

The sprawling expanse of al-Hawl takes form in Peter's mind: A place originally meant to temporarily shelter those caught in the Syrian civil war, it has now transformed into a looming purgatory for its inhabitants, many of whom are trapped through their association with ISIL, however directly or indirectly that may have been. The images of women in black veils, children with lost eyes, and makeshift tents against the Syrian desert backdrop fill Peter's mind.

"Why al-Hawl?" he asks, breaking the brief silence.

"The mastermind of the group has ties there," Knight answers cryptically. "Specifically, a wife he married in Raqqa. She's hidden somewhere deep within the camp—and could be the key to identifying him."

SIX

NEW YORK

Kara's source, Amy Harris, worked for Lumina auction house. Her role there had always been multifaceted. On the surface, she catalogued art and liaised with clients. But beneath that façade, she'd become something more dangerous: an informant. She'd witnessed firsthand the house's illicit dance of deceit, where clients laundered their shadowy fortunes through phantom auctions. Canvases that never existed and sculptures that no one ever saw were bought and sold for millions, turning dirty money into ostensibly clean assets. Amy's conscience couldn't sit well with the charade, leading her to Kara, a beacon of justice in a world shrouded in shadows.

Kara's Subaru Outback skids to a halt in front of Amy's apartment complex, a gray, looming structure that seems to merge with the night itself. Without hesitation, she jumps out, her heels clicking against the wet pavement, and approaches the glass doors. She jabs at the intercom's buttons for Amy's apartment, holding on to the hope that maybe, just maybe, Amy will answer.

Silence.

She tries again. More silence.

A creeping dread begins to fill Kara as she repeatedly buzzes, the shrill noise echoing in the otherwise quiet street. However, she's just about to call the police, her phone in her hand, when the intercom is answered. "Hello?"

Kara's heart leaps into her throat. "Amy? Are you okay?"

"What's all the noise?" Amy sighs. She sounds half asleep.

"Amy, I got the email you sent me. What happened?"

She waves off the question dismissively. "Oh, it was nothing. I had an accident at work. I fell over on the loading bay."

"But what was it you were filming? The men filling up the barrels."

"I was playing a prank on the guys from the garden center next door," she says quickly. "Pretending to spy on them while they were unloading fertilizer."

"One of them seemed pretty upset to see you there," Kara points out in a dubious tone.

"He was just laughing, pointing me out to the others. That's when I fell over. They helped me up, got me home."

Kara still feels uneasy. "Can I come up?" she asks.

"I'm in bed, Kara."

Kara sighs. Keeping her voice low, she asks, "Are you sure you're okay?"

"Of course, Kara. It's silly for you to come all this way just because you couldn't get through on the phone."

"Why weren't you answering?"

"I hit my head pretty bad. One of the guys from the garden center gave me something for it. It knocked me out. I was asleep."

Kara takes a step closer to the intercom, her worry evident. "Amy, are you really okay? Is anyone pressuring you at Lumina?"

"No one is suspecting me. Nothing."

"And the video?"

"Just men unloading fertilizer," Amy repeats, a bit more forcefully this time.

Kara nods slowly, her eyes narrowing in thought.

"Good night, Kara," Amy says. "I'll call you in the morning."

"Good night, Amy."

Kara's intuition churns. But in the end, she lets her breath out, lets it go, and walks back to her car, hoping that it's just another weird night in New York City.

SEVEN

CIZRE, TURKEY

THE FIRST GLIMMER OF DAWN PAINTS THE SKY A pale hue of lilac as the Gulfstream's wheels screech gently against the tarmac of a Turkish runway. The plane then taxis its way to a discreet hangar on the fringe of Cizre airport, the closest place to the Syrian border that they can safely land. The hangar's shadowy interior contrasts with the rapidly brightening day outside.

Peter, shoulders slightly hunched from the long journey, steps off the plane right behind Ben Knight. Both men pause for a moment, letting the chill morning air refresh them. Before them stand three individuals, each distinct in appearance and demeanor.

During the journey, Knight gave Peter the rundown on the team he'd be working with. To the far left, there's Paul Bennett, his sandy blond hair catching the morning light. Knight had mentioned, with a mix of professional acknowledgment and familial warmth, that Paul is his nephew. He nods at Peter, an acknowledgment between professionals. Behind Bennett's bespectacled eyes, Peter knows there's a mind brimming with knowledge of the region's complex geopolitics—as well as a sharp tactical thinker under fire.

A few steps away stands Aria Patel. Her silhouette is small but confident. She offers a slight smile, the pen behind her ear a testament to her analytical nature. Though primarily behind the scenes, her presence here indicates the gravity of their mission.

Then there's Tom Cohen. Impeccably dressed, his posture screams diplomacy, though Peter knows he has special forces training. A leather-bound notebook clutched in his hand, he greets Ben Knight with familiarity, their previous collaborations evident in the easy way they interact.

Peter sizes them up quickly. "Team," Ben Knight starts, not one for unnecessary preamble, "this is Peter."

Paul Bennett offers a hand, firm in its grip. "Uncle Ben's told me a lot about you. Glad to be working together."

Peter can see from the way they look at him—almost with awe—that they know exactly who he is and what he is capable of.

Aria's nod is respectful. "We've got a lot to unpack. Ready when you are."

Tom simply smiles, extending a hand to Peter. "Welcome to this side of the world. Let's get you briefed on how we're gonna approach this thing."

MOMENTS LATER, their Land Cruiser is winding its way through the streets of Cizre. Birds, awakened by the dawn, chirp in sporadic melodies, but the town itself feels as though it's holding its breath. Its strategic position, at the nexus of Syria, Iraq, and Turkey, makes it a simmering hotbed of tension.

Peter, still adjusting to the stark contrast from the hangar's shadowy environment, gazes out the passenger window. Children are already at play, kicking balls in alleyways, while older residents begin opening shops and stalls, preparing for the day's trade. Despite the semblance of normalcy, the presence of armed checkpoints and patrolling soldiers tells a different story.

Driving the vehicle, Ben Knight's expression is tight, his lips set in a thin line. He is no stranger to volatile zones, but each one carries its own weight, its own set of unpredictable variables. In the truck's rear, Paul, Tom, and Aria remain vigilant, their senses heightened, their postures alert. The town's complex dynamics are palpable, and every alleyway or unexpected honk makes the team instinctively grip their concealed weapons tighter.

Noting the rising sun's reflection off a building, Aria leans toward Tom Cohen, murmuring, "Golden hour in a fireworks factory."

Cohen gives a brief nod, eyes never leaving the street. "Makes you appreciate the calm before the storm."

After a few more turns, the pickup eases into a side street, halting outside an unassuming two-story structure. To the uninformed eye, it blends seamlessly with its neighbors. But to those in the know, it's a pivotal base of operations for the CIA.

"We're here," Ben Knight announces tersely, killing the engine.

Peter steps out, squinting slightly against the morning sun.

"The closer we are to danger," Knight tells him, "the further we are from harm. It's the last place they'll think to look."

Bennett, jumping out, surveys the building and its surroundings. "A stone's throw from Syria. Perfect."

They enter the safe house, greeted by their Kurdish contact, Hozan. His face is inscrutable, but his nod is one of respect and understanding.

The transition from the outdoors to inside is jarring. The warm sunlight is replaced by cooler, artificial light, revealing a makeshift operations hub. In a living room, maps and images litter the walls and a table in the center.

Bennett, rolling his shoulders to release the tension, beckons everyone closer. "Let's not waste daylight. Time to get down to business."

As the team gathers around him, the weight of their mission settles heavily upon them. The room's ambiance darkens slightly as Bennett lays out the plan. Maps, satellite images, and surveillance shots of al-Hawl are spread out before them.

"We've got one shot at this," he begins, his voice low and heavy with the weight of the mission. "We're entering the lion's den. This isn't just about extracting the Wolf Pack leader's wife; it's about maneuvering through a maze of shifting allegiances, prying eyes, and potential betrayals. It's a tinderbox, and we're potentially the spark."

Peter's eyes fix on a photograph of the woman they intend to extract, her face poking out of a black hijab.

"Sonya Khan," Bennett says. "Through extensive interviews with ex-ISIL fighters and other Islamic entities, we've been able to confirm that she was indeed married to the man we believe is the true mastermind behind the Wolf Pack collective. The two met in Raqqa, introduced by the Islamic State. They married in a secret wedding and lived secretly, hidden in the heart of the city. They had two children."

"Are they still alive?" Peter asks.

"Unfortunately both died before she could make it to al-Hawl. But recently," he adds in an undertone, "she's reached out to us, making contact through a secret phone at the camp. She claims to be in possession of a photograph that shows the mastermind's true identity."

"And you're sure you can trust her?" Peter puts to him.

"She knows her life, and that of her children, hangs in the balance. We need to trust her just as much as she needs to trust us."

Aria interjects, her eyes darting over the images of al-Hawl, "There are still many in the camp who are both armed and deeply loyal to ISIL. They won't let her go without a fight. We've identified three men who are reportedly watching over her inside the camp. It is through them that we have arranged the meeting. All of them have returned from the frontlines, battle-hardened and vengeful. They're not to be underestimated. Currently, they think she's meeting with reporters. They only agreed because we're paying them. But if they think for one second that we're CIA there to take her, they will attack."

Bennett, always the strategist, points to the cluster of

tents. "We need to be wary of the women too. While some are victims, others have become watchdogs, enforcers in their own right. The line between ally and enemy here is blurred."

Tom Cohen nods in agreement. "Peter and I will pose as reporters from the New York Times. Having greased enough palms, they're allowing us to interview her under the pretense of discussing her journey from Sweden to Raqqa as an eighteen-year-old."

Peter, fingers lightly drumming the table, asks, "How are we gonna isolate her from the others?"

"That's where the photo op comes in," Bennett continues. "Tom's the reporter, you're the photographer. You tell them you need to take her somewhere with a view in the background for the article. Insist on the need for a controlled environment, away from the camp's center. It's a risk, but it's our best shot at getting her to the extraction point with minimal attention."

Peter raises a brow. "And if it all goes south?"

Knight and Bennett exchange glances, understanding the unspoken reality. "Then you shoot your way out," Bennett confirms, his voice grim. "That's why it's best if it's you and Tom. You're the sharpest shooters. We'll be relying on you both to provide the necessary cover and distractions if they are needed, using the chaos to your advantage."

Peter smirks. "Always did love a good exit strategy."

The group nods in unity, the room buzzing with the energy of the impending mission. The stakes are high, the risks higher, but each knows the importance of their role.

As they gather their equipment and finalize details, the

sun outside continues its ascent, unaware of the storm brewing in the hearts of the operatives.

EIGHT

NEW YORK

THE FOLLOWING AFTERNOON FINDS KARA ensconced in her editor's plush Manhattan office, her gaze drifting to the view of Fifth Avenue below. Traffic moves by in an orchestrated dance, a scene she's witnessed countless times. Heidi, her editor, is engrossed in Kara's latest article, habitually murmuring under her breath with every line she reads.

This article should be the only thing on Kara's mind, her crowning achievement—a culmination of four grueling months. Yet the triumph evades her. Weary to the bone, she recalls the preceding night. After not getting back from Amy's, she'd spent another six hours crafting the article. A mere four hours of rest later, she'd dashed to the office to make her one o'clock deadline.

Finishing the piece, Heidi leans back, nodding approvingly. "It's strong. Front page material. You've outdone yourself, Kara. Another compelling story."

Such praise should elicit a surge of elation, yet a heavy shadow tugs at Kara's heart—Amy and the events of last night.

Though exhaustion suggests that an immediate retreat to her apartment is her wisest next move, Kara is pulled in another direction. As she leaves her editor's offices and navigates the familiar path to the subway station at Fifth Avenue and 59th Street, her fingers instinctively reach for her phone. She dials Amy's number once again, hope waning with each repeated attempt. After all, she'd promised to call Kara this morning. Something she hasn't done.

Yet again, it goes to voicemail.

Twenty minutes later, Kara approaches Amy's apartment complex, and straight away she's hit with a wall of dread. As she gets closer, the distant wail of sirens grows louder and more pronounced. A chill runs down her spine; the universe seems to be screaming at her that something is wrong. She quickens her pace.

Arriving at the building, Kara is met with a scene that drains the color from her face. Blue and red flashing lights from police cruisers light up the area, painting the onlookers in eerie, alternating shades. Paramedics rush around, their faces a mask of somber concentration.

A police officer stands at the entrance, keeping bystanders at bay. Kara, her voice trembling, manages to ask, "What happened?"

The officer, a middle-aged man with graying hair, looks at her with a mix of pity and weariness. "There was a woman found dead in her apartment."

The world seems to spin around Kara. She feels her knees go weak. "Amy... is it Amy Harris?"

The officer's eyes search hers, seeing the desperation. "Are you a relative?"

Before Kara can answer, the building's main door opens, and a team of paramedics emerge. They're wheeling a stretcher with a body bag strapped on top. The scene feels like a macabre parade in slow motion.

"No!" Kara's voice breaks as she tries to rush forward. The police officer's arm shoots out, blocking her path, but not before she gets a closer look at the body bag. A familiar heart-shaped silver necklace dangles out from the zipper, caught in the teeth. Kara recalls commenting on it once when they met up to speak regarding the fraud at Lumina.

"What happened to her?" Kara demands, tears filling her eyes, her voice a mix of anger, grief, and shock.

One of the paramedics, a young woman with a kind face, approaches Kara. "We believe she was assaulted, ma'am. I'm so sorry."

Kara feels the weight of the revelation pushing her to the ground. The world around her becomes a cacophony of conflicting noises—the murmurs of onlookers, the distant sirens, the soft-spoken condolences. All she can focus on is the cold, hard reality: Amy is gone.

NINE

AL-HAWL REFUGEE CAMP, SYRIA

DUST SWIRLS AROUND THE RAGGED TENTS AS THEY make their way through the sprawling expanse of the al-Hawl refugee camp. Peter and Tom Cohen, despite their Western attire and conspicuous presence, walk with a steely determination. Both have adopted the guise of New York Times journalists, each wearing vests laden with what appear to be camera gear, but which in reality is hiding a lot more than lenses.

Beside them strides a local guide, a wiry man with sun-weathered skin and a sharp gaze, who they met just outside the camp's entrance. As they delve deeper into the heart of al-Hawl refugee camp, the devastation its inhabitants have faced, and go on facing, becomes increasingly palpable. Emaciated children, their eyes hollow from hunger, dart between the makeshift tents. The elderly, too feeble to fend for themselves, lie listlessly on threadbare rugs, their quiet suffering punctuated by occasional, heart-wrenching coughs. Everywhere there is a sense of despair: lives on hold, dreams shattered, a people displaced.

Peter's eyes drift to a gaunt child gnawing on what seems like a piece of cardboard, her feet blackened by the dusty ground, her face smeared with grime. His heart clenches, but he forces himself to focus on the mission.

As they journey farther in, the squalor gives way to a more organized, albeit foreboding, structure. Men with thick beards and hardened eyes stand guard before a large dome made from tarpaulins stretched over a wooden frame tied together. Every one of the men in this part of the camp has an AK47 slung over his shoulder, a hand resting on the wooden butt. The contrast couldn't be starker: Children play in the dirt, giggling and chasing after one another, while just feet away, the looming threat of violence hangs like a storm cloud.

Both Peter and Tom Cohen shift subtly, aware of the hidden firearms on their persons. At the entrance of the domed tent, two bearded fighters eye them with suspicion. Their guide, without hesitation, pulls out a roll of dollar bills, passing it to the guards. After a cursory count, the guards nod, allowing the trio to proceed.

Inside the tent, the atmosphere is tense. People sit cross-legged in the center, conversing in a low murmur. Among them is the woman they have come to see. Sonya Khan. Her once vibrant eyes now hold a weariness, her skin drawn tight over high cheekbones.

Sitting beside her, a woman of notable authority

commands the space. Her dark hair is covered by a richly embroidered scarf, and her piercing eyes assess Peter and Cohen critically. Around the tent, the armed men look on, their Kalashnikovs ever present and within reach.

Peter and Cohen exchange a glance. This is the moment they've prepared for. The stakes couldn't be higher.

The inside of the tent, dimly lit and sweltering, becomes a pressure cooker of tension. Cohen begins the "interview," asking carefully rehearsed questions about life in the camp, the challenges faced by the people, the hope and despair that resides within its confines.

While Cohen's words flow smoothly, keeping the attention of the woman of authority and the Wolf Pack leader's wife, Peter is locked in a dance of silent observation. His piercing eyes, having seen more than their fair share of combat zones and tense encounters, scan the armed guards. The glare returned to him is cold, filled with a loathing that chills Peter to his core. He can feel the raw animosity emanating from them, an unspoken promise that given the slightest reason, violence would be their answer.

The interview goes on, a mere façade, a smokescreen behind which both sides play their part, waiting for the right time to introduce the photo op. The camp's ambient noise fades, replaced by the pregnant silence in the tent, each word, each glance carrying weight.

Cohen, sensing the need to conclude the interview, gestures toward Peter. "We should head outside where the light is better," he suggests, pointing to the entrance of the tent. "My cameraman needs to take some shots."

They expected this to be the easy part, getting Sonya out

of the tent. But it soon becomes apparent that it will be anything but. It's as if a trigger has been pulled. The guards step forward, menace emanating from them. "You will take photos here, and we will accompany you," one of them growls.

"That wasn't the agreement," Cohen argues.

He is trying to maintain a calm façade, but the slight quiver in his voice betrays him.

The guide, sensing the escalating danger, springs to life, engaging in a fierce debate with the guards in Arabic. Their heated exchange is punctuated by gestures, finger pointing, and the unmistakable sound of Kalashnikov safeties clicking off.

The air in the tent grows even heavier, a tangible dread settling over everyone. Peter, his instincts on high alert, subtly reaches behind, slipping his hand between his body armor and his torso, fingers grazing the cold steel of the SIG Sauer P229 Elite taped to his back.

Sonya is fast becoming overwhelmed. Her eyes, wide with panic, dart between her captors and the strangers who have promised her escape. Suddenly, her fear gives way to action. With a desperate scream, she bolts for the entrance. One of the guards, reacting in a frenzy, raises his weapon, but Cohen lunges forward, pushing the barrel aside just as the trigger is pulled. The tent erupts in pandemonium. Bullets rip through the fabric, finding the guide and the authoritative woman.

Amidst the cacophony, Peter draws the pistol. Two quick shots, two guards down, including the one wrestling with Cohen. The rapid-fire event leaves a grim tableau:

Cohen and Peter, guns drawn, surrounded by chaos and the pained moans of the dying.

Outside, the shouts and commotion continue. Cohen, catching his breath, turns to Peter. "What now?"

Peter's face, smeared with dust and blood spatter, hardens. "Now we go get her."

The camp transforms into a warren of danger. Sporadic gunfire crackles in the air, creating a manic soundtrack. As Peter and Cohen split up, Peter's instincts take over. His movements are fluid, like a spirit gliding through the maze of tents and makeshift shelters. More jihadists emerge. But they are so loud and clumsy that it is easy to stay out of their way.

The structures of the camp become his allies, the flapping sheets of fabric, the wooden poles, and the makeshift pathways. Yet in such chaos, danger lurks at every corner.

As Peter spots Sonya through the gaps in the tents, relief threatens to cloud his judgment. It's this brief lapse that nearly costs him his life. A massive figure bursts out from a nearby tent, using the element of surprise to tackle Peter to the ground and knock the SIG Sauer out of his reach.

Amidst the windswept landscape of the Syrian refugee camp, a blinding whirlwind of dust and debris rises, shrouding the two men locked in deadly combat. Peter's opponent, once an ISIL fighter who has known battle, is a tower of muscle and menace. He unsheathes a wicked-looking knife—a machete. The glint of its steel, illuminated by the fleeting sun, is a clear and present omen: a cold intent to end Peter's life.

He explodes at him, forcing Peter to duck beneath the arc of the blade.

Twisting around, Peter has little time to breathe, the machete dancing at him again, the sunlight blinking off it.

Too slow.

The cold bite of the blade grazes the skin of his forearm, inching perilously closer with each slash. His arms flail as he dives along the ground to escape another barrage, and with his assailant coming after him, Peter's hand scrambles along the ground, searching for something, anything. His fingers find the handle of a pot, its contents bubbling over an open fire. In a desperate move, Peter whirls around and flings the scalding water at his attacker. The man's pained scream is both horrifying and vindicating.

The attacker's grasp slackens around the machete just long enough for Peter, with lion-like swiftness, to snatch it from him and drive it with a heart-wrenching chop into the soft flesh of the man's neck as though burying it in a tree trunk.

For a moment, everything stops.

The life drains from the jihadist, and his hulking form collapses to the ground, the machete stuck in his flesh where the neck meets the shoulder, blood pouring down the blade.

Wasting no moment, Peter picks up the SIG Sauer and breaks into a sprint, heart pounding in his chest, fueled by adrenaline and an unyielding resolve to find the woman they're here for.

Through the turmoil, Sonya stumbles, her burka hampering her movements. Just when she thinks she might have evaded her pursuers, a firm grip yanks her backward. The cold steel of a knife presses against her tender throat, and she gazes into the bulging eyes of her captor. But just as the blade is about to make its cut, a gunshot pierces the air, reverberating through the camp. The man's grip slackens, his lifeless body falling away from her. Before Sonya can even register what has happened, a strong hand pulls her upright. Peter's face—grimy, bloodied but determined—meets hers.

"Come on," he commands, his voice brooking no argument. "We're leaving."

TEN

NEW YORK

THE ROOM FEELS MORE LIKE A CAGE THAN A detective's office. Harsh overhead lights gleam off the white walls, giving it a surreal glow. Despite the muted colors, everything seems too bright, too stark. The only break in the silence is the soft rhythmic ticking of a clock somewhere down the corridor and the faint sound of distant conversations, muffled through the thick walls of the precinct.

Kara paces the floor, her heels resounding sharply against the cold tiles. She can't believe that Amy is dead.

A soft click breaks her reverie as the door to the office swings open, revealing a detective. He's tall and broad-shouldered, with salt-and-pepper hair cropped close to his head. His face, lined with age and experience, holds a pair of sharp eyes that have likely seen too much of the city's underbelly.

"Ms. Tate?" he inquires softly, a touch of genuine

concern in his voice. "I'm Detective Diaz. Would you like a fresh coffee? Something to eat, perhaps?"

Kara shakes her head, pulling herself together. "No, thank you, Detective. I'm all right."

He nods, taking in her composed demeanor with a hint of respect. "All right. Let's get started then."

With that, they both take their seats, facing each other across a battle-scarred desk.

Detective Diaz clears his throat. "Before we begin, is there anything you want to ask me?"

"When did it happen?"

"Coroner says it was some time around midnight."

Kara closes her eyes and breathes, "Right after I left."

There is a moment's silence, the detective giving Kara some time to compose herself. Then she opens her eyes, nods her head, and tells him she's ready.

"All right, Ms. Tate," Diaz begins. "Let's start from the top. You said earlier to the officers that you're a journalist writing a piece about financial fraud, and that the victim was connected to this. What is that connection?"

Kara takes a deep breath. "I've been working on an exposé about financial fraud in New York's Arts District. Amy, she... she was my primary source at the auction house she works at. She had insider information about some of their illicit dealings."

The detective's eyebrows rise slightly. "Which auction house is this?"

"Lumina."

He writes this down. Then, "And was there any chance someone at Lumina could have discovered her involvement with your article?"

Kara shakes her head emphatically. "That's the thing. The article hasn't even been released yet. It's slated for next week. No one should know anything about it. We're not even contacting Lumina for comment until the day before it goes to print." She pauses, pulling out her phone. "But there's this," she says, playing the video for him.

Detective Diaz leans forward, watching the footage from the loading bay intently. His face remains impassive, but his eyes show concentration. As the video ends, he looks up. "Looks like fertilizer to me."

"Yes. Lumina is right next to the Eden Project," Kara adds.

"That's the garden center in the Arts District, isn't it?"

"Yes."

"So it might be for them."

Kara takes a moment before replying. "That's what I thought. But why would she film it unless she thought something was off? Later on, I went to her apartment. I spoke with her over the intercom."

"You didn't see her?"

"No. She wouldn't let me in."

The detective's pen moves rapidly across his notepad, scribbling down every detail. "Did she give you any reason?"

"She said she was sleeping. That I'd woken her up."

"What about the video? Did you speak about that?"

"She brushed it off, said she was playing a prank on the guys from the garden center, that she fell and accidentally sent it to me. But she was real off." Kara's voice breaks slightly. "Scared. Like somebody was in the apartment with her."

"And you're sure it's not something to do with the work she did for you?"

Kara shudders before speaking. "I hope not. But you might want to look into it."

The detective nods slowly. "I will. Anything else you think I should know?"

"That's all I have."

They sit in silence for a moment before Kara eventually musters the courage to ask the one question she's wanted to ask this whole time but was too terrified to. "How did Amy... How did she die?"

Detective Diaz pauses, the weight of the question pressing down on him. He meets her gaze with genuine sorrow. "Her throat was cut, almost down to the bone."

Kara feels the room sway. She nods slowly, her eyes glistening. "Thank you, Detective. Please find who did this."

ELEVEN

TURKEY

THE JOURNEY FROM THE CHAOTIC MIRE OF AL-Hawl to the Turkish border is fraught with tension. The hush of the night, punctuated only by the hum of the Land Cruiser, belies the dangers that still lurk in the shadows. Every bump on the dirt road feels like a potential landmine, every distant light a possible threat. Inside the vehicle, everyone is speechless.

At the border, they hand over their paperwork. The guards cast suspicious glances their way, but after a seemingly interminable wait, they are waved through. Turkey, with its promise of safety, welcomes them, and the tension in the vehicle lessens, if only by a fraction.

The winding roads eventually lead them into the town of Cizre. As they pull up to the nondescript safe house, they're met by their Kurdish contact, Hozan, his deepset eyes betraying traces of worry. He's been expecting them, and without a word, he ushers them inside.

Upstairs, familiar faces greet them. Aria, with her sharp features, radiates an aura of calmness, while Paul Bennett, with his stocky build, immediately starts taking inventory of their supplies. And then there's Ben Knight, the lynchpin of this operation, his tall frame towering over the others.

Sonya is ushered into a dimly lit lounge, the curtains heavy and drawn, cocooning them from the outside world. The room holds a somber atmosphere, as if it's absorbed all the pain and sorrows of those who have been there before.

As Sonya sits, eyes wary, Ben Knight takes a seat opposite her. The room becomes a world in itself, the weight of the mission, the hope, the risks all converging in this one space.

Knight leans forward, his eyes fixed to those of Sonya, the leader's wife. "Sonya," he says gently, "the photo you promised. Do you have it?"

Sonya hesitates, taking another deep breath before admitting, "I'm sorry. I don't."

"Why not?"

She looks down, guilt evident in her eyes. "I lied. I needed to get out. I'm sorry."

There is a tense pause. Knight exchanges a glance with Aria, who stands by the door, her posture alert. Peter, who is leaning against a wall, lets out a soft sigh. Everyone in the room knows how critical a clear visual of the man they are hunting would have been.

Knight exhales deeply, letting the weight of the revelation sink in. Then, "All right. Describe him to us."

Sonya hesitates for a moment, then begins, "His skin... it's like coffee. A warm, medium shade. His eyes are brown, and his hair is curly and jet black." She pauses, "He's Middle Eastern. Originally, anyway."

"Originally?"

"Yes. But only by race. Even though he spoke Arabic well, he didn't sound Arabic. He sounded American."

"One of our own," Tom Cohen mutters in the corner.

Knight glances momentarily over his shoulder at him. Then his eyes are back on Sonya. "How old?"

"Thirty, I think."

"You think?"

"He would never tell me his exact age. Never tell me his birthday or his star sign. He was very secretive. I mean, God, we'd met only twice before getting married in Raqqa. A week later, I was pregnant, and he was going off to fight jihad against the infidels in their homelands."

Knight takes a deep intake of air through his nostrils. Then he prods, "Any distinguishing features?"

She nods. "He has a scar, right over where his appendix would be."

Knight jots down the details. "Did he go by a particular name?"

Sonya replied, "Yes, he used the kunya name Abu Musa. It's Moses in English."

"Abu Musa?"

"Yes."

Knight and Bennett share a look, before Knight returns his attention to Sonya, continues, "And you mentioned he was American?"

"Yes," Sonya confirms.

Knight leans back, considering the information. "Did he ever speak about his family? His background?"

Sonya's eyes take on a distant look. "Not much. He really didn't talk about his past at all. All he would say is that his family were kaffir, infidels. That they had chosen their path to hell."

"What about places he lived near? Landmarks, that sort of thing."

Sonya's eyes brighten. She sits up in the chair. "He did once tell me about hiking in the Appalachians. He mentioned it was right on his doorstep."

In the background, Tom Cohen muses aloud, "That's spread across a large area. There's at least fourteen states that cover the Appalachians."

Ben Knight focuses on Sonya. "Did he mention any mountains in particular?"

She takes a moment, brows furrowing as she digs deep into her recollections. "He spoke about a blue mountain," she finally shares.

"Blue Ridge?"

"That's it."

"Could be Virginia," Knight surmises, narrowing down the options.

"Could be Georgia," Paul Bennett interjects, "Tennessee, Maryland, or any number of states that have the Blue Ridge mountains."

Having turned to look over his shoulder at his nephew, Knight turns back to Sonya. "Anything else you can remember?"

"His family were originally Muslim," Sonya discloses, "but they converted to Christianity. I know that because he told me."

Bennett, leaning against the wall, pipes up, "So he's a

migrant?"

Sonya glances at him. "Maybe his parents. But not him. He was born in America."

"Where?"

"I don't know."

Knight nods, then asks, "Did he ever mention names, friends or acquaintances from his past?"

She ponders for a moment, then shakes her head. "No. He seemed to harbor deep resentment towards his past. As if he wanted to erase every trace of it."

"How about in Raqqa?" Knight asks, leaning forward. "Did Abu Musa, your husband, have particular confidants or allies within the group? Anyone he seemed particularly close to?"

Sonya's gaze drops to her lap, where her hands are clasped tightly. "He was rarely ever in the caliphate. Mostly abroad. He only returned to meet the leaders. But when he did come back..." Her eyes shift upward, as if recalling those moments. "It was as if he were royalty. They revered him, the heralded disruptor from the West. As if he wielded the very wrath of Allah. It's laughable," she adds bitterly, locking eyes with Knight. "They play at being invincible, but they're just misguided boys."

Knight narrows his eyes, considering her words. "What about outside the caliphate? Did he have contacts or allies living in the West, perhaps not directly part of ISIL but in league with their ideology?"

A spark ignites in Sonya's somber eyes. "Yes. There was one man he spoke to. Imam Malik al-Nasri."

Knight jerks slightly. It's imperceptible to most people in the room. But not to Peter. He spotted it.

Knight's voice drops an octave. "You're sure it was Malik al-Nasri?"

She nods. "Yes. Musa mentioned him several times by name. I believe they planned things together."

Refocusing, Knight continues, "Did Musa ever mention specific places he frequented, either for operations or as refuges?"

Sonya furrows her brow. "What do you mean?"

"Operatives often have safe houses, places they source materials from or spots to lay low post-operation. Anything like that ring a bell in regard to Musa?"

She pauses, then slowly shakes her head. "Like I said, he was guarded, never spilling details about his assignments for ISIL. He was... distant. Most of the time, it felt like he was a world away."

Knight taps his pen, contemplating her words. "What about his future plans?"

She sighs, looking defeated. "No. The last time he left coincided with intensified bombings and drone strikes. I never heard from him again. He didn't even reach out during the evacuations to inquire about his own children. But you know what always struck me about Musa?"

Knight leans forward slightly. "Tell me."

She takes a breath, choosing her words carefully. "I sometimes doubt he was genuinely committed to Islam or to the words of the Prophet. I don't think many of them were. For them, Islam was a tool."

"A tool for what?"

"To channel their rage, their disillusionment with the world they were born into. The fact that it has never appreciated them in a way they demand it to. Whenever I tried to delve deeper into Musa's family or his history, he would deflect, grow agitated. I often felt that he was wandering adrift, searching for an identity. That's why he can adapt so seamlessly, moving fluidly from one role to another." She pauses, the weight of her emotions pressing down on her. "I still love him, though," she confesses, her voice tinged with a mixture of pain and affection.

Tears pool in her eyes, but she hastily wipes them away.

———

THE DIM LIGHT in the Cizre safe house casts an eerie hue over the rustic living room. Sonya is in one of the bedrooms, sleeping off today's drama. The atmosphere she leaves behind is thick with anticipation.

Peter's gaze sharpens as he turns toward Ben Knight. "Ben, what can you tell me about Malik al-Nasri?"

Knight, a bit taken aback by the directness, pauses for a moment. Then he sighs. "You noticed my reaction, then?"

Peter nods.

His face grim, Knight begins, "On the surface, Imam al-Nasri is an influential figure in Chicago's Muslim community. Beneath it, he's an informant who's been on our books for nearly two decades."

Murmurs ripple through the room. Eyes dart between team members, seeking clarity.

"That's the catch," Knight continues, taking a deep breath. "If al-Nasri is indeed the Wolf Pack's contact, we've got a serious problem. He's not just an informant. He's one of the best, most reliable assets the US intelligence community has ever had."

Tom Cohen, looking puzzled, pipes up. "If he's playing both sides, he's not just leaking information. He's manipulating the entire game."

The room falls silent, the magnitude of the situation sinking in.

Paul Bennett asks, "How are we going to approach this, unk? Confront al-Nasri?"

Knight sighs, rubbing his temples. "That's the challenge. If he's a double agent, confronting him could jeopardize years of intelligence work. But we can't just let it slide either. We need a strategy, and we need it fast."

TWELVE

MADISON AVENUE, NEW YORK

Kara's fingers drum impatiently on the tabletop, her eyes scanning the café's entrance for a face she's only seen in online photographs. Her excitement peaks as one of Amy's friends, whom she'd contacted on Facebook, walks in. Her name is Lisa. Lisa is slender with auburn hair that cascades in soft waves to her shoulders, framing a face that wears a mix of apprehension and determination. Her green eyes scan the café, finally locking on to Kara. As she approaches, her heels clack rhythmically and deliberately against the tiled floor.

Without uttering a word, Lisa pulls out the chair opposite Kara and takes a seat. The next chapter in this dark puzzle is about to begin.

"Thank you for meeting me, Lisa," Kara begins, urgency lacing her voice.

"Of course. Amy... She meant a lot to me. This is all just... hard to process. How can I help?"

"I want to understand what happened. Amy trusted me, gave me the video I sent you earlier."

"I saw it. Creepy as hell," Lisa comments with unease.

"I think she sent it to me because I'm a journalist. Because I can look into it. But there are gaps I can't fill. Your profile says you and Amy were best friends."

Lisa shivers, takes a quick intake of air. "Yes. Since freshman year of high school."

"Is there anything you can tell me about her that has happened recently? Anything strange. Did she tell you she was scared of anything?"

"She told me a little about the work she's doing for you. She said it was dangerous, but I never thought it could get her hurt."

"The police have already cleared them," Kara says.

It's true. Detective Diaz called last night to tell her that he doesn't think it has anything to do with them. They seemed genuinely surprised and upset at her death.

"Did Amy have a boyfriend?" Kara asks next.

A dark cloud appears to cross Lisa's face. "Yeah, she did. Joseph."

"Joseph who?"

"Joseph Dalton."

"How well did you know him?"

Lisa hesitates, picking at the edge of the café menu. "Joseph? He was... different. Amy only met him a few months back. Everything was so rushed with him. But honestly, I never got a good vibe. I told her as much. She laughed it off, said I was too protective."

"How many times did you meet him?"

Lisa sighs. "That was another red flag. I only ever met him once, and that was by accident. See, he'd never meet up with any of her friends at social occasions. In the two months they were together, he never once came to a party or get-together with her—casual or otherwise. The one time our paths crossed was a fluke. I was in her neighborhood, returning a book. I just knocked, unannounced. When she answered with the chain latch still on, I could see that I'd interrupted something."

Kara's memory involuntarily flits back to the other night: Amy hesitant to open the door.

Lisa's voice breaks Kara's train of thought. "When she finally let me in, I was introduced to her 'boyfriend.'"

"What was that like?"

"Weird."

"Weird, how?"

"He was friendly. Introduced himself. Shook my hand. Which I found real formal. Then he kept quiet. Like he was just waiting for me to leave. Amy grabbed the book and did her best to get me out the door."

"Did Amy share anything about his background? His roots?"

"Vaguely. New York, but she hinted he liked to travel. That he was a bit of a traveler. She always said he had this air of mystery, keeping things close to his chest. That day, he barely acknowledged me. Just stood there, sizing me up. His look was, I don't know... unsettling."

Electricity bursts up Kara's spine, her investigative instincts salivating. "You think Joseph could have anything to do with it?"

Lisa tips her head, scrunches her nose. "I don't know. Being a bit creepy doesn't make you a killer."

"You know where he lives?"

"No. But he works at that garden center next to Luminar. The Eden Project. That's how they met."

Kara's mind is whirring. It is like a great big piece of the puzzle just slotted into place.

THIRTEEN

CHICAGO

IMAM MALIK AL-NASRI IS A DISTINGUISHED FIGURE said to have a wise gaze and a graying beard. He stands out not just for his spiritual leadership in Chicago's Muslim community but for his brave affiliation with the CIA since the aftermath of 9/11. Born in Alexandria, Egypt, he moved to the US during his early twenties, embracing the dual identity of an American Muslim.

From the outside, Imam al-Nasri's daily life appears centered around the serene mosque in Chicago's south side. Here he leads prayers, conducts community gatherings, and mentors a vibrant group of young Muslims. However, behind closed doors, he has been the eyes and ears for the intelligence community, playing a pivotal role in curbing extremist ideologies.

The imam's efforts have been fruitful in multiple ways: Many potential extremist plots have been thwarted thanks to the intelligence he has provided. He has also succeeded in mediating between disgruntled individuals from his community and law enforcement, ensuring rehabilitation over retribution.

His relationships with both the American intelligence community and his local Muslim community are built on a fragile balance of trust. For Imam al-Nasri, the mission has always been clear: to protect his community and his adopted country from the inside out. This dual allegiance, while often testing his personal and ethical boundaries, underlines his belief that the true essence of Islam is peace and service to humanity.

Or so it would seem.

The Chicago night blankets the affluent suburb in a serene quiet, broken only by the occasional distant bark of a dog or hoot of an owl. Elegant homes, each with meticulously manicured lawns and vibrant trees, line the streets. They are testimonies to the area's wealth and exclusivity. One such home, with its pale beige bricks and intricate woodwork, belongs to Imam Malik al-Nasri. Large windows overlook the leafy road, with tall oaks casting elongated shadows across the driveway.

Several houses away, a nondescript black Ford Transit sits inconspicuously. To any passerby or neighbor, it would seem just like any other van one might find in such an upscale neighborhood. But inside, it's a different story.

From the driver's seat, Peter scans the surroundings, his fingers drumming the steering wheel in anxious anticipation. Ben Knight sits rigidly beside him, eyes locked on al-Nasri's residence about a hundred yards down the street. The back of the van is a maze of equipment. From there, Paul Bennett coordinates the surveillance, earpiece firmly in place, murmuring softly into the comms system. Across from him, Aria, with her dark hair pulled into a tight bun, is engrossed in her work at a surveillance console.

The center of her attention is taken by an IMSI-catcher, a complex device that intercepts mobile phone traffic and tracks the movement of phone users. Essentially, it can trick phones into believing it's a legitimate cell tower, enabling Aria to activate cameras and microphones remotely and listen in on conversations. Beside the screen of the IMSI-catcher, a laptop displays the interior of al-Nasri's house. Using a malware she planted earlier, Aria has hacked into the home's security system. The screen shows grainy footage from inside the house—living rooms, hallways, and even the ornate dining area, all of it caught on the imam's own CCTV.

A slight rustle over the comms brings Bennett's attention back. "You in position yet, Viper Two?"

Hidden in the bushes on the property's edge and camouflaged by the night, Tom Cohen peers through night vision goggles, keeping an eagle eye on the back of the Imam's house. "Roger that, Viper One," he whispers back, his voice barely audible.

"Good. Keep yourself alert in case this turns sour."

On Aria's monitor, the grainy figure of Imam Malik al-Nasri becomes clearer. Dressed in a simple white kurta, he carries a bowl of popcorn into the living room and takes a seat next to a woman identified as Fatima al-Nasri, his wife. They cuddle together, both reaching into the bowl for fistfuls of popcorn. The team listens in on their harmless conversation, made barely audible through the IMSI-catcher.

Ninety-nine percent of all surveillance operations is nothing more than watching people do boring, normal, everyday stuff. Tonight is no different. Aria and the others watch as al-Nasri and his wife eat popcorn and watch television—a quiet intimacy between two people who've known each other for a long time. Neither showing one iota of suspicion that they're being watched.

Outside, the team silently observes. Peter's gaze never wavers from the screen he and Ben Knight watch in the front of the van. For him, every detail, every gesture could be a clue, an insight into the man they're investigating. But all he sees now is a mundane evening in a family home.

Aria leans in, adjusting a frequency. "This is... very ordinary," she murmurs.

Ben Knight nods, leaning back slightly in his seat. "Often the most dangerous people hide behind the mask of ordinary."

Paul Bennett, eyes still trained on his equipment, adds, "Or maybe sometimes, they just watch TV with their wives."

The van falls into a contemplative silence.

Peter eventually breaks it, his voice quiet but decisive. "Ben, you ready?"

Knight straightens up, his features hardening into determination. "As ready as I'll ever be." Taking hold of the handle, he turns over his shoulder to Peter and adds, "Time to kick the hornet's nest."

He opens the van door, stepping out into the night. The evening air is cool against his skin, but he barely notices as he makes his way purposefully toward al-Nasri's front door. Every step is calculated, every movement deliberate. The night waits with bated breath as Ben Knight prepares to meet Imam Malik al-Nasri.

The plan is simple. Al-Nasri is their best lead to the man they're after. So Ben Knight is going turn up out of the blue, introduce himself as CIA, and ask for intel on the Wolf Pack. He'll make sure to drop a few details, too. Like that they know he called himself Abu Musa in Raqqa, and that he's American. If al-Nasri is involved, the mere hint that the CIA knows something will force him to reach out to the Wolf Pack. If he does, Aria's tech will give them a potential trace —or at least lead them to the next bread crumb. If al-Nasri makes a call or sends a message, the IMSI will catch it.

The stillness of the affluent Chicago suburb is broken only by the soft chirping of crickets and the faint rumble of distant vehicles. Stepping onto al-Nasri's property, Knight's moves toward the front door of the house with measured and intentional strides. Every footfall seems to echo in the quiet of the night, growing louder in his own ears. As he nears the ornate door, the muted sounds of laughter and the hum of the television suggest a typical evening within.

Drawing a deep breath, Knight hesitates for a moment. Looking back toward the van, his eyes lock on to Peter's, a silent exchange passing between them—trust, responsibility, anticipation. In the darkness, the distance between the two men feels vast, filled with the weight of what's to come. The night air grows thick. With a final nod to Peter, Ben Knight reaches out and firmly presses the doorbell.

Everything changes.

Instead of the gentle chime one would expect, the night instead erupts into chaos. A deafening roar fills the air as a massive fireball engulfs Knight and the front of the house. Windows shatter outward, sending shards of glass in all directions. In mere moments, the once elegant home is reduced to rubble, its interior consumed by roaring flames.

In the van, the shockwave knocks Peter and the team off their seats, the vehicle rocking violently, their screens going bright with static. As the initial shock subsides, a haze of smoke and dust fills the air. Peter scrambles out of the van into the road.

"Knight!" he shouts, his voice choked with panic and disbelief.

The radio crackles to life in his ear, Paul Bennet's voice filled with urgency. "Viper Two! Report! Are you okay?"

Nothing but static comes from Tom Cohen's radio. Peter's eyes glow with the fireball rising from the backyard.

"Tom?!" Bennett calls out down the radio. "Tom? For God's sake, Tom, answer!"

Just when hope seems extinguished, a strained cough breaks the haunting silence of the radio. It's followed by a series of ragged breaths, wheezing through the static.

"I'm here..." The voice is weak, spluttering but alive. It's Tom Cohen.

"Tom! Are you hurt?"

More coughs, the sound of someone battling through a throat full of smoke and ash. "No... A little shaken... But I'm good. What happened?"

Next, Bennett's voice is filled with emotion. "Uncle Ben?"

The raging inferno that was once al-Nasri's residence casts a harsh, unyielding light over the scene. Flames, a cruel shade of orange, dance manically, consuming the remnants of the home and everything in it. The sharp scent of burning wood and something more sinister fills the air, making breathing arduous.

Peter, momentarily paralyzed by the shock of what he's witnessed, finally forces himself to move. He begins running toward the fire, the desperate hope that he might find some sign of Ben Knight still alive driving him forward. Each step closer to the blaze feels like a step into the mouth of hell, the waves of heat threatening to singe his flesh.

"Ben!" he yells hoarsely, his voice rough with anguish. But the fire roars back at him, drowning out his cries. It's a savage, merciless force, and it's clear to Peter as he stands there that Knight couldn't have survived the explosion.

"Ben..." he murmurs again, more to himself this time, feeling a profound sense of loss.

The sudden ring of his phone cuts through the cacophony, jolting him from his grief. Cautiously, he retrieves the device from his pocket, squinting at the unfamiliar number displayed on the screen. Hesitating only for a moment, he answers, "Hello?"

The voice on the other end is chillingly cold, devoid of any emotion. "Did you like it?" it taunts. "Did you like watching him die? Watching Ben die?"

Peter's grip tightens around the phone, his knuckles white. Rage bubbles up, but he forces it down, trying to remain calm. "Who is this?"

The briefest pause, then, "Goodbye, Azrael."

And with that, the call ends, leaving Peter surrounded by the crackling of the fire and the weight of a new, terrifying reality. The Wolf Pack knows him, knows his team, and is out for blood.

FOURTEEN

ALBANY, NEW YORK

Kara's Subaru Outback hums smoothly beneath her, its headlights slicing through the early evening gloom. The city of Albany in Upper New York rises up ahead, a cluster of twinkling lights that slowly becomes more defined as she draws nearer. The familiar rhythm of her car's engine is broken only by the soft, dulcet tones of the radio announcer.

"...breaking news from Chicago. An explosion has rocked a suburb a short while ago, with early reports suggesting it was a targeted bombing. Details are still emerging, and no official statements have been released yet, but we'll be sure to keep our listeners updated as we learn more."

Kara frowns, adjusting her grip on the steering wheel. Another bombing? The world seems to be spiraling faster and faster out of control. She briefly contemplates the implications of such an attack, then shakes her head, refocusing on the task at hand: Amy.

A call coming through her hands-free interrupts the radio. Kara, expecting it, answers. "Detective?"

"Yes, Ms. Tate. This is Diaz. You've been calling my office all day, leaving messages, and I'm returning your call."

"Do you know about the boyfriend?"

"Joseph Dalton?"

"Yes. That's him."

"We know about the boyfriend," Detective Diaz says.

"So you've spoken to him?"

"Not yet."

"What does that mean?"

Detective Diaz sighs. "It means he's skipped town."

"You've tried his workplace, right?"

"Yes. He hasn't shown up at the garden center since the night of the killing."

"And you've considered that it could have been him that night when she was recording the loading bay?"

"Yes." Diaz sounds tired. "The footage is too grainy to make an ID, but it could be him. And that, unfortunately, is where we're at. A lot of coincidences adding up to one big 'unfortunately.'"

"But you've checked his address?"

"Empty."

"And you don't find that suspicious?"

"I do. It places him at the top of the leaderboard of suspects. However—and this is a big however—the name he gave your friend, his landlord, and his employer, this Joseph Dalton, is nothing more than an alias. The guy doesn't exist. All I've got is that he worked for two months at the Eden

Project, was a good worker, kept to himself, dated the victim during that time, rented an apartment under a false name, and is now gone."

"Can't you find him?"

"Oh, we're trying, all right. His details, or at least what we have, are in the system, but I haven't even got a decent photo of the guy. I've got nada. Now if you'll excuse me, I gotta go."

The call ends and the name Joseph Dalton runs through Kara's head like a freight train. She is convinced that the name holds significance. As the road unwinds before her, anticipation builds—the people awaiting her arrival might hold vital insights into Joseph Dalton.

Turning off the main road, she enters a quiet suburb. Rows of well-kept houses line the streets, their gardens carefully manicured and windows warmly lit from within. The quintessential image of domestic tranquility.

Amy's parents' home is easy to spot, a charming two-story colonial with a wraparound porch. The warm yellow of the house's exterior paint seems to beckon you in, a stark contrast to the unfolding chaos in Chicago.

Kara parks on the curb, taking a moment to collect her thoughts before disembarking from the Subaru. This is going to be difficult. Meeting the family of someone you know, under such tragic circumstances, is never easy.

She pulls her coat tighter around herself and heads up the walkway, the crunch of her footsteps on the gravel path loud in the still night. As she nears the door, it opens, revealing a middle-aged couple. They share Amy's gentle features.

Kara swallows hard, steeling herself for the difficult conversation ahead.

The living room is a cozy space filled with the soft, diffused glow of table lamps. Family photos dot the walls, and Kara notices a younger, freer Amy in many of them. Her heart twinges with sympathy.

"Please," says Amy's mother, gesturing toward the couch, "sit."

Kara does, settling into the plush cushions. Amy's father disappears briefly into the kitchen and returns with a tray bearing three glasses of lemonade. Kara takes a sip, grateful for the refreshing coolness.

Then she takes a deep breath, searching for the words. "Thank you for allowing me to come here tonight. I can't imagine how hard this is for you both. I'm so sorry for your loss. Amy was... she was a good person."

Amy's father places a hand on his wife's shoulder, trying to provide some semblance of comfort. She reaches over to a side table and retrieves a photo album. Opening it, Kara is presented with a montage of Amy's life: young Amy with braces, prom night Amy with a high school sweetheart, graduation Amy beaming in her cap and gown.

The mother's voice trembles as she speaks. "We were so proud when she graduated from art school and moved to New York City. Amy had always dreamed of living in the Big Apple."

Kara listens intently, absorbed in the shared memories. Each snapshot, each story a piece of the puzzle that is Amy.

The woman's voice grows softer, more reflective. "She was always so ambitious, full of life and dreams. Living in New York, working there—it was everything she wanted."

Seeing the family's pain, Kara softly says, "I'm so sorry to intrude like this."

"It's okay," Amy's father reassures her. "We want to help in any way we can. You said on the phone that you were helping the police."

"I am."

This is technically a lie. Nonetheless, if she does find anything of worth here, she will take it straight to Detective Diaz.

Kara hesitates before asking, "Did you ever meet Amy's boyfriend, Joseph?"

Both parents shake their heads. "No," Amy's mother replies.

Instant disappointment.

She goes on, "I know they got serious pretty quick, but whenever we asked to meet him, there was always an excuse. But she talked about him. Said he was the most disciplined person she'd ever met, very set in his ways."

Curious, Kara presses, "Did she mention anything else about him?"

The father's face reddens slightly. "Yes, she mentioned that he'd taken her to a local mosque."

"A mosque?"

"Yes. Joseph was a muslim. I didn't think much of it, though. Each to their own, and all that. She was always such a curious girl, always trying new things. I put it down to this."

"Do you remember where the mosque was?"

"I do," Amy's mother butts in. "She showed me it once when I was visiting. It's on West Broadway. It sounded like he was there a lot. Maybe the people there will know something about him."

Kara nods, taking it all in. The pieces of the puzzle slowly form a clearer picture in her mind. The soft patter of rain outside makes the atmosphere heavy as she broods over the information.

———

AN HOUR LATER, Kara is leaving. The quaint suburb, with its charming houses and gentle drizzle, holds an eerie stillness as she walks back to her car. Though she's filled with newfound determination from her conversation with Amy's parents, there's a prickling sensation at the back of her neck, a feeling of being watched.

The dim glow from the distant lampposts barely illuminates the outline of her Subaru, parked in the shadows.

As she slips the key into the lock, a swift movement to her left catches her attention. Before she can react, a strong hand grips her, trying to pull her into the deeper shadows of the tree-lined road. Another hand, gloved, clamps over her mouth, muffling her startled scream. Panic courses through her, but she fights against the immobilizing fear.

In a desperate scramble, Kara's hand dives into her handbag. She grasps the cold metallic body of a taser and, without hesitation, jams it backward into her assailant's face. A muffled scream of pain erupts, the grip on her loosening instantly. The masked figure convulses, then crumples to the ground.

Without wasting a second, Kara dives into her car, her fingers trembling as she turns the key in the ignition. The engine roars to life and she speeds off, tires squealing on the wet road.

Reaching for her phone, she dials 911. As the call connects, the outline of an approaching vehicle in the rearview mirror fills her peripheral vision. Suddenly, a car—lights off, nearly invisible in the rain-soaked darkness—slams into her. The impact jolts Kara, sending a searing pain through her body as she's thrown forwards. The phone flies from her hand, cutting the call short.

The Subaru veers off the road, narrowly avoiding a tree, before Kara wrestles it back onto the street. Taking a few seconds to orient herself, she fights off the dizziness, breathes deeply, and focuses on getting away from her pursuer.

Gripping the steering wheel, she weaves through the narrow lanes of the suburb, her rearview mirror filled with the ominous silhouette of the pursuing car. The streets blur around her, becoming a dizzying cascade of color and light. Every time she thinks she's gained some distance, she feels a jarring thud as the car behind rams into her back bumper.

Her breathing quickens. The dampness of her palms makes it hard to grip the wheel. She pushes her car to its limits, engine growling in response. The neighborhood lights fade, giving way to the intermittent beams of moonlight that dapple the winding country roads that lead out of Albany.

A narrow bridge approaches, and she tries to use it to her advantage. But just as she speeds across, her pursuer closes the gap and delivers a brutal slam to her side. The world tilts as the Subaru loses traction, tires shrieking against the asphalt.

Veering off the highway, the world outside her window

becomes a terrifying blur of dark trees and the rapid approach of a deep embankment leading to a river. She braces herself as the car plows through the underbrush, the shattering of glass and the crunch of metal echoing in her ears. With a final jarring thud, the Subaru slams into a tree, the airbag deploying and leaving Kara dazed.

Shaking off the disorientation, she realizes the immediate danger she is in. Gathering her strength, she wrenches the door open and tumbles out just as a series of gunshots break the silence, splintering the wood of the tree she has crashed into.

Gasping in pain and fear, she sprints toward the river. The sharp stones underfoot and the cold rush of the water do little to hinder her. With the water up to her waist, she dives beneath the surface, swimming with all her might until she reaches a cluster of rocks. Taking cover, she struggles to catch her breath, her entire body trembling from shock and cold.

Every rustle of leaves, every splash of water, heightens her anxiety. But as the minutes tick by, a distant sound catches her attention over her hammering heart: the muffled rumble of another car. The gunman, sensing the imminent arrival of potential witnesses, hastily retreats, the roar of his engine fading into the night.

When she is certain he is gone, Kara carefully emerges from her hiding spot, taking in the mangled wreck of her car. The night's events weigh heavily on her, leaving her feeling vulnerable and shaken. She needs to get to safety and fast. But more than that, she needs answers.

FIFTEEN

CHICAGO

THE EARLY MORNING SUN CASTS A PALE, ALMOST ghostly light on the destruction. Police tape flutters in the breeze, marking a boundary around the obliterated remains of what was once the home of Malik al-Nasri. Evacuated residents, their faces pallid and eyes wide with shock, are held at a safe distance. Bomb squad members, flanked by trained dogs, methodically sweep the nearby buildings.

The Wolf Pack's meticulous planning is evident. The walls of the house, now just shattered remnants, had been packed with explosives. Whether they were detonated by Knight's simple act of ringing the bell or a remote trigger is still a mystery lost among the debris. But Peter, his face stained with soot and eyes weary, is fairly certain it's the latter: that one of the Wolf Pack detonated it himself remotely.

Something about this guy tells Peter that he would have wanted to be the one to physically pull the trigger.

Seated on the curb opposite the smoking rubble, he can't shake off the feeling that the Wolf Pack had been watching, waiting for that exact moment when Ben Knight would step up to the door.

As he reflects on the horrifying events, Peter's thoughts then turn to Imam Malik al-Nasri. He's pretty sure that the cleric wasn't in on it. Nothing suggests al-Nasri had any inkling of the impending doom. No signs of foreknowledge whatsoever. This isn't the aftermath of a suicide bombing. Al-Nasri, like Knight, was merely another target. But the question that gnaws at Peter, refusing to let him find peace in the chaos, is why did the guy reach out to him of all people? And to call him by his old codename, too. Like he knew him from before. But as far as Peter can recall, he's never encountered the collective, only heard about them.

While he sits there thinking, Paul Bennett approaches, taking a seat alongside him on the curb.

Bennett takes a deep, ragged breath, his voice laden with grief. "You knew Uncle Ben the longest, didn't you?"

Peter's eyes remain unfocused, staring at the ruins. "Yeah, I did." A slight hitch in his voice as memories flood back. "Ben was... he was one of the good ones. Always fair. You could trust him. And considering the shit we went through in the Fallen Angel program, that was a rare thing."

Bennett's eyes glisten, a mixture of pain and nostalgia. "I looked up to him ever since I was a kid. Every summer at his cabin, fishing, listening to his stories... I thought the world of him. Following him into the CIA—it was all I ever wanted."

The weight of loss hangs heavy between them. The chirping of early morning birds seems almost out of place amidst the devastation around them.

"I remember the first op we were on together," Peter's voice, though shaky, carries a tone of deep respect. "Straight away I knew Ben was reliable. His hands were steady, his eyes focused. He had that way about him, you know? Made you believe everything was going to be alright."

Bennett nods, his throat tightening, struggling with the emotions threatening to spill over. "He had faith in people, saw the good in them. It's something I always admired. And now..." His voice breaks, the reality of the loss hitting hard.

Peter finally turns to look at Bennett, eyes red-rimmed but determined. "We need to find who did this. We need to find him and make him pay."

Bennett's jaw clenches, his resolve palpable. "The Wolf Pack won't get away with this. We're going to catch them, no matter what it takes." The solemn pledge, underscored by the shared history and reverence for the man they've lost, binds them in the silent early dawn.

The moment is interrupted when Aria strides toward them, her usual light-hearted demeanor replaced with an intense seriousness. Brow furrowed, her eyes dart between Peter, Bennett, and Tom Cohen, who has just joined them, his face ashen, still processing the shock of losing their commander.

"Okay," she begins, her voice tense. "So I've done a couple of little checks. Turns out we weren't the only ones to have hacked into al-Nasri's security system. Someone else hacked into it four days ago and has been watching remotely ever since."

Bennett's jaw tightens, his gaze sharp. "Can we get a trace on it?"

Aria's frustration is palpable. "Encrypted IP address that could be anywhere."

"That's how he was watching," Peter murmurs, piecing the puzzle together.

Aria tilts her head slightly, eyes narrowing. "So he knows we're after him."

"It would appear so," Bennett says, his tone grim.

Tom Cohen, who has been silently listening, his eyes still fixated on the ruins, finally speaks. His voice, though quiet, carries an edge. "We're in his crosshairs now."

"That's not all," Peter adds. "He called me. Right after it happened."

"What did he say?" Aria asks.

"Not much. But it was definitely him."

"Did you trace it?" Cohen asks.

"Yeah. Got me nothing more than a standard burner phone that pinged off a nearby cell tower around the same time."

"He was right here," Aria breathes, glancing about the street.

"Or at least close enough to feel the explosion," Bennett adds.

Peter's thoughts race, his mind connecting dots that previously seemed unrelated. "One thing's for sure," he declares, a cold determination in his voice.

"What's that?" Cohen asks, his gaze turning to Peter.

"The wife set us up. It was all a trap to get us here."

Without missing a beat, Bennett nods. "Already on it."

Cizre, Turkey.

Outside the Turkish safe house, two CIA operatives gather. One of them, a tall man with graying temples and cold blue eyes, steps forward and rings the buzzer.

Silence.

He tries again, pressing harder, but there's still no response. The sense of urgency grows palpable between him and his partner. As well as this, they have been unable to reach the Kurdish contact, Hozan, via phone.

With a nod from one of the men, the two operatives move swiftly into position on either side of the door. In one synchronized motion, they kick it in forcefully. The door flies open with a crash, the lock giving way under the combined power of their blows.

Inside, the house is eerily quiet. The telltale signs of a hasty exit are everywhere: clothes scattered on the floor, an overturned chair, a meal half-eaten on the table. But it's the scene in the living room that draws their immediate attention.

Lying in a pool of his own blood is Hozan, a solitary figure placed in charge of keeping Sonya safe. The gory tableau is all too clear—multiple stab wounds speak of a brutal end.

"She stabbed him," one of the men remarks.

"Search the house," the other commands tersely.

The two of them move swiftly, checking every room, closet, and potential hiding spot. But Sonya Kahn is nowhere to be found.

SIXTEEN

ALBANY

KARA IS STILL TREMBLING FROM THE AFTERSHOCKS of the night's events. She sits in an ER cubicle. The muted, sterile light casts a pallor over her face, illuminating a freshly stitched cut above her eye. A blanket, coarse yet comforting, is draped over her shoulders, attempting to shield her from the coldness that has seeped deep within.

The soft rustle of the curtain being drawn aside breaks the silence. A female police officer steps in, her eyes filled with a mix of professional concern and curiosity. She settles onto the chair opposite Kara, flipping open her notepad.

"You claim you were assaulted," she begins, her voice even but not unkind.

Kara nods, her voice coming out shaky. "I was. At first on the street, while trying to get into my car. Then he pursued me in his own vehicle."

The officer glances at a report. "There are marks on the

rear bumper of your vehicle, and we found traces of another car's paint. Did you get a clear view of the man who targeted you?"

The memories flood back: a masked figure, eyes filled with intent. "His face was hidden, but I caught a glimpse of brown eyes," Kara says.

The officer nods, jotting this down. "And the car? Can you provide any specifics?"

Wracking her brain, Kara feels a pang of frustration. She can only recall the enveloping darkness and the car's silhouette. "It was pitch black, and he drove without headlights. I couldn't catch its make or model."

Trying to jog her memory, the cop asks, "Was it an SUV? Or maybe a sedan?"

Kara shrugs, despair evident. "I really can't recall. The darkness and my panic masked a lot."

A sigh escapes the officer. "Well, we'll review any available CCTV footage. Anything else you might remember?"

A battle wages within Kara. She holds fragmented truths, but is it worth sharing? Maybe later, with Detective Diaz, if she decides to. For now, she keeps her cards close. Shaking her head, she murmurs, "No, not at the moment. I'm still trying to process everything. Maybe later, something might come back."

The officer gives a sympathetic smile, standing up. "Take your time, Ms. Tate. Just know that we're here to help."

As the officer leaves, determination replaces the fear in Kara's eyes. If the assailant believed this would deter her, they are gravely mistaken. Kara Tate is relentless in her pursuits.

SEVENTEEN

CHICAGO

In the dim morning light of the bombed-out street, Peter and the rest of the team rally with a fierce determination, pooling every available resource to trace even the faintest of leads. The recent tragedy has made their pursuit deeply personal, amplifying the weight of each ticking second. For mobility and discretion, they maintain their position in the nondescript Ford Transit, still parked a short distance from the devastation.

Inside the back of the van, monitors flicker, and the hum of processors working at full capacity fills the air. Aria's fingers dance over her keyboard as she dives deep into the digital labyrinth, hunting the elusive encrypted IP address the Wolf Pack were using to monitor Malik al-Nasri's home security cameras.

At the front of the van, the soft glow from a lamp illuminates Peter's, Bennett's, and Cohen's faces, the urgency of their conversation cutting through the ambiance.

"So we have to consider," Peter begins, "that everything Sonya Kahn told us was either a lie or a manipulation. For one, I don't think we can count on her physical description of him."

"You don't think he's Middle Eastern?" Bennett interjects, his brow furrowed.

Peter shakes his head slightly, lost in thought. "I'm not sure. Subterfuge is often foggy. She may have offered some accurate details while obscuring others. But I think it's best to stick as loosely to it as we can."

Bennett nods slowly, processing the implication. "Well, it would make sense to lie. Send us on a wild goose chase. You think the Blue Ridge mountains and all that is real?"

"Probably not."

Bennett hesitates for a moment before continuing, "Well, I've still got a team combing records for men in their thirties, raised as Christians in those states, who are of Middle Eastern descent and have appendix scars."

Cohen, who had been silently following the conversation, chimes in, "Any leads?"

"A few, but nothing concrete. There was a significant wave of adoptees from Afghanistan in the mid to late two thousands, especially after the fall of the Taliban. The local churches spearheaded many of these initiatives, bringing in hundreds of kids. A substantial portion were teenagers, which matches our suspect's age profile if he's thirty now."

Peter rubs his temples, weighing the new information. "But if Sonya was lying about his age, which seems likely, it might not lead us anywhere."

Bennett exhales deeply, frustration evident in his tone. "Then we're back to square one."

The soft crackle of the radio interrupts the quiet hum inside the van, and Aria's voice cuts through, breaking the chain of their thoughts. "Come join me in the back. I think I may have found something."

With a mix of hope and urgency, Peter, Bennett, and Cohen swiftly make their way toward the rear of the van. The interior lights gleam over Aria's workstation, illuminating her face as it reflects the glow of multiple screens. Her fingers are poised, ready to display the results of two hours' painstaking work.

The small space feels even tighter as they all huddle around her. Aria, not waiting for their questions, dives right in. "So I've managed to narrow the IP down to three states."

"Which ones?" Peter asks, leaning in.

"Pennsylvania, New Jersey, and New York."

Bennett raises an eyebrow, clearly expecting more. "Okay. Is that it?"

Without lifting her eyes from the monitor, Aria responds, a touch of annoyance evident in her voice. "Do you really underestimate me that badly, Paul?"

Bennett rolls his eyes, his impatience growing. "Get on with it."

With a knowing smirk, Aria continues, "So I've been studying the specific times he accessed al-Nasri's house security feed. There's a discernible pattern, though subtle."

Peter's brow furrows. "What is it?"

Aria leans back, visibly fatigued from her meticulous work. "This guy's disciplined," she explains, pointing to a series of timestamps. "He always logs into the feed at the same time, like clockwork."

"Shift pattern?" Bennett wonders aloud, piecing together the puzzle. "Could he have a job with regular breaks?"

Aria nods, the pieces aligning for her too. "That's exactly my line of thinking. For example, he never logs in between eight and four. Only during lunch hours—and never for long during those times."

Peter's eyes sharpen, processing the revelation. "So he's likely blue collar."

"But can we use it?" Bennett asks, his gaze now fixed intently on Aria.

"If he's sticking to a strict schedule," she states, "we can make some educated guesses. First, if he's logging in during lunch hours and not between eight and four, it implies he's on a job that prevents access during working hours but grants him a set break."

Cohen listens intently, his experience as an operative kicking in, "So a factory job? Construction? Something that involves tight monitoring or limited tech access?"

Aria nods. "Could also be retail, service industry. I know it's not much, but we should start by identifying major factories, construction sites, or commercial hubs in those three states which match the break timings."

Peter leans forward, the wheels in his mind turning rapidly. "We could cross-reference this with any known activity of the Wolf Pack's or places we suspect he might have been."

Aria gestures at the screen, to another window she has opened. "Already on it. And if he's using any personal device or even a company device to access al-Nasri's feed, there might be a digital footprint."

"We can work with local law enforcement," Bennett suggests. "Request employee records, look into any anomalies or individuals who might fit the profile."

Aria smirks. "That's the plan. And once we have a list of potential workplaces, we can dig deeper, check out alibis, movements. He's smart, but this pattern gives us an opening, a vulnerability."

"Fantastic work, Aria," Bennett says. "We might be closer than we think."

Cohen adds his own nod of approval. "Smart girl."

The atmosphere in the van shifts from despair to determination. They have a lead, a genuine chance to track down the elusive Traveler. The team knows the road ahead won't be easy, but with every piece of the puzzle they uncover, they're one step closer to justice.

EIGHTEEN

NEW YORK

MORNING SUNLIGHT FILTERS GENTLY THROUGH the window, casting a soft glow over the café's wooden tables and mismatched chairs. The soft hum of conversations, the clink of porcelain, and the aroma of freshly brewed coffee fills the space. Michael sits impatiently, drumming his fingers on the table as he waits for Mayu.

"Michael." His girlfriend's voice rings out, cheerful and bright, as she approaches the table. A couple follows close behind her—Mayu's college friends, he presumes. The woman has a warm, welcoming smile and wavy auburn hair that cascades over her shoulders. Beside her is a tall man, a good head above Michael, with neatly combed blond hair, sporting glasses and an air of confidence—or is it arrogance?

"Michael," Mayu continues, "this is Hanna and Brad. We're taking a few classes together this semester."

Hanna extends her hand, her grip firm and friendly. "It's nice to meet you."

Michael smiles, feeling at ease. "Likewise."

As for Brad, he merely nods, a brief acknowledgment, as he takes a seat opposite Michael. His blue eyes, though framed by intellectual-looking glasses, seem to hold a constant, critical evaluation of everything they land on. Mayu has described the couple before. Hanna is the real friend, Brad just a hanger-on, though Hanna really likes him. Brad is also older, a mature student.

As the foursome settle, conversation turns, quite naturally given the gathering, to the current classes Mayu and her friends share at Columbia.

"I think Professor Stanton's take on political philosophy is so passé," Brad declares, pushing his glasses up the bridge of his nose with an air of superiority. "All that rubbish about social contracts and man needing to surrender his freedom to escape his nature. That's for the sheep. Those of us who can think for ourselves should embrace our nature. Embrace our instincts away from the numbing effects of everyday society."

Hanna, trying to involve everyone, turns to Michael. "What do you think about the relationship between freedom and authority?"

Michael hesitates. "Well, I haven't given it much thought, to be honest."

Mayu squeezes his hand under the table, a silent word of encouragement.

Brad's lips quirk up in a small, knowing smile, and Michael feels his face heat up a bit. The older student continues, "It's essential, really, to consider these aspects in our rapidly evolving world. Western civilization is due a rebirth."

Michael tries to engage. "Freedom's important, of course. But so is having some rules. It's a balance, isn't it?"

Brad leans back, assessing Michael. "It's far more nuanced than that," he declares.

Hanna, sensing the rising tension, quickly jumps in. "Oh, look, the carrot cake here is amazing. Anyone want to share?"

Mayu, trying to change the topic, says, "Michael and I are thinking of traveling around Asia over the summer."

Michael perks up, grateful for the shift in conversation. "Yeah, we're gonna start in India and work our way across to Vietnam."

"That sounds amazing," Hanna comments.

But Brad, perhaps intentionally, steers the conversation back to academia. "You should read Inglorious Empire by Shashi Tharoor while you travel India. It's a very good polemic on British rule. Have you read his work?"

Michael, feeling cornered, replies, "Can't say I have."

Brad's eyebrows rise slightly, a silent 'I thought as much.' The rest of the conversation blurs for Michael. Brad's steady stream of academic jargon and name-drops feels less like friendly banter and more like a subtle challenge or perhaps even a rebuke.

The hour can't pass quickly enough. When it's time to leave, Hanna gives both Michael and Mayu warm hugs, her genuine nature shining through. Brad, ever the enigma, merely nods, his goodbye as brief as his initial greeting.

Outside, Michael takes a deep breath of fresh air. "Your friend Hanna's nice enough."

Mayu chuckles, wrapping her arm around his. "And Brad?"

"He's... something," Michael replies, choosing his words carefully.

Mayu grins, leaning into him. "He certainly is."

The vibrations from Michael's phone interrupt them. Pulling it from his pocket, he sees Dad flash across the screen.

"Hey, Dad," he greets, trying to keep his voice light. But there's a heavy pause on the other end.

"Hey, Mikey." Peter's voice finally comes through, sounding not only weary but raw, like someone who's been through an emotional wringer.

"Dad, you okay?"

Peter lets out a heavy sigh. "It's been a rough twenty-four hours. But I wanted to hear your voice. How have you been?"

Michael senses the weight of his father's fatigue, a depth of emotion that's unusual for the typically unflappable Peter. "I'm good, Dad. Just had coffee with some of Mayu's... friends."

Peter chuckles weakly. "Making new friends, huh?"

"Yeah, something like that," Michael replies, his thoughts still on the earlier encounter with Brad.

There's another weighted pause. The son's intuition, honed from years of knowing his father's moods, tells him something's off. "Dad, what's going on?"

Peter takes a moment, then says, "Ben Knight... he's dead." His voice trembles for the first time, and it cuts through Michael like a knife. "There was an operation, and things went south. It was... It was sudden."

The weight of the words sink in, and Michael can feel his heart pounding in his chest. "Oh, Dad... I'm sorry."

Peter's voice is thick with emotion. "He was a good man."

Michael feels a tight knot in his stomach, the kind that only comes with grief. "I know," he replies, his voice barely a whisper.

There's another pause as father and son share a moment of silent mourning.

"Dad, I wish I was there with you," he says.

Peter's voice is thick with fatigue. "Me too, son. Me too."

The call ends, and Michael stands there, stunned. Mayu, who's been observing quietly, steps forward, wrapping her arms around him. The warmth of her embrace provides a momentary respite from the pain.

"It'll be okay," she whispers, her words filled with gentle assurance.

For now, Michael simply lets himself be comforted, grateful for Mayu's presence and the simple truth that, even in the face of grief, he's not alone.

NINETEEN

YASIN'S CONSCIOUSNESS IS A SLENDER THREAD, weaving through the darkness that engulfs him. Sounds are distant murmurs, muffled and haunting as they drift in and out of perception. The scent of antiseptic burns, a stringent intrusion that drags him, unwilling, towards awareness. Pain, visceral and raw, claws at his abdomen, but it's a distant whisper, an unreal specter amidst the heavy fog of sedation.

His eyelids flutter, the assault of bright lights painting the darkness with bursts of luminescence. The shadows of two figures loom over him, their forms indistinct, their distant voices pulling him toward wakefulness.

"Yasin," the name reverberates, an anchor hauling him into the stark reality of the pain, the light, the presence of others. His heavy eyelids rebel before conceding, opening to unveil a room of hushed tones and somber light.

He's not alone. Umar and Ayoub stand sentinel, their eyes casting a mixture of disdain and concern.

A bandage adorns Yasin's cheek, a testament to the

taser's savage bite. But that's nothing compared to the discomfort in his stomach. Thick stitches cover a line of torn flesh that is four inches in length, the wound bloated and fresh. The searing agony in his abdomen comes in waves of pain.

As he instinctively feels the wound, a shiver runs down his spine. Ayoub's voice is sharp, the hard edges of his tone cutting through the morose silence of the room.

"You know it has to be this way, Yasin," he says. Each word is a dagger, drawing lines of accusation and condemnation. Umar stands beside him in silent agreement. "You did well acquiring us the ammonium nitrate," Ayoub goes on. "But now your purpose has changed."

"You should never have got with that girl," Umar adds. "You showed her too much."

Anguish and bitterness flare; a dance of fire and ice. "I killed her, didn't I?" Yasin spits back, his voice a poisoned chalice.

Ayoub's nod is somber. "Yes, but you let her friend go. That is why Musa has chosen you to be a martyr, Yasin."

A martyr. The word is a monolith, casting a shadow that swallows the room, the men, the pain. In its dark recesses, the lines between victim and perpetrator, saviour and damned, are ghostly threads, weaving a destiny that none can escape.

The storm in Yasin's eyes is both birth and death; the genesis of a destiny and the culmination of choices made and unmade. His hands, trembling and reluctant, journey to his wounded abdomen. Underneath his soft touch, the line of stitches is a tale of darkness yet to be told. One which the whole world will hear soon enough.

TWENTY

THE SOFT HUM OF THE G650'S ENGINES IS A constant, comforting background noise. Above the clouds, the team is en route to the city that never sleeps: New York. Inside the jet's plush cabin, sleek tables are littered with laptops, cables, and sheets of paperwork.

Aria's eyes are glued to her laptop screen. After hours of meticulous work and advanced algorithms, she's managed a significant breakthrough. She has successfully narrowed down the IP address, once spread across the entirety of the East Coast, to a concentrated four-mile radius around New York City. Essentially, Aria has just significantly reduced the size of the haystack.

Bennett, Peter, and Cohen gather around her, drawn to the glowing map on her screen. Tiny blue markers pinpoint the locations where the Wolf Pack had accessed al-Nasri's security system. The team's task now is to cross-reference these locations with any discernible patterns that might give away the Wolf Pack's habits or routines.

"Okay," Bennett begins, eyes tracing the digital map. "They accessed the security feed at specific intervals, almost like clockwork. We're looking for any businesses, residences, or points of interest that fit the pattern within this radius."

Tom Cohen adds, "If we can correlate the times he accessed the feeds to the locations, we might be able to piece together a routine or even pinpoint a base of operations."

"Did the Wolf Pack always access the feed near a specific café during his lunch break?" Bennett continues. "Or perhaps near a gym in the evening? The key is in the details."

The team members work systematically, dividing the map into sections and looking for patterns. With New York approaching, the stakes are high. But with every click, every pattern discerned, they inch closer to pinpointing the terrorist's location.

Half an hour later, amid the low hum of the jet's engines and the intermittent click of laptop keys, Peter's voice cuts through the silence. "I think I found something," he announces.

Immediately, Aria, Bennett, and Cohen swing their chairs around to peer at his screen. The display showcases an internal messaging system exclusive to the maintenance department of the New York Subway.

"So I was looking at possible targets," Peter says.

Laid out before them is a list detailing a series of maintenance jobs: tasks, faults, and issues reported.

"Look here." Peter taps on the screen, drawing the team's attention to a series of timestamps. "What caught my eye is a pattern of consistent anomalies with the subway's security apparatus, specifically, camera blackouts. These blackouts consistently occur in the same area and at the same time. Moreover, each malfunction or outage aligns almost exactly with the times our suspect checks al-Nasri's feed."

Aria tilts her head, processing the information. "So you're saying at the same time each day, he heads to the subway and... what? Sabotages the system?"

Peter nods. "Seems like it. Either he's directly involved in these outages, or there's a major coincidence here. He even got pinged several times on a cell tower close to the entrance of the subway maintenance tunnels while accessing al-Nasri's security system on a burner phone."

Cohen, leaning in to get a closer look, comments, "It could be part of an escape route or something else we haven't considered yet."

Bennett, leaning back thoughtfully, taps his fingers on his laptop's surface. "So the New York subway becomes his playground after hours. We've got a timeline and a location. It gives us a point to start."

Aria narrows her eyes, her analytical mind in overdrive. "The subway system is vast. He could be doing anything from planting devices to simply using it as a mode of transportation. We need to figure out his purpose."

Bennett stands, determination setting his features. "Well, there's only one way to find out." He looks at the team with renewed vigor. "We're heading to the New York subway."

TWENTY-ONE

NEW YORK

THE MOSQUE AMY'S MOTHER MENTIONED, THE ONE on West Broadway, is named Masjid al Farah. Kara settles into a corner of the bookstore, her chosen vantage point concealed yet clear enough to give her a direct view of the mosque's entrance across the street. The establishment she sits in, named "Page Turner's Haven," has the familiar scent of old paper and leather, blending with a hint of freshly brewed coffee from the in-store café.

From her corner, she can hear the muffled sounds of New York's ever-busy boulevard: honking taxis, the distant chatter of pedestrians, the occasional siren. Every now and then, the mosque's doors open, releasing a small group of people into the sunlight, their shoes clicking on the pavement as they head off in different directions.

A gentle call to prayer floats through the air, its soothing rhythm bringing a brief serenity to the bustling street. Kara, however, is barely aware of it. She's been at this post beside the window for nearly three hours now, and each minute seems longer than the last. The spine of the book she's clutching—some mystery novel she picked up without much thought—is creased from the tension in her grip. She hasn't turned a page in almost an hour.

As the minutes drag on, Kara's attention starts to drift. Maybe this is a dead end. Maybe she's following the wrong lead. But just as these doubts begin to take root, fresh movement at the mosque's entrance catches her eye.

A man steps out, momentarily pausing to adjust the collar of his shirt. His appearance is unremarkable, save for one glaring detail—a white bandage stark against the tan of his cheek. Memories flash through Kara's mind: the glint of metal, the electric hum of the taser, the muffled scream of her attacker, his hand reaching up to his cheek. Two prongs, two marks.

She strains her eyes, trying to discern any sign of two dark scorch marks beneath the bandage. But the distance and her discreet position don't afford her a clear view.

She realizes she can't just sit and wonder; she needs to act. Quietly, she sets the book down on the table, careful not to attract attention. Slipping on her large-rimmed hat and adjusting her sunglasses to shield most of her face, she swiftly exits the bookstore.

The man, oblivious to Kara's intense gaze, heads down the street, lost in the sea of pedestrians. But Kara's eyes don't lose him, not for a second. Every step she takes is calculated, maintaining a safe distance yet never letting him out of her sight. The hunt is on.

THE RAIL CONTROL Center buzzes with a muted cacophony of low hums of machinery, sporadic radio chatter, and the click-clack of keyboards. Amidst this orchestrated chaos stands a monolithic wall of monitors, each screen flashing with camera feeds from different corners of New York's sprawling subway system.

Peter and the rest of the team are escorted into the center's inner sanctum: a security hub that houses the nerve system of the entire underground network. Bathed in the cold, bluish glow of the screens, the four of them feel the weight of the room's importance.

They're greeted by Officer Ted Spinelli, a portly, middle-aged transit cop with a thinning hairline and the weary eyes of someone accustomed to late shifts and countless cups of coffee. He gestures toward a cluster of monitors, which flicker intermittently with static, drawing a frown from the seasoned officer.

"Been like this for two weeks," he grumbles, adjusting his belt which seems to be perennially fighting a losing battle against his belly. "Always the same time, feeds go dark along the same stretch of tunnels. And then, right on cue, they light back up a few hours later. Like clockwork. Never seen anything like it."

Aria, eyes darting between the screens, takes note. "Two to three hours, you said?"

Spinelli nods. "Every single night. Strange, right?"

"Outside cyber attack?" Cohen suggests, leaning in closer to the screens.

"Could be, but our IT guys haven't found anything yet," Spinelli responds.

Peter, arms crossed, studies the pattern, his mind racing. "Someone is using that window for a specific task. Maybe to do something undetected inside the tunnel."

Spinelli raises an eyebrow, impressed by Peter's deduction. "Exactly what I was thinking. Someone knows the system well enough to exploit it."

"Has anyone been down there to take a look?" Bennett asks.

"Nope," is the answer. "We got too many problems on our hands to send people running around those tunnels."

Bennett steps forward, his tone urgent. "Then we need to go down there. Take a look around the locations of these cameras. Can you take us there?"

Spinelli looks momentarily taken aback by Bennett's intensity but nods in agreement. "Sure thing," he says, reaching for the nearby rack to grab his heavy-duty coat, the fabric worn from years of service.

Aria, Peter, Bennett, and Cohen exchange glances. They may just be on to something, and in the labyrinth of New York's subway, they're about to delve deeper into the mystery. Every second counts.

———

KARA'S FOOTSTEPS barely make a sound as she tails the man from the mosque through the maze of New York streets. The steady hum of traffic is punctuated by distant sirens and the occasional shout, but her world narrows to the rhythmic tap of his heels against the pavement.

The air feels thick to Kara, not just with pollution but with tension. She can taste the grit of the city on her lips and feel the weight of its energy pressing on her, urging her forward.

He suddenly turns, leading her to the gaping maw of a subway entrance. The metallic scent of the underground hits her immediately, a mix of iron, grime, and stale humanity. Her heart thunders in her chest, each beat mirroring the urgency of her pursuit.

She slips in just behind him, using a cluster of people as a natural barrier. The fluorescent lights overhead cast an unnatural glow, making the shadows deeper, more deceptive. As he boards a train, she's right on his heels, darting into the adjacent carriage. Through the grimy connecting window, she watches him. Every movement he makes sharpens her focus, tightening the knot in her stomach.

Then he does something that sends a jolt running through her: he reaches up to his cheek, lifting the bandage slightly to scratch the wound. Beneath it, two dark scorch marks mock her—the damning signature of her taser.

The train's brakes squeal, announcing an impending stop. He rises, and she's immediately on the move, shadowing him as he leaves his carriage. The platform is dim, lights flickering. She's unyielding as she follows him along it, using every pillar and advertising board as makeshift shields.

Suddenly, he does the unexpected. He doesn't head for the exit at the end like she had presumed. Instead, he drops onto the tracks, glancing around only once before vanishing into the foreboding darkness of the tunnel.

Her breath catches, the cold, stale air stinging her lungs. For a split second, Kara hesitates. But determination propels her forward. Descending onto the tracks, the city's familiar noise fades, replaced by her own ragged breathing and the distant, ominous hum of a train. Whatever secrets he holds, she's now more determined than ever to uncover them.

———

PETER, Bennett, Aria, and Cohen move cautiously through the belly of the subway system, the beams of their flashlights cutting through the darkness like sabers. Officer Ted Spinelli leads the way, the transit cop's familiarity with the tunnels evident in the confidence of his every step. The muted crunch of gravel beneath their feet fills the dank space. Occasionally, it's joined by the distant screech of metal against metal as trains ply their routes somewhere above or below them.

The damp, stagnant air carries the unmistakable scent of mold, intermixed with the metallic tang of old, rusting tracks. A chilled wind finds its way through the passages, curling around their bare necks, making them shiver as they're pulled deeper into the heart of the underground.

Distant rumbles ebb and flow, a symphony of subterranean activity. Sometimes the vibrations under their feet grow pronounced as a train draws near, only to fade into silence, replaced by the soft, eerie rush of the wind.

"We get plenty of vagrants down here," Ted Spinelli remarks. "They climb the fence or cut a hole. Come seeking shelter, especially on cold nights."

As he says this, Peter notices remnants of makeshift beds —a filthy mattress with holes burned in it, old newspapers, tattered clothing—and empty food containers. There's a desolate, forgotten feel to the place, remnants of stories left unfinished and untold.

Cohen steps closer, shining his flashlight on the abandoned belongings. "It shouldn't be like this," he comments grimly.

Turning a bend, the tunnels open up into a wider service area. Officer Spinelli stops and motions with his flashlight. "This is it. Where the cameras keep acting up."

In this space, the air feels heavier, colder. Peter's flashlight sweeps over the ground. He immediately picks out a set of deep grooves in the gravel. They stand out because they're the only ones in the inch-deep layer of crud that covers the ground. "Tire tracks?" he muses aloud, a quizzical frown forming.

"A truck by the look of it," Cohen adds.

"Do people still drive down here?" Bennett questions Officer Spinelli, gesturing at the evidence beneath their feet.

Spinelli shakes his head, clearly puzzled. "They shouldn't. Not for at least ten years, anyway."

Tom Cohen kneels, running his fingers over the tracks. "And yet, here they are. As clear as day," he adds, his voice echoing ominously through the tunnel.

"But someone could get access?" Aria inquires, trying to piece together the clues.

"I guess," Ted admits, his uncertainty palpable. "There are still ways in if you know where to look."

Peter's flashlight beam follows the tire tracks as they snake into the foreboding shadows of another passage. "What's down there?" he asks, a note of urgency in his voice.

Officer Spinelli swallows, the dry click audible in the

silent expanse. "Mostly old storage areas. No one's used 'em in years."

The group exchanges uneasy glances, the weight of the unknown pressing on them. Every rumble and whisper is amplified in the suffocating silence, and the mystery of what awaits them in the depths of the tunnel hangs heavy in the air.

———

KARA'S BREATH comes in short, measured bursts as she stealthily tracks her assailant through the shadowy confines of the subway. The murky lighting, an uneven blend of distant station lights and the occasional dim overhead bulb, casts menacing shadows that dance on the damp walls. Every far off sound down the long, dark tunnel amplifies the tension, reminding her of the danger lurking right in front of her. She begins to question her sanity: Why is she following a man who clearly tried to kill her literally hours ago?

Maybe he knows I'm following him, she thinks. Maybe he's drawing me into a trap.

As she proceeds, her target pauses, his silhouette visible against a faintly lit section of the tunnel as he leans against the wall. Holding her breath, Kara quickly tucks herself into a nearby alcove, her heart pounding against her chest.

He appears to be in pain, clutching at his side with his other hand. As he lifts his shirt, she catches a glimpse of bandages adhered to his side. A pang of confusion hits her— she doesn't recall inflicting a wound in that area during their previous encounter. But given the chaotic nature of their confrontation, there's no telling what injuries she might have inadvertently caused.

The man lifts the bandages, revealing a nasty looking set of stitches across his stomach. Kara is certain—she never gave him such an injury. This is something else.

Resuming his journey, the man she is sure is her assailant leads her deeper into the city's subterranean labyrinth. The musky scent of damp and the distant, perpetual thrum of the city above them accompany their descent. Kara feels like she knows where they're heading: Times Square, a bustling hub even beneath the ground.

Kara gets little time to reflect on this fact, however.

Suddenly, the roaring sound of an approaching train fills her ears, and its bright lights loom closer at breakneck speed. Caught off guard, she has no choice but to throw herself back and press herself as close as possible to the cold, rough concrete wall of the tunnel. The wind generated by the train's speed buffets her, tugging at her clothes and hair. As the massive beast rushes past, mere inches from her face, she feels the power and fury of the city racing through its veins.

When the train finally vanishes into the distance, leaving only its lingering rumble behind, Kara takes a moment to catch her breath. But the assailant's form is moving ahead, and she knows she must press on. The stakes are too high, and every shadow, every noise becomes a part of the chase, driving her deeper into the bowels of New York City.

———

THE COLD, damp tunnels give way to a distinct smell, sharp and invasive. Peter, well-acquainted with that scent from his years in the field, stops in his tracks. His heart rate quickens as recognition sets in.

"That smell," he murmurs, his voice barely above a whisper.

Bennett takes a deep breath through his nose, his face contorting in concern. "Ammonium nitrate."

Aria, her normally composed face now etched with worry, nods in agreement. "It's strong. Must be nearby."

Cohen pulls the collar of his shirt over his nose, the acrid scent stinging his nostrils. "We need to move cautiously," he warns.

They follow the pungent odor until they arrive at a large open shutter. The tire tracks they had been following vanish into the opening. Their senses on high alert, they unholster their pistols with a synchronized motion.

Peter signals to Ted Spinelli. "Wait here."

The transit cop nods.

Cautiously, the four agents take their positions at the entrance, pistols raised. With silent coordination, they step into the underground storage area, every sense heightened. The overpowering stench of ammonium nitrate envelops them, making it hard to breathe. Yet there are only the residual signs of the powder having been present; the floor is smeared with it, the walls, too. Whatever was in here, though, has been largely removed.

Aria's sharp intake of breath draws the others' attention. She's staring straight up, eyes widened in horror. Following her gaze, Peter, Bennett, and Cohen tilt their heads upward, their faces paling at the sight.

Strategically placed explosives line the ceiling, each attached to a sturdy rafter. Right above their heads is an intricate web of destruction, ready to take down the very foundation of the city. A deafening rumble interrupts the chilling silence as a train moves overhead, causing a shower of dust to rain down on them.

Peter swallows hard. "This... this is enough to take out the entire station."

Cohen's jaw tightens, and his voice is strained. "This is premeditated. Meticulously planned."

Bennett shouts, panic evident in his voice, "Ted!"

"Yeah?" comes the resounding reply from the officer.

Bennett's voice trembles as he asks, "What's directly above us?"

"Times Square," Ted responds, confusion evident in his voice. "Why? What's going on?"

Bennett's reply is urgent, his voice desperate, "You need to get on your radio. Evacuate the entire area. And get us backup, NOW!"

———

THE DAMP SUBWAY air seems to be getting thicker. Kara's senses are on high alert. The soft padding of her shoes against the wet ground and the distant rumbling of trains create an eerie symphony. Her focus is on the man she's tailing. She slows her pace as he rounds a corner, taking a moment to gather herself. A myriad of distant noises reverberate through the cavernous space, some sounding like what Kara is sure are hushed voices, but they're so indistinct amidst the other noises of the underground that she can't be sure.

With bated breath, she turns the corner, only to find herself immediately trapped. The man's hand shoots out, and he grips her tightly, slamming her against the cold, damp wall. Before she can even register what's happening, the cold steel of a blade is pressed menacingly against her throat. Fear pierces through Kara, her breath coming in rapid, shallow gasps.

"Why are you following me?" he hisses, his eyes gleaming with malice. A flash of recognition darkens his features further. "You?" Rage twists his face, making him even more menacing. He pulls back his hand, readying the knife for a lethal strike.

Every second stretches out, as if time itself is holding its breath, the weight of impending doom hanging in the balance. But then, out of the enveloping darkness, a commanding voice cuts through the tension. "Hold it there!"

Both Kara and her attacker turn their heads, squinting into the gloom. Emerging from the shadows, a man strides confidently toward them, the distinct shape of a pistol pointed directly at her attacker.

Kara's heart pounds in her chest, her mind racing, hoping that this new arrival is an ally rather than another threat. The tension in the dimly lit subway tunnel becomes increasingly tangible. The soft hum of electricity and distant rumbles of passing trains are drowned out by the thudding beat of Kara's heart.

"Let her go," the newcomer orders firmly, his voice reverberating in the cavernous space.

Emerging from the inky shadows of the subway tunnel, Peter Black's silhouette stands tall and unwavering, every line and muscle of his body radiating a lethal determination. The muted light casts a cold gleam on his SIG Sauer, which is almost as cold as the gleam in his steel-gray eyes.

Tom Cohen is just steps behind him, his own weapon raised and ready, his eyes fixed on the assailant with unyielding intensity.

But the assailant is quick. Shoving Kara in front of him, he uses her as a human shield, the knife's cold blade pressing ominously against the skin of her throat. "Seems like you're closer than I thought," he taunts, his voice dripping with menace.

Peter's expression is one of pure focus. "Let her go," he demands once more, the force behind his words evident.

Cohen, mirroring Peter's unwavering stance, adds his own voice to the command. "You're not walking out of here."

The situation escalates further when the assailant uses his free hand to pull a dead man's switch from his jacket pocket, holding the fate of everyone in the tunnel in his hand. "You recognize this, don't you?" he challenges, his gaze locked with Peter's and then flicking to Cohen.

Both men nod, their eyes never leaving the device.

"You've seen the C4 packed into the rafters."

Another nod from both Peter and Cohen, the weight of understanding visible in their eyes.

"Then you understand the stakes at play."

As the assailant backs away with Kara, keeping her close and the knife pressed to her neck, Peter's determination is unwavering. "You can't leave with her," he asserts.

It is then, from the darkness of the tunnel, that Bennett and Aria emerge. Both of them have pistols raised and trained on the assailant. Kara's eyes widen in fear, an involuntary scream escaping her lips and piercing the tense silence as the knife bites into her skin, drawing a thin line of blood.

With a swift move, the assailant backs up to an emergency door and pushes it open, the metal clanging loudly as the two of them slip through it.

Peter, calculating quickly, says to the others, "I'll trail them. You three, try and cut them off. He won't risk setting the explosives off while he's still in range. We have to keep him inside the station."

With the plan set, Bennett, Aria and Cohen split off, taking a different route. Peter, with determination fueling his steps, enters the stairwell, where the rhythmic shuffle of hurried footsteps spirals upward. Each echoing cry from Kara sends an icy jolt of anticipation down his spine. With his senses heightened, the moist, cool air in the stairwell contrasts sharply with the sweat forming across his body.

Emerging onto the Time Square platform, a scene of controlled chaos unfolds before Peter, the evacuation already underway. Overhead lights buzz and flicker intermittently, casting sporadic light over the massive expanse of tiles. The faint scent of body odor, mixed with the metallic tang of the subway, fills the air. People, in various states of panic, move like a flood over the platform, pushing past each other to get as far away from danger as possible. All the while, cops and transit workers try to usher them out.

At a distance, Peter catches a glimpse of the assailant—a shadowy figure moving deliberately backward, clutching

Kara closely with one hand while the other grips the dead man's switch. Peter's every instinct screams at him to charge forward, but he forces himself to move methodically, pacing his steps, trying not to escalate the situation any more than it already is.

Suddenly, a swarm of transit police in navy blue uniforms converge on the platform. The metallic glint of their badges is visible even from a distance, their radios crackling with urgent chatter. Several officers, upon spotting the ongoing standoff, instinctively draw their firearms, their expressions a mix of fear, determination, and confusion.

"It's under control!" Peter shouts, his voice resonating above the din, carrying an authority that belies his mounting anxiety. "Focus on the evacuation!"

The officers, taking Peter's cue, put their guns away and redouble their efforts, ushering panicked passengers toward the exits. The ever-present hum of subway activity is punctuated by cries of distress, the rhythmic thud of boots, and the occasional barked order.

Drawing ever closer to the turnstiles, the first hint of daylight can be seen from the stairs leading to the street above—but Peter can't let him get that far. Once he's out of reach of the bombs, he'll drop that switch. Peter is sure of it.

Yet before any idea of how to stop that can fully form in his head, a phalanx of heavily armed NYPD officers storm down the steps, their black tactical gear stark against the bright lights of the platform.

"Freeze!" they bellow, weapons trained on the assailant.

He twists around to see them. Seizing the moment, Kara drives her elbow into the wound on his stomach with all her might, managing to break free when he goes weak with pain. Her desperate sprint carries her straight into Peter's arms. He holds her briefly, ensuring she's safe, before turning his attention back to the immediate threat.

Unfortunately, there's a problem, one that becomes apparent pretty quickly. The NYPD isn't in the loop about the dead man's switch. Their demand is a loud, unyielding, "Drop it or we'll shoot!" Their intentions are clear, their posture aggressive.

For a heart-stopping moment, everything seems to freeze. The assailant's face breaks into a wicked grin as he locks eyes with Peter. "Okay," he says in a tone dripping with malice. "Have it your way."

With a swift motion, he drops the switch and raises his hands.

The moment lingers like the breath before a storm, where everything is deathly still. Then, a tremendous roar shakes the very foundations of the station. The ground quivers beneath them, a violent tremor that feels like the very earth is rebelling. Beneath the weight of the explosion, the concrete floor cracks, spiderweb patterns racing outward, growing, expanding.

Chaos erupts.

The ground, once solid and dependable, starts buckling, sending people into a frenzied panic. Some dive desperately for cover, arms over their heads. Others are not so fortunate, their feet sliding out from under them, swallowed by the widening chasm, their cries piercing the cacophony of destruction. Overhead lights flicker and burst, showering the pandemonium below with a hail of glass.

Amidst the turmoil, a large chunk of debris strikes Kara,

knocking her to the ground, her body instantly going limp. Peter, fighting against the bucking tremors and his own panic, lunges for her. With a grunt of effort, he lifts her unconscious form, throwing her over his shoulder in a fireman's carry.

As another violent shake threatens to tip him over, Peter catches sight of a piece of concrete flooring that's now angling upward. Without a second's hesitation, he dashes for it, every step a battle against the forces threatening to pull him under. Dust and smoke form a blinding, choking veil around him, making every breath a labor. His footfalls mirror his heartbeat—urgent, pounding, desperate.

The tilted concrete, unstable and shifting, begins its treacherous slide into the gaping abyss as the station caves in on itself. Peter's boots scurry for purchase, searching for any crack, any grip to propel him forward. Time seems to slow, every second an eternity of risk as he clings to Kara on his shoulder, her presence adding an extra, desperate dimension to the scramble.

Then, just as the entire station seems destined to collapse into the ground, Peter reaches the edge. The stairs to the street beckon like the promise of salvation. Drawing on reserves he didn't know he had, he bolts up the steps, Kara's weight a testament to his resolve.

Emerging into the light of day, he's greeted by a new scene of disorder and confusion. Times Square, usually a bastion of life and energy, is in utter turmoil. People are scattering in every direction, their screams intermingling with the wail of sirens. As Peter pauses to catch his breath, a monstrous plume of dust and debris bursts from the subway exits, enveloping everything in its path.

Tom Cohen appears, helping Peter with Kara, ensuring they both get out of immediate danger. Peter's chest heaves, each breath a mix of relief and dread as he takes in the transformed landscape.

Cohen, sharing the weight of the moment, looks at Peter. Their eyes lock, a silent recognition passing between them of the gravity of what's just unfolded and the uncertainty of the ordeal that lies ahead.

———

THE ASSAILANT, driven by a cocktail of adrenaline and dread, slips through the subway exit amidst the frenzy of falling debris and choking dust. He's greeted by the pandemonium of Times Square. Amidst the cacophony of cries and the rush of panic, he strides purposefully, a stark contrast to the fleeing masses.

Nevertheless, it's not long before he senses a presence behind him. The realization doesn't come from seeing or hearing. It comes from the icy touch of cold metal pressed menacingly against the back of his neck. He freezes, every muscle tensing.

Standing behind him is Paul Bennett, his face a mask of steely determination, his gun unwavering. A few paces away, Aria Patel, equally grim-faced, aims her pistol at the assailant, her gaze locked on to him with an intensity that brooks no defiance.

"Put your hands behind your head and get down on your knees," Bennett commands, his voice cold and unyielding.

For a moment, defiance flits across the assailant's eyes,

but Bennett's unwavering glare snuffs it out. Slowly, the man complies, the weight of his situation sinking in.

As he drops to his knees, Aria approaches, handcuffs in hand. In the midst of the madness surrounding them, the trio creates a pocket of stillness, the climax of justice slowly unfolding.

TWENTY-TWO

NEW YORK

IN THE HEART OF MIDTOWN PRECINCT SOUTH, THE interrogation room is quiet, save for the faint hum of the overhead lights. Its battleship gray walls, devoid of decoration, close in oppressively. The old scent of tobacco lingers, a grim reminder of past confrontations held within these confines.

The bomber, chained to a heavy metal table via a pair of handcuffs, sits forward, his posture tense. His eyes dart between the two FBI agents facing him.

Agent Foley, sitting directly opposite the bomber, is a striking figure. Tall with sharp cheekbones, her chestnut brown hair is pulled taut into a bun, highlighting the icy intensity of her blue eyes. Every inch of her screams authority, from her crisply ironed suit to the polished Star-Spangled Banner pin stuck in her lapel.

To her right, Agent Johnson provides a stark contrast.

His compact frame, topped with sandy hair that's seen a touch too much sun, suggests years of fieldwork. Though the lines on his face speak of experience, his hazel eyes still retain a spark of youthful curiosity.

Being that they're all stateside, it's the FBI's show.

Clearing her throat, Foley begins, "You've caused quite a commotion today. It would be in your best interest to cooperate."

Johnson, leaning slightly back in his chair, adds with a hint of menace, "Because right now, you're looking at charges that will keep you behind bars for multiple lifetimes."

Inside the observation room, Tom Cohen leans forward, whispering to Peter. "Watch his hands," he advises, pointing out the bomber's subtle movements that betray his fluctuating emotions.

"Then what would be the point in cooperating?" the bomber asks. "If I'm doomed anyway."

The two agents share a sideways glance before retraining their gazes on the assailant.

"You understand what happens next, don't you?" Foley puts to him.

The bomber says nothing. Just stares back at her.

When Foley continues, her voice is low and ominous. "You get this one chance to explain yourself here, before we hand you over to the CIA and they put you on a one-way trip to Guantanamo. See if their guys out there can't persuade you to tell them everything you know in their own unique style."

The assailant swallows hard. But behind his fearful gaze,

there's a glint of defiance. The interrogation is only just beginning.

Next door, inside the observation room, the dim lighting casts shadows over the intense expressions on the faces of Peter and the rest of the team. From the speaker above, tinny and slightly muffled voices from the interrogation room filter through, making the atmosphere even more intense.

Bennett, one hand firmly gripping a radio, looks authoritative as he instructs the FBI agents inside. Both Foley and Johnson wear earpieces, receiving Bennett's ongoing guidance. As they converse, every word, every hint of an intonation is keenly observed and analyzed by the three watchers outside.

"Take his cuffs off," Bennett whispers into the mic. "Let him feel a little more comfortable."

Inside, Foley, with deliberate care, comes around the table and unhooks the cuffs from the bomber. The faint clinking of the chain resonates in the room, a marked difference to the otherwise heavy silence. The bomber sighs, leaning back, his wrists red and chafed. Dust, a dark reminder of the subway explosion, cascades from his short curly hair onto his shoulders as he moves.

Johnson attempts to break the ice. "You want a coffee?"

"I don't drink coffee."

"Tea, soda?"

The bomber shakes his head firmly.

Inside the observation room, Peter's eyes never leave the man beyond the glass. "He looks just like how Sonya described him."

"And he sounds like him, too," Aria continues. "His

accent is typical of the Appalachians. Also not liking coffee. Could be Mormon. Would explain the conversion."

Peter rubs his temples, his unease palpable. "But if she was telling the truth, why did she lead us into a trap, then?"

The other side of Peter, Tom Cohen thoughtfully murmurs, "Maybe she told some of the truth. Or maybe she didn't know it was a trap. Maybe someone else took her and killed Hozan."

Inside the interrogation room, tension hangs thick in the air. Foley's gaze is inflexible as he addresses the bomber, voice firm. "So you gonna tell us your name?"

"No, Agent Foley," the bomber retorts with a smirk, eyes gleaming with mischief. "I am not going to tell you my name. You will have to use your resources to find it out."

They've taken his fingerprints. Nothing came back on the Integrated Automated Fingerprint Identification System (IAFIS). He doesn't have a police record at least.

Bennett murmurs into the radio, "Ask him if Abu Musa rings any bells."

Foley touches her ear, then asks the question. The result is chilling. The bomber turns to the one-way and smiles before returning his gaze to the agents.

Johnson assesses him, trying a different angle. "You sound American. Midwestern?"

The bomber's grin widens, clearly enjoying the guessing game.

Behind the one-way mirror, Aria shakes her head, rolling her eyes at the agent's inability to place the accent correctly. As for Peter, his gaze remains focused, his features tightening with each second. The more he observes, the more he finds himself drawing connections to Sonya's description of the man behind the Wolf Pack. And with every moment, an unsettling sensation inside him grows more potent.

"Ohio?" Johnson ventures, looking to catch the man off guard.

The bomber's chuckle is cut short, replaced by an exaggerated eye roll. But his amusement quickly dissipates as a sudden sharp pain forces him to clutch his side.

"You hurt yourself," Foley points out, noting the man's reaction.

Nodding in agreement, the bomber raises his eyes to meet Foley's, hand still pressed firmly against the injury. There's an evident discomfort in his demeanor.

Foley's attention shifts to the bomber's bruised face. "Same as your face."

Johnson, curious and persistent, probes further. "How'd it happen?"

The bomber's defiance returns, his voice cold. "It doesn't matter."

Inside the dim observation room, Bennett's voice whispers through the earpieces of the two agents, guiding their line of questioning, the room electric with tension.

"Ask him about the bombing of al-Nasri," Bennett's voice instructs.

Foley leans forward. "Tell us about Malik al-Nasri. What do you know about him?"

The bomber smirks. "You mean the time Malik al-Nasri tipped your government off about the wedding of the daughter of an important al-Qaeda member, and your subsequent drone strike killed the entire wedding party in Yemen?"

Johnson interjects, "What about Abu Musa's involvement in the recent attack in Beirut?"

The bomber retorts, "Like when American-made weapons raze schools in Palestine?"

Bennett's voice again guides them. "Ask him about his time in Raqqa."

Johnson, not missing a beat, says, "Tell us about Raqqa."

The bomber's eyes darken. "You mean when children starved in Syria because of your sanctions?"

The questioning continues in this manner, with the bomber turning every question into an accusation about some real or fabricated atrocity. The wound on his flank continues to cause him occasional discomfort, each wince a grim reminder of the violence he's endured for his god.

"Your wife," Foley pushes. "She executed a Kurdish contact in Turkey. You know where she is now?"

"What is one traitor to Islam when your government murders thousands of my brothers and sisters?" the bomber fires back. "When they turned a blind eye to the corruption of the men they put in charge in Afghanistan, so that entire villages suffered from contaminated water supplies, while the government spent the money?"

The atmosphere in the room thickens. The questioning reaches its climax when Johnson, leaning over the table, asks in a stern tone, "What do you know about the Wolf Pack?"

The bomber turns, his gaze fixed intently on the one-way mirror. It's as if he's looking directly at Peter. "What do I know?" he asks. The silence is chilling. "I know that the sword of Allah comes in many forms." The venom in his voice when he says this sends a chill down everyone's spine.

Shaking off the discomfort, Agent Foley attempts to regain control. "Let's get back to the subway bombing."

The bomber dismissively shakes his head, turns back to her from the one-way, then looks up at the stained ceiling tiles. "I'm getting bored of this," he groans in a tired voice. "I want to enter Paradise now. I want to go home."

As the tension reaches its zenith, Bennett's radio comes alive with a message. "Kara Tate is awake."

Bennett glances at Peter. "This is just going around in circles," he whispers. "You wanna come with me and see what she's got to say?"

"Sure," Peter replies, his voice shaky. The weight of the obscure interrogation lingers as he stands, but he shrugs it off, ready to face another challenge.

———

NYU Langone Tisch Hospital stands just a stone's throw away from the precinct. The walk takes less than five minutes. The sterile, white light of the hospital corridors contrasts sharply with the dim interrogation room they've just left behind. The faint smell of antiseptic fills the air, and the soft hum of medical equipment serves as the backdrop to the scene before them.

Inside a private room, Kara lies against immaculate white pillows. Her usually vibrant olive skin seems washed out against the crisp sheets. A small bandage over her right eye contrasts starkly against her raven hair, now pulled back to reveal her face. There's a certain weariness in her eyes, but also a fire—a determination that tells anyone who looks at her that she's not easily defeated.

Kara's focus shifts from the outside world as Peter and Bennett enter. Recognizing her rescuer, her lips hint at a smile. "I owe you a thanks," she murmurs. "They said you carried me out of there."

Peter nods toward her cut forehead, his voice laced with concern. "You okay?"

Her eyes sparkle with a hint of mischief. "Just a scratch. I've had worse playing softball."

Peter doubts that. She's being glib and using humor to deflect the fact that she's in shock and possibly concussed. It's a common technique.

Bennett clears his throat, drawing her attention. "Ms. Tate, we need to debrief you. Can you walk us through everything that happened up until the point we found you in the subway? Every little detail might help."

Kara sighs, adjusting herself to a more upright position. "All right," she begins. "Here goes."

As her narrative unfolds, Peter settles into a nearby chair while Bennett stands, arms folded, maintaining a respectful distance. They hang on every word, interjecting occasionally for clarity. Her recounting paints a vivid image of Kara's harrowing last few days.

"So you think the man who set off those explosives," Bennett inquires, "could be this Joseph Dalton guy your friend was dating?"

Kara nods. "Yes. He's also the guy who attacked me. And even though the footage was really grainy, I'm sure it was the same guy who pointed at Amy on the loading bay."

Peter interjects, "It means the others are out there; the rest of the collective."

Kara agrees, "At least three men were on that loading bay."

Bennett pauses before revealing, "There's more." Their eyes fix on him. "Preliminary findings suggest the subway bombs contained C4. Plastic explosive. That means we still don't know where the ammonium nitrate is."

"Then," Peter adds, "we need to get back to the bomber. Find out where his accomplices are."

———

BUT THEY DON'T GET to do that.

Back in the interrogation room, a sudden, eerie ringtone slices through the air, the piercing tone of a call not expected but ominously timely. The air grows cold, and the FBI agents exchange wide-eyed glances, hands instinctively moving to check their own devices.

Neither is receiving a call, and yet the tone goes on. They're professionals, trained to expect the unexpected, but nothing has prepared them for what is coming next. A cold shiver runs down their spines as they pinpoint the source of the sound: It is coming from the man before them.

They are sure he was searched thoroughly when he came in.

It's then that both agents realize the ringing is coming from the wound in the bomber's stomach—from inside the bomber. He lifts his gaze, that familiar spark of malevolence now accompanied by a hint of triumphant glee. "Seems my time is up," he murmurs, the corners of his lips stretching into a sinister grin. "Paradise is calling."

Aria and Tom Cohen, positioned behind the one-way mirror, feel their heartbeats reverberate in their ears. Panic surges within them as they turn sideways, their eyes meeting, an instinctual knowledge that every second counts.

But destiny doesn't wait.

A blinding flash ignites, followed by a deafening roar that violently shakes the building's very core, tearing through metal, glass, and brick.

———

PETER AND BENNETT are just reentering the precinct when the bomb goes off. Several floors below, they feel the blast's furious might as it rattles through the building. The emergency lights flicker into life, painting the haze-filled corridors in a menacing crimson hue. Smoke alarm sirens pierce the smoky air, the cries of nearby officers joined by the haunting chorus of shouts and terrified screams.

With hearts racing and dread weighing heavily upon them, Peter and Bennett charge up the stairs to the interrogation suite, the smoke and dust getting thicker. The floor is a jagged mosaic of debris and shattered glass, testament to the malevolence that has just transpired. The interrogation room is obliterated, its former confines now a grotesque image of twisted destruction, the bomber and the FBI agents vaporized.

The first person they find is Tom Cohen. Amidst the scene of devastation, he lies crumpled in a corner. The force of the explosion and the subsequent collapse of the room have left his body limp and still. Bennett, his hands trembling, barely registers the ash and dust that smears across Cohen's face as he checks for a pulse. A heavy silence ensues; the absence of a heartbeat confirms the dread that swells within. Every silent feature, every still gesture of Cohen's lifeless form echoes with the unutterable tragedy of a voice and a presence forever silenced. Bennett's expression, taut with anguish, veils the surge of emotions as the glum realization dawns—Tom is gone.

Just as the gravity of Cohen's death begins to cement, a muffled cough pierces the suffocating silence, redirecting their attention. It's Aria. The debris of shattered walls and splintered furniture bury her, yet that feeble sound of life sparks an urgency that propels both men into action. They toil together, hands bleeding and lungs choked with dust, to lift the rubble from her.

Beneath the wreckage, they find her. Aria. Her clothing is blackened and charred, and her body bears the brutal marks of the explosion's wrath. A nasty cut to her forehead leaks blood that mats her hair and streaks down the side of her face. Unconscious, there is an undisturbed serenity to her features—she's alive, the vitality within her prevailing against the moment's cruelty.

The juxtaposition of emotions is overwhelming. Tom's stillness and Aria's silent, yet affirming life render the room a silent testimony to the undiscriminating nature of terror, where life and death are neighbors, separated only by the fragile veil of fate. In this aftermath, the haunting duality of loss and survival hangs heavy in the smoky air.

Grief and shock intertwine, forming a cold grip around Peter and Bennett as they stand amidst the rubble, the grim reality of Tom Cohen's loss settling deep within them, even when considered alongside the fierce relief of Aria's survival. The room, now a mausoleum of destruction and a testament of life's fragility, bears silent witness to the unutterable collision of loss, survival, and the haunting specter of terror that now casts its shadow over every surviving soul.

TWENTY-THREE

CHINA TOWN, NEW YORK

The chilling aftermath of the explosions at Times Square and Midtown Precinct South hang heavy in the air. The city, usually unyielding and robust, now finds itself trembling on its foundations, an unsettling quietude snaking through its streets. On a typical Saturday night, the heartbeat of the city would be palpable, a rhythmic pulse of life and energy. Tonight, however, the scenes are markedly different; the usual hustle and bustle replaced by a somber reticence.

China Town, always a flurry of lights, sounds, and scents, feels the change acutely. The neon-lit streets, ordinarily awash with a vibrant mix of tourists and locals, are noticeably quieter. Vendors, who would normally be immersed in the frenetic energy of hawking their daily deals, find their calls echoing back, their enthusiasm met with an unusual stillness.

It's amidst this muted atmosphere that Michael, Mayu, Brad, and Hanna find themselves seated in their chosen eatery. Nestled among a row of similarly vibrant establishments, marked by red paper lanterns swaying gently in the evening breeze, the restaurant seems to hold its breath. Inside, a sight that would be an anomaly on any other night greets them—empty tables. The porcelain plates, steaming teapots, and glasses of water gleam under the yellow hanging lights, untouched and waiting. The soft, melodic tune of a traditional Chinese zither can be heard in the background, its haunting melody piercing the uneasy quiet.

"I swear, Professor Palmer's lectures get longer every week," Brad starts, adjusting his glasses and leaning forward as if presenting a thesis. "I thought I was going to fall asleep during his discourse on post-war economic policies."

Hanna nods in agreement, rolling her eyes playfully. "I swear, half of our class was falling asleep. But you know, his thoughts on globalization really resonate with the modern East-West dynamic. Especially considering the cultural influences we've seen recently."

Michael tries to engage. "You know, I've read a bit about—"

But Brad quickly cuts in. "Oh, and don't even get me started on his views about the socio-economic disparities in East Asia. I mean, it's so obvious that he's basing his theories on outdated data."

Michael's cheeks redden, a knot forming in his stomach. He feels the distance between him and the conversation grow. He doesn't need a PhD to see Brad's blatant attempts at overshadowing him.

Underneath the tablecloth, Mayu's fingers intertwine

with his. She offers him a sidelong, empathetic smile, her eyes conveying a silent promise: I'm here with you.

Brad continues on, seemingly oblivious. "I mean, at Columbia, we're constantly on the forefront. It's like we're in this academic bubble, always pushing the boundaries."

It's in these moments that Michael fantasizes about ways to shut Brad up. Not hurt him, but maybe stuff a dumpling in his mouth or something.

The sound of his phone vibrating breaks through his spiraling thoughts. Checking the caller ID, he sees it's his dad. "Excuse me for a moment," he says, rising.

He retreats to a quiet alcove, away from the lively ambiance of the restaurant. The traditional zither music now sounds distant, replaced by the muted hum of a ceiling fan.

"Hey, Dad," he answers, anxiety lacing his voice. "What's up?"

"Mikey." Peter's voice trembles slightly, betraying an underlying unease. "I just needed to hear your voice, is all."

Michael swallows hard. "You weren't anywhere near today's bombings were you?"

Peter exhales audibly. "I was."

"Jeez. What's going on?"

"I don't know, son. Things are getting complicated."

"You okay?"

"I'm... shaken. But I'm alive." There's a brief pause. Then, "Promise me you'll stay safe, Mikey. Things are... unpredictable right now."

"I promise," Michael assures him, though the weight of the situation presses on him. "And you? You need to be careful too."

"I will," Peter replies. "Just... wanted to hear your voice."

"I'm here, Dad. Always."

Their conversation ends, but Michael remains in the alcove a moment longer, gathering himself. As he turns back toward the table, Brad's loud voice hits him like a wall, making him groan under his breath before he begins walking over.

———

One Police Plaza, New York.

They've moved to a more secure location. The digital forensics room of One Police Plaza buzzes with electric tension. Powerful computers, their cooling fans working overtime, form a semi-circle around the room. At its epicenter stands a state-of-the-art fingerprint analysis system, an intimidating machine rigged to scour various international databases for matches.

Within the mechanical hum of computers and servers, Bennett stands tall and focused, addressing the team with a voice that, despite its steadiness, barely conceals the under-tones of frustration and urgency. Aria Patel, fresh stitches glimmering above her eye, stands with him and Peter. Having regained consciousness soon after her rescue from the rubble, Aria's presence alone attests to her grit and resilience. Paramedics had insisted she should go to the hospital, but after stitching the deep cut above her eye and conducting a cursory check that confirmed a light concussion and some bruising, Aria had insisted on returning to duty immediately.

"We're coming up empty on our usual suspects with his fingerprints," Bennett says. "But consider this: He might've gone through international checkpoints. Our angle should be to dig into global passport and immigration databases."

Peter, his posture stiffening with the weight of the situation, counters, "It's a wide net to cast. Not all countries are open books. Many won't readily hand over such guarded information."

"That's where Interpol comes in," Aria points out. "I've already pushed through a priority request, demanding access to prints from customs checks. He might have evaded our local nets, but traveling leaves footprints. Or in this case, fingerprints. Every time he's been aboard, he'll have had his prints scanned at immigration."

While she speaks, Peter silently appraises Bennett and Aria. In the face of Tom Cohen's haunting demise and the tragic loss of Ben Knight, his uncle, Bennett stands resilient, his spirit unyielding. Aria, stitches and all, mirrors this resilience, a woman forged in the crucible of terror and tragedy, yet unbroken. The grim images of Tom's final moments are barely an hour in the past, and yet here they are, driving the mission forward. It's a testament to their iron-clad wills under duress.

Aria takes a seat at the console. "Uploading the prints to Interpol now," she reports, her fingers flying across her workstation with lightning speed. On her screen, the unique pattern of the bomber's fingerprints enlarges, a kaleidoscope of lines and swirls that may hold the key to unlocking his identity.

A thick tension blankets the room, everyone holding their breath in suspense. The agonizing wait stretches on, each moment elongating as if time itself is holding its breath. Then, suddenly, the atmosphere is pierced by the triumphant chirp of an incoming notification. Aria Patel, with eyes that mirror the collective anticipation of the room, clicks open the file, ready to decode the bomber's enigma.

Every eye widens. "We have a hit," Aria declares. The computer screen showcases an ID match for the prints. "Yasin Farid. American."

"He on any radars?" Bennett asks.

"No. Nothing. No loose links to extremist groups, either. He's moved through Turkey, Jordan, and Lebanon in the last three years. But apart from that, nada."

With a few expert keystrokes, Aria summons Yasin's passport photo onto the screen. The familiar face of the man who detonated himself, ending the lives of Tom Cohen and the two FBI agents, stares back at them, cold and detached.

Bennett's eyes blaze, a potent cocktail of fury and determination. "Where's he from?"

"He's been living in New York for the past ten years," Aria reads, her gaze scanning the data, "but he's originally from Fairfax, Virginia."

Bennett and Peter exchange a heavy, weighted glance, the gravity of the situation pressing down on them.

"That'd cover the Blue Ridge mountains," muses Bennett, visibly rattled. "Looks like our guy. Sonya must've been telling some of the truth, at least."

"So close to home," Aria adds, referencing the fact that Fairfax is within spitting distance of CIA Headquarters in Langley. Many of its staff have homes there.

"Any family in the agency?" Peter asks.

"No. None," Aria replies.

The room falls into a stifling silence, questions and theories hanging in the air. All eyes eventually converge on Yasin Farid's image, still hauntingly present on the monitor, offering no answers.

Bennett leans forward, narrowing his eyes at the screen. "What more can you tell me about Yasin Farid?"

Aria delves deeper into his profile. "Born to parents originally from Lebanon. They hailed from wealth. His father worked as an engineer, while his mother practiced law."

Recalling earlier conversations, Peter chimes in, "Did the family convert to Christianity at some point?"

Rapidly sifting through the records, Aria responds, "Yes. Their religious orientation is registered as LDS."

Once again, Peter and Bennett share a look.

Aria asks, "Are we making his identity public?"

Bennett's voice cuts through. "Hold off for now."

The room's low hum is then interrupted by a knock on the door. A uniformed police officer stands at the threshold.

"Kara Tate wants out. Says she wants to go home," the officer reports.

Bennett's response is swift and firm. "She can't go home. She could still be in danger."

The officer seems almost amused. "Reckons she's got a right to leave whether we like it or not."

Feeling the tension, Peter steps in, placing a reassuring hand on Bennett's shoulder. "I'll take her back to her place. I need to get some fresh air anyway."

Bennett nods. "Fine. But hurry back. We need to gear up

for Virginia. Time to find out who in the hell Yasin Farid was."

———

NIGHT BLANKETS NEW YORK, the city's glowing lights casting a dim illumination on the streets. Peter maneuvers a borrowed FBI car seamlessly, Kara beside him, her form shrunk into the passenger seat. Since departing, her voice has been conspicuously absent, lost in a torrent of thoughts.

As the silhouette of her Williamsburg apartment emerges a few blocks away, she breaks the heavy silence, her gaze still distant. "I get a feeling this isn't over yet."

Peter's grip on the steering wheel tightens slightly. "I have the same feeling," he acknowledges, keeping his focus on the asphalt ahead.

Kara's eyebrows furrow as she pieces together the puzzle. "There has to be more of them. What about the other two men on the video Amy sent?"

Peter nods, his mind racing. "It's not just that. You said earlier that he was working at the garden center."

"The Eden Project."

"Right. Well, the FBI looked into it. They confirmed Yasin Farid was Joseph Dalton. But there's more. Someone hacked the place's ordering system to get extra loads of ammonium nitrate. The night your friend took the video, they didn't have an official delivery. And there's another thing. The storage facility in the subway... it was thick with the smell of ammonium nitrate—like it had been kept there —but the explosives he used? C4 charges, not ammonium nitrate."

Kara's eyes meet his across the car, searching for answers. "So where's all the fertilizer?"

"Exactly," Peter acknowledges, glancing in her direction. The streetlights illuminate her features, and in this dim light, he's struck by her beauty. They share a fleeting, intense moment, eyes locked. But almost as soon as it begins, they both blush and divert their gazes, caught off guard by the unexpected intimacy.

When the car comes to a halt outside her apartment, Peter's protective instincts kick in. "Let me walk you up," he offers.

She gives him a weak smile. "It's okay. You don't have to."

But Peter's already unbuckling his seatbelt. "I insist."

The ambient hum of the city fades as they ascend the stairs, replaced by a stifling quiet that heightens Peter's senses. Each step resonates with an echoing thud, the building itself seeming to exhale slow, anticipatory breaths. Kara follows closely behind, her breaths matching the pace of Peter's, both conscious of the eeriness slowly enveloping them.

As they approach her landing, an unsettling chill dances down Peter's spine. His seasoned instincts flare, warning him of potential danger. Silently, he slips his hand beneath his jacket, fingers closing around the reassuring grip of his SIG Sauer. His posture stiffens, every nerve alert and ready.

"Kara, give me your keys," he instructs, voice low and authoritative. "Stay here."

She nods, the weight of the situation evident in her eyes as she hands him her keys. Approaching the apartment door, Peter notices something amiss. Fresh scratch marks mar the door's keyhole. They aren't random markings, but deliberate and recent, hinting at forced entry. The realization tightens his grip on the gun, the stakes of the night growing ever more perilous.

The door groans softly as Peter pushes it open, revealing a scene of disarray. Once tidy shelves and drawers now lie gutted, their contents strewn haphazardly across the floor. It's as if a whirlwind has torn through the apartment, leaving a trail of personal belongings in its wake. The faint scent of a musky, foreign cologne lingers in the air, and mixed with it is the unmistakable metallic smell of fear.

A breeze, cold and biting, drifts in from an open window, ruffling the sheer white curtains that dance like ethereal ghosts. The city's muted sounds, distant sirens, and hushed voices from below filter through the opening. Peter swiftly moves to the window, peering out into the gloom of the night. The fire escape is empty.

He secures the window, locking out the cold night, and then checks the rest of the apartment. When he's sure it's empty, he calls out softly, "Kara, it's clear. You can come in."

She enters, and the moment her gaze lands on the ransacked living room, she releases a choked gasp. The weight of violation hangs heavy in the air. She hurries to her bedroom.

"My laptop..." she murmurs, her voice tinged with panic. "It's gone!"

Peter follows her in, immediately understanding the significance of what's been taken. "I'm sorry, Kara," he says, his voice heavy with empathy and concern. "It looks like someone wants to know what you know."

She turns to face him, her eyes glistening with tears of

frustration and vulnerability. "My entire life was on that computer. And he just... took it."

Peter steps closer, placing a comforting hand on her shoulder. "You couldn't have known. But one thing's for certain."

She turns to him. "What?"

"You can't stay here tonight. It's not safe."

Kara nods, defeated. "Where will I go?"

"You're in luck. I have a place in Brooklyn. It's not much, but it's safer than here."

As she gathers a few essentials into a bag, Peter dials Bennett. "It's Peter," he begins. "Kara's apartment's been turned over. They took her computer. We're headed to my place in Brooklyn. She'll be safer there."

"Well, no need to hurry back. Director McLean is on her way."

Peter's face contorts slightly. "Oh?" he mutters. "What's happening?"

Bennett sighs audibly over the phone. "She's coming in to brief me. I've got a bad feeling she's gonna tell us to hand everything we have over to the FBI and leave it alone."

Peter takes a breath, lets it out through his nose, then speaks. "I've been thinking."

"Dangerous," Bennett remarks.

Peter smirks, goes on, "You get the feeling that we're being targeted?"

Bennett takes a second or two to answer. When he does, his voice is a little unsteady. "Yeah, I've thought about that too," he says. "It was like he was waiting specifically for Uncle Ben to ring that bell." He pauses, the memory haunting him. "Plus, the way Farid looked at the one-way... like he knew we would be there when the bomb detonated."

"And Sonya, too," Peter adds. "The fact that she reached out specifically to the CIA. Not the State Department or anything like that, but directly to American intelligence."

Bennett sighs again. "Well, I'll let the FBI know. Take tomorrow off. I'll fill you in when I can. Let you know our next step. The FBI is already in Fairfax, talking to Farid's parents. Let them deal with it."

Peter's eyes narrow. "There's gonna be more," he says.

"We'll see," Bennett responds, his tone non-committal. "I'll update you in the morning."

As the call disconnects, Peter's attention shifts. Standing nearby, Kara clutches a compact overnight bag.

"Let's go," Peter urges, and together, they make their way out of the apartment.

———

PETER's small Brooklyn apartment is bathed in the mellow golden hue of city lights filtering in through the partially open blinds. The untidy environment of a bachelor is disrupted by their sudden presence. Peter had completely forgotten about the state of the place: a pile of discarded magazines here, a random sock there, the dining table sporting an unflattering collection of dirty plates and coffee mugs.

As he rushes around, embarrassed, Peter quickly shovels the magazines into a drawer and sweeps the dishes into the sink of his kitchenette. "Sorry about the mess," he huffs, running a hand through his wavy hair. "Haven't had anyone over in a while."

Kara, still shaken from the evening's events, glances around the apartment, taking it all in. "Do you have any wine?" she asks, her voice quivering slightly.

Peter freezes, eyes darting to the kitchen cabinets. "No wine," he admits, a sheepish grin appearing on his face. "Just beer."

Kara gives a small smile, the tension in her shoulders easing a bit. "Beer's good."

He grabs two cold bottles from the fridge and hands one to her. They find themselves on his old, slightly sagging couch, the distant hum of city life a gentle background chorus.

As they take tentative sips, Peter watches Kara's gaze as it drifts across the room, perhaps taking in the mismatched cushions or the random assortment of books and CDs. Maybe judging his taste in outdated music.

"Why journalism?" Peter inquires, gently interrupting the silence in an attempt to distract her attention away from his apartment.

She seems taken aback for a moment but then sighs, a melancholic look in her eyes. "My father," she starts, "was a small business owner. He ran a bookstore down in the Village. But he got pushed out by the bigger chains. I watched as these corporate bullies just... took over everything. And it wasn't just him. In high school, college, everywhere, I saw the same thing. The big guy stepping on the little guy. It broke my heart."

Peter nods slowly, engrossed in her words. "You wanted to give the little guy a voice."

She nods enthusiastically, her passion palpable. "Exactly! To champion the underdogs. To stop the bullying. America's built on principles of standing up for what's right, isn't it? But more often than not, it feels like those principles get lost."

He leans back, taking in her fiery spirit. "Too true. Might often equals right in this world. That shouldn't be the way."

Their conversation flows effortlessly, from stories of Peter's adventures to tales of Kara's escapades in journalism. They find themselves laughing over shared experiences and common gripes about the city.

As the beers make them warmer, their physical distance narrows. Their knees touch, and there's a shared jolt, a spark. Slowly, they both lean in, eyes locked. A stray strand of Kara's hair falls into her face. The world outside fades, the hum of the city growing distant. It's just the two of them, tired but filled with a yearning neither had expected.

Their lips meet, tentative at first, then more confidently. It's a passionate, raw, and intense connection. Before they know it, Peter is lifting her into his arms, their beers forgotten on the coffee table.

The rest of the world ceases to exist as they journey into the night, two souls seeking solace and warmth in each other's embrace.

TWENTY-FOUR

BROOKLYN

PETER AND KARA'S PEACEFUL MORNING SLUMBER IS abruptly broken by the unmistakable sound of a key turning in the lock, followed by the apartment door creaking open. The position of the bedroom, with its door wide open, gives whoever enters an immediate view of its occupants.

Before Peter can fully process the intrusion, his feet hit the cold floorboards, and he springs out of bed, clad only in a pair of rather worn boxer shorts with a faded Superman logo. In a single fluid motion, he dashes out of the room, ensuring that he shuts the bedroom door securely behind him, leaving Kara, still slightly disheveled from sleep, clutching the bedsheet to herself with wide eyes.

Michael walks in and stops when he sees his father, slightly taken aback. "Whoa. Didn't expect to see you here."

Peter adjusts himself. "Yeah. I stayed in New York last

night. Don't know for how long, though. What brings you here?"

"I need your tennis racket," Michael replies, adjusting his baseball cap. "Mayu's using mine."

Peter arches an eyebrow. "Who are you playing?"

Michael rolls his eyes, a mock grimace on his face. "Brad and Hanna."

A grin sneaks onto Peter's face. "Brad? As in, the Brad?"

"Ah huh. The very one. I swear he's even more competitive about tennis than he is about proving his intellectual superiority."

The two men engage in a staring contest, Peter clearly playing gatekeeper in front of the bedroom door.

Michael breaks the silence. "You planning on moving away from the door anytime soon?"

Peter looks innocent, feigning confusion. "Oh, am I blocking it?"

"Yes. You are blocking it. The racket's in there."

A brief glance over his shoulder at the closed door is followed by a smirk. "How about I play butler and get it for you?"

Michael narrows his eyes, leaning in slightly. "There's someone in there, isn't there?"

Peter's complexion takes on a shade reminiscent of a tomato.

Bingo, Michael thinks. "Spill the beans, old man."

Peter sighs, his shoulders sagging. "It just happened, all right? No need for the third degree."

With a twinkle in his eye, Michael leans even farther forward. "Can I say hi?"

Peter's face looks none too pleased. "No, Mikey," he says

in a deadpan. "You can't say hello. She's still asleep. Just... give me a second."

Peter slips back into the room, making a grand effort to shield the view from Michael, who's straining to look, clearly trying to catch a glimpse as Peter makes it through the smallest of gaps between the door and the frame. Inside, Kara sits up, hair a wild cascade around her. The two share an amused glance before Peter rummages around, locating the racket.

Back outside, he thrusts it into Michael's hands. "Here, go unleash your fury on the tennis court."

Michael chuckles. "Maybe I can take some out on Brad."

Peter nods, patting his shoulder. "Then I wish you the best of luck."

"Much appreciated, old man," Michael shoots back, already heading out. But just before he leaves, in a voice loud enough for the entire floor to hear, he calls out, "Oh, and morning to you too, mystery lady!" He throws a wink over his shoulder and disappears from the apartment, leaving Peter both embarrassed and amused.

The soft click of the bedroom door signals Peter's return, his face slightly flushed from the unexpected rendezvous with his son.

"Was that your son?" Kara inquires, her tone light and teasing as she pulls the sheet around herself a little tighter.

"Yeah," Peter replies, his chuckle blending with a hint of pride.

She tilts her head, squinting as if doing some quick mental arithmetic. "He seems mature for his age."

"He's twenty-one."

Kara's eyebrows shoot up in genuine surprise. "Seriously? You really don't strike me as old enough to have a twenty-one-year-old son."

Peter chuckles, the corners of his eyes crinkling. "Well, his mom and I were still kids ourselves when we had him."

Kara's playful demeanor wanes, replaced by genuine curiosity. "And where is she now? His mom?"

The question, though innocent, pierces through him like an arrow, bringing memories he's tucked away to the forefront. "She's not with us anymore," he says, the weight of the words evident in his tone.

Kara's mouth forms an 'o,' and she murmurs with sincerity, "I'm sorry." Her words carry the automatic response society expects, but the softness in her eyes suggests genuine empathy. "Must've been hard. For both of you."

"It was," he acknowledges, lost in thought for a moment. His gaze, which had momentarily become distant, is suddenly refocused on something at the corner of the room. His steps quicken as he strides over to pick up a small box with a replacement grip that had been delivered just a few days prior.

Without missing a beat, he rushes to the living room window, cranking it open. Looking three stories down, he spots Michael on the pavement, chatting with Mayu and another young woman.

"Hey, Mikey!" Peter shouts, his voice echoing slightly. "Don't forget this! The old grip's almost worn away."

Mayu, hearing the familiar voice, looks up, her face breaking into a bright smile. "Morning, Peter!"

"Hey, Mayu!" Peter replies, the warmth in his tone evident.

With a deft toss, he throws the grip down, and Michael, ever the athlete, catches it effortlessly.

As Peter watches them, another figure enters his line of sight—a tall man with curly blond locks, sporting a retro turtleneck and black Ray Ban shades, giving off strong vintage Bob Dylan vibes.

Ah, that must be Brad, Peter muses to himself. Just as the thought crosses his mind, Brad, as if feeling Peter's gaze, removes his sunglasses. Their eyes lock in a brief moment of mutual acknowledgment. The silent exchange is cut short as Brad slips his shades back on, and the previously disjointed group melds into a harmonious quartet, strolling away and leaving Peter with his thoughts.

It is then that the subtle vibrations of his cell phone create a gentle rhythm against the sleek surface of the breakfast bar counter, pulling him out of his momentary reverie. Picking it up, he takes a look at the screen. The caller ID shows "Bennett."

He swipes to answer, and before he even gets a chance to say hello, Bennett's voice erupts from the other end, frustration dripping from each word. "Well, that was a shit show," he practically snarls.

Confused and a bit taken aback, Peter responds, trying to keep his tone neutral, "What was?"

He can almost hear Bennett clenching his teeth in exasperation. "Director McLean waltzes in first thing this morning. I swear, my head had barely touched the pillow for what felt like three hours, and she's demanding a full briefing."

Peter could picture the scene: the bustling office, Bennett's barely caffeinated state, and Sandy McLean, presumably looking fresh and poised for confrontation.

"We painstakingly go over everything," Bennett continues, his voice growing more strained, "she listens, occasionally gracing me with her insights, and then, right at the bitter end, she drops the bombshell: She's handing the entire operation over to the FBI. Just like that."

"Well, we knew it would be passed on. After all, stateside is Federal territory."

"Yeah, but I at least thought we'd be working side by side. Not sending us as far from the action as possible."

"And where's that?"

"Turkey," Bennett says, the word heavy with implications. "Sonya Khan has resurfaced in the East of the country. It's the only solid lead we've got, and apparently, the only one Director McLean is willing to let us chase. Aria's heading back to Langley, while you and I are flying out. I'll see you at Kennedy in, say, an hour. That should give you just enough time to... wrap things up with Ms. Tate," he adds in a sly tone that makes Peter's cheeks warm.

Chuckling with part incredulity and part embarrassment, he asks, "How'd you know?"

Bennett's voice carries a smirk. "You're one of mine, remember? I keep tabs on my people. Now seal it with a kiss and hustle over to Kennedy. Plane's waiting."

The call clicks off, leaving Peter with the static of his thoughts and the lingering scent of Kara's perfume enveloping him. She's standing in the bedroom doorway. Peter looks at her, his eyes heavy with the gravity of the situation. "I'm being called to Turkey," he announces, his voice slightly shaky.

Kara, her journalistic instincts always alert, tilts her head. "Who's Sonja Khan?"

"The wife of the man we believe is orchestrating all of this."

Kara's breath catches. "The Wolf Pack?"

Peter nods, the weight of the name evident in his demeanor. "Exactly. Sonya could be the bridge to unraveling this all."

For a moment, the room is still, filled only with the charged air between them. Kara takes a step, closing the distance, and in an impulsive motion, they find themselves locked in a deep, soulful kiss.

She pulls away slightly, a hint of sheepishness coloring her cheeks. "Sorry," she murmurs, her eyes shimmering. "I just couldn't help myself."

Peter grins, slightly breathless. "It's okay. Listen, while I'm gone, make yourself at home here."

She raises an eyebrow playfully. "Mmm... Okay. But only if you're sure about it."

"Of course I am. You can stay as long as you want." Opening a drawer from the kitchenette, he retrieves a set of keys and hands them to her. "The alarm is 2001."

A warm smile graces her lips, gratitude evident in her gaze. Their faces inch closer, and as their lips meet again, time seems to halt.

Breaking the moment, Peter sighs. "I need to shower. Got a plane to catch."

Kara, mischief dancing in her eyes, coyly asks, "Is there room in that shower for two?"

Peter grins mischievously. "There is. But we have to be quick."

TWENTY-FIVE

DIYARBAKIR, TURKEY

Less than ten hours later, the wheels of the G650 are screeching down against tarmac, the harsh sound breaking the otherwise peaceful day.

Peter and Bennett quickly disembark, their eyes hidden behind dark sunglasses despite the lateness of the hour. The weight of their mission presses down on them as they find their pre-arranged vehicle: a sturdy-looking Jeep, slightly worn from the desert sand. Its engine roars powerfully to life in the airport parking lot.

Driving into Diyarbakır, the city reveals itself as an intricate blend of modernity and antiquity. Tall, modern buildings stand juxtaposed against ancient walls and ruins. Like Cizre, the city's Kurdish history whispers in the wind, stories of resilience and resistance echoing in the maze-like streets.

Peter turns the Jeep onto a side street, parking outside a quaint café named Kaya's. Its stone exterior, adorned with creeping ivy, exudes rustic charm. Warm light spills from its windows, hinting at a cozy interior.

The duo enters, navigating through the café's lower floor, where locals enjoy late-night tea and pastries. The rich aroma of Turkish coffee mingles with the sweet scent of baklava. Through a wooden archway, a staircase leads them to an upper balcony.

Against the wrought-iron railing stands their contact: Akam. His tall frame is silhouetted against the city's ancient ruins, dimly lit by the moonlight and streetlamps. The impressive stone walls, remnants of a time gone by, frame the backdrop.

Bennett approaches first, hand extended. "Akam."

The Kurd grasps it firmly, nodding. "Bennett. And this is Peter?"

"It is."

Peter and the Kurd exchange a brief nod.

The men settle into plush chairs, the old wood groaning slightly. Overhead, a string of fairy lights casts a soft glow over their clandestine meeting.

Bennett leans in across the café table, eyeing Akam intently. "So your people have a hook in her?" he questions.

"Yes," Akam affirms with a solemnity that carries the weight of a vendetta. "They are watching her as we speak. She does not move without our knowledge."

Bennett's eyes, sharp and evaluating, acknowledge the Kurd's response. "Good. Good," he mutters, accompanied by a brisk nod. "Thank you, Akam. I know how hard it is for you to hand her over to us."

Moonlight spills onto the balcony, casting a glow onto Akam's chiseled features, which momentarily contort with a visceral pain. "It has taken every ounce of strength not to avenge my brother," he declares, voice dripping with rage and anguish. "Not to drive a knife across her throat as she did to Hozan."

It is then that Peter recognizes the similarities between this man and their former Kurdish contact in Cizre, the one who was killed during Sonya Khan's escape. Peter, previously a silent observer, inches forward, his intrigue palpable. "Your brother was Hozan?"

Meeting Peter's gaze with a heavy sadness, Akam nods slowly. "Yes. He was my little brother."

"She will face justice, Akam," Bennett interjects, a steely determination in his voice. "Now tell me about where she is."

Regaining his composure, Akam retrieves a smartphone from the depths of his jacket. With a swift motion, he displays on its screen an aerial image of a fortified compound.

"I have two of my best men ready to help with the assault," he informs them. "I take it the CIA are only providing the two of you?"

"That would be true," Bennett confirms.

Akam's dark eyes assess both men. "Then it is good that I got us assistance in catching this she-dog. Because she is currently guarded by five armed men. Though I suspect it could be more as the surrounding buildings are also owned by the same people who owns the bitch's current den."

"Who are they?" Peter asks.

Akam turns to him. "Criminals. Not Kurds, Turks. Ones you don't want to meet, ever. They've come all the way down from Istanbul for this."

"So they were the ones who took her?"

Akam nods.

Bennett asks the next question. "Are they working along-side the Wolf Pack?"

"We don't think so. Intercepting some of their telephone conversations, we've established that they're holding her for ransom to the group. They say that if they are not paid within twenty-four hours, they will hand her over to the CIA."

"Then why don't we just wait?" Peter puts to Bennett.

The Kurd has an answer for this. "Because the son of a bitch is going to pay them what they want."

Peter's eyes back on Akam. "And, what? They'll hand her over to him?"

Akam shakes his head. "No," he says grimly. "He's paying them to kill her."

Peter and Bennett look at each other, a shared under-standing traveling between them.

Bennett says it first, "Then she must know something that can lead us to him."

As the two CIA operatives take this in, Peter's phone vibrates with an incoming call. Extracting it from his pocket, Kara's name illuminates the screen. The ambient sounds of the café seem to fade as he stands. "I need to take this," he mutters, casting an apologetic glance toward Bennett, who simply nods.

Peter slips from the open balcony into the dim interior of the café. Neon lights cast a subdued glow, playing tricks with the shadows. Around him, patrons sit immersed in conversation or lost in thought, tendrils of hookah smoke meandering upwards from their pipes, diffusing the mood.

"Hey," he murmurs, pressing the phone close to his ear, the warmth of her voice a stark contrast to the cool Turkish evening.

"Firstly," Kara begins, her tone a blend of assertiveness and vulnerability, "I just wanted to make it clear that I don't usually sleep with strangers."

A momentary silence hangs between them before Peter chuckles softly, his voice low and husky. "Me neither," he admits, leaning against a carved wooden pillar.

The brief pause is filled with the gentle clinking of tea glasses, bubbling hookah water, and distant chatter. Kara's voice continues, quivering just a bit. "I guess it was the circumstances. I'd almost lost my life. You'd saved it. Then you were so sweet letting me stay at your apartment, and I guess the whole experience got the better of me and... well, my defenses were down..."

Peter's gaze drifts to the intricate tilework of the café floor. "Kara, you don't have to explain. It's okay. I get it. I shouldn't have taken advantage of you."

Kara's response is swift, almost defensive. "You didn't take advantage of me," she asserts. "I was very much... into it. Both times. I just didn't want you thinking that I was easy."

His voice softens. "I'd never think that."

Their words bridge the gap, establishing mutual understanding, until Kara shifts the topic. "I went back to al-Nur Mosque. Asked around."

A frisson of unease courses through Peter. "Kara," he interjects, disappointment evident in his tone, "you need to leave this alone."

But she's relentless. "The imam I spoke to there told me

the FBI had spoken to them and that they talked about Yasin Farid. About him attending the mosque for the last two months. That he used it to pray and nothing else. Didn't have any friends there. But the FBI hadn't shown them a picture of Amy. When I did, the guy recognized her."

Her revelation halts him. "What else did he say?"

"She visited a few times with Farid but also once with another man, too."

"Who?"

"A white man. American. Not dressed like a typical Muslim, but still very knowledgable about the Quran. The man I spoke to at the mosque said he was also impressed by the man's Arabic. Said that he spoke it with an Afghani accent. Which was weird being that everything else about him was so typically American."

Peter's mind is racing. But as he thinks about it, the night is interrupted by Bennett's sudden appearance. His impatient expression conveys a clear message: Time's up, get back to the table.

Breathing deeply, Peter attempts to draw a line, "Look, Kara," he exhales, the weight of the mission heavy on his shoulders, "I gotta go. Hand everything you have to the FBI. Go straight to their field office now. Please, Kara. Stay out of this."

He disconnects, thrust into a storm of thoughts and emotions, with the ever-present question: What does this mean?

––––––––

NEW YORK.

THE STEADY THRUM of water hitting tiles is punctuated by the rhythmic snip-snip of toenail clippers. The room is clouded with steam, the scent of Michael's shampoo lingering in the air. Mayu perches on the toilet seat, a towel wrapped securely around her slender frame, her long wet hair creating rivulets down her back as she focuses on giving her toenails a trim.

"Seriously, Brad talks so much, you'd think he was on a mission to never let anyone else speak," Michael groans, his voice slightly muffled by the shower curtain.

Mayu chuckles. "I've noticed. And the thing is, he mostly just talks about himself."

"Exactly!" Michael exclaims, running a hand through his wet hair. "Every time I try to talk about a game or anything else, he somehow steers it back to his latest academic success or some supposedly exotic trip he took. It's exhausting!"

Mayu leans back, her hands pausing in their work. "You know, I think he's just insecure. People who always talk about themselves are usually trying to prove something."

Michael sighs, considering Mayu's words. "But Hanna seems smitten with him. The way she hangs on his every word."

Mayu smirks. "Well, opposites do attract. Hanna's the quiet type, and Brad... isn't."

There is a brief pause in their conversation, only the sound of water and Mayu's clippers filling the room. Then Michael speaks again, his voice lower. "You know what creeps me out? The way he stares at me sometimes. Like he's trying to figure me out or something."

Mayu widens her eyes at him, genuinely surprised. "Really? I haven't noticed."

"It's weird," Michael reiterates, shifting a bit as if he could shake off the memory of Brad's gaze.

"Well, I guess you're gonna be upset about what I've got to say next."

Michael pulls the shower curtain to the side and arches an eyebrow at her. "Why?"

She turns to him with a big, cheesy smile. "Because Hanna's invited us to dinner tonight, and I kind of said yes."

"Kind of?"

"I did say yes," Mayu says, nodding.

Michael groans, his face disappearing back behind the curtain. "Okay. I'll go. But can we make this the last one for a while?"

"Sure." After a few more snips of her toenail clipper, Mayu sighs in contentment. "There! All done."

———

DIYARBAKIR, Turkey.

THE OLD PART of the city comes alive in a different way at night. The ancient walls, a symbol of the city's rich past, cast long shadows on the cobblestone streets. Yellowed street-lights give the old buildings a sepia hue, painting them in an atmosphere of nostalgia and secrets. It's here that Peter and Bennett have chosen to rendezvous.

Three Kurdish men stand waiting in an alleyway, their silhouettes barely distinguishable in the dim light. They're different in age, stature, and demeanor, but a shared sense of purpose binds them. The eldest, Akam, with his salt-and-pepper hair, is tall and imposing. His eyes, weathered by years of resilience, hide a storm of memories. Beside him stands a younger man with a lean frame and sharp features, his brow furrowed in concentration. His name is Dara. The third, Ferhad, is slightly stocky, with a beard and a perpetually watchful gaze. Their allegiance to the PKK, the Kurdish Worker's Party, has been their identity and their fight. But occasionally, they take a little freelance work from the CIA. After all, revolutions cost money.

Peter and Bennett pull up in a pitch-black SUV, dressed in a manner to blend into the background—plain clothes, no noticeable accessories, their caps pulled low. Their meeting is covert, for the PKK is outlawed in Turkey, and neither party wishes to attract unnecessary attention.

Diyarbakır, often dubbed the 'unofficial capital' of the Turkish Kurds, bears a complicated history. Kurdish identity, language, and culture have long been suppressed by the Turkish state. The very walls and stones of this city have seen Kurdish uprisings, tales of oppression, and relentless resistance. It's in these streets, rich with memories, that Kurdish poets penned verses of their struggles, and activists plotted against the oppressors.

The three men get in the back of the SUV and they drive off into the city. Inside, the conversations are earnest and low-pitched. The streetlights outside provide fleeting illumination, briefly highlighting the intense expressions on their faces.

The van glides smoothly over the asphalt, occasionally jostled by the unevenness of ancient, weathered cobblestone streets. Akam, his voice edged with tension, speaks up. "The compound is near the eastern walls. Secluded, guarded, and from what we know, very well-fortified."

The van begins to ascend, its engine straining as they climb a hill. Peter's eyes, sharp and assessing, gaze out the window, taking in the surroundings. They're approaching the outskirts of the city, where the mighty ancient walls of Diyarbakır stand tall, their stones carrying tales of countless sieges, peace treaties, and betrayals.

The scenery begins to change. The dense urban sprawl gives way to more spaced-out structures. Square, stone villas dot the hilly landscape, signs of affluence and power. The compounds they pass are grand, with tall, imposing walls protecting them. Some have watchtowers, hinting at the need for vigilance, while others flaunt their wealth with ornate gates and fountains.

The van turns off the main road onto a gravel pathway that leads to a vantage point overlooking one such villa. It sits regally atop a hill on the other side of a steep vale. The villa's compound is expansive, surrounded by those signature tall walls. Olive groves stretch out on one side, the silvery leaves of the trees shimmering under the pale moonlight.

Bennett turns to Akam. "And you're sure she's in there?"

Akam nods. "Our people are watching her now. She hasn't stepped out in days, but we've seen activity. She likes to go out in the garden at night."

Peter, ever the strategist, murmurs, "We need a plan. We can't just storm the place."

Bennett agrees, "Especially without backup."

Peter kills the engine, and the men huddle into the back, a set of building plans spread out before them. In the darkness, their faces are illuminated in garish light by the iPad Bennett holds out. On it are detailed satellite images.

Peter, Akam, and the other two Kurdish fighters, Dara and Ferhad, lean in, their expressions a mix of determination and concern.

"Okay, gentlemen," Bennett begins, his voice commanding their attention. "Sonya is being held here." He points to a detailed image of the villa about a hundred yards away. "And your reconnaissance has it that there are five armed men stationed within the compound with her. I'm thinking if we go in quietly, it should be an easy in-and-out job."

Akam's eyes, however, show doubt. "That's if there really are just five men. The criminal gang who owns the compound she's in own many of the properties around here. There could be more men in more houses."

Peter acknowledges the concern. "We'll come to that if and when it happens. For now, though, we have to operate on the intelligence we have. Bennett, run through the approach."

Bennett traces a path on the satellite image of the compound. "You three will enter the gardens by going over the west wall here. Peter and I will take the west, the front of the villa. If we're quiet and efficient, we'll get to her before the Wolf Pack pays the ransom and we lose Sonya Kahn forever."

Dara, the younger of the Kurds, asks, "And once we get to her?"

Peter replies before Bennett can. "We get her out, quickly and quietly. If she resists, we subdue her."

Bennett nods in agreement. "The element of surprise is our advantage. Five guards shouldn't pose a problem if we stick to the plan."

Akam takes a deep breath and addresses his companions. "Remember, this is not just about the she-dog. This is for my brother and every Kurd that's fallen to these Daesh bastards."

The room goes silent, each man lost in his thoughts, knowing full well the stakes of the operation. After a moment, Bennett breaks the silence.

"Time to gear up. We move as soon as we're ready."

TWENTY-SIX

NEW YORK

THE SOFT PATTER OF RAIN AGAINST THE WINDOWS of Peter's apartment fills the silence. Kara sits curled up on the couch, the ambient light from the city outside casting faint, moving shadows across the room.

Lost in thought, she absently watches television. The events of the past few days play on a loop in her mind, each revelation more bewildering than the last. The FBI had appeared bored earlier when she'd seen them. In a monotone, the agent she'd spoken to had told her that the Amy Harris homicide investigation had been looked at, but that was all he was willing to say on the matter. The agent took down what she had to tell him about the two attending the same mosque she'd followed Yasin Farid out of and left it at that. Kara had felt a little numb when she'd left the FBI's New York field office, a feeling that still grips her now.

The soft trill of her phone breaks the spell. Reaching for

it, she glances at the screen. She doesn't recognize the number. Her heart skips a beat. Could it be another lead? Hesitating for a split second, she swipes to answer.

"Hello?"

"Ms. Kara?" The voice on the other end is vaguely familiar, a touch of warmth and gravitas. "This is Imam Rahim from the al-Nur Mosque."

Kara straightens, her grip on the phone tightening. "Imam Rahim, hello. What can I do for you?"

"I've been asking around, as I promised," he begins, his tone indicating the gravity of his findings. "About the other man with your friend and Yasin Farid."

She nods, even though he can't see her. "Yes?"

"It seems he rented an apartment not far from the mosque, in Greenwich Village," he reveals, pausing to ensure she's following. "Apparently, he invited some of the younger men amongst our followers to his place, where I'm afraid he shared some disturbing films about American atrocities in Iraq. I have the address."

Kara scrambles for a pen and paper from the coffee table, scribbling down the details as he relays them. The weight of the information is palpable, each word heavy with potential.

"Thank you, Imam Rahim," she breathes, her voice laced with gratitude. "I can't tell you how much this means to me."

His response is solemn, yet kind. "I hope you find the person who murdered your friend," he says, a hint of sadness in his tone. "A good Muslim does not kill the innocent."

Kara swallows hard. "Thank you for your help."

They exchange a few more words, pleasantries filled with shared concern, before ending the call.

The room feels both still and electric, a nexus of possibility. With newfound determination, Kara realizes she's one step closer to the answers she's been searching for.

She'll go to Greenwich Village. She'll find out the truth. Whatever it takes.

———

Diyarbakir.

Under the cloak of night, five figures clad in shadow-black clothing close in on the compound's ancient stone barriers. The atmosphere is dense, thick with both the weight of the humid night air and the tension of the mission at hand. Crickets, oblivious to the men's purpose, lend their rhythmic cadence to the silence, their song only broken by the subdued sounds of careful breathing and stealthy footsteps on gravel.

Bennett takes the lead, his experienced eyes scanning the surroundings before issuing a series of swift, deliberate hand signals. In response, the Kurds disperse, each taking a strategic position along the garden's three walls, ensuring no blind spots. It's at the main entrance, the compound's singular gateway to the outside world, that Bennett stations himself.

He firmly grasps a Mossberg 590. Even in the dim light, the shotgun's breacher configuration stands out—a design tailored to tear down barriers. The very sight of it in Bennett's hands promises unforgiving force.

Peter, in contrast, opts for a different kind of power.

Strapped securely to his back is an M4A1 Carbine, a weapon revered and chosen by the world's most elite military forces. Known for its deadly precision and adaptability, it's a statement of intent in Peter's hands.

Silently, he scales the rear wall of the three-story compound, drawing closer to a previously scouted open window on the second floor. Its iron bars, though slim, present an obstacle—one the compact bolt cutters dangling from his belt hold the promise of swiftly solving.

Balanced precariously on a window ledge, Peter deftly unslings the bolt cutters from behind him. One foot finds purchase on a modest outcropping just above a lower window, while his other foot is stabilized by an inconspicuous waste pipe protruding from the stone façade. Cautiously, he cranes his neck to glance through the bars, ensuring that only the topmost part of his forehead and keen eyes breach the windowsill.

Inside, the scene is bathed in the silver glow of the 3 a.m. moon filtering in through an opposite window. It casts a soft light upon an ornate rug and accentuates the detailed frames of the paintings lining the walls. The landing is a pocket of stillness—no signs of movement, no breath but his own.

"Echo One in position now," Peter murmurs, his voice barely above a whisper.

"Proceed once you're past the grill," comes Bennett's hushed reply through his earpiece, tension evident even in the restrained volume.

Working with practiced efficiency, Peter employs the cutters, snipping through four of the window's vertical bars right at their base. This creates just enough space for him to squeeze through. Gently, he bends the freed bars upwards, the metal offering little resistance to his force. Moments later, he's carefully placing one boot on the interior wooden landing, then the other. Each step is taken with painstaking care, Peter trying to distribute his weight evenly to avoid any betraying creak from the old floorboards beneath.

"Echo One, I'm in," he whispers, his voice low and urgent. The M4A1 Carbine nestles securely in his shoulder, its silhouette even more menacing with the suppressor fixed to its end—turning the weapon's potential roar into a lethal hush. His footsteps, deliberate and nearly silent, carry him farther down the corridor, drawn to the faint sound of a television.

Rounding the next corner, the faint blue hue of artificial light splays onto the corridor's hardwood floor as Peter approaches a doorway. His fingers instinctively brush against the Picatinny rail system of the carbine, feeling the reassuring familiarity of the weapon's design. With the adjustable butt-stock snugged tightly to his shoulder, he feels agile, ready for the split-second decisions that might lie ahead.

Edging closer, he can discern the television's audio clearer now: it's playing a cartoon. Amidst the playful dialogue and zany sound effects, he detects another sound—the rhythmic rise and fall of someone snoring.

With the gentlest push of his fingertips, Peter slowly inches the door open farther. It reveals a modest-sized bedroom. The television, casting its vibrant glow, stands atop a chest of drawers facing the foot of a bed. And there, on the bed, lies the very target of their mission: Sonya.

"Echo One?" Bennett's voice filters through the earpiece, hushed and alert. "Report."

"I've got eyes on the target," Peter murmurs, voice barely above a breath.

"Can you extract without causing a scene?" Bennett's inquiry comes, just as hushed.

Peter is about to reply when a telltale creak coming from behind cuts him off. He spins on instinct, the M4A1 snapping up in a fluid motion. He's met by wide eyes and an open mouth; one of the guards up for the bathroom and clearly about to sound the alarm. But Peter is quicker. With the suppressor muting its roar, the carbine dispatches a rapid succession of shots. The intruder's intended shout morphs into a stifled grunt as he crumples to the ground. The metallic chatter of spent shell casings hitting the floor seems loud in contrast, punctuated by the dull thud of the fallen body.

Whipping back to face the room, Peter's heart sinks. Sonya is upright now, alarm evident on her face. Her scream pierces the silence, and soon the hasty sounds of footsteps and muffled voices echo from the hallway.

"Echo Two," Peter urgently communicates, "we've been made. Go loud."

Almost on cue, the ground shudders, and a deafening blast reverberates throughout the compound. The front door, once a solid barrier of oak and iron, has been obliterated by a breaching round from the Mossberg. The operation has shifted gears; stealth is no longer on the table.

Amidst the haze of gunpowder and adrenaline, Peter moves with surgical precision. The dim corridor, only intermittently lit by the flash from his carbine, becomes a dangerous dance floor. Two men rush him from a side room. One attempts to raise his weapon, but Peter is faster, putting a controlled burst into the man's upper torso. The other, reaching for a sidearm, barely clears the leather holster before he meets the same fate.

Downstairs, the reverberation of Bennett's Mossberg is unmistakable. A single shot from the breaching shotgun meets an assailant head-on, obliterating him in a gruesome display of power. The fearsome report of the shotgun echoes, a testament to its raw, unbridled strength.

Simultaneously, the sounds of rapid Kurdish commands mix with the footfalls outside. The trio, adept climbers from years of rugged terrain in their homeland, surmount the compound walls with practiced ease. A lone silhouette dashes across a second-floor balcony. One of the Kurds takes aim and fires. The figure crumples, falling over the railing to land with a thud on the stone below.

Amidst all this, Peter's main focus is Sonya. He bursts into the room, finding her eyes wide, her demeanor a mix of rage and fear. As he lunges for her, she fights back, teeth bared, a wild energy emanating from her. It takes every ounce of Peter's strength to overpower her, finally securing her wrists with zip ties.

Peter's eyes meet Bennett's as he reaches the bedroom door. They share a quick, silent consensus: they need to extract her—now.

The ragtag group—Peter, Bennett, Sonya, and the three Kurds—make a break for the front of the house, intent on reaching their extraction vehicle parked two blocks away. But as they emerge from the busted door, the distant roar of engines fills the street. Headlights pierce the night from both sides, and two vans screech to a halt from opposite ends, flanking the compound entrance.

The back doors fly open, and armed men spill out, AK47s raised, eyes locked on their targets.

"Back into the house!" Peter's command is immediate, mirroring the urgency of their situation. The team, with their precious cargo, is forced to retreat, knowing that the real fight is just beginning.

———

New York.

THE RATTLE and hum of the subway car fills the air as it speeds through the darkened tunnels below the city. Water slips steadily down the windows, a constant reminder of the heavy rain that has been pelting the city all day. The lights inside the carriage flicker occasionally, casting transient shadows on the passengers' faces.

Michael sighs audibly, adjusting his coat collar and glancing at the wet footprints on the floor. "We could've taken a cab, you know," he grumbles, peering outside at the tunnel's gloom.

Mayu chuckles softly, her eyes dancing with mischief. "Come on, it's an adventure! Besides, think of all the money we're saving for dessert."

Michael shoots her a sideways glance. "Brad's cooking. We're already saving on the meal. The least we could have done is taken a cab."

She nudges him playfully. "Isn't it romantic, though? Riding the subway together, just like in those old movies?"

He smirks. "In those movies, it wasn't pouring with rain outside, and they usually had an umbrella."

Mayu feigns shock. "Oh no! Did we forget the umbrella?"

Michael nods, trying to maintain a stern face but failing. "Seems so."

The subway slows as they approach their stop. The dim platform comes into view, populated by a handful of people flipping open their umbrellas in anticipation of the world above.

As the doors slide open, the distant sound of rain reverberates through the station. Michael and Mayu exchange amused glances.

"Ready for a run?" she asks with a grin.

He groans, taking her hand. "Lead the way."

Hand in hand, they dash out into the rain-soaked evening, laughter trailing behind them as they make their way to Brad and Hanna's.

———

DIYARBAKIR.

THE CLASH of bullets and the pounding of boots echo through the claustrophobic corridors of the large house. Every corner they turn is a calculated risk, every glance back a heartbeat longer than the last.

Upstairs, Peter and the others make their way through the second floor toward a back staircase. The six of them move fluidly, Sonya being shoved along by Peter, Bennett at the back with Akam, their weapons drawn. Almost in choreographed precision, they ascend the steps two at a time when they reach the back stairs. With each blast of gunshots that follows them, they become acutely aware that they are vastly outnumbered by their pursuers.

Reaching the top of the house, a brief moment of respite is granted by a solid oak door, which Bennett promptly bolts. The illusion of safety is quickly shattered, however, with the crackling roar of gunfire. The enemy is just a floor below and closing in fast.

They cross the master bedroom toward an open door. The cool night air greets them as they step out onto a balcony. The tight cluster of Diyarbakır rooftops stretches out before them, offering a lifeline.

Sonya's face contorts with fury and anguish, her voice raw. "You're trapped! They'll—"

But before she can finish, a shout comes from below. Someone has spotted them from the street. Bullets spray upwards, their deadly trajectory marked by puffs of dust and stucco, chipping away at their cover.

"Don't you get it?!" Sonya shouts at Peter, suddenly lunging at him. "This is all part of his—"

Bennett, making a split-second decision, swings the butt of his Mossberg, striking the hysterical woman on the side of the head. Her eyes, wide and full of betrayal, lock with Peter's for a heart-wrenching moment. A single droplet of blood then traces a path down her cheek before she goes limp.

"She'll be easier to handle now," Bennett points out.

The next house is a story shorter. The gap to its rooftop is the width of a narrow alley.

"We'll have to throw her across," Peter says, gazing down at Sonya.

Bennett turns to Akam. "You three go across first. Get ready to catch her."

With renewed urgency and bullets seeking them out, the Kurds make the leap first. One after the other, they jump, their silhouettes framed by the torrent of bullets slicing up through the air. They land on the adjacent rooftop, roll, and quickly find their feet.

Peter and Bennett grasp Sonya firmly, one on each side. The weight of the situation presses as heavily on them as the woman they're holding. Six feet separates the building they're on from the adjacent one. On the other side, Akam, Dara, and Ferhad brace themselves, ready to make the catch of a lifetime.

Below, the rhythmic burst of gunfire pierces the night. Bullets zing past, ricocheting off brick and metal as assailants shoot upwards, aiming for them. The thunderous roar of another barrage of bullets is much closer, hammering on the thick oak door that leads to the balcony. Every thud signals that their time is rapidly running out.

With a shared, silent nod, Peter and Bennett sprint forward, using the momentum to propel the woman across the perilous gap.

They let go.

Sonya's limp body soars through the air, a silhouette against the moonlit sky. For a breath-halting second, uncertainty hangs thick.

Then the trio on the opposite side lunges forward, their arms outstretched. The woman lands in their grasp, the force pushing them back a step, but they hold steady. The five men share a fleeting moment of relief amidst the chaos, knowing the danger is far from over.

The blast of a grenade sends the last of the door into splinters as Peter and Bennett jump the gap, joining the others. Once across, Peter hauls Sonya onto his shoulder, and the five of them rush onwards, chased by the rat-a-tat-tat of machine gun fire.

The rooftops of Diyarbakır become a frantic ballet of movement and gunshots. The city lights illuminate the frenzied chase, casting an eerie glow on the group as they navigate the treacherous jumps and narrow pathways between the buildings.

Dara and Ferhad, taking positions on either end of the current rooftop, spray covering fire, their weapons barking loudly at the mass of chasing men running along the alleyways below them. The rhythm of the team's own shots mixed with the constant hail of bullets from below paints a deadly symphony. The attackers are relentless, their shouts and orders a constant presence in the narrow streets below.

As Dara holds their ground, Akam and Ferhad throw Sonya across another perilous jump. The gap is wide, and for a heart-stopping moment, it seems as if she might not make it, her body flopping through the air. But Bennett and Peter throw themselves forward, grabbing her and hauling her to them.

Leaving Sonya on the ground, they immediately turn to provide cover fire, their stance firm, their faces etched with fierce determination.

It's now the three Kurds' turn. They exchange a quick nod with Akam—and the three of them sprint toward the edge, pushing past their exhaustion.

But as they leap, a barrage of gunfire rises to meet them. Akam and Ferhad clear the gap, their bodies jerking from the momentum, but Dara is less fortunate. A bullet finds its mark, and a guttural scream pierces the night. Instead of reaching the edge, Dara's body violently collides with the side of the building. The impact is brutal, and he starts a spiraling descent into the alley below.

Time seems to slow for those watching from above. Dara's fall feels both swift and agonizingly long. The sound of his body crashing into the cobblestones reverberates through the still night air.

Before the group can even process the horror of what's happened, a swarm of attackers descends upon Dara's crumpled form. Even in his weakened state, he attempts to sit up, to defend himself, lifting his carbine. But it's futile. A hail of bullets ensures he won't ever rise again.

The rooftops, once their escape route, now feel more like a trap. The weight of loss is heavy on their shoulders, but hesitation can prove deadly. Their path is clear—forward, always forward—even as the echoes of Dara's final moments haunt their every step.

The narrow pathways of Diyarbakır's rooftops resound with the rapid pounding of boots. Just as they seem to be gaining distance, a barrage of bullets erupts from their left. A shadowed figure emerges onto the roof of the opposite building, his silhouette briefly illuminated by his muzzle flash. He and Peter run parallel, locked in a race where the prize is survival.

As Peter narrows his eyes on the moving target, he squeezes the trigger of his M4A1. The enemy collapses, no match for Peter's trained precision. But victory is short-lived.

As another takes the fallen attacker's place on the opposite rooftop, the M4A1 gives a hollow click—empty.

Desperation and adrenaline combine in Peter as he reaches for a spare magazine stowed in his armor. But before he can reload, a door to his right flings open with a bang. The chilling sight of an AK47 muzzle greets him, the glint of its metal a stark contrast against the dimly lit surroundings.

Without missing a beat, Peter lunges forward, using the momentum of his run to slam the door shut with his shoulder. The force jolts the rifle from the surprised assailant's hands, causing it to skitter across the rough surface of the rooftop. In the chaos, Peter's spare magazine slips from his grip, clattering somewhere out of sight.

He is briefly disoriented, but the glint of a blade quickly refocuses his attention. The attacker is undeterred by the loss of his rifle, now brandishing a wickedly sharp knife. Their eyes lock, both recognizing that this is a fight to the death.

Bennett, Akam, and Ferhad move ahead, their priority Sonya. Their faith in Peter's abilities is evident as they leave him to fend for himself against his adversary.

The knife-wielding attacker lunges, his blade glinting ominously. Peter parries, their limbs clashing in a brutal dance of desperation. The edge of the rooftop becomes the boundary of their battleground. Every step is both a risk and an opportunity. They grapple, the man's hot breath and wild eyes inches from Peter's face. Each tries to gain the upper hand, to send the other hurtling into the abyss below.

Peter parries the arm holding the blade, then counters with a knee to the man's midriff, trying to buy some time to reach the discarded magazine. The attacker rebounds quickly, his knife flashing in a vicious arc aimed straight at

Peter's throat. Reacting purely on instinct, Peter catches the man's wrist with both hands, struggling to keep the gleaming blade from making contact with his skin. Their locked grips turn into a dangerous dance, with each trying to throw the other off balance—and therefore off the roof.

Their breathing becomes ragged, faces twisted in determination and grit. With a sudden force, the attacker uses his weight to push Peter backward, pinning him against a raised ledge. The cold, hard edge of the bricks presses into Peter's back, reminding him of the dangerous drop just inches away. He feels the knife inching closer to his jugular, the man's triumphant sneer spreading across his face, the odds stacking more and more in his favor.

But Peter Black wasn't trained from a boy to surrender to such odds. Mother and Magda didn't teach that lonely little boy in the wilderness of Alaska about giving up and dying on some rooftop in Turkey. No. They taught him to fight, no matter what.

Just when the situation appears dire, he recalls his training, grounding himself with the knowledge that he can still turn the tables. Using the man's momentum against him, Peter twists his body sharply to the side, forcing the attacker off-balance. Using this window of opportunity, he delivers a sharp elbow to the man's face, feeling the crunch of contact.

The assailant stumbles, momentarily disoriented, giving Peter the crucial seconds he needs. He dives for the fallen magazine, fingers wrapping around its cold metal. The attacker, realizing the change in tide, rushes at him one final time, blade poised for a fatal strike.

But Peter is quicker.

He snaps the magazine into the M4A1 in one fluid

motion and swings it up. Before the attacker can close the distance, Peter pulls the trigger. The murmur of the suppressed gunshot whispers in the night. The attacker is hit, a sudden jolt of shock etched on his face as he clutches the impact site, staggering back from the force, before crumpling to the ground, the knife skittering away uselessly.

Peter stands, chest heaving, the weight of the moment sinking in. The night is still around him, but the pulse of danger remains. Re-armed and refocused, he hurries to rejoin the others, determined to complete the mission.

The narrow alley below is shrouded in shadow, a perfect hiding spot for their getaway van. As they drop down, a sense of urgency grips the team; their extraction must be swift if they are to evade the escalating threat.

Bennett wastes no time, swinging open the driver's door and starting the van's engine, which rumbles to life. Akam, his body brimming with adrenaline, lowers the unconscious Sonya into Peter's waiting arms. She feels lighter than she looks, a stark contrast to the weight of the situation.

It is as Peter secures Sonya in the back of the all-black panel van that the ominous sound of rapidly approaching footsteps reverberates through the alley. The sharp shout of a command in a foreign tongue is followed by the unmistakable, chilling chatter of automatic weapons.

Ferhad, ever the protector, positions himself to cover their escape, his weapon trained on the alley entrance. But the attackers are many, and they come in with a ferocity born of desperation. The first burst of bullets finds its mark, ripping through Ferhad's side. He cries out, collapsing to the ground.

"No!" Akam screams, reaching for his fallen comrade.

But in his anguish, he exposes himself for just a second too long. Bullets tear through the night, hitting him in the shoulder and spinning him around.

Peter reacts on instinct. Grabbing Akam, he pulls him into the back of the van, blood smearing across the metal floor as bullets punch the sides. Bennett jams the accelerator. The van lurches forward, its tires shrieking in protest against the ancient cobblestones.

Bennett grips the wheel tightly, every muscle in his body tensed as he weaves them through the maze-like streets of Diyarbakır. The headlight beams of two pursuing sedans suddenly burst in the van's mirrors, their intensity matching the relentless determination of the attackers.

Akam, despite the pain radiating from his wounded shoulder, shouts directions to Bennett. "Left, left! There's a very narrow alley ahead."

Bennett nods, taking the sharp turn with screeching tires. The van's sides graze the stone walls of the tight space, sending sparks flying. Behind them, the menacing roars of the sedans' engines grow louder, drawing nearer.

Peter, his face set in grim determination, kicks open the back doors of the van, providing himself a clear line of sight. As the first sedan comes into view, he takes aim with the M4A1 and fires a precise burst. The car's front tire explodes, sending it crashing into the walls, blocking the path of the second sedan.

They escape the alley.

But the attackers are not so easily deterred. Another sedan, sleeker and faster, appears from a side street, its occupants firing wildly as they hang from the windows. Bullets ping off the van, creating a deafening cacophony.

Bennett swerves, narrowly avoiding an empty market stand.

Peter spots a gas canister near a roadside café. Taking a deep breath, he aims and fires. The canister explodes in a brilliant fireball, engulfing the pursuing sedan. As the explosion's shockwave shakes the van, Bennett skillfully maintains control.

With a glance in the rearview mirror, Bennett sees no more pursuers, only a trail of chaos and destruction. "We're clear," he announces, his voice heavy with relief.

Peter pulls the back doors closed, finally allowing himself to catch his breath. Akam, pale and clutching his wounded shoulder, gives Peter a weak nod of thanks.

As the city lights become distant dots in the van's rearview mirror, the silence is palpable. The reality of the night's events weighs heavily on them all.

"What a night," Peter mutters, wiping the sweat from his brow and staring into the vast darkness ahead.

"It's not over yet," Bennett says from the front. "Not by a long shot."

———

New York.

An inviting aroma wafts through Brad and Hanna's home, a tantalizing mix of roasted spices and the faintest hint of seared meat. Michael takes a cautious breath, impressed despite himself. In the soft, ambient lighting, the dining table stands elegantly set, the silverware gleaming.

Brad, often so imposing and domineering, seems to have taken a step back this evening. He greets Michael with a nod and even cracks a joke about the bad weather. Michael, waiting for the other shoe to drop, finds himself gradually relaxing as the evening progresses.

Brad, in his element in the kitchen, brings forth the main course: perfectly seared duck breasts accompanied by a tangy cherry sauce, buttery mashed potatoes infused with roasted garlic, and a medley of crisp, lightly sautéed seasonal vegetables. The colors play brilliantly off each other, the reddish hue of the duck contrasting with the vibrant greens and yellows of the veggies.

Michael leans over to Mayu, whispering, "I have to admit, this looks amazing."

Mayu chuckles softly, "I told you you might enjoy yourself."

Brad seems to pick up on Michael's approval, a small smile tugging at his lips. "It's actually Hanna's recipe," he reveals modestly, serving the dishes to each guest. "So you should compliment her."

"I could eat this every day," Mayu comments as she takes another bite, the rich flavor of the duck mingling harmoniously with the sweet tanginess of the sauce.

Michael nods, genuinely surprised. "This might just be the best duck I've ever had."

Hanna beams at the compliment. "Thank you. Brad actually hunted the duck himself."

Brad shrugs modestly, a far cry from his usual self. "It's a hobby. And when you have a chef like Hanna at home, it's worth it."

The group exchanges stories, laughs at shared memories,

and enjoys the delicacies on their plates. The atmosphere remains pleasant and warm, much to Michael's relief. For the first time, Brad feels less like an overbearing figure and more like a genuine host.

As they finish their entrees, Hanna hints at the dessert. "If you liked the main course, just wait until you taste Brad's chocolate fondant."

Brad raises an eyebrow, playfully reprimanding, "Now, now, don't spoil the surprise."

Michael can't help but smile, thinking that perhaps Brad isn't so bad after all.

———

New York.

Kara stands in front of a faded brick building, her eyes taking in the worn façade of the apartment block in Greenwich Village. The windows are lined with grime, and the sounds of muffled conversations and music waft down from open windows, hinting at the lives within. A deep breath calms her nerves as she checks the address Imam Rahim provided.

From the entrance, an elderly woman with silvering hair emerges. She limps toward Kara, her expression neutral but curious. "You the one looking for Terry's place?" she asks, her voice raspy with age.

Kara nods, her eyes scanning the woman's wrinkled face. "Yes, I'm Kara. Imam Rahim said you might be able to help."

The woman's name is Shaniya. She manages the building.

Shaniya lets out a soft chuckle. "Help? Maybe. Let's see." She begins to lead Kara through the building, her slow gait making it clear that every step takes effort.

As they walk, Kara breaks the silence. "So his name was Terry, then?"

"Yeah. But I can't tell you if it was real or not. I never got a surname."

"Why not?"

"He paid up front for six months. He's still got a month left. Just turned up at my office with the money. Didn't want to go through any of the usual processes. Just needed an apartment for a while. In the end, though, it was hassle."

Kara's curiosity is piqued. "Why do you say that?"

The old woman gives her a sidelong glance. "Well, when he was around, which was rare, there were complaints."

Kara arches an eyebrow. "Complaints? What kind?"

The manager's face darkens, her voice dropping to a whisper as they reach a landing. "Strange visitors at odd hours, chanting, just... weird stuff."

Kara pulls her phone out and brings up a photograph of Yasin Farid, displaying the screen to the woman. "Have you ever seen this man?"

The old woman squints to see. "Maybe he was around," she murmurs. "I don't know."

Kara slips the phone back in her pocket. "And the neighbors?" she pushes. "Did he get on with them?"

Shaniya sighs deeply, her face etched with weariness. "The neighbors liked to complain. Loudly."

She leans closer to Kara, the scents of old perfume and

mothballs mingling in the dim light. "Some of them don't like Muslims," she murmurs conspiratorially. "Even if they're white like him."

Kara's heart tightens at the comment, the underlying prejudice all too familiar. "You don't mind letting me into his apartment?" she asks.

The woman's gaze meets Kara's squarely. "Been wanting an excuse to see how he lives," she confides. "Check if those complaints hold any weight."

TWENTY-SEVEN

DIYARBAKIR

THE SAFE HOUSE IS SITUATED ON THE RURAL outskirts of Diyarbakır, providing a complete contrast to the chaotic chase they've just escaped. The small villa stands silent, a stone edifice against the night, only disturbed by the approaching rumble of their vehicle. The gate creaks open as Bennett steers the van in, killing the headlights immediately.

Akam's gritted teeth and ragged breaths break the silence, the pain evident in his eyes. He uses Bennett's shoulder as a crutch, every step a reminder of the ordeal they've just been through. Peter, in the meantime, supports a recently awoken Sonya; her gaze cold and unyielding, her eyes burning with a bitter intensity.

The urgency in Bennett's movements underscores the gravity of the situation. The front door is barely closed before he's instructing Peter to clear the nearby dining table. The wood groans under Akam's weight as he's laid on top.

His once-pristine shirt, now stained with blood, is quickly torn open to reveal the bullet wound.

"Peter, get rid of her, then grab the medic kit. Chest of drawers by the door." Bennett's command is crisp, each word heavy with urgency.

Peter guides Sonya into another room, a hand gripped firmly around her upper arm. The whole time, she stares at him, a mix of defiance and hatred burning in her eyes. He cuts away the zip-ties binding her wrists and replaces them with handcuffs. After that, he secures her to a radiator. Even constrained, she doesn't break her piercing gaze.

"You can't trust your friends," she tells him as he reaches the door to leave, the bitterness in her voice filling the silent room.

Peter, ignoring her, closes the door firmly and returns to the others. With focused haste, he retrieves the medic kit, passing it to Bennett.

As Bennett works, cleaning the wound, he finally speaks. "You're damn lucky, Akam."

A pained chuckle escapes Akam's lips. "I sure don't feel lucky."

With a smirk, Bennett replies, "Bullet went straight through. Missed everything vital. Some stitches and you'll be complaining about other things in no time."

Akam's relieved sigh is palpable. "That's something at least."

Bennett's gaze sharpens, his voice dropping to a near-whisper as he leans towards Peter. "Move her upstairs," he murmurs, nodding in the direction of Sonya. "There's a room at the end of the hallway, on the left. You'll find what you need there. It's about time she gave us some answers."

New York.

The musty smell of old paper hits Kara as she steps into the apartment, with Shaniya the curious building manager right behind her. The windows are masked with sheets of yellowing paper, preventing any hint of the outside world from entering. The rooms feel stifling, compressed.

Every step Kara takes reverberates in the quiet emptiness of the studio apartment, the lack of furniture amplifying her movements. She pauses to take it all in. The emptiness is paradoxical because the walls are the exact opposite.

Photographs—so many photographs—cover them from top to bottom.

Kara steps closer, her gaze narrowing onto the familiar face that pops up in image after image. Peter. Candid shots of him walking, him talking on the phone, him laughing with someone she doesn't recognize. There are images of him looking directly at the camera, his eyes cold and guarded, as if he senses the prying lens.

Shaniya, stepping beside Kara, lets out a sharp intake of breath. "Goodness," she whispers, staring wide-eyed at the walls.

Next to Peter's photos, more faces. One she recognizes from photographs in Peter's apartment: Michael, his features distorted in some pictures from being captured mid-motion. And then there's Mayu, Michael's girlfriend. Some photographs capture her alone, and in others she's with Michael, their hands intertwined or sharing a secret whisper.

It's a mosaic of obsession, a clear focus on Peter, but with Michael and Mayu not far behind. It is clear: Peter appears to be this man's target, his obsession.

Kara's fingers twitch as she reaches out, touching one photograph of Peter. There's an intimacy in the way he's been captured, like a lover's gaze. Yet, knowing what she knows, the display feels invasive, creepy.

Drawing a breath, Kara realizes she needs to document this. She pulls out her phone, starting to record the pictures. The depth of this obsession hints at something far more sinister than she'd initially suspected. Every click of her camera only deepens her resolve to unravel this mystery.

Behind her, Shaniya shifts uncomfortably, her expression a mix of curiosity and concern. "I never imagined... all of this," she murmurs, her voice barely above a whisper. "He really was up to something."

———

Diyarbakir.

The dullness of the room envelops Sonya. The air feels heavy to her, and a stale mustiness stings her nostrils. As she shifts her weight, her movement is restricted by the straps binding her to a chair, the leather biting into her wrists. The room seems to swallow any sound she makes, the padded walls absorbing each gasp and rustle.

Her vision homes in on the two figures standing in sharp contrast against the muted gray palette of the room. Peter, his silhouette tall and imposing, stands slightly behind

Bennett, whose creased forehead is a testament to the storm brewing inside him.

Sonya smirks, summoning every ounce of bravado she can muster. "So this is how the USA conducts its foreign affairs," she says, her voice dripping with disdain.

Bennett, unmoved by her sarcasm, replies, "Do you understand what is about to happen?"

Sonya's defiance doesn't waver. "Do you?" she retorts.

The room's atmosphere is electrified with a palpable energy that wraps around each person. Sonya's gaze darts rapidly between the two men, before locking on to Peter.

"He used to talk about you, you know," she murmurs, her voice a soft needle, poking and prodding at the taut membrane of the room. "He was obsessed with you."

"You don't know me."

"No. I don't. But he does."

The sudden shift draws Bennett into their verbal dance. "And that's what we're here to find out. Who he is."

As Sonya's attention swings to him, her eyes, previously animated, turn icy. "Even I don't know that. The woman who bore him two sons," she chokes out, her voice quivering, a hint of vulnerability cracking through her façade. "Two dead sons."

Bennett's voice becomes urgent, his patience wearing thin. "Tell me everything you know, Sonya."

Her eyelids flutter, moisture pooling at the edges, and then a single tear breaks free, carving a trail down her dirt-streaked face. "You know, even now, when he wants me dead, I still love him. Will still…"

"Is he planning more attacks?"

She regards Bennett, then says, "Why would he share that with me?"

"Who is he, Sonya?"

"I told you. I don't know any other name than Musa."

"What does he really look like?"

"He's white, American. Looks like you."

A surge of frustration moves Bennett into action. From the shadows of the room, a glint of metal catches the dim light as he pulls a cloth sack from a tool chest. The rustle of fabric is a soft whisper, contrasting sharply with the increasing intensity of Sonya's breaths as her eyes follow him.

Against one wall, a rusted tap drips intermittently, each drop echoing like a muffled drumbeat. Bennett seizes a weathered plastic watering can, its spout crudely amputated, and begins filling it. The room becomes heavy with impending doom.

———

NEW YORK.

SOFT CANDLELIGHT CASTS a warm glow in the dining room. Michael, Mayu, and Hanna sit around the elegantly set table, their stomachs almost full and anticipation palpable in the air. It's the moment they've all been waiting for—Brad's famous chocolate fondant.

Michael smirks, beginning a soft drumming on the table's edge with his fingers. Mayu giggles and joins in, their rhythm setting a playful tone. Hanna hesitates for just a moment, then, grinning, joins the impromptu drum roll.

The sound of footsteps from the kitchen grabs their attention. Through the door's frosted glass panel, a tall silhouette can be seen, prompting more eager drumming.

Brad's shadow grows larger and closer, and as the kitchen door swings open, the three friends anticipate a tray full of delectable desserts.

Instead, they are met with a chilling sight.

There's no tray. No fondant. Brad emerges, cradling a canister in one hand. A gas mask obscures his face, making his features grotesque and unrecognizable. The playful atmosphere shatters in an instant.

Reacting first, Michael surges to his feet, the weight of sudden realization pushing him into action. But before he can get far, a jet of gas shoots out, hitting him squarely. With a muffled cry, he crashes backward, dragging the tablecloth and dishes with him in a cacophony of crashing ceramic.

Mayu, driven by instinct, lunges toward Brad. But she too is met with a cloud of incapacitating gas. She slams into the wall, her world spinning as she slides down and into unconsciousness.

Hanna remains frozen, her face a mask of horror and disbelief. "Brad, what's going on?" she manages to whisper, her voice quivering.

Brad's eyes, cold behind the gas mask, fix on her. "It has been fun, Hanna," he says emotionlessly.

The glint of a silencer catches the dim light as Brad pulls out a pistol. Without hesitation, he fires a shot directly into her heart. As Hanna's eyes widen in shock and she slumps to the floor, he coldly walks over, and without emotion or pause, shoots her again in the head, ensuring she won't get up.

The room, only moments ago filled with laughter and camaraderie, is now eerily silent.

———

DIYARBAKIR.

AMID THE STARK, soundproof walls, Peter watches in grim silence as Bennett methodically pours water onto the cloth sack, which is now over Sonya's face. The muffled gasps and spluttering are a disturbing counterpoint to the room's sterile ambiance. Each tortured gasp sends a shiver of unease up Peter's spine—the internal war waging inside him between duty and morality.

Bennett, eyes on his wristwatch, sees it reach twenty seconds and stops pouring. Lifting the wet cloth hood just enough so only her mouth is revealed, he begins barking questions. "Who is he? Where's he from? Which state? How old is he? Tell me about his family?"

She can't speak immediately, too busy trying desperately to catch her breath, gasping and choking, her arms and legs tugging at the restraints. Eventually, her chest stops heaving long enough for her to talk. "He's got a brother... He told me that once... an older brother in America..."

"Now we're getting somewhere. Did he tell you his brother's name?"

Sonya thinks long and hard, but it's no good. So the sack is pulled back down and Bennett picks the watering can up again.

The shrill ring of Peter's phone pierces the heavy

atmosphere. Glancing at the screen, Michael's name flashes before him. He immediately dismisses the call, but it buzzes back to life instantly, the relentless ringing adding to the tension in the room.

"You'll have to excuse me," Peter mutters.

As he steps out, he's barely aware of Bennett's frustrated shouts from behind, his demands to Sonya for a name, a piece of information, anything.

Peter stands on the landing, taking a moment to center himself before answering the phone. "Look, Mikey, this isn't a good time," he begins, impatient.

The voice that responds is not Michael's familiar tone. Instead, it's chillingly cold, devoid of emotion. "This isn't Michael," it states.

A bolt of dread shoots through Peter. The walls appear to close in and the weight of the phone seems to double, the screen lighting up with incoming photo messages. Peter's heart plummets as he glimpses the previews. Two images— Michael and Mayu, both bound, their eyes blindfolded. His fingers tremble as he expands the photos, the details too cruelly clear.

"You could have Photoshopped those," he retorts, trying to keep his voice from shaking.

"Then why would I have his phone?"

"You could have stolen it."

The man on the other end chuckles coldly. "Not likely. Look, if I were you, Azrael, I'd work on the basis that I've got your son and his girlfriend and that I will hurt them if you do not do everything I am about to say."

The distant, stifled sounds of Sonya's struggling breaths reaches Peter's ears. It's a muffled echo of horror, serving as a haunting backdrop to the nightmare unfolding on the phone.

"What do you want?" Peter's voice is gravelly, strained.

"You have my wife, correct?"

Peter remains silent, every muscle taut, his mind racing to comprehend the situation and identify the voice.

"Well, you have. She is probably being tortured right now. She's got a strong will, but not strong enough to avoid eventually giving you and your partner everything she knows. Therefore, I want you to go back in that room, and I want you to shoot her dead."

Peter's face contorts in disbelief. "What?"

"You heard me. I want you to march in there and put a bullet in her heart or her head. As for your partner, I will allow you to deal with him however you want. Kill him or incapacitate him. My advice would be to kill him. Much easier to escape afterwards. After all, doing this will make you a fugitive and certainly put an end to your recently resurrected CIA career. The choice is simple. Kill my wife or I will kill your son. Keep me on the phone. You have ten seconds to do it. Tick tock."

A thick haze of desperation hangs in the air. The corridors of the safe house seem to narrow, and a relentless ticking in Peter's head begins, in tandem with his racing heart. The impossible choice before him threatens to shatter Peter.

Then he makes it.

Peter steps back into the room, the SIG Sauer already in his hand. With his back to him, Bennett is too busy pouring water over Sonya's clothed face.

"Kill her," the voice on the other end of the line hisses. "Kill her or it's your son and his bitch."

Peter makes a split-second decision. He pulls the trigger.

The echo of the gunshot lingers in the dim room, a stark contrast to Sonya's lifeless form, now slumped against her restraints. Bennett's eyes dart between Sonya and Peter, disbelief battling with understanding. The world seems to have tilted on its axis, and reality feels distorted.

Peter, hand shaking slightly but still firm, keeps his gun pointed at Bennett, who still holds the watering can. The weight of the decision presses down on him, a life taken to potentially save another.

Bennett's gaze is sharp, calculating. "Peter, what the hell's going on?"

"Put your hands out," Peter orders, his voice breaking slightly. His mind reels, desperately trying to stay ahead, to find a way to save Michael.

"I can't believe you're doing this," Bennett says, his eyes on the pistol. Then he does exactly what Peter expects him to do. He lunges for the gun with a sudden burst of energy, swinging the watering can in a wide arc aimed at Peter's head. But Peter, anticipating the move, deftly dodges the makeshift weapon and, with a swift, practiced motion, smashes the butt of his pistol into the side of Bennett's head. Bennett collapses to the floor, unconscious.

With a surge of adrenaline, Peter quickly moves to secure Bennett's hands behind his back with the zip ties. He can't help muttering, "Sorry" as he tightens them. His heart pounds in his chest, a drumbeat of regret and determination as he braces himself for the next step in this treacherous dance.

He places the phone back to his ear. "Now what?" The question hangs heavy, filled with despair and desperation.

There's a pause, a smirk evident in the voice that responds, "Now we play a game. The rules are simple. You do as I tell you."

"And what's that?"

"You're a man of exceptional talent, Peter Black. A skilled survivor of any situation."

"Stop blowing smoke up my ass and tell me what you want."

"I want you to use your unique skillset to get back to the United States while remaining a fugitive. You have forty-eight hours to reach Texas."

"Where in Texas?"

"Anywhere you wish. Just contact me on this number once you're there. If you are late, your son dies."

Peter senses he's about to put the phone down. "Hey."

"What?"

"Whatever it is I did to you," Peter says in a solemn tone, "I'm sorry."

"Tell that to your son."

The line goes dead.

TWENTY-EIGHT

NEW JERSEY

THE DESOLATE EAST STATE HIGHWAY UNFURLS beneath the cold grip of night, devoured mile after mile by the predatory advance of three sleek black vans. Each vehicle moves with a singular purpose, their headlights slicing through the encompassing darkness, casting eerie luminescence over the road's fog-kissed surface.

Inside the lead van, Musa's hands, clammy with a sheen of sweat, cling tightly to the steering wheel. The dashboard's sickly green glow casts ghostly light over his weathered face, revealing the map of anxiety etched into his skin. Periodically, he steals glances into the rearview mirror. The sight that meets his eyes is haunting: dozens of plastic drums standing in regimented rows, reflecting cold light. Each one represents potential destruction, but it's the secret beneath them that truly unsettles Musa. They have a falsified permit for the ammonium nitrate. They don't for what is underneath it.

As the van jostles over an uneven patch of road, there's a faint muffled sound—a stifled whimper, almost lost among the drone of engines. Unknown to anyone else on this road, beneath the drums in the first van, under a cunningly constructed false floor, lie Michael and Mayu.

Gagged, bound, and drugged, they are trapped in a nightmarish limbo.

The radio crackles to life, tearing Musa from his grim reflections. "All good up there?" Ayoub's voice, from the second van, carries a note of apprehension.

"All clear," Musa manages to reply, though his voice is laced with undeniable tension.

Silence reigns once more, punctuated only by the constant drone of engines.

In the third van, Uma's eyes dart nervously, every shadow beyond the windows a potential threat. Fields, blanketed in darkness, seem to watch him with a thousand unseen eyes. He's on edge, every nerve raw, anticipating danger at every turn.

"Remember, no stops. No matter what," Musa's stern voice cuts through the radio static, each word heavy with unspoken dread.

Trying to break the tension, Ayoub quips, "Wouldn't want our precious cargo being late." Yet, the humor falls flat, the silence that follows more oppressive than before. The magnitude of their task, the devastation they could unleash, looms large in each of their minds.

Time stretches, every second an eternity. The dark landscape rushes past, yet dawn is still a distant promise. As the horizon slowly starts to light up, the impending realization of what the future will bring becomes increasingly chilling.

———

New York.

Kara sits across from the agent, a table between them—the surface cluttered with documents, some of which have familiar faces on them. The New York FBI field office buzzes outside the room, but in here, there's an uneasy silence.

After taking pictures, Kara had called the police. It wasn't long before the FBI arrived. Now she's here.

"I was looking for an accomplice of Yasin Farid," Kara starts, her voice wavering slightly. "I didn't expect to find those photos."

The agent leans in, her eyes sharp. "So you claim. But how did you get access to the apartment?"

Kara's irritation is clear. "I told you, the building manager let me in."

"Why didn't you call the police when you suspected whose apartment it was?"

Kara goes red. "I don't know. Look, your guys are up there, you've looked into the place, seen it. Have you found out who this Terry guy is?"

"It's something we're looking into," the agent replies in a monotone.

"Okay. What about the pictures of Peter and Michael Black all over the walls? Michael's girlfriend? Why are they there? It's like he's stalking them."

The agent arches an eyebrow, her lips tightening. "Again, that's something we're looking into. Now, you should trust us to do our job."

Kara's patience wears thin. "Then do it."

Before the agent can respond, Kara's up and out, her heels clicking briskly against the marble floor.

She's barely outside the looming façade of the building when the soft buzz of her phone in her purse startles her. Pulling it out, she hesitates for a split second over the unknown number before answering.

"Kara." Peter's voice rushes through, sounding ragged.

"Peter! Where are you? What's happening?"

"Long story," he says breathlessly. "I'm in Turkey, trying to make my way back. But it's complicated. I need something from you, and I don't have much time."

Her heart races, her fingers gripping the phone tighter. "What do you need?"

"I need to know who he is, Kara. The man we're up against. Can you do that for me?"

There's a heavy pause as she processes his plea, the noise of New York swirling around her. Finally, she replies, "Yes. I'll find him, Peter. But there's something else you should know. I went to his apartment and found the walls covered in pictures of you and your son."

There's a brief pause, an intake of air. Then, "It's always been about me."

Kara is frowning. "How do you mean?"

"He's kidnapped my son and his girlfriend."

"Oh my God," Kara gasps, her hand coming involuntarily over her mouth.

"Back in Cizre," Peter goes on, "Sonya said something

that caught my attention. I think she was actually speaking the truth for once. She said that he wasn't really a Muslim. That he used Islam for his own purposes. I think that's true. I think this has nothing to do with jihad or a caliphate. This is about him and me. About his revenge."

A shiver runs through Kara before she speaks. "So maybe she was telling the truth about other stuff, too."

"That's what I think. I'm sure Sonya was telling the truth about Fairfax. That's where it all links back to."

"You mean Fairfax, Virginia?"

"Yes. That's where she said Musa was from. It's also where Yasin Farid is from. I think they knew each other from before. There's something about their pasts that's crucial, Kara. Start there."

Kara's eyebrows knit together, thinking. "So you're saying there might be a connection from their time growing up in Fairfax?"

"Exactly. Look into Farid's past, see who he was associated with, and cross-reference that with any recent movements or people connected to the Wolf Pack. And look for any connection with me from before when I worked as a cleaner."

"A cleaner? Does that mean what I think it does?"

"Yes. I cleaned up for the United States government. There were a lot of hit jobs against Islamic groups from 2001 to 2017 I was involved in. I'm thinking I may have killed someone he was close to during that time. It's a guess."

Kara exhales, jotting down notes. "It's not much to go on, but I'll do my best."

"Another thing."

"What?"

"Sonya said he had a brother. I think that was true, too. The person you're looking for has a brother."

"I'll look into it."

"Thank you," Peter says, gratitude evident in his voice. "But be careful, Kara. These people don't mess around. If they think you're digging too deep, they'll come for you."

"Trust me, Peter. I can look after myself. I'll find the answers and help get Michael and Mayu back," she assures him, her voice filled with determination. "I'll go pack and be on the first flight out of here."

———

ANKARA, Turkey.

IN THE GRIMY bathroom of an Ankara hotel room, Peter places the burner phone on top of the sink and stands facing a cracked mirror. The flickering overhead light casts uneven shadows, and for a moment, he hesitates, taking deep breaths to steady himself. Memories of his training surge back; he knows he can do this.

Gritting his teeth, he cleans a pair of tweezers with a lighter, the flame turning the metal red-hot for a brief moment. He cools it under the tap, then carefully sets it aside on a folded towel. A bottle of local raki is uncapped next, and Peter takes a long swig, letting the burning liquid steel his nerves. He then pours some over the tweezers, sanitizing them.

Using his left hand, he gently pulls back his right upper eyelid, his blue-gray iris stark against the bloodshot white.

The knowledge of the bug, hidden somewhere behind his eyeball, spurs him on.

With a suppressed groan, he carefully begins to maneuver the eye forward, using the cleaned tweezers to coax it gently out of the socket. His breathing is ragged, sweat beads on his forehead, but determination powers him through the ordeal. As the eye displaces, he catches a glimpse of the tiny metallic speck behind it. The bug.

With swift precision, he grasps the device, no bigger than a grain of rice, and pulls it free. It clinks lightly as he drops it into the porcelain sink. After taking a moment to catch his breath, Peter carefully guides his eye back into its socket. The pain is intense, but the sense of relief is even more overwhelming.

Splashing his face with cold water, he checks the eye in the mirror. Red and irritated, it will need time to heal, but it's back in place. The bug is out of him. The CIA no longer have an exact position on him.

Stepping back into the main room, he's greeted by the sight of money spread out on the bed. He picked it up this morning from the safety deposit box he'd dropped it in years ago—remnants from his days working for Pat Hughes, emergency funds he'd never thought he'd need. He gingerly sits down beside the money, a man with a mission, ready for his next move. The room is dim, the soft hue from a solitary bulb illuminating the stacks of dollars beside him.

Pulling out a burner phone, he dials a number he knows by heart but hasn't called for many years. The man's name is Dimitri, a known forger tied to the criminal underbelly of Istanbul.

"How long for a UK passport with a US visa?" Peter asks the second the call is answered, urgency evident.

"Peter Black," Dimitri answers in a warm tone. "It is so long since I heard your voice."

"How long?"

"Four days," Dimitri states matter-of-factly.

Glancing at the money, calculating, Peter wanders to the window, peering through the curtains. "Make it one and I'll triple the price."

Silence, but only for a moment. "Okay. But I need the money now."

"No. On completion," Peter challenges, his gaze fixed outside. "Can you do it or not?"

There's a grumble on the other end, undoubtedly Dimitri wrestling with greed and caution. Then, "I can."

Down below on the street, a car pulls to a stop. Peter's been expecting it. Bennett and his team disembark, heading for the hotel entrance. Peter's heart races.

"I'll contact you in a day," he mutters, quickly disconnecting the call.

Hastily, he scoops the money into a rucksack. Securing a chair against the door, he dashes into the ensuite. The bathroom window leads to a ledge, a pathway to the next building's balcony that he's already sketched out in his mind.

He leaps.

Crashing onto the balcony, he lets himself into the room, interrupting an intimate moment. The couple's shouts and screams fill the musty air, but Peter's already out the door, disappearing down the corridor.

Back in his own room, Bennett's efforts to break down the door culminate just as Peter slips out the back service door of the neighboring establishment. Merging with the alleyway's shadows, he's nothing more than a whisper in the wind by the time they finally make it through the door.

Bennett quickly scans the interior of the dimly lit room, the crumpled sheets of the bed, the curtains open slightly on the window like someone was standing there only a minute ago. But it's the open bathroom door that draws his attention. The tracking app on his phone is buzzing incessantly, an indicator glowing bright on the screen. He strides over, his two man team following close behind.

In the stark white of the bathroom sink lies the tiny metallic bug, still and inert. Bennett's eyes narrow in frustration. The tracking app beeps, the icon on the screen hovering directly over the sink, indicating the bug's position. It's as if it's mocking him.

He reaches down and picks up the bug. Its minuscule size contrasts sharply with his anger. "Damn it!" he curses, crushing the tiny device between his fingers. The remnants of the bug fall back into the sink, and the signal on the tracking app disappears.

Bennett takes a deep breath, feeling the weight of the missed opportunity. "He's already one step ahead," he mutters, his voice tinged with both admiration and frustration. The room, with its signs of a hasty departure, serves as a reminder of just how elusive Peter Black can be.

TWENTY-NINE

SOMEWHERE IN THE USA

Relief washes over Musa, Ayoub and Uma as they reach their destination: a private lockup hidden within a wasteland of closed businesses; tool repair shops, mechanics. The lead van skids to a halt just in front of the shutter. Without hesitation, Musa leaps out, his boots ricocheting sharply against the asphalt. Swiftly, he maneuvers the lock, the shutter door rattling as it starts to lift. Dust and shadows dance in the dim light as he dashes back to his van. The gears crunch, and with the other two vans trailing behind, they roll into the lockup, the heavy shutter descending in their wake.

Stepping out of the vans, the men stretch their stiff limbs and then, one by one, embrace each other. There is a sense of camaraderie in their hugs, a shared understanding of the risks they are taking and the importance of their cause.

Musa's voice cuts through the stillness, calm yet

commanding. "You have excelled, brothers. The next phase is soon. Now help me remove the kafir from the floor of my van."

Moving with efficiency, the three men unload the barrels, placing them methodically to the side. Their attention then turns to the van's floor panels, hidden beneath accumulated dirt. Working together, they expose the concealed compartment.

Beneath the panels, Michael and Mayu lay motionless, their skin ghostly pale in the meager light. IV lines tether them to bags filled with sedative, ensuring their unconscious state.

Musa approaches, checking each captive's pulse and eyes. The lockup's atmosphere tightens as the men await his verdict.

"Still heavily sedated," Musa confirms, satisfaction evident in his tone. "Stable."

Michael and Mayu are carefully lifted by the men and placed on makeshift stretchers, ensuring that their IV lines remain undisturbed. As one of the men monitors the sedatives' flow, Musa's gaze remains unwaveringly on the captives.

The lockup, only moments ago drenched in silence, now resonates with activity as the group readies itself for what comes next.

———

Fairfax, Virginia.

. . .

THE MORNING SUN is bright when Kara arrives on Eden Way, an otherwise quiet suburban road now lined with press vans, their satellite dishes sticking out their roofs. Reporters scuttle around with cameras in tow, everyone eager for a glimpse, a comment, anything from the Farid family. After all, their son is now the latest big bad enemy of the free world.

She parks her airport rental a few houses down, far enough away not to draw attention but close enough to keep an eye on the front of the Farids' home. Through the car's tinted windows, the once-vibrant blue of their house now seems to sag under the weight of scrutiny. Their curtains, closed tightly, give away nothing, and their front lawn is vacant save for a forgotten bicycle, a sign of lives disrupted.

Kara knows there's little chance the Farids will let her in —not with this media circus encroaching on their doorstep. But with the desperation of the situation, needs must. She looks around, spotting a tall wooden fence that separates the Farids' neighbor's house from the street. Another fence, out of sight from the road, divides the two properties. A quick scan assures her that no one's looking in that direction. Or indeed hers.

Taking a deep breath, she hustles toward the fence, her sneakers cushioning her steps on the soft lawn. In one fluid motion, she hoists herself up and over, landing softly on the other side. The neighbors are thankfully out, meaning the route to the opposite fence is unopposed.

The Farids' backyard is serene, a stark contrast to the chaos out front. Concealed by a series of tall shrubs, Kara crouches, wondering what to do now. The soft buzz of the cicadas does little to calm her racing heart.

Before she can plan her next move, the door creaks open. Mrs. Farid steps out, a woman once vibrant and cheerful, now sporting shadows under her eyes and a weariness that weighs her down. Her trembling fingers place a cigarette in her mouth, and she lights it. Then she glances around her backyard.

Their eyes meet, and for a split second, both women are frozen where they are.

Kara steps out from the bushes, raising her hands to show she means no harm. "Mrs. Farid," she starts, her voice soft but insistent, "I'm not here to exploit your pain. I just want to help. To tell Yasin's story, your story."

Tears pool in Mrs. Farid's eyes, but her gaze remains wary. "Why would you care about my son's story?" she finally whispers.

"Because," Kara exhales slowly, searching for the right words, "Yasin isn't the first American to be brainwashed into terrorism, and unless we address this, he won't be the last. Your son was radicalized, Mrs. Farid. And I believe America needs to understand how and why."

A heavy silence falls between them, broken only by the distant hum of the media frenzy out front. After what feels like an eternity, Mrs. Farid motions for Kara to come inside.

As the door closes behind them, Kara feels a weight of guilt settling over her. After all, most of what she just said is untrue. She has no intention of writing anyone's story, merely finding out anything she can on the men now stalking Peter: the Wolf Pack.

———

Istanbul, Turkey.

As evening descends upon the Istanbul skyline, casting a dusky glow across the minarets and domes, Bennett and his team lie hidden, having positioned themselves discreetly for the stakeout of Dimitri Malenkov. The fading light refracts off the waters of the Bosporus, providing a serene backdrop to the tense operation.

Dimitri Malenkov is a man well known to the CIA. Formally a contact of Pat Hughes, it wasn't hard to connect the dots to Peter.

Originally from Leningrad, Malenkov was born in 1965. His history is intricately woven with the underbelly of the black market, a legacy from his father, a notorious black marketeer of the Soviet era.

Dimitri, however, was a cut above even his illustrious 'papa.' He had inherited more than just his father's penchant for the underground; he delved deep into the world of people smuggling—a lucrative trade during the tumultuous 1980s. Along the way, he was introduced to the intricate art of forgery. This newfound passion led to the formation of a sprawling network, including master forgers and covert operatives embedded deep within the Bureau of Consular Affairs. These were men who could lay their hands on the seemingly unattainable: pristine materials for the forgery of the most secure documents, such as a coveted box of blank US passports, sourced directly from the echelons of government.

With the Cold War's curtain call, Dimitri, ever the opportunist, expanded his horizons. He set up operations in

Istanbul, a city synonymous with mystery and secrets, the sort of place that attracts the types of people desperate to vanish. And for the right price, Dimitri is the man who can facilitate any disappearance.

The air crackles with almost tangible tension, as Bennett's team keenly observes the entrance of Dimitri's workshop from a nondescript apartment across the street. Nestled within Istanbul's winding alleys, Dimitri's workshop stands out: arches reminiscent of Byzantine grandeur frame the entrance, while the walls, built of Ottoman bricks, wear their age with a patina of grime and soot. The eyes of the two operatives in the apartment, sharp and unblinking, are glued to the workshop's sturdy oak door, while Paul Bennett and Aria Patel sit in a nondescript car nearby, their muscles coiled like springs, ready for action.

The moment they've been waiting for arrives as the target, Dimitri Malenkov, finally emerges from the building and strides with purpose toward his car. The operatives in the apartment, their hands trembling slightly with adrenaline, quickly relay this information via radio to Bennett. The message whispers in his ear, and without a moment's hesitation, he kicks the car into gear and begins to trail behind Dimitri, his and Aria's hearts pounding against their rib cages with the weight of what they might uncover and the consequences that could follow. The chase is on.

——

FAIRFAX, Virginia.

. . .

THE FARIDS' living room is filled with soft, muted light that filters through the drawn curtains. Mr. Farid, a tall man with deep-set eyes and a graying beard that speaks to his Qatari roots, stands by the window, occasionally peeking out of the blinds at the press outside. Mrs. Farid, with her olive complexion and expressive hazel eyes, sits gracefully on the couch. Ornate trinkets are arranged on the mantelpiece, standing alongside framed photos of a smiling Yasin at various ages. The room is suffused with a sad quietness, broken only by the occasional sipping of tea.

Kara, shifting uncomfortably in an old but elegant armchair, speaks up. "Thank you for allowing me into your home. I'd really like to share your story, and Yasin's story, with the world."

Mrs. Farid, clutching an old photo album, looks up with weary eyes. "We don't recognize the man in the news. The one who killed all those poor, innocent people. We only know the Yasin from these pictures." She opens the album to show a young Yasin in a boy scout uniform, his badge-laden sash hanging proudly. The next photo shows him outside a Mormon church, arm in arm with his parents.

Kara, glancing at the photos, says, "He looked like any other young American boy. What changed?"

Mr. Farid takes a deep breath. "He was such a quiet, thoughtful boy. Always polite, always respectful. But after he went away to college, he became obsessed with his Lebanese roots. His Islamic roots. After his conversion, he became distant. We didn't understand it. He'd never previously shown any real regard for the old country."

Kara, trying to sound gentle, presses on, "When you say conversion, you mean his conversion to Islam, right?"

Mrs. Farid nods. "Yes. We converted to the Church of Latter Day Saints around three years after we arrived. We weren't exactly what you'd call strict Muslims before that. But we fell for the local community so much that we decided to convert and were baptized."

"So Yasin grew up in the church?"

"Yes. But as he grew older, he became curious about other religions, and because of our roots, he felt a connection with Islam."

Kara, trying to dig into any connections, asks, "Did you notice any change in his behavior or the types of friends he was keeping during this time?"

Mr. Farid looks down. "He became isolated. Started keeping to himself. His friends from church, from school— he stopped seeing them. We wanted to be supportive of his new faith, but then he started expressing some... extreme views. We didn't know where they were coming from."

Kara, sensing a lead, asks, "Did he mention anyone, any group or particular mosque, that might have influenced him?"

Mrs. Farid shakes her head. "No. We asked him multiple times, worried about him. But he just became more distant. Shut us out until he no longer even answered our calls. That was five years ago. We haven't spoken since."

"Do you think there's a chance he may have been influenced by someone outside of your community, maybe online?"

Mr. Farid rubs his temples as he tells her, "We don't know. When he was here, he used to spend a lot of time on his computer, but we assumed it was for school. We never imagined... this."

Kara tries a different angle. "Were there any signs, any hint of his intentions? Anyone he might have been working with?"

"Our son was a good boy," Mrs. Farid insists, teary-eyed. "But over time, he became a stranger to us. If he had accomplices, we truly do not know. I wish we did. Maybe then we could have prevented all of this."

Kara, realizing she won't be getting the answers she's looking for, softens her tone. "I'm truly sorry for your loss. I can't imagine the pain you're going through."

Mrs. Farid closes the photo album. "We just want people to remember the Yasin from these pictures, not the monster he became."

Kara can almost feel the pain in her eyes. It's clear that the Farids are grappling with the choices their son made and the actions he took. She thanks them for their time and leaves, knowing she has more pieces to the puzzle but still many questions left unanswered.

Kara slips out through the back gate, eager to avoid the cluster of journalists camped at the front door. In the alley, where the shadows of the adjacent houses cast long, dark shapes across the ground, she spots a young man around Yasin's age loitering close to the Farid's backyard. He has a scruffy beard and wears a hoodie that almost hides his anxious eyes. And if that's not at all suspicious, he begins skulking off the second Kara makes eye contact with him, glancing around nervously as if he expects to be followed.

Not wanting to disappoint him and sensing a potential lead, Kara quickens her pace and follows him to a house at the end of the street.

As he reaches the door, she calls out to him, "Hey!"

Hurriedly, he fumbles with his keys, trying to open the door and get inside. But Kara gets there just in time to shove a foot in the door, preventing it from closing.

"Did you know Yasin Farid?" she asks as he looks at her from the gap in the door.

His eyes dart from her face to the foot in the door. "You the cops?"

"No." Kara shakes her head, keeping her voice steady.

"Press?"

"Yes. But I'm not with those other vultures."

The two stare at each other, worry evident in the man's eyes.

"You never answered my question," Kara adds.

Looking down, he replies, "Yeah. I knew Yaz."

"How well?"

"Almost my whole life. Well, before he went all off grid, anyway."

"Then I need to speak with you. Can I come in?"

He stares at her a while, clearly weighing his options. Then, with a resigned sigh, he nods and opens the door wider to let her in. As she steps inside, she offers her hand. "Kara."

"Eddie," he says, taking it.

———

Istanbul, Turkey.

Inside his car, Dimitri grips the steering wheel with one hand while holding his phone in the other, his voice steady as he speaks. "I'll be there soon," he assures, casting a glance at the rearview mirror as he turns onto a road that passes underneath a causeway.

"Where are you now?" comes Peter's voice in his ear.

"Underneath the causeway," Dimitri tells him, before adding derisively, "Where all Istanbul's forgotten children come to live."

The streets in this part of the city are a canvas of human despair, filled with the homeless who have found a semblance of shelter under the concrete arches of the causeway. Men and women with faces etched in lines of hardship, their emaciated bodies wrapped in tattered clothing, huddle around small fires in makeshift camps. Hollow with defeat, their eyes follow the cars passing by. Their faces are a silent plea for compassion in a world that seems to have forgotten them. A disheveled mother cradles a crying baby, her eyes vacant, while an old man with a grizzled beard and matted hair rummages through a trash can, vying with the street cats for anything that might ease the gnawing hunger in his belly.

As Dimitri drives along, he can't help feeling a pang of guilt at the sight of so much suffering. During his childhood, his father had told him about the Siege of Leningrad, when the Nazis had blockaded the city, slowly starving its inhabitants to death. This reminds him of those stories.

But it isn't long before it passes, the pang quickly suppressed by years of hardened resolve. After all, he has his own problems to deal with.

In the car trailing Dimitri, Aria Patel casts a sympathetic glance at the homeless as they pass them. "It's hard to see, isn't it?" she murmurs, her voice tinged with sadness.

Bennett, eyes fixed on Dimitri's car, gives a curt nod. "It is," he agrees. "But we have a job to do."

Aria nods, her expression determined as she focuses on the road ahead. They can't afford any distractions, not with so much at stake.

Up ahead, a crossroads is bathed in a hazy glow, the red stoplight illuminating the shadows of the underpass with an otherworldly hue. As Dimitri rolls to a stop, Bennett and Aria maintain their distance, stopping three cars behind—a standard precaution drilled into them during training. The intersection is bustling with activity; pedestrians darting across the road, vehicles humming with impatience, the tramps wandering between the cars, begging for a few coins. Their disheveled appearance and desperate demeanor obstruct Bennett's line of sight, making it difficult to keep a close watch on Dimitri's vehicle.

A particularly disheveled tramp, reeking of stale sweat and unwashed clothes, approaches Dimitri's car and unceremoniously douses the windshield with a bucket of murky water. Annoyed, Dimitri rolls down his window and barks in Turkish, "Hey! Fuck off."

Undeterred, the tramp leans into the window and does something that surprises Dimitri: He tosses in four thick bricks of US dollars.

"What the hell?!" Dimitri exclaims, his eyes widening in surprise as he recognizes the face behind the layers of dirt and grime: It's Peter.

"Long time, no see," Peter murmurs, smirking slightly.

A wave of shock washes over Dimitri's face, momentarily displacing his hardened exterior before he quickly regains his composure. "You smell awful," he mutters, reaching under his seat and retrieving a manila envelope, which he passes to Peter.

Peter quickly checks the contents.

"You don't trust me?" Dimitri asks.

"No," Peter snaps back as he flicks through the pages of the passport.

Simultaneously, Bennett and Aria are engaged in a battle of wills with two persistent tramps who are insistent on cleaning their windshield.

"We don't need our car cleaned," Bennett snaps, trying to wave them away.

One of the tramps replies in Turkish that Bennett doesn't understand, rubbing his stomach in a universal plea for food.

Aria leans out of the passenger window. "Not now!" she shouts in Turkish.

Peter, now satisfied with the contents of the envelope, leans in closer to Dimitri. "Give my friends the runaround, will you?" he instructs.

As the traffic light flicks to green, Dimitri nods subtly, and the vehicles lurch forward. "Always a step ahead, aren't you?" the Russian comments as he pulls away.

Peter, clutching the passport in his hand, retorts, "Always." He then melts into the crowd, disappearing into the sea of pedestrians in his ragged disguise.

Finally, the persistent tramps leave Bennett and Aria alone.

Hurriedly, Bennett puts the car in gear, muttering curse words to himself as they move along with the traffic. He presses on the gas, with Aria responding, "Let's not lose him now" as they resume their pursuit of Dimitri.

Peter watches from the corner of an eye as their vehicle disappears into the distance, swallowed by the thrumming city traffic. A smirk creeps across his face as he reaches into his pocket and pulls out a wad of bills. He approaches the two tramps who had aided his deception, their eyes widening as he hands them each a generous sum.

"Thanks for the help," he tells them.

As Peter walks away, blending into the urban sprawl, he can't help but feel a sense of satisfaction. Despite the close call, he has managed to outwit Bennett and his team once again. Nevertheless, the game of cat and mouse is far from over, even if for now he has the upper hand.

———

FAIRFAX, Virginia.

IN THE HEART of Eddie Smith's dimly lit living room, the weight of anticipation presses heavily. Soft light seeps in through the heavy drapes, casting a gentle glow on the worn-out furniture and revealing walls adorned with traces of a life once full of vibrancy.

Kara, with her sharp, analytical eyes, sits across from Eddie. He's a lanky figure, bones stretched tall and thin, with hair that looks like it hasn't met a comb in days. His eyes dart around nervously, each quick movement betraying a sense of unease.

On the coffee table between them, lies a slightly creased photograph, a frozen moment from an age gone by. It captures Eddie and Yasin Farid in their youth, grinning ear to ear, joined by two other boys. All four are swathed in Boy Scout uniforms, badges meticulously sewn on, faces radiating youthful exuberance.

Eddie had presented the photo shortly after they'd sat down. Like the Farids, he appears to want Kara to see Yasin as something other than a murderer. As they sit there, her gaze keeps drifting back to it, an attempt to reconcile the beaming boy with the man who, just two days prior, had held a knife to her throat before blowing himself up in a police precinct.

Returning her focus to Eddie, Kara initiates the interview. "Were you still close to Yasin, before he... did what he did?"

"Not really," Eddie mutters, recalling his past with Yasin. "Not since he went off to college. That was when he began to question everything."

"Is that when he converted to Islam?"

"Yeah. It was after that stupid class he took. The one on cultural assimilation. After that, he became obsessed with his heritage, his identity. Claimed his natural one had been taken away from him. I tried to support him, thinking it was just a phase. But then he started sending me stuff."

"Stuff? Like what?"

"Videos and documents about the American government."

She leans forward, her pulse quickening. "Such as?"

Eddie shifts uneasily in his chair. "Stuff like how back in the fifties, the US government tricked a bunch of African American syphilis patients, giving them placebos instead of medicine during an outbreak. Basically, using them as guinea pigs to track the disease's progression."

"The Tuskegee Syphilis Study," Kara remarks.

"You mean it's true?"

"That one is, but it's more complicated than that. Did Yasin ever mention being involved with any group or person? Anyone he might've trusted?"

Eddie's eyes dart away. "No. But I couldn't tell you about any of his recent activity. Me and Yasin haven't spoken for years. It just got worse over time, Yasin getting more and more radical. And then, about four years ago, he just cut me off. Stopped communicating, blocked me on social media."

"What about before that?" Kara pushes gently. "Was there someone else he might've spoken to? Someone influencing him?"

Eddie's dull eyes glimmer as he thinks about it. Then he answers, "No one I can think of. I mean, he kept that stuff private from me because he knew I didn't approve."

Desperation creeps into Kara's voice. "If you know something that can help find out who was working with him, now's the time."

"All I can give you is the stuff he sent me. Maybe you'll be able to find something in that."

Frustration growing, Kara takes a moment, deciding on her next move. "Well, make sure to send it to me right away. Here's my card."

She takes the aforementioned card from her handbag and hands it over.

Eddie hesitates, then takes it, nodding slowly. "I'll email it to you."

She nods back, a silent agreement between them. "You do that. And thank you, Eddie."

Kara takes one last look at the picture of Eddie, Yasin Farid and the two other boys. All that innocence, lost.

Eddie observes her, his own gaze falling on the photo. "We were inseparable back then," he recounts, his voice tinged with a mix of nostalgia and regret. "Called ourselves the Wolf Pack."

Electricity races up Kara's spine, the name echoing inside her skull, ringing innumerable bells. Her eyes snap up to meet his. "What did you say you called yourselves?"

"The Wolf Pack."

Picking up the photograph, she points to the boys. "This is the Wolf Pack."

"Yes."

"And who are these two?"

"That's Jimmy and Max. They're brothers. That picture was taken right before they went missing."

"Missing?" Kara's heart jolts once more.

"Yeah. Their dad went crazy and ended up kidnapping them both when Max was ten and Jimmy was twelve. They were never seen again. It was all pretty messed up. I guess you could say the rest of us took it real bad. Especially Yasin."

"And you have no idea where they are now?"

"No. No one does."

———

ISTANBUL, Turkey.

. . .

Peter finds himself in the dingy bathroom of one of Istanbul's many rundown establishments. The tattered wallpaper is peeling at the edges, and the faucet leaks in a slow, rhythmic drip. It's not much, but for now, it's a much safer haven than any of the upmarket places in the city, where he's sure his picture has been circulated among the staff.

A single dim bulb hanging from the ceiling casts a muted yellow glow over a cracked mirror. He peers at his reflection, mentally preparing for the transformation he's about to undergo.

From a bag, he retrieves the tools of his new identity. A well-worn cleaner's uniform—faded blue with streaks of dirt and patches sewn in haphazardly. He slips it on, adjusting the fit. The clothes hang a bit loose on his athletic frame, but they'll do the job.

Next comes the false beard. Each strand is carefully designed to blend seamlessly into his skin, making the disguise as authentic as possible. The adhesive is strong, bonding quickly to the contours of his face. He meticulously positions each section, ensuring that it adheres properly. As he looks in the mirror, his familiar face morphs into that of a stranger. The transformation is almost complete.

He then smudges fake tan over himself, creating the illusion of a hard-working Turk. His striking blue eyes are the only remaining trait of his former self, so he pulls on a worn-out baseball cap low, letting the shadow of its bill veil them.

Peter exhales, his breath clouding the mirror. The city outside beckons, filled with both danger and opportunity. He knows the streets will be swarming with agents looking for him, but in this getup, he's just another face in the crowd. Another janitor, trying to make ends meet in the bustling metropolis.

His burner phone vibrates with a call. Peter eagerly answers it. "Kara?"

"Peter, I may have found something." Kara hesitates before tentatively asking, "This might be out on a limb, but does the name David Harrison ring any bells for you?"

Peter is silent, a thick pause filling the space between them as his mind whirs with the name.

"Peter?" Kara prompts, her voice edged with concern. "Did I lose you?"

When he finally breaks the silence, his voice is hushed, cautious. "Yes, I know him. But what has David Harrison got to do with this?"

"You know him?" She sounds taken aback.

"Yes. What did you find out about him?"

"That he was working for the US diplomatic office in 1994 when he was captured by the Taliban. Spent almost five years in an underground cell hidden in the Hindu Kush. That was before he was released as part of a 1999 prisoner exchange with the Taliban, an event that was facilitated by a Chicago Muslim leader named Malik al-Nasri. The same Muslim leader who was killed along with his wife the other night in a bomb attack. I mean, this guy is ringing bells all over the place."

"How did you get to David Harrison in the first place?"

She tells him about bumping into Eddie Smith at the back of the Farid's place. "Eddie was friends with Harrison's sons," she continues, "Jimmy and Max. So, too, was Yasin Farid. And get this, they called themselves the Wolf Pack."

Peter feels his heart pounding in his ears. Memories flooding back to him, a boy lying face down in the dirt, eyes fixed to the body of his dead father.

"Six years after David Harrison got back," Kara's voice goes on, "he took those two boys with him to Afghanistan. They've never been seen since. That was 2005." She stops speaking a beat, waiting for his reply. "Peter?"

He breathes out. Then, "He didn't work for the US diplomatic office. That was just cover. He wasn't a diplomat. He was CIA."

"CIA?"

"Yes. He was out there recruiting double agents when he got captured. But I never knew him then. I only got to find out about him much later, in 2007, when David Harrison had become Abu Yusuf al-Amriki." There's a weighted pause. "By then, he had fully embraced the Taliban's ideology and was a full-blown member."

The sounds of Kara inhaling sharply fill the line. "Eddie said that he converted both his sons soon after returning to America. That he took them out of school, out of their church, the Boy Scouts."

Peter's sigh is a weary one. "It went beyond faith."

"How so?"

"After his release, the CIA allowed him to come back, thinking his experience and knowledge of the Taliban's inner workings would be invaluable assets. But we were blind. His release was a ruse, a carefully constructed ploy. He was the Taliban's Trojan horse."

"What do you mean?" Kara asks.

"The Taliban didn't care about the prisoner they

exchanged for Harrison. Their only goal was getting him back to the US. By the time agents across the Muslim world started to vanish, the pieces fell into place. David, or Abu Yusuf, had hacked our database, sharing intel with various extremist factions. Our operatives, most of them with families, were hunted down. Many met brutal, unspeakable fates."

A cold dread seeps into Kara's veins. "Where did Harrison go after that?"

Peter's voice is laced with bitterness. "He got wind we were on to him. Fled to the Afghan badlands with his boys. And then nothing. Until we picked up his trail two years later."

"You found him?"

"Ben Knight and I tracked him to a remote valley in northern Afghanistan," Peter confirms. "He and his Taliban buddies had taken three humanitarian workers. They were about to execute them when I showed up and neutralized the threat."

"Neutralized the threat? Does that mean David Harrison is dead?"

"Very," Peter agrees.

"What about the boys?"

"The youngest kid was there. Max. After taking out Harrison and the rest, I secured him. The older one, Jimmy, he wasn't there. I heard we lost him to the Taliban."

Kara's breath catches. "Wait. One of the brothers was there?"

"Yeah. He was out there in the desert with them. I guess the old man wanted to show him the ropes."

"What happened to him?"

"I got him to the extraction point and handed him to Ben Knight. Beyond that, I can't tell you what happened to him."

Kara's voice trembles, but her words carry an unmistakable urgency. "Peter, it has to be them. It has to be the sons or at least one of them."

Peter thinks about it before responding, the gravity in his voice palpable. "Are you absolutely certain?"

She closes her eyes, trying to recollect every detail, every hint. "I... I'm not entirely sure. But the pieces fit."

It is then that Peter comes to a decision. His voice turns resolute. "I'm going to give you the number of a contact in the CIA. Her name's Kirsty Lang. I've worked with her more than anyone else in the agency. You can trust her. Pass on everything you've got and find out what Ben Knight did with Max Harrison after I handed him over. Remember that name, Ben Knight. Maybe it's in a report somewhere and Kirsty can take a look."

"Understood," Kara replies. "Ben Knight. I'll call her."

"I'll text you her number the second this call ends."

Trying not to sound desperate, Kara asks, "When will I hear from you again?"

Looking at the stranger in the mirror, Peter replies, "I'm preparing to make my move. If everything goes the way I want it to, I should be back stateside in a day."

There's a slight pause. Then, "Peter?"

"Yes?"

Her voice softens. "Just... take care of yourself."

A moment's hesitation, then a soft exhale. "Same goes for you. And Kara... thank you."

The call ends and Peter takes one last look at his cracked

reflection, adjusting the cap. The image staring back at him is of a man ready to vanish, to become a ghost. With a final nod, Peter steps out of the bathroom, mind buzzing with fresh revelations, but ready to navigate this next chapter of his precarious existence.

THIRTY

UNDER THE SOFT GLOW OF STREETLIGHTS, MUSA, Ayoub, and Umar sit huddled inside a weathered work van that is very different from the three they came down in. This one isn't black, and it isn't indistinct. It is white with the words "Fairfax County Department of Public Works and Environmental Services" emblazoned down the side.

The worn fabric of the three men's coveralls strains against their tensed bodies. Every detail of their attire—from the faded logos to the smudges of dirt—paints a picture of workmen at the start of a long day. Yet beneath this façade, their eyes betray them. Sharp and alert, they dart around, taking in the tranquil scene of the suburban neighborhood that spreads out around them.

The van's engine rumbles softly as it maneuvers through the tree-lined streets, casting fleeting shadows on quaint houses with manicured lawns. The eerie silence of the late evening is punctuated only by the occasional chirp of a cricket or the distant bark of a dog.

As they pull up beside a discreet sewer entrance, the trio exchanges a weighted glance. The night's true mission is just beginning. Without a word, they climb out, each movement calculated, their every step reverberating softly against the backdrop of the sleeping suburb.

In a choreographed rhythm, they quickly assemble a safety barrier around the manhole, ensuring its sturdiness. With synchronized precision, they heave the heavy lid off, revealing the inky abyss below. The atmosphere hardens, the very air seeming to thicken as they descend the ladder into the vast sewer tunnel beneath the street.

The oppressive stench immediately assaults their senses, a mix of decay and damp accentuated by the slick, algae-coated walls that glisten in their flashlight beams. Each step squelches, their boots sinking slightly into the muck, but the men move forward with unwavering determination.

Musa unfurls a water-stained map, the lines and markings delineating their path. With each stride, the weight of their mission hangs heavier. Suddenly, he stops, his eyes scrutinizing the dank surroundings before he confidently points to a seemingly insignificant patch on the tunnel wall. "This is it. Just the other side is where we need to be."

Their eyes gleam with a mix of anticipation and purpose as Musa brandishes a can of white spray paint, marking their chosen segment on the tunnel wall with a big X. After that, they ascend to street level, where they methodically retrieve the specialized tunneling gear and essential bracing supplies from the van. One piece at a time, the equipment is carefully lowered into the gaping hole.

The usually serene ambiance of the sewer, previously marked only by the intermittent plop of water, is soon dramatically transformed. The thunderous roar of heavy-duty hammer drills reverberates, aggressively challenging the integrity of the aged, moisture-laden bricks. As each man finds his rhythm, they begin a haunting, rhythmic chant of the Takbir, their voices echoing in determined unison: "Allahu akbar. Allahu akbar."

The chant, a rhythmic incantation, melds with the mechanical drone of the drills, creating a hypnotic cadence that reverberates through the tunnel, filling the void with a sense of purpose. Sweat courses down their faces, muscles scream in protest, yet their spirits soar, buoyed by the chant, the knowledge that with each passing moment, they inch closer to their objective.

———

CIA HEADQUARTERS, Langley, Virginia.

IN THE BUSTLING environment of the George Bush Center for Intelligence, analyst Kirsty Lang sits engrossed in her work, her eyes darting across the dual screens in front of her. The analytical software she's using is running its algorithm, highlighting potential connections between a new Syrian terrorist group and known militant leaders. Every line of data, every possible connection, is vital.

Her concentration, however, is repeatedly broken by the incessant chatter of her two co-workers. They're huddled together, their words a mix of whispers and emphatic expressions.

"Man, you heard about the shit going down in Turkey?"

the taller one, Alex, asks, his eyes wide with a mix of concern and excitement.

Sitting up on Alex's desk, Mark, the other, leans in closer, his voice a hushed tone. "Yeah, they said we lost a key source. Shot by one of our own, can you believe that?"

Kirsty's fingers pause above her keyboard, her irritation building. She takes a deep breath, trying to focus on the data unfolding on her screens, but their words penetrate her concentration.

"I heard it was one of Paul Bennett's team," Mark adds, his words laced with a sense of revelation. "And so soon after losing Tom Cohen, too."

Kirsty can't hold back anymore. She swivels her chair around, her eyes narrowing. "Do you guys mind?" she interrupts, her voice icy. "Some of us are trying to work here."

Alex and Mark exchange a look before Alex replies, "Sorry, Kirst. It's just crazy, ain't it? Our own operative pulling the trigger on a source?"

Kirsty's jaw tightens. "Who? Who pulled the trigger? What source?"

"You haven't heard?" Mark's eyebrows lift in surprise.

Kirsty shakes her head. Unlike the others, she'd bypassed the morning ritual of water cooler gossip, opting instead for an immediate dive into her work. "No," she responds, her tone absent, her focus still partially anchored to the lines of code on her computer screen.

Mark opens his mouth to answer, but his gaze shifts past Kirsty, his posture stiffening. "Ma'am," he greets, respect laced in his voice.

Director Sandy McLean's sudden presence fills the room, a formidable energy that silences the buzz of casual conversation. "Shouldn't you be somewhere else, Mr. Williams?"

Mark's voice falters a little, "I was about to leave."

"Then do."

As Mark makes a hasty exit, the Director's piercing gaze settles on Alex. "And how about you, Mr. Frost? Isn't it time you took your lunch break?"

"Yes, ma'am," Alex responds. There's a brief, almost imperceptible pause, before he collects his jacket and follows Mark out of the room, leaving Kirsty and the Director alone.

Kirsty swivels in her chair to face Director McLean. The contrast between them couldn't be starker—the Director, a picture of traditional authority in her neatly tailored bespoke suit, her graying blond hair tied in a long ponytail, and Kirsty, a vibrant embodiment of the unconventional with her bubblegum-pink hair and Japanese cosplay clothing.

"You've heard the rumors, right?" The Director's voice is soft yet commanding as she takes a seat on the edge of Kirsty's desk.

"Kind of," Kirsty admits, a sheepishness lingering in her voice.

Director McLean's eyes, sharp and discerning, probe for more. "What have you heard?"

"Well, those two were just yammering on about some source being shot in Turkey."

The revelation hangs in the air for a moment, charged and waiting.

"And did they say who did the shooting?"

"No. I don't think they knew."

There's a potent pause. Director McLean's next words,

heavy with gravitas, punctuate the silence. "At twenty-one hundred hours our time yesterday, the operative Peter Black murdered the source Sonya Kahn during an interrogation. He then subsequently attacked a fellow operative and is now on the run."

"But why?" Kirsty's voice is a blend of disbelief and confusion.

The Director's eyes darken—a storm of emotions and unanswered questions rolling behind them. "That's what I'd like to know. He's currently doing everything he can to evade our people, and I don't know why."

Kirsty's voice quivers slightly, "There has to be an explanation for it. Peter wouldn't just kill someone and disobey orders for no reason."

Director McLean's gaze shifts downward, her fingers intertwining as she grapples with the haunting aftershocks of Peter's sudden betrayal. The air, heavy with silent revelations, seems to hold its breath as she inhales deeply. Each word is measured, carved from a mix of stern authority and concealed vulnerability. "Now I'm going to ask you this once, Kirsty," she says, "and I want you to tell me the truth."

"Okay." Kirsty's reply is almost a whisper, the weight of the moment pressing down upon her.

The Director's gaze, piercing yet searching, never leaves Kirsty. "After Ben Knight, you know Peter the most."

"I do, and he always came across as straight up. Reliable."

"Yes. And that's why I need you to be truthful now." The intensity of Director McLean's eyes bore into Kirsty. "Has he contacted you?"

"No," is the immediate answer, Kirsty's voice a testament to the truth. "I've not spoken to Peter since our last job together, at least a month ago."

The Director's eyes, inscrutable yet discerning, linger on Kirsty, as if attempting to peel back the layers, to unearth truths unspoken. After what feels like an eternity, she nods, "Okay. Good."

As the Director rises and begins leaving, the atmosphere is charged. She halts at the door, her hand casting a shadow on the handle. "And it goes without saying, Ms. Lang," she tells her in a firm voice, "that if you do hear from Peter, or have any information pertaining to his whereabouts, then you will come straight to me."

She doesn't wait for an answer, merely steps out of the room. The Director's departure leaves a resounding silence in her wake, the gentle click of the door sealing Kirsty in a room that suddenly feels too large and too suffocating all at once. She's alone with revelations that whisper through the silence, a haunting dance of knowledge and uncertainty that churns in the space around her. The screens before her pulse with data, but their ordered chaos is a distant hum against the tumult of her recent, more imposing thoughts: Peter— and what had propelled him down this incomprehensible path?

The unexpected vibration of her phone shatters the eerie quiet, causing her to jump. An unfamiliar number blinks ominously on the screen, and an instinctive unease compels Kirsty to glance over her shoulder, half-expecting Director McLean's scrutinizing gaze to be staring right back at her from the door. But the coast is clear. So she answers. "Peter?"

"This isn't Peter," a female's voice replies.

Confusion furrows Kirsty's brow. "Then who is it?"

"My name is Kara Tate."

"And who the hell is Kara Tate?"

"It doesn't matter. What does, is that I'm calling because Peter Black needs your help."

Kirsty's spine stiffens, and she again twists around to check the door. The Director's stern warning, only seconds ago, reverberates in her mind, her heart pounding against her ribcage.

Huddling into the confines of her desk and leaning over the phone, she says in a hushed whisper, "I should report this straight away."

"No don't!"

"You know what Peter did, right?"

"He had to. They have his son."

Kirsty's anger dissolves into concern. "Who have?" she asks, her voice sharpening.

"The Wolf Pack."

Kirsty's eyes widen in shock. "But the Wolf Pack was Yasin Farid. That's what the preliminary investigation is saying. Everyone who helped him is abroad. Disbanded."

"No! They're not. There's more coming. They're using Peter as a smokescreen. Please, Kirsty, let me explain."

"Okay," Kirsty Lang says in an even tone. "Explain."

Kara tells her everything she found out in Fairfax. Each revelation weaves through the ominous quiet; David Harrison, the two sons, a narrative of hidden truths and veiled secrets that pulse in the silence.

"Find out what happened to the sons," she says at the end. "Find out what Ben Knight did after Peter handed him Max Harrison, and what happened to the older brother

Jimmy. Please, Kirsty. We're his only hope. Michael's only hope."

A resolve, fierce and unyielding, ignites within Kirsty. "Okay," she says. "Leave it with me. I'll see what I can find out. And Kara?"

"Yes?"

"If he contacts you again, tell him to call me. I can help."

"Okay. Thank you, Kirsty."

As the call ends, the room pulsates with the latent energy of unveiled secrets and looming enigmas.

Then, having given herself a second or two to comprehend it all, Kirsty turns back to her screens, gets rid of the data, and begins.

———

Istanbul Airport, Turkey.

The vastness of Istanbul Airport reverberates with the energetic hum of travelers arriving and departing. Their myriad languages and conversations create a lively cacophony. The white gleam of floor tiles, polished to perfection, reflects the overhead lights, illuminating the transient world of travelers.

Against this backdrop, Paul Bennett, Aria Patel and the two other members of their team move with purpose, singular in their mission, seemingly impervious to the distractions around them. Their keen eyes never waver, scanning the teeming crowds for the slightest anomaly.

Ahead, the metallic sign for the security office gleams

under fluorescent lights, and they head into a narrow corridor. En route, they pass a janitor, an elderly man with a beard that seems to tell tales of a life lived long and hard. His eyes barely lift from his task as he methodically mops the passage. Yet there's a subtle alertness in his furtive gaze, a sense that he sees much more than one would suspect.

Upon reaching the office, Bennett doesn't waste a moment. With a swift, practiced motion, he presents a photograph of Peter to the officer on duty.

"This man." Bennett's voice is steely, demanding attention. "He'll be here, but not as you see him. He's a master of disguise and in possession of fake documentation."

The officer, a stern-faced man with salt-and-pepper hair, studies the photograph intently. "You know the name he's traveling under?"

"No."

"Then disguised or not, it'll be like finding a needle in a haystack."

Bennett's eyes narrow, determination evident in his features. "Then we need a magnet. Every moment we waste gives him an advantage."

In the background, the old janitor's mop moves rhythmically, swishing over the tiles of the doorway.

"Keep this photo close," Bennett instructs the officer. "He's dangerous, and we need to find him before he disappears again."

As the team moves away from the office, the janitor's mop slows, his eyes momentarily glancing up at Bennett. However, he fails to spot Aria Patel holding up the rear as he turns back to his bucket. Their shoulders bump, and the janitor's mop clatters to the gleaming floor, splashing water.

"I'm so sorry," Aria murmurs, bending down to help retrieve the fallen mop. As their hands briefly touch, there's an electric charge, a sense of recognition. Her eyes meet the janitor's, and for a split second, the well-practiced mask of Peter's disguise slips, revealing a hint of the man beneath.

The instant recognition flickers in her eyes, Peter knows he has to move, and fast. Her hand, trained and instinctual, reaches for her pistol, but Peter, with reflexes honed through years of training, gives a deft flick of his mop. It connects with Aria's hand, sending the gun clattering to the polished airport floor. She lets out a startled cry, the sound sharp and piercing in the cacophony of the airport, causing the others to whip around sharply. Time seems to suspend itself, each second stretching out infinitely as their eyes lock on to the scene unfolding before them. Their training, drilled into their muscle memory, kicks in as they swiftly assess the situation and prepare to react.

In that singular, heart-stopping moment, the bustling airport—with its throngs of travelers, announcements over the loudspeaker, and the hum of activity—fades into an inconsequential background murmur, and all that remains is the pulse-pounding tension that crackles electrically in the air between them. The world narrows to this singular moment, teetering on the edge of eruption.

With the nimbleness of a much younger man, Peter pivots on his heel and bolts down a side corridor. Bennett and his team spring into action, lunging forward with an athlete's grace, their strides eating up the distance between them and their quarry.

Emerging into a food court, Peter weaves deftly through the crowds, narrowly avoiding a collision with a family towing a cart laden with luggage. Ducking into a duty-free shop, he sends a cascade of perfume bottles crashing to the floor in his wake. The acrid scent of alcohol fills the air as the agents close in, dodging the shattered glass and startled shoppers.

Aria, still smarting from the humiliation of being disarmed, is a woman possessed. Her determination fuels her speed as she gains on Peter. He can feel her breath on his neck as he bursts out of the shop and onto a moving walkway. He leaps onto the handrail, running along it with the balance of a tightrope walker, while the agents are forced to shove their way through the throng of startled passengers filling up the travelator.

Bennett and his two colleagues, a wiry man named John and a solidly built woman named Maria, fan out, trying to cut off Peter's escape routes. With Aria in close pursuit, they're able to herd him into a dead end: a balcony overlooking the vast airport atrium. It's a dizzying sight, with travelers like ants below and the distant hum of conversations merging into a white noise. Peter skids to a halt, his back to the ledge. The balcony offers no escape, save for the staggering drop behind him. His eyes scan the area, homing in on some bunting that hangs nearby.

Aria, eyes ablaze, storms up, her recovered pistol aimed directly at Peter's heart. Bennett and the others quickly converge, forming a semi-circle around him, every exit covered, every angle watched. John, breathing heavily, keeps his gaze and gun fixed on Peter, while Maria subtly motions for the nearby Turkish airport security. Within moments, they join the operatives, their guns also drawn and aimed.

Peter's gaze sweeps over the assembled forces—CIA and

Turkish security alike—understanding the gravity of his predicament. The breeze from the open terminal lightly tugs at his fake beard, hinting at the freedom just beyond reach.

Bennett steps forward, his voice cold. "There's nowhere left to run, Peter."

For a moment, everything seems to stand still. The deafening hum of the airport fades to a whisper as all eyes lock on to the standoff on the balcony. Peter's gaze drifts over his shoulder, catching glimpses of the oblivious travelers below, their faces tiny and distant, all the time contemplating his next desperate move.

Bennett takes another step forward slowly, his gun trained on Peter. His face is a storm of emotions—anger, betrayal, determination.

"You've run far enough, Peter. But it ends here," Bennett declares, his voice steady.

Peter doesn't reply immediately, taking a moment to let out a shaky breath. "You think I want any of this, Bennett? You think I enjoyed pulling that trigger?"

"You had a choice!" Bennett's shout almost drowns in the cacophony of travelers.

"Yes. My son's life or Sonya's. What would you have done?" Peter's voice is raw, a man grappling with the weight of his actions.

Bennett's face tenses. "You should've trusted the agency. We could've saved them both. You betrayed us all, Peter," Bennett continues, his grip tightening around the pistol. "Now place your hands at the back of your head and get down on your knees."

Peter's voice cracks with sheer desperation. "Don't you see, I can't! He's got Michael! If I don't do what he says, if I don't keep running, he'll kill my son!" The raw emotion in his voice is palpable.

Bennett, however, remains unwavering, his voice a low rumble. "Put. Your hands. Behind your head. Now."

As the team advances, tightening the circle around him, Peter's eyes dart rapidly, calculating his slim chances. His gaze locks on to the vibrant bunting strung along the balcony. With the team only a few steps away, Peter's decision is sudden and bold.

"Not today," he breathes, and with a quick push, he vaults over the railing, clutching the bunting. The cloth rips away from the railings, creating a makeshift swing that propels him through the vast expanse of the terminal.

Releasing his grip, Peter tucks and rolls, minimizing the impact and bouncing back to his feet in a fluid motion. Bennett and the others can only watch in momentary disbelief from the balcony above as he slips farther away from their grasp.

Spotting an abandoned luggage cart, Peter leaps onto it without breaking stride, sending it careening down a wide corridor that leads to the exit. Security officers give chase, dodging and weaving through the crowd, but the cart gives Peter the edge he needs. He barrels down a flight of stairs, sending it flying into the air, and lands hard but rolls to his feet, sprinting for the exit.

Outside, the bright sunlight is momentarily blinding, and Peter squints as he scans the area for a getaway vehicle. He spots a taxi idling at the curb and makes a beeline for it. With a final burst of speed, Peter leaps into the backseat of the taxi and waves a wad of cash at the driver.

"Get me out of here. Now!"

The cabbie nods, puts the car in gear, and speeds away, just as several security come bounding out of the airport. All they can do is pound their fists in frustration as the taxi disappears into the distance.

Peter slumps in the back seat, a heavy realization settling within him: Any conventional exit from Turkey is now an impossible dream.

———

Langley, Virginia.

Kirsty's hand hovers before the stern, mahogany door of Director McLean's office. Taking a deep breath, she raps her knuckles against the wood. "Come in," comes the crisp response. The door creaks open under Kirsty's touch, revealing the Director, stern and unyielding, glasses perched on her nose, pen moving meticulously over a sea of paperwork.

"Director McLean." Kirsty's voice is a mix of rehearsed authority and nervous apprehension.

The Director's gaze, piercing and incisive, lifts from the papers. Eyes locking onto Kirsty, she places her pen down with measured grace. "Ms. Lang, I wasn't expecting you. Something I should know about Peter?"

Kirsty shifts, the polished floor beneath her feeling unstable. "No, ma'am, it's not about Peter. Or at least not in the way you might think."

Director McLean removes her glasses, the atmosphere

charged with anticipation. "Then what can I help you with?"

"It's about David Harrison," Kirsty starts, the name hanging in the silence between them.

The Director's eyebrows knit together. "David Harrison," she repeats almost to herself. "That's a name I haven't heard in years. Why are you digging into a termination that happened over a decade before you even joined the agency, Ms. Lang?"

Kirsty hesitates, her lips drawing into a thin line before the confession spills from her. "I've been looking into things, and I can't believe no link has been made yet."

Director McLean leans back, her gaze sharp, unyielding. "A link to what, exactly?"

Kirsty breathes, each word punctuating the charged silence. "To the Wolf Pack."

The Director's eyes narrow, her voice a blend of curiosity and caution. "What link?"

Kirsty leans forward, the intensity of her gaze matching the gravity of her words. "I think that David Harrison's sons, or at least one of them, might be behind the Times Square bombing. But when I looked into the file on their father's termination, it's all redacted, even for my level five security clearance. So can you tell me what happened after Peter handed the youngest son Max over to Ben Knight?"

Director McLean's face is an enigmatic mix of guarded composure and faint echoes of unvoiced emotions. For a fleeting second, a shadow of something—guilt or remorse, perhaps—passes across her eyes. It's ephemeral, barely there, then swept away by a resurgence of stoic professionalism. The faintest quiver in her voice is the only betrayal of the storm beneath the calm as she answers. "Max Harrison is dead. So is his brother. What you're looking into, Ms. Lang, is a dead end."

Kirsty's face is awash with confusion, the pieces of the enigmatic puzzle clashing, refusing to align. "Are you sure?"

The Director's affirmative is as cold as ice. "Yes."

"But how did they die?"

There's another flicker of something unsaid, a storm of secrets, regrets, and unutterable truths, swirling behind the Director's eyes. "I'm afraid I can't tell you. It's classified, and way above your clearance grade. But I can assure you, Ms. Lang, both Max and Jimmy Harrison are dead."

Kirsty's lips part, a retort, a question on the verge of spilling from her mouth when a sudden knock startles them both into silence. Their heads turn, eyes sharpened, as the door opens.

Mark Williams steps in, an ominous pallor to his skin, eyes ringed with the shadows of unspeakable revelations. His voice, though steady, is tinged with an undercurrent of alarm. "Ma'am, I've got some real bad news."

Mark's gaze flits to Kirsty then back to the Director.

"It's okay," Director McLean says. "You can speak in front of Ms. Lang."

Walking to her desk, he extends a sheaf of papers he's holding. "Ma'am, we've got a serious security breach. These are some screen grabs I got of it."

The Director's hands, steady yet imbued with an unutterable gravity, take the documents. Placing her glasses back on, her razor-sharp eyes scan the content. "And what am I looking at exactly?"

"These are the names and addresses of hundreds of our

sources and contacts living inside the Middle East and Africa. They were recently recovered from he dark web."

The revelation slices through the room, a cutting edge of betrayal and vulnerability. Director McLean's voice, an alloy of alarm and command, demands clarity. "You mean to say they're in the public domain?"

Mark's nod is as heavy as the silence that follows.

"And you know the source of the leak?"

Again, Mark nods. "It's come from inside. One of our own has done it."

"Who?"

"The leaks were sent from the same IP address operative Black uses. It was Peter Black, ma'am."

Across the desk, denial and shock weave through Kirsty's features. "No. It can't be."

The denial hangs, suspended amidst a tumult of unspeakable betrayals, and in that moment her heart stops when she feels her phone vibrating in her pocket. Pulling it out, she sees a number she doesn't recognize and is straight away sure: It's Peter.

"I have to take this," she mumbles, getting up from her chair. "It's my mom."

Mark and Director McLean hardly register her exit, too engrossed in the unraveling narrative of betrayal before them, until she reaches the door. At that moment, Sandy McLean looks up from the papers on her desk. "Remember, Ms. Lang," she says with an icy precision. "If Peter so much as sends you a text, I want to know about it. You're either for or against us here."

The phone continues to vibrate in Kirsty's hand as she gulps down a dry lump and nods. "Of course, ma'am."

Once in a nearby stairwell, she finds a private corner where she is unlikely to be overheard. Taking a deep breath to steady her nerves, she answers the call. "Is this who I think it is?" Her whisper, delicate yet charged, drifts into the phone.

"Kirsty," comes the familiar voice of Peter Black, a mix of desperation and relief in his tone, "I need your help more than ever."

Her anger flares instantly. "You have a lot of nerve calling me. They're saying you've been leaking classified documents. What the hell is going on, Peter?"

"That's a new one to me," Peter's retort, laced with a blend of disbelief and urgency, resonates within the confining spaces of the stairwell.

Kirsty presses, "Well, did you?"

"No," he says, his voice cracking slightly. "All I'm doing is trying to keep Mikey and Mayu alive long enough for me to find the bastard doing this and end him. If I'm not back in the USA in twenty-four hours, he'll kill them. But, Kirsty, I need your help to do that. Bennett and the others are on my ass. Airports are a no go. I need you to get me passage back to the US quick and unseen."

"Then why don't you just hand yourself into them? Explain things. Paul Bennett has always come across as a reasonable guy. I'm sure he'll understand so long as you tell them everything instead of running."

"If I don't remain a fugitive, he'll kill them," comes Peter's panicked reply. "It's one of his little rules."

Kirsty takes a deep breath in, then out, trying to stay calm in the face of the mounting crisis. "Okay," she says eventually. "Then give me an hour. I might have something for you." She ends the call, her mind already racing with possible plans to get Peter out of Turkey and into the United States.

———

Istanbul, Turkey.

Peter is sitting in a dimly lit bar waiting for Kirsty to call him back. It's a dingy place where the light seems to be absorbed by the walls rather than reflected. He's tucked away in a corner where the shadows hang heavy, offering a cloak of anonymity. He nurses a lukewarm beer, the condensation from the glass wetting his fingers, the bitter taste a poor distraction from the storm of thoughts raging in his mind.

It's pretty clear, the Wolf Pack are trying to frame him, bring him to disgrace. But how did they get access to his computer, to his CIA security? Surely, they're not so good at hacking that they can gain access externally.

Then that would imply someone inside the agency. But who?

Peter sips his beer. He's wearing another disguise—a bucket hat pulled low over his forehead, a scruffy ginger beard glued to his face, glasses that he doesn't need. The disguise is uncomfortable and itchy, but it's necessary. Every time the door of the bar creaks open, he tenses, preparing for the worst—for Bennett and the others to pour inside.

The air is thick with the smell of stale beer and sweat. The low hum of conversation is punctuated by the occasional burst of laughter, creating a sense of normalcy that

Peter can't help but envy. He fidgets in his seat, his knee bouncing up and down as the seconds tick by, each one stretching out interminably.

One excruciatingly long hour later, his burner phone lights up with a call and he snatches it off the table. "Kirsty?"

"I've got you something," she says without preamble, her voice a lifeline in the dark. "But you'll have to source a boat. You know Burgaz Island?"

"Yeah. It's not far from here."

"Can you be off its coastline in an hour?"

"I can try."

"Good. I'll text you the exact coordinates. Make sure you're there. They won't be waiting around."

Peter has to ask, "Who won't be waiting around?"

"You'll find out when you get there."

———

Dulles, Virginia.

Kara glances at the clock on the wall for the innumerable time, the monotonous tick-tock echoing in the confines of the small, dimly lit motel room. She shifts uncomfortably in the armchair she sits in, the anticipation carving a restless energy in the silence. Every now and then, the distant rumble of an airplane taking off from Dulles International Airport punctuates the quietude, a reminder that the world is all movement beyond these four walls.

In this space, however, time seems suspended—each moment stretching into eternity as she waits for Kirsty Lang to call. The continued ticking of the clock is the only accompaniment to her anxious breaths. The information she had imparted all those hours ago still hangs heavily in the room, an invisible specter that colors the atmosphere with sinister hues.

The shrill ring of her phone slices through the silence, startling Kara. She lunges for it, her hands trembling slightly. "Kirsty?" Her voice is laced with an urgent expectancy.

"Yes, it's me," Kirsty's voice, though distant, is a balm to the anxiety twisting Kara's insides. "I talked to Director McLean."

"And?" Every cell in Kara's body is on edge, electrified by the anticipation of revelations.

A pause. A breath. "The files on David Harrison and his sons are redacted. Heavily. And from what the Director told me..." Kirsty hesitates, the silence pregnant with unsaid words. "Max Harrison is dead, and Jimmy is missing, presumed dead."

A cold, sinking feeling anchors in Kara's stomach. "But that can't be..."

"I pushed for answers," Kirsty interjects, her voice a mix of frustration and determination. "But she wouldn't tell me how it happened. Just that they were dead."

"Then it must be the older boy, Jimmy," Kara's words are quick, a desperate attempt to piece together the jigsaw of secrets and lies. "If Max is dead, then his brother must have survived. Now he's getting revenge against Ben Knight and Peter."

"Maybe. Look, I didn't get many answers," Kirsty says, "but I did find something else. David Harrison's former wife —the boys' mother. She lives in Virginia still."

A sliver of hope, precarious yet palpable, pierces the heavy air. "You think she might know something?" Kara's voice, though hushed, is laced with an intense urgency.

"It's worth a shot, isn't it?" Kirsty's rhetorical question hangs between them.

"It sure is," Kara declares, the determination rendering her voice steely.

"I'll send you the exact address," Kirsty assures her, and though miles apart, a silent consensus binds them—a shared commitment to unveil the veiled, to illuminate the obscured. "Good luck, Kara."

———

THE SEA OF MARMARA.

IT'S NIGHTTIME. Peter sits in a small dinghy he stole from a nearby marina, the darkness around him almost suffocating, the craft slowly heading out to sea. Checking his coordinates and seeing that he's almost there, he cuts the outboard engine, the sudden silence ringing in his ears. Eyes on the smartphone in his lap, the screen's glow illuminating his face with an eerie light, he uses a paddle to get himself right on top of the X. Once there, he waits. The only sound is the gentle lapping of water against the stolen boat.

He doesn't have to wait long.

The still waters of the bay are suddenly shattered by an undercurrent of turbulence. Bubbles rise, followed by a deep, resonating vibration that shakes the dinghy. The silvery sheen of moonlit water bulges upwards, and with a powerful surge, the black, leathery form of a submarine breaches the surface. Displaced water runs down its sleek form in torrents, causing ripples that fan out in every direction.

The submarine, a leviathan of steel, glistens under the pale glow of the moon. As the remnants of water slide off its hull, a hatch on its conical tower begins to rotate, gears grinding. A blinding ray of artificial light spills out, momentarily illuminating the night. Against this stark brightness stands a figure, his features obscured by the contrast of shadow and light. "Peter Black?" he calls out.

Peter doesn't say anything. Adrenaline pumping through his veins, he approaches with cautious speed. As he nears, he stands up, the boat floating toward the tower under its own sway. Then he's stepping onboard, the frigid metal of the submarine's ladder chilling his palms, each rung a cold reminder of the world he's stepping into. With every step upwards, his heart hammers louder, mirroring the uncertainty and urgency of the moment.

Once inside, he is led through the narrow corridors of the USS Trident by its captain, a stern-looking man with a no-nonsense demeanor. "You'll be staying in my cabin," he says, his voice clipped and professional. "You're under strict orders not to interact with my staff. Not to leave the cabin."

Peter stops him. After all, this man is essentially saving the life of his son by giving him this ride. "I can't thank you enough for this," he tells the captain.

The captain's reply catches him off guard.

"I'm only doing this," he says, "because twelve years ago you rescued an oil tanker captain who'd been kidnapped in the Indian Ocean. Somali pirates had taken him and his crew hostage, held them for eight weeks. That's when you infiltrated their compound and rescued the whole group. That captain was my brother. Today he lives because of you. That's why I'm risking my entire career and liberty to get you to your next location."

Peter's throat tightens with gratitude, but before he can say anything, he asks, "And where is my next location?"

The captain gives him a measured look. "You'll soon find out."

THIRTY-ONE

AFTER ALMOST A DAY OF CONSTANT WORK, THE three men finally break through the sewer wall, dust and debris falling around them as they step into the space beyond. It is an old chamber, covered in cobwebs that cling to every surface. In the center of the room stands an old industrial generator, silent and still. A long tunnel stretches out before them on the other side of it, swallowing the beams of their flashlights in inky darkness.

Musa begins speaking, his voice filling the confined space. "The main building has four of these external generator rooms linked by long underground tunnels on each side of it. One on the north, one on the south, one on the east, and this one, on the west. That tunnel," he adds, flicking his beam at the long corridor of darkness, "takes you right underneath the building."

Umar, squinting into the darkness, asks, "How far is it?"

"Half a mile. See these cables?" Musa says, pointing his flashlight beam at thick cords that snake along the wall.

"They're so long that there's almost a hundred tons of copper inside of them."

Umar frowns, puzzled. "Why's it so far from the actual building?"

"Well," Musa explains, "when they built the place in the 1950s, the United States was in the middle of the Cold War. They wanted to protect it from blackouts caused by bombings. So if the area ever got hit with a bomb, they'd still be able to get power from outside the blast zone. That's why this room is so far underground and surrounded by reinforced concrete."

Ayoub grimaces, rubbing his sore arms. "Tell me about it. I've just spent the last day breaking through it."

The men chuckle gently, then look down the tunnel, the darkness an ominous void.

Umar, still uneasy, asks, "And you're sure there's no security cameras down there?"

Musa nods confidently. "In the nineties, they decided it was too expensive to maintain, so they bricked up the entrances and decommissioned the generators. There is zero security around here because it's almost thirty years since anyone even thought about these tunnels. It is a blindspot. They will not see us coming, brothers."

He smiles, and it catches on, his companions sporting broad grins.

"Okay," Musa then says, pausing and drawing his gaze to Ayoub. "You should leave now, get to Texas."

Ayoub nods, a solemn determination etched on his face.

Musa is the first to step forward, pulling Ayoub into a firm embrace. The warmth of their bond radiates through the dank chamber, a fleeting moment of solidarity before the upcoming separation. Ayoub's breath is steady but laden with the gravity of their mission, every inhale mirroring the impending danger and every exhale affirming their unwavering conviction.

Umar follows suit, and the intensity of his grasp speaks of the two's bond. Words are not enough for the storm of emotions swirling within them—fear, anticipation, loyalty.

As Ayoub steps back, the traces of their contact linger—a connection of brotherhood that defies the encroaching darkness. Then, with one last shared look, he leaves.

"And we," Musa says, his gaze transitioning from the receding figure of Ayoub to Umar, "will stay here and finish what we've started."

Umar's gaze is filled with anxiety but also resolution. "Do you think he'll make it to Texas?" he asks, referring to Peter's race against time.

"It looks like it," Musa replies, before his attention then shifts. "I almost forgot, I need to leave soon, too."

"Why?"

"I've got to check on our prisoners."

———

SOMEWHERE OFF THE western coast of Morocco.

THE INKY WATERS of the North Atlantic churn tumultuously, reflecting the gray of the overcast sky above. From its fathomless depths, the USS Trident, its matte black hull cutting through the water with predatory sleekness, surfaces with a barely audible hiss.

Not far away, an imposing aircraft carrier, the USS Nimitz, dominates the horizon. Resembling a floating city, its enormous frame is an intricate mosaic of steel, weaponry, and high-tech equipment. As the submarine gracefully approaches its behemoth counterpart, the rhythmic thumping of rotor blades grows louder. A helicopter, its blades slicing through the mist-laden early morning air, lifts off from the carrier's deck and with practiced precision, hovers above the awaiting submarine, ready to bridge the gap between the two maritime giants.

Peter, squinting against the wind generated by the helicopter's blades, steps out of the hatch and onto the top of the submarine. The captain stands beside him, offering a salute as Peter is hoisted up into the helicopter. As the aircraft begins to ascend, Peter takes one last look at the captain, who waves him off, a mixture of respect and concern in his eyes.

The chopper carries Peter over the expanse of water, the submarine shrinking into a speck below them before disappearing entirely into the vastness of the ocean. As they approach the aircraft carrier, Peter feels a surge of adrenaline. He is dropped onto the runway, the helicopter hovering just long enough for him to jump out before it zooms away again.

As he stands on the misty flight deck of the USS Nimitz, the distant hum of aircraft machinery envelops him. Out of the dense fog, a silhouette gradually takes form. It's a fighter pilot, tall and lean with chiseled features, confidently striding toward him, his helmet visor reflecting the dim light around. "Ever been up in a Hornet before, sir?" he inquires, a teasing smirk playing on his lips as he extends a helmet and oxygen mask toward Peter. Taken aback by the sudden shift of circumstances, Peter merely nods, a mix of anxiety and excitement coursing through him.

Together, they walk toward the menacing shape of the F/A-18 Hornet, its sharp lines cutting through the mist. Climbing up the ladder, Peter finds himself stepping into the tight confines of the jet's cockpit, the heart of this aerial predator.

"The closest I can get you," the pilot says, his hands deftly flicking switches and adjusting dials as Peter straps himself in and pulls on the helmet, "is an airfield in northern Mexico. See, it's an act of treason to go into US air space without permission—even for me. The Mexicans are a little less switched on about it, though. Easier to sneak in and out."

"Just get me close to the border," Peter replies, his voice muffled by the mask.

"Will do. And, sir?"

"Yes?"

The pilot hesitates for a moment before continuing, his tone sincere. "I'd like to thank you personally from the bottom of my heart for what you did for me back in Iraq."

Peter, surprised, turns to look at the pilot. "What did I do?"

"You don't remember?"

"No."

The pilot lets out a soft chuckle, shaking his head in disbelief. "Back in '04, I got shot down over Baghdad, right before the fall of Saddam. It was you that came and carried me out of an Iraqi torture chamber. I'd be dead if it weren't for you, and my boys would've been raised without their old man. This here journey is me paying you back. So thank you, sir."

Peter, touched by the pilot's words, nods. "You're welcome."

"Now hold on to your britches," the pilot says, a grin spreading across his face as he throttles up the engines. "Because we're about to go yee-hah."

The jet roars to life with a fierce intensity, its vibrations resonating deep within Peter's core. With a sudden thrust, they're catapulted down the carrier's deck, the immense g-forces pinning Peter firmly against the cushioned contours of his seat. Within seconds, they're airborne, the carrier shrinking beneath them as the endless expanse of ocean sprawls out. The cerulean waters seem to meld seamlessly with the sky at the horizon, creating a mesmerizing canvas of gradients. Drawing in a sharp breath, Peter inhales the crisp, oxygen-enriched air, steeling himself for the daunting path that lies ahead. Amidst the lurking dangers, an undeniable rush courses through him as they ascend, piercing the very fabric of the atmosphere. The enormity of his mission weighs on him: This, he realizes, is the beginning of the end.

———

THE SEDATIVES ARE WEARING OFF. Michael's eyes flutter open to the cold, harsh light reflecting off the gray concrete walls. Every muscle in his body aches as he pushes himself upright, quickly taking stock of his surroundings. There isn't much. A thick metal door with no handle on the inside, the cot he sits on, a plastic bucket. That's it.

It's pretty obvious what's happened. But why? And who in the hell is Brad?

His next thought is: Mayu?

Frantic, he throws himself at the door, pounding on it with all the force he can muster. "Hello? HELLO? Anyone?!"

A soft cry from the cell next to his captures his attention. "Michael?"

It's Mayu. Panic laces her voice.

His heart leaps in his chest, terror and relief warring within him. "Mayu!" he shouts. "Are you okay in there, baby?"

"Yeah," she replies, voice quivering. "I think so, anyway."

Michael tries to wedge his fingers into the narrow gap around the door. "We have to get out of here."

His desperate efforts are interrupted when a small hatch at the bottom creaks open and a tray with meager food offerings, plastic cutlery, and a paper plate is pushed into the room.

In a surge of rage, Michael kicks the tray away, sending the sparse contents flying. Without a second thought, he throws himself at the hatch, trying to squeeze through or at least get a look outside. But the gap is too small. His shoulders jam in the narrow space, and before he can pull himself free, a forceful boot meets his face, sending him reeling backward.

"You son of a—" Michael's voice trembles with rage as he unleashes a tirade, convinced the man on the other side is Brad.

"Michael, stop!" Mayu pleads from her cell. "Please! Brad, if you're there, just tell us what you want."

The eerie silence stretches on, until finally, a voice pierces the quiet, chilling Michael to his core. "My name isn't Brad. My name is Abu Musa."

"I don't care what your fucking name is," Michael shouts out, leaning against the door, his voice reverberating back at him off the cold metal. "You let me and Mayu out of here right this fucking instant. You hear me?"

There is a long silence in which all Michael can hear is his own hurried breathing and the beating of his heart, the daze of the drugs still swelling in his head, making it all echo.

"You know, Michael," Musa finally says, "you and I aren't so unlike each other."

"I am nothing like you, you fucking creep," Michael gasps.

"You're wrong. We're both men living in the shadows of our fathers."

Michael frowns, confused. "What do you even mean?"

"My father was once in the CIA. That was until Allah came to him through the Prophet and opened his eyes. Then he became committed not to American greed but to the great global caliphate. Your father, on the other hand," he adds in a cold tone, "has only ever been a shield to that greed."

Michael's eyes narrow. "You know nothing about my father."

Outside the cell, Musa smiles, a thin, cold smile that does not reach his eyes. "That's where you're wrong. My brother and I are experts on your father. Ever since my brother first laid eyes on him in that valley, the day he killed our father, we have been obsessed."

Michael feels a chill run down his spine. "Who are you, really?"

Musa's smile widens, but it is a smile devoid of warmth. "Your father knows me as the leader of the Wolf Pack. But I am so much more than that. I am the end of his world."

———

Coahuila, Mexico.

The sun blazes down on a lonely dirt airfield in the arid wastelands of the Chihuahuan Desert. The heat distorts the air, making the horizon shimmer like a mirage. Standing amidst the dust and scrubland, Peter feels the sweat trickling down his back as he watches the F/A-18 Hornet scream away into the sky, leaving a trail of dust and a deafening roar in its wake. He feels oddly bereft as the plane disappears from sight, a tiny speck against the vast expanse of blue. Peter is alone now, in a foreign land, with danger lurking around every corner.

He pulls out his burner, the cool plastic a stark contrast to the heat of his hand, and dials Kirsty's number. "I'm in Mexico," he says the second she answers, his voice rough with exhaustion and the dry desert air. "Now what?"

"Your contact should be there shortly," Kirsty replies, her tone brisk and efficient. "He's helped us out over the years, and he should help you out now. He goes by the name the Coyote. He's Mexico's number one people smuggler. If anyone can get you across the border undetected, it's him."

Before Peter can ask for more details, a cloud of dust on

the horizon catches his eye. A pickup truck is approaching, bouncing along the rough track at a speed that suggests the driver is well-acquainted with the terrain.

"I think he's here," Peter says into the phone.

"Then I'll leave you to it," Kirsty replies. "Call me once you're back on US soil."

She's about to put the phone down when Peter stops her.

"Kirsty?"

"What?"

"How's the stuff going with Kara?"

Kirsty Lang's reply is sharp and to the point. "If I had something I'd tell you." Then the call goes dead.

As the pickup pulls up beside Peter, the dust momentarily obscures his view, until the wind clears it away, revealing a large Mexican man with gang tattoos covering every inch of visible skin. He's wearing a battered cowboy hat that casts his face in shadow, but his eyes are sharp and assessing as they lock on to Peter's. This, Peter realizes, must be the contact.

"Coyote?" he asks, stepping forward.

The man nods, his gaze never wavering. "You the gringo Kirsty sent?"

Peter nods. "I am that gringo."

With a grunt, the Coyote jerks his head toward the truck. "Get in."

As they drive off along the rough, winding track, the truck jostling with every bump and pothole, Peter can't help but feel a flicker of hope. He knows he's far from safe, and there's a long, perilous journey ahead of him, but with the Coyote's help, he might just make it back to the US, to his son and Mayu. And then, he vows with a surge of determination, whoever's behind all this will pay.

———

FAIRFAX, Virginia.

IN A PICTURESQUE SUBURBAN NEIGHBORHOOD, the sun lazily descends toward the horizon, painting the sky with warm hues of orange and pink and casting elongated shadows that dance across the asphalt. The gentle twittering of birds mingles with the soft rustling of leaves, creating a soothing symphony that fills the air.

Kara's rental glides to a stop in front of a quaint, meticulously maintained house that is nestled amidst a sea of lush greenery. Stepping out of the vehicle, she strides purposefully toward the front door. The garden, a carefully curated explosion of colors, seems to welcome her as she passes. Reaching the doorstep, she takes a deep breath and knocks.

The door is answered by a small woman in her late-sixties with a face that shows a lot of wear and a lot of sorrow. Her eyes, once bright, now have a dullness to them, as if they have seen too much.

"Mrs. Harrison?" Kara asks, trying to keep her voice steady.

"Yes?" the woman replies, her own voice tremulous.

"I'd like to speak to you about your ex-husband, David Harrison. May I come in?"

The woman's expression becomes deeply sad, then angry. "I'm sorry. I can't."

She goes to close the door, and in a desperate move, Kara places a foot in the way. "Please," she says when the woman's swollen eyes are back on her. "Lives are in danger. I need answers, Mrs. Harrison, and I think your ex-husband is the key to that."

"David's dead." She practically spits it.

"But I don't think your sons are."

Debra Harrison stares at her a while. Then, gradually, she relents, her expression softening and the door widening.

CIA HEADQUARTERS, Langley, Virginia.

THE OVERHEAD LIGHTS inside the George Bush Center for Intelligence hum softly, casting a muted, luminescent glow in the dimly lit room. A multitude of screens illuminate the shadowed space, displaying an array of encrypted messages, live satellite feeds, and active chat windows. Prominently on the main screen, a real-time satellite image shows a vehicle tearing through the desert, its exact location pinpointed as it approaches the Mexico-USA border.

Kirsty Lang leans forward, her eyes sharp and fingers dancing over the keyboard. Every so often, her gaze flits to maps of potential routes, border checkpoints, and safe house locations scatter her desk. She glances at a smaller window on her screen—a secure line of texted communication with the Coyote. A recent message from him reads: "Approaching the final checkpoint. Standby."

The scent of a familiar cologne reaches her just before

she feels the cold shadow of a presence behind her. Without turning, she knows who it is—Paul Bennett.

"Impressive setup you have here, Ms. Lang." His voice is deceptively casual, but the underlying threat is unmistakable.

Kirsty's heart races, but she forces a calmness into her voice. "Just wrapping up a few things," she replies, quickly minimizing the windows and praying he hasn't seen too much.

She takes a slow, deliberate breath and turns her chair to confront him. There, framed by the dim light filtering through the blinds, stands Bennett, flanked by Aria Patel. Their expressions are unreadable, a deadly calm masking any intention.

Bennett's cold gaze meets Kirsty's, and the air grows thick with the weight of unspoken accusations and secrets. Slowly, with the authority and confidence of someone who's caught their prey, he steps forward.

"Ms. Lang," he intones with chilling precision, the edges of his mouth turning up in a faint, sardonic smirk, "we'd like to speak with you."

"W-what about?" she stammers.

"I think you already know," he says in a chillingly even tone.

Kirsty swallows hard, feeling the walls close in. She knows she's been found out. The chase, it seems, is not just reserved for the arid wastelands of Mexico.

———

FAIRFAX, Virginia.

THEY SETTLE into the living room, a cozy space adorned with paintings of landscapes and a medley of trinkets lining the walls. Yet amidst the Pottery Barn charm, there's a notable void: not a single family photograph is in sight.

"David," Debra's voice breaks through the silence, a fragile whisper. "He was everything to us—a loving husband, a doting father. But Afghanistan..." her voice falters, "it stole him from us."

The room breathes silence before Debra continues. "He came back a stranger. I didn't notice it at first, but maybe I was just kidding myself. I mean, of course he was going to be different. He'd spent five years in an underground room no bigger than a cupboard, chained to a bed by the ankle. If that doesn't change you, what will, right?"

"It must have been hard," Kara states. "For all of you."

"It was really hard for the boys."

Kara's heart thumps at their mention.

"Boys need their father," Debra Harrison goes on. "Jimmy was eight and Max only six when David went away. The first couple of years were hell. It was like he was dead, but not. Stuck in limbo, I called it. After three years, I never expected him to come home. I mentally detached. Then he came back." Her eyes film over and her face droops. "But it wasn't him, not anymore. And no matter how much I wanted it to be my David, he wasn't the same."

"Tell me about that," Kara says, her line of questioning following the pattern of a reporter as opposed to a detective.

"It started with small things. He would ask me to cover up, even if we were at the beach. He'd say that a wife's skin shouldn't be for the eyes of other men. But it never bothered him before. He even used to encourage it when we were at college." Her face darkens further as she adds, "Then, about three months after he got back, when he'd returned to active duty at Langley, I caught him praying in the garage. Kneeling on a prayer mat performing salat. That's when he confessed he'd converted to Islam while he was captive. I said that was ridiculous. That they had made him convert, he wasn't a real Muslim. His faith was with Jesus Christ, with the church. You know what he said to that?"

Kara gently shakes her head.

"He told me that Muslims followed Christ, too, as a prophet. He called our savior Isa. He tried to convert me, there and then."

Debra Harrison looks up from her hands at Kara, eyes brimming with tears.

"What about the boys?" Kara asks.

Debra goes to speak but her lips quiver instead, nothing but a hiss escaping them, and all she can do is look out the window, tears slipping down her cheeks. Kara leans forward, taking a tissue from a box of them that lies on a glass coffee table. Debra Harrison takes it from her, mouthing a thank you as she dabs at her face.

Eventually she can speak. "Those boys idolized their father." She wipes away more tears. "Max had barely known him before David was taken, so when he returned, it was like an orphan being gifted a father. David was no longer the stories of his older brother, he was there for real. Those boys would have followed him into anything, so it wasn't long before both stopped coming to Sunday mass with me."

"David converted them?"

"Yes. Made them pray with him five times a day. Took them out of school, too."

"Did David ever overtly display his change of religion?"

Debra Harrison shakes her head. "Oh no. See, when the CIA debriefed him, they asked about it. The Taliban were well known for trying to brainwash captives and turn them into assets. This isn't something new. The KGB used to do it all the time; turn an agent's political ideology, thus turning him against the USA. With Islamic extremism, they do it through religion. It obviously worked on David. So he was never going to tell them during debriefing, was he? And when I found out, he made me promise to keep it a secret. Said that it was only the religion, that he was still a patriot. So I kept his secret."

A glimmer of shame works its way across her features. Kara nods, encouraging her to continue.

"Not long after that, David began to act strangely, disappearing for days at a time. Sometimes taking the boys with him. Then he started to call them by new names. Musa and Ali, he called them. And he was Yusuf. I mean, what could I do to stop him? They hardly knew their father. It was crucial they spend time together. If I'd known what they were up to, though, I would have never left them alone."

Kara inquires, "What were they up to?"

"He was turning them against their own country, their own religion, their own people. Poisoning their minds until my own sons were calling me disrespectful for not covering my hair." Her lip quivers as she stares hard at Kara. "My own sons," she repeats in a trembling voice. "Jimmy and Max were both smart boys. Real smart. But when it came to their father, they couldn't see any wrong. That's why it was so easy for David to take them after I got the injunction."

"The injunction?"

"After a while, I just couldn't bear it any longer. I filed for divorce and for sole custody of the boys. That's when David... became vicious." Debra's voice quivers. "I was forced to get an injunction just to keep him from showing up all the time." She takes a shaky breath, her voice dropping to a whisper. "Not long after that, the FBI came knocking. They informed me David had maintained contact with certain individuals from his time in captivity. He'd been disclosing the identities and locations of Afghan allies to the US." Tears flood Debra's eyes, and she struggles to continue. "It had resulted in the deaths of over fifty people. The Taliban... they didn't just kill them. They beheaded their children." Overwhelmed, she buries her face in her hands, sobbing inconsolably. Instinctively, Kara leans in, offering a consoling touch on her trembling hand.

"David was smart, though," she goes on. "He was one step ahead and got away. Got himself to Afghanistan with both boys using false passports." She takes one big, quivering breath in, then exhales, the tears running down her face. "And I never saw my sons again."

The only sound for a while is that of Debra Harrison crying.

When she thinks she's ready, Kara says, "Debra, this may sound odd, but I think your sons are still alive."

Debra involuntarily shudders.

Kara goes on, "And I think they're in the United States. Have you had any strange contact with anyone recently?"

Debra Harrison thinks. "I don't think so."

"No unexpected calls or odd characters lurking around?" Kara persists, her eyes searching Debra's for any hint of recognition. "Or just something happening that has struck you as strange and out of place?"

Debra hesitates for a brief moment, her gaze distant as she revisits her memories. "Wait," she finally responds, her voice low, brow creased. "There may be something... But it could be nothing."

"Anything," Kara prompts.

Debra Harrison begins getting up from her seat. "I'll show you," she says, making her way to a bureau and opening a drawer.

"Show me what?" Kara can't help asking.

When she returns, Debra Harrison is carrying a bundle of envelopes filled with greetings cards. Handing them to Kara, she says, "I get one every birthday and Mother's Day. I thought it was a prank... I still think it's a prank or just a wrong address."

Kara opens the first envelope and pulls out the card. "Happy Birthday Mom" is printed on the front along with a generic picture of some birds. Inside there is no writing, no message, just the card.

"See what I mean," Debra Harrison says.

"And how long have you been getting them?"

"Oh, about six years."

"And you have no idea where they come from?"

"No. I've never looked into it."

"Do you mind if I do?"

"Sure. Be my guest."

Kara, swallowed in the depth of Debra's pain and the enigma of the silent cards, finds herself at the precipice of an abyss. An unsolved puzzle that beckons, promises, and threatens.

———

CHIHUAHUAN DESERT, Mexico.

PETER FOCUSES his attention on the scene unfolding beyond the pickup's windshield. Dusk is settling over the arid landscape, painting the sky with deep purples and inky blues as the last rays of sunlight fade away. Peter and the Coyote speed along a rugged dirt road toward the US-Mexico border. The large Mexican, his skin etched with Aztec-style gang tattoos, grips the wheel of the battered pickup truck with hands that have seen a lifetime of hard work and illicit deals. Peter sits beside him, nerves humming like a live wire, eyes scanning the horizon for any sign of trouble, more nervous than ever.

A minute ago, he tried getting ahold of Kirsty, let her know he was going radio silent for the next hour. But she didn't pick up, merely texted him good luck. It's not much, her texting instead of picking up, yet it pulls his nerves tight like the strings of a violin.

Then they snap!

Without warning, the thudding whirr of helicopter blades chops through the air, a discordant note in the quiet of the desert evening. A sleek black helicopter looms into view, rising up from behind a sand dune with an air of menace. Inside, Bennett, his face a mask of determination, grips the microphone connected to the chopper's Tannoy.

"Peter," he announces, his voice distorted by the loudspeaker but still unmistakably his, "give yourself up before it's too late."

As the helicopter hovers overhead, casting a dark shadow over the truck, two all-terrain vehicles burst into view on the horizon, kicking up clouds of dust as they barrel toward them at breakneck speed. Bennett's team, a cadre of elite operatives trained for high-stakes scenarios like this one, are inside, their faces set with grim determination.

Peter's heart pounds in his chest as he and the Coyote exchange a tense glance. There's no turning back now.

The desert stretches out like an endless sea of sand, undulating dunes giving way to rocky outcrops and sparse scrub. It's a barren, unforgiving landscape, and as the sun sinks lower in the sky, casting long, golden rays across the sand, it feels as though the entire world has been reduced to this one desolate place.

In the battered pickup truck, the tension is palpable. The Coyote's knuckles are white on the steering wheel, his eyes flicking constantly between the rearview mirror and the road ahead. Peter, for his part, is doing his best to stay calm, but the adrenaline coursing through his veins is making it difficult. He knows that Bennett's team won't give up easily, and as the helicopter continues to hover ominously over-head, the two all-terrain vehicles close in from behind.

"I'm not sure we'll outrun these pendejos," the Coyote says. "You're gonna have to do something, gringo." Reaching into the side of the door, he pulls out a Beretta M3 and hands it over.

Peter makes a split-second decision. Tucking the pistol in his waistband, he opens the door and climbs out of the speeding pickup. Gripping the sides of the vehicle for support as the Coyote swerves to avoid an oncoming dune, he sidesteps along the running board and clambers into the back. Drawing the M9, Peter takes careful aim at the tires of the first ATV. He knows that he needs to incapacitate the vehicles without harming the drivers—these men are just doing their jobs, after all, and he has no desire to kill them.

The wind whips his hair into his face as he squeezes the trigger. The gunshots are sharp and loud in the still desert air. The first shot misses, sending a spray of sand into the air, but the second hits its mark. The front tire of the ATV explodes in a cloud of rubber and dust, sending the vehicle careening off course. The driver struggles to regain control, but it's too late—the ATV flips, sending its occupants sprawling onto the sand. Peter allows himself a moment of relief before turning his attention to the second vehicle.

As the ATV draws closer, Peter takes aim again. This time, he's more successful—two quick shots, and both front tires are blown out. The vehicle skids to a halt, its occupants jumping out and taking cover behind the dunes. But Peter knows that it won't be long before they regroup and continue the chase. For now, at least, they have a small reprieve.

Turning his attention to the helicopter, Peter feels a jolt of panic. Bennett is leaning out of the side, a pistol trained on the pickup. Before Peter can react, a bullet whizzes past his ear, narrowly missing him and hitting the bed of the truck. He ducks down, cursing under his breath as he scrambles for cover behind the cab. Another shot rings out, this one grazing his arm and leaving a burning, stinging sensation in its wake. Peter grits his teeth against the pain, knowing that he can't afford to lose focus now.

It is then, however, that the Coyote suddenly yells through the open driver's window, "Fortune's on our side, gringo. Look ahead!"

From his hiding spot behind the cab, Peter risks a glance, aware of the chopper's persistent presence looming above them. On the distant horizon, a sandstorm rises, painting the sky a deep, foreboding amber. With every passing moment, the towering cloud of sand grows more imposing. As it looms ever closer, another shot rings out, echoing through the vast expanse. "Get in!" the Coyote yells, just as more rounds from Bennett whip past, perilously close.

In a rush, Peter scrambles back into the safety of the cab, both men hurriedly rolling up the windows. The Coyote, his gaze fixed on the approaching storm, turns to Peter, eyes blazing with a heady blend of fear and thrill. "Hold on," he shouts over the roar of the wind. "We're going in!"

They drive headlong into the storm, the world turning a hazy shade of orange. The wind howls like a banshee, sand ricocheting against the pickup as it whips past. Looking out the back window, Peter squints through the murk, trying to keep an eye on the helicopter, but it's almost impossible to see anything in the swirling chaos. The pickup jolts and shudders as the Coyote navigates through the storm, the engine roaring in protest, but the Mexican knows the way, even when blind.

Inside the chopper, Bennett's face is a mask of frustration. The pilot steadies the chopper, holding it precariously at the fringe of the swirling tempest. "It's a no-go, sir," he announces grimly.

The sandstorm is providing Peter with the perfect cover to escape, and there's nothing Bennett can do to stop it. With a curse, he signals to the pilot to pull back. The helicopter changes trajectory, disappearing into the distance as the storm rages on.

Back in the pickup, Peter and the Coyote exchange relieved glances. It's not over yet—they still have a long way to go before they're safe—but for now, at least, they've managed to evade capture.

THIRTY-TWO

WACO, TEXAS

IN THE FADING LIGHT OF THE SETTING SUN, ABU Ayoub al-Amriki maneuvers a nondescript sedan down a barren highway. The desolate landscape is awash in the soft, golden hue of twilight, casting long shadows that dance eerily along the sun-parched earth.

Once Daniel Foster, a Brooklyn native, Ayoub's past life seems like a distant memory—faded, tattered, and buried.

He had once been a young, optimistic soul who, not wanting to follow his older brothers into drug addiction, enlisted in the U.S. Army. Sent to Iraq at twenty, Daniel was initiated into a world of unspeakable horrors while stationed at Abu Ghraib prison. The grotesque spectacle of the gang rape of a young Iraqi woman by US soldiers seared an indelible scar into his soul.

The sound of his impassioned pleas for his fellow soldiers to stop still ring in his ears today as he drives through this barren, twilight land of Waco towards the setting sun. Reporting the rape to his superiors had been a haunting testament to his naiveté. Nothing was done, and then came the backlash. Ostracized and branded a "snitch", the boy who had entered the war with dreams of valor emerged years later as a jaded soldier, a soul marred by rejection and betrayal. Discharged onto the streets, bitter and filled with hatred towards his country, he found himself hustling drugs with his older brothers. By the time he was serving a four-year stretch for possession with intent, the future seemed bleak. Daniel Foster was lost.

However, the prison bars of Attica Correctional Facility became his chrysalis. Within those cold, hard confines, Allah whispered the divine symphony of salvation into his ears. Amidst the hopeless cries and chilling silence, Daniel discovered Islam and was reborn as Abu Ayoub al-Amriki, the soldier rechristened a warrior in the unholy battalion of vengeance.

When he left prison, ISIL was just starting their recruitment drive. Having witnessed firsthand the barbarity of his fellow countrymen in Iraq, it seemed fitting that a group hailing from the same country would be the one he chose to join. As a six-year veteran, Ayoub's expertise was essential, and he quickly climbed through the ranks of ISIL.

As the faded sign of a private airfield emerges from the twilight gloom, he recalls his first meeting with Abu Musa. Musa amazed Ayoub because he had survived amongst the Taliban from the age of fourteen. He was the only foreign white man Ayoub ever saw that the Arabs treated the same as each other. He was accepted by all as their own. Then came his expertise in planning. Musa's father had been CIA, and before his death, had taught Musa everything he knew about planning attacks and operations.

Ayoub's military expertise, forged in the blood-soaked fields of Iraq, coupled with Musa's intricate knowledge of covert operations and espionage, birthed the Wolf Pack. Musa was the schemer, a weaver of intricate plots, his mind a labyrinth of secrets and stratagems. Ayoub, on the other hand, was the warrior, forged in the crucible of combat, his instincts sharpened in the unforgiving theaters of war.

The Wolf Pack, though, was never destined to remain a duo. Soon, others came to join them. Like a magnet, their fierce reputation and indomitable spirit drew others into their fold. Among them was Umar, a soldier of formidable prowess as well as a master with computers.

Yet, it was the arrival of Ali, Musa's younger brother, that completed the pack. Ali is a ghost. Even Ayoub has never laid eyes on him. His only connection to the group is through his brother, Musa. Ali operates in the ethereal spaces between light and shadow, an invisible hand manipulating things.

But soon, they will all be together—in paradise.

The outline of the modest airfield emerges from the gloom. It's not much; just a battered shed for a hangar, an office, and a dirt runway. Ayoub turns off the road, taxis the sedan down the airfield's driveway, the vehicle kicking up clouds of dust as it pulls onto the rugged terrain.

The evening breeze that flows in through the windows seems to synchronize with the storm raging within Ayoub's soul. The lights are on in the hangar, and, out here in the untethered expanses of Waco's outskirts, the airfield appears as a semblance of civilization against the wild.

The shriveled figure of an old man, his white hair shining in the sepulchral light, waits beside a Cirrus SR22. It's a small, single-engine, five-seater plane. Its somber silhouette casts long, spectral shadows in the diminishing light as Ayoub pulls into the hangar, parks beside it, and gets out.

"Howdy," the old man says.

Ayoub has no time for pleasantries; he only has eyes for the plane. "Is it fueled with reserves like I asked?"

"Yes, sir. It's filled to the brim. Can't take no more fuel."

"And you're sure it will make the trip without refuelling?"

"So long as the weather forecast is correct and there's no unforeseen storms or wind conditions."

"And all the permits are in place?"

"Yes, sir. They're expecting us in Virginia tomorrow morning."

"Good. And your family doesn't expect to hear from you until then?"

The old man frowns. "No, sir," he says in a dubious tone, unsure why the client would ask this. "They don't expect to hear from me until tomorrow."

"Good," Ayoub says, reaching into his jacket.

When he retrieves his hand, the pistol in it shines dimly in the electric light. The old pilot gets a second to think about it before one shot is fired, and he's falling to the dirt.

———

THE BLEAK CELLS of Michael and Mayu are separated by a

foot of thick, cold, reinforced concrete. Both rooms are almost identical in their grim design.

The two of them sit with their backs to the shared wall. Even through a foot of reinforced concrete, Michael can sense his girlfriend's presence behind him.

"Mayu?" he calls softly, his voice edged with desperation.

There's a pause before her voice comes through, faint but unwavering. "I'm here."

He leans closer to the shared wall, letting the coolness press against his skin. "I think we should be honest. I don't know if we'll get out of this, Mayu. But before... before whatever happens, I want you to know how much I love you."

"I love you too, Michael," she whispers back. Her voice trembles, but her resolve is clear. "More than you'll ever know."

"I want to tell you how much I love you," Michael goes on.

"I know. I know."

"But I want to tell you anyway. I don't know if I'll ever get another chance." He pauses to take a deep breath, then starts, "It's the little things with you, babe. You know that? Like the way your eyes light up when you're talking about something you're passionate about. The way you scrunch up your nose when you're concentrating. I love the way you twirl your hair around your finger when you're nervous."

Mayu lets out a choked laugh. "And I," she replies, "adore how you chew on the inside of your cheek when you concentrate. How your eyes crinkle at the corners when you smile."

"You've noticed that?" Michael sounds genuinely surprised.

"Of course," Mayu replies. "I've always seen you, Michael. Everything about you. Like how you always pause just a moment before taking my hand, as if relishing the anticipation. Or how you always tie your left shoe before your right."

He chuckles softly. "And you, with your mismatched socks, claiming it's a fashion statement. How you always place your hand over your heart when you hear a sad story."

There's a pause, a collective breath in the heavy atmosphere of their prison.

"Mayu," Michael continues in a whisper, "every moment I've spent with you, every laugh, every tear, has been the best part of my life."

"We may not have tomorrow," Mayu murmurs. "But we have now, and our memories. And I cherish every single one of them."

Michael rests his head against the wall, closing his eyes. "So do I, Mayu. So do I."

In the stillness of their concrete cells, their love is a beacon, a testament to the human spirit's ability to find hope even in the bleakest of moments.

After a moment of silence, where each breath seems louder and the distance immeasurably more profound, Michael's voice pierces the uneasy hush. "We can't stay here, Mayu. Waiting... it's not an option."

Another silence, but this one is different—it's charged, potent, a precursor to a storm of decisions made in the name of life, love and death.

"I can't bear the thought of losing you, or of you losing

me," Michael continues, his voice steady. "Dad... he's out there somewhere trying to get to us. But we can't just rely on him, or anyone else. Right now, we only have each other, Mayu."

On the other side of the imposing wall, Mayu's breath hitches. Desperation and hope, intertwined, pulse through the cold, stale air of confinement. She rests her forehead against the concrete, a silent gesture reaching across the imposing barrier.

"You're right," she responds, her voice imbued with a tenacity born from love and the instinct to survive. "We can't be passive. But I'm scared, Michael. Promise me that no matter what, we'll find our way out of this nightmare together."

"I promise, Mayu." The words aren't just a vow; they're an unspoken pact sealed in the quiet, resolute spaces between heartbeats. "We will escape this hell," he assures her, "and we will do it together."

———

UNDERNEATH THE MEXICO-AMERICA BORDER.

THE AIR IS DAMP, clinging to their skin like a second layer. It's been a while since Peter tasted true darkness, the kind that envelops and constricts, where even breathing seems like a conscious effort. Yet, here in this underground passage, it is this very darkness that promises freedom.

The cramped tunnel stretches on like a scar beneath the earth, its damp walls exhaling cold, musty breaths. Peter's boots squish into the soft ground, remnants of previous rains long trapped in this subterranean world. The ceiling joists hang low, causing him to hunch, the grit of the earthen ceiling brushing against his hair.

With each step, the immense weight of the earth above feels right there, pressing down like an ocean of dirt and stone. The occasional drip of water echoes loudly, splashing onto the floor and mingling with the sound of their synchronized footfalls. In this cocoon of darkness, their senses are amplified. The scent of wet soil, a mixture of decay and life, lingers heavily.

Guiding him, the Coyote moves like a phantom—quiet, efficient, every movement born from countless trips through this very passage. Even in the near total darkness, Peter can sense the man's alertness, the keen awareness that has earned him his title among those desperate for passage.

A hint of cool, fresh air begins to tickle Peter's face, an enticing promise of what lies just ahead. The light at the tunnel's end, once a mere speck, now broadens, casting silhouettes that dance with each step they take. As they near the exit, the once suppressed sounds of the night come alive —the distant hoot of an owl, the rustle of desert plants in the breeze.

Stepping out from the tunnel's maw, they are embraced by the vast desert night. The moon, nearly full, bathes the landscape in a pale light, rendering sand and shrubs in hues of silver. Peter tilts his head back, taking deep lungfuls of the fresh air, the chillness of the night erasing the stifling feel of the tunnel.

With his features sharply defined by the moonlight, the Coyote takes a moment to scan the horizon, every muscle taut and poised. After a few tense seconds, seemingly satisfied with their isolation, he reaches into the depths of his coat, producing a gleaming magazine for the Beretta M9 which he offers to Peter. "You're probably going to need this," he warns as Peter takes them.

The weight of the magazine in his hand, cold and real, brings the gravity of Peter's mission crashing back. He nods, eyes wide with both gratitude and apprehension.

"This is where I leave you," the Coyote murmurs, his voice blending seamlessly with the whisper of the desert wind.

Peter's voice wavers slightly, rich with emotion. "Your help has been invaluable. Thank you." He lets a brief silence settle between them before extending a callused hand. "Peter."

The Coyote's eyes, typically guarded with layers of caution, soften for a fleeting moment. "Raul," he responds, clasping the offered hand.

Their handshake evolves into a brief but tight embrace, the kind shared between men who've journeyed through peril together. As they part, mutual nods of respect pass between them, then Peter is gone, Raul watching him all the way until he has faded into the night.

———

LANGLEY, Virginia.

KIRSTY LANG SITS IN A CORNER, the murmurs of muted conversations and the rhythmic tapping of computer keyboards rendering her surroundings into a symphony of activity. The George Bush Center for Intelligence is abuzz with intelligence officers, their eyes scanning screens and ears tuned to encrypted transmissions; their collective energy permeating the air.

Aria Patel watches her with hawk-like precision. Each move, each gesture Kirsty makes is meticulously observed, cataloged. The atmosphere, thick with tension, hangs heavy and oppressive.

The sudden trill of Kirsty's phone causes Aria's senses to go into overload. Both women jolt; eyes lock, suspicion and alarm gleaming in Aria's gaze. The phone sits on a nearby desk. Grabbing it, Aria brings it to Kirsty and holds it out. Her voice steely and resolute, she commands, "Answer it."

The screen displays an unknown number. It could be Peter. Kirsty's fingers tremble as she swipes to answer, Aria's eyes unyielding.

"Hello?" Kirsty's voice, a mixture of apprehension and anticipation, wavers.

"Kirsty, it's Kara," comes the quick reply.

Aria's body tenses; her breath hitches imperceptibly.

"Kara, where are you?" Kirsty implores, her voice a low, anxious murmur.

"Debra Harrison has been receiving anonymous cards," Kara's voice, brisk and determined, imparts information at a breakneck pace. "She's been getting them for years, Kirsty. On birthdays, on Mother's Days. Nothing inside them. No messages. No signatures."

Aria listens, her features inscrutable, but something—a flicker of uncertainty, a shadow of intrigue—passes through her eyes.

"I traced it back," Kara continues, breathless. "An online company sells these cards. So I called a guy I know who's good with computers."

"You mean a hacker?"

"Yes. And guess what? I've got the IP address address of the account holder, and even better, I got a physical address linked to that."

"Where?" Kirsty presses, the rapid unfolding of revelations spurring her heartbeat into a frenetic tempo.

"Fairfax," Kara's voice is a combination of excitement and apprehension. "I'm almost there. The address is 927 Ellery Street."

Kirsty's brow furrows; something about that address niggles at the corners of her memory. Aria too, her gaze intent, appears struck.

"It sounds familiar," Kirsty mutters, her voice almost drowned in the chorus of ambient sounds.

"But the cards, Kirsty," Kara goes on. "They have to mean something. Who would send her them? It has to mean at least one of the brothers is alive."

"Alive..." Kirsty's voice, a mere whisper, trembles with the magnitude of implications.

"Look, I'm there now. I'll call you after." Kara's voice, resolute and final, leaves no room for protest.

"No, Kara, don't hang—" but the line goes dead; silence, profound and ominous, ensues.

Aria's eyes, stormy and unreadable, lock onto Kirsty. "That address is familiar," she muses. "What was she talking about? The cards, Debra Harrison, an address..."

"That's what I'm telling you about," Kirsty insists, the

fervor in her voice slicing through the ambient noise. "There's more to all of this."

In the soft hum of a room lit by computer screens, Aria Patel's intense gaze meets Kirsty's. Secrets and revelations, silent yet persistent, linger between them as they step together into an abyss of covert truths.

———

FAIRFAX, Virgina.

THE TRANQUIL SERENITY of the Virginia night is disrupted by the muted noises of movement and activity. A beautiful house, nestled comfortably in a neat suburb, is alive with light, illuminating the darkened silhouettes of moving men and their panel vans. The scene, a dance of coordinated chaos, is markedly different to the silent, sleeping neighborhood around it.

Kara's rental car pulls to a gentle stop before the spectacle. She sits for a moment, her gaze penetrating the shadows, observing the orchestrated dance of figures moving boxes. The garage, ajar and revealing, spills illumination onto the driveway, and the silhouettes of the removal men move to a silent rhythm within the light.

Kara gets out, making her way along the driveway with measured steps. The night air, crisp and silent, wraps around her as she casts an elongated shadow that mingles with those dancing around the home.

The general quietude of the sleepy suburb is punctuated by the muted commands of a woman directing the workers.

"That's for storage," she says, her voice, authoritative yet tinged with a latent sorrow. Her silhouette, defined against the backdrop of the illuminated interior of the garage, lends an air of solemnity to the scene.

Kara's steps are purposeful and resolute as she approaches. The woman before her stands fragile yet steadfast. Her silver hair, a testament to her years, cascades in gentle waves, reflecting the moon's tender light. "Excuse me," Kara calls out, her voice a blend of determination and inquiry.

The woman turns, her gaze sharp, piercing the darkness. "Yes?" she responds, her tone a mix of impatience and curiosity.

"Do you live here?" Kara asks, the question hanging in the air and infusing the night with an aura of anticipation.

"No," the woman replies curtly. "My brother did. But he passed away recently. We're clearing it out."

Kara's senses are heightened; every word, every nuance resonates with profound significance. "May I ask who your brother was?" she inquires, her voice steady yet infused with an inexplicable apprehension.

"Not that it matters, but his name was Ben Knight." The woman's words, stark and unembellished, cut through the silence.

Kara's spine straightens, a jolt of realization electrifying the tranquil air. Peter's voice comes back to her—Remember that name, Ben Knight.

Surely it's not the same guy.

"He worked for the CIA, right?"

The woman, taken aback, regards Kara with a mix of

suspicion and bewilderment. "Yes, he did," she replies in a dubious tone. "I'm sorry, who are you?"

"I'm Kara Tate." The introduction, simple yet laden with unspoken context, hangs in the air, before she adds, "And you are?"

"I'm Pamela Bennett. Are you going to tell me what this is all about, Ms. Tate?"

———

DEL RIO, Texas.

THE NEON LIGHTS of the Pilot Travel Center bathe the parking lot in a soft glow. Trucks and pickups line up neatly along the asphalt, their drivers taking a break at the nearby all-night diner. Peter's footsteps are soft as he moves from one truck to the next, his eyes scanning for any that might have a vulnerable gas cap. Time is of the essence, and Peter needs a diversion.

Finding a promising-looking older truck, he reaches into his pocket, pulling out a piece of discarded electrical wire he found along the way. Peter strips back the plastic covering to reveal the copper wire within. His fingers then deftly work on the gas cap's lock. The wire slides in, manipulating the mechanism until, with a satisfying click, the cap unlocks. Quickly, Peter uncaps it and starts to tear his shirt into strips, twisting them into makeshift rope. He dips one end into the fuel tank, allowing the cloth to soak up as much gasoline as it can. The other end, he leaves hanging out, a makeshift fuse ready to be ignited.

Before lighting it, he looks around. The coast is clear. The soft chattering from the diner and the distant hum of an interstate form the backdrop to his activities. With a flick of his Zippo, he sets the cloth ablaze. It's a slow burn at first, but it's only a matter of time.

The lights of the diner beckon. Peter adjusts his jacket and heads toward it, just as the truck's fuel tank reaches its ignition point. It's upon reaching the door that a deafening explosion fills the air, flames shooting up high, thick black smoke billowing upward. The shockwave rattles the windows of the diner.

"Hey, Jerry, ain't that your truck?" someone yells from inside.

The man in question, a burly guy in a worn-out Rangers cap, jumps to his feet, disbelief all over his face. "Gosh darn it!" He bolts out of the diner, racing toward the now-engulfed vehicle.

The explosion has drawn the attention of every patron. Waitresses stop in their tracks, their pens hovering over their notepads, customers leave their half-eaten meals, and everyone either rushes outside or gathers at the windows, gawking at the inferno that was once a truck. The confusion is electric, the crowd noisy and panicked. Several drivers, fearing for their own vehicles, scramble out of the diner to move them away from the blaze.

Peter, on the other hand, remains calm amidst the storm. Slipping inside the diner, he starts checking the jackets hanging on the backs of chairs. One after the other, he feels the pockets, searching. Time is ticking. Finally, in a leather jacket, he feels the unmistakable shape of car keys and an old mobile phone—a Nokia, sturdy and reliable. Swiftly pocketing both items, he scans the lot through the diner's window. Pressing the fob on the keys, he spots the Toyota that matches the key when its indicators light up. As luck would have it, the pickup is parked on the opposite side of the lot to the fire. All attention is elsewhere.

Exiting the diner, he makes his way to the Toyota, unlocking it. He starts the engine, which roars to life. Gravel crunches beneath its tires as Peter maneuvers it out of the lot.

The truck stop, with its lights, fire, and shocked patrons, fades into the distance behind him. Soon, all that remains in the rearview mirror is a fiery glow that eventually dims to nothing. Nevertheless, the adrenaline in Peter's veins burns brighter than ever. He's made his escape with nobody the wiser.

It is now that he retrieves the Nokia from his pocket and dials a number. It's answered almost immediately.

"It's me. I'm back," Peter declares, his voice tight with tension before adding in a chilling undertone, "Which one are you—Jimmy or Max?"

A cold laugh resonates from the other end. "She got you that far, did she?"

"I killed your father," Peter interjects.

"Yes. You did."

"I'm sorry for that."

"No you're not," the man on the other end of the line retorts flatly. "In your mind, my father was a traitor who deserved to die."

"Don't make my son and his girlfriend suffer for what I did," Peter snaps back.

There's a brief pause. Then it's business as usual. "Where are you?" he asks.

"Just leaving Del Rio."

"Good. That's close enough. You know the town of Hondo?"

"Just outside San Antonio."

"That's it. I'm going to send you the address of a junction there. That's where you'll meet someone who will take you the rest of the way. If you arrive with company or if he suspects you're not alone, he won't hesitate to send the word and your son and his girlfriend are dead."

The call ends sharply, leaving Peter with a cold dread that snakes its way down his back. The stakes have never been clearer, and fear tightens its grip on him.

———

FAIRFAX, Virginia.

PAMELA BENNETT'S GAZE, a mix of confusion and skepticism, remains fixed on Kara as the investigative journalist finishes recounting the labyrinth of events that has led her here. The distant sounds of removal men can be heard in the background, their footfalls resonating through the hollowed spaces of the nearly emptied house.

"And so," Pamela's voice is tinged with incredulity, her eyes reflecting the internal struggle to reconcile the narrative just laid out before her, "these greeting cards led you here?"

Kara nods. "Yes. The account that sent them was being used from this address."

Pamela leans back against a sideboard, her eyes flitting across the room they stand in, tracing the outlines of sheet-covered furniture and stacks of boxed memories. "But that's awful. Why would my brother want to taunt this woman?"

"I don't know," Kara admits. "None of it really makes sense."

It is then that the glimmer of something draws her attention; amidst the orchestrated chaos, a photograph lies, uncovered and unpacked, on top of a bureau. Kara reaches over, fingers brushing against the cool surface of the frame. Faces frozen in a moment of past happiness gaze back at her. One face is particularly familiar.

"This is Paul Bennett," Kara's voice, almost involuntarily, slices through the room's silence.

"Yes," Pamela acknowledges, her gaze falling upon the captured moment. "He's my son."

A cascade of realizations and connections threaten to overflow Kara's thoughts, but before she can articulate them, Pamela interjects.

"Look," she says, her voice a delicate mix of vulnerability and curiosity, "I'd like to help you, but I know nothing of my brother's career. As you probably know, it was top secret. Plus, with us living all the way up in Montana, we only got to see each other during the holidays. It was only once Paul joined the agency and moved down about six years ago that we got to see more of each other. He always did idolize his uncle."

Kara's fingers tighten around the edges of the picture frame. She's about to probe further when the abrupt burst of headlights through the windows stops her.

Cars screech to a halt, their sudden arrival throwing

stark, oscillating shadows against the interior of the house. Silhouetted figures march out, purpose and authority in their strides, their outlines sharp against the pools of light.

The door swings open, and Aria Patel, a picture of composed sternness, steps into the house. Her gaze locks onto Kara.

"Ms. Tate," she practically growls. "Come with me."

In the suspended heartbeat of imminent confrontation, Kara hands Pamela Bennett her card. The touch of their fingers is transient yet charged.

Aria escorts Kara out, her grip firm yet not unkind, the two moving towards a nondescript black sedan awaiting them at the end of the drive.

The ghosts of unfinished conversations and unveiled secrets hang heavily in the air as the car pulls away, leaving Pamela Bennett standing amidst the boxed remnants of her brother's existence—a sentinel to the mysteries that dwell in the shadowed spaces of Ben Knight's life.

THIRTY-THREE

THE SOUND OF GRINDING METAL REVERBERATES ominously through the tunnel as Musa pries open the lid of one of the large barrels, revealing the granulated white substance of ammonium nitrate within. It's a volatile precursor to what they have planned, and the sheer amount suggests the scale of devastation they intend will be vast and all-powerful.

Umar is responsible for moving the barrels. Using an old, rugged sack barrow, he transports the heavy containers one by one from the breach in the sewer wall. The wheels of the barrow groan under the weight, echoing eerily in the long, dark stretch of tunnel. His flashlight illuminates the thick cables that run along the wall, a constant reminder of their end goal.

At the other end, Musa supervises the positioning of the barrels. He ensures that they're spread out evenly beneath the building's foundation, maximizing the potential impact.

He knows the importance of the task, and while his hands are steady, there's a tension in his eyes.

Once a barrel is in position, Musa begins the meticulous process of connecting wires to it, interlinking them in a daisy-chain fashion. The thin red and black wires stand out starkly against the pale ammonium nitrate.

As Umar is moving another barrel into place, Musa leans in close to him, his voice a whisper. "I just received a text. Ayoub is at the rendezvous."

"Then it is almost upon us, brother," Umar replies in a similarly hushed tone, a smile rising up his cheeks.

Musa looks at his friend, the fire of conviction burning in his eyes. It's the same flame that burns in so many of their hearts—one lit from a history of grievances, stories of heroism, and tales of sacrifice passed down through generations.

"Soon," Musa murmurs, placing a firm hand on Umar's shoulder, "we will give our people new stories to tell."

The two share a moment of understanding before the relentless pace of their mission takes over again and they go back to work. With each barrel that's wired up, the gravity of their actions becomes more apparent.

Hours seem to pass, the silence only broken by the soft scraping of barrow wheels and the occasional whispered instruction. As the last barrel is set in place and the last wire connected, the two men take a moment to stand back and assess their work.

"We're almost there," Musa murmurs, wiping sweat from his brow.

"Yes we are," Umar agrees. "Yes we are."

The weight of their next steps hangs heavy in the air, but

the determination is evident in each man's eyes. They've come this far, and there is no turning back now.

––––––

Hondo, Texas.

It's daybreak when Peter approaches the outskirts of Hondo in the stolen Toyota. Under the emerging sunlight, the town's modest skyline stands stark and silhouetted against the lightening sky. The gentle glow of dawn illuminates the distant buildings, casting long shadows that stretch out over the asphalt.

He parks on a barren corner at the very edge of town, where old signs waver in the cool, early morning air, their metallic surfaces gleaming with the first light of day. Shutting off the engine, Peter takes a deep breath, trying to adjust to the brisk air that greets him when he steps out into the dawn.

He doesn't have to wait long. A black sedan, its tinted windows dark against the soft morning light, emerges from a side street less than a minute after he gets out of the car. It slows as it nears him, finally coming to a stop alongside the Toyota.

The driver-side window hums down to reveal a man with a serious, almost haunting countenance.

"Peter?" he asks, his voice devoid of emotion but the word sharp and clear.

"Yes," Peter responds.

"Do you recognize me?"

Peter nods. "You're Daniel Foster."

"That's a name from a previous life," the man at the window retorts.

"Yes. Of course. You're Abu Ayoub al-Amriki now."

"Just Ayoub will do."

Swiftly, Ayoub gets out the sedan, pistol in hand, using the vehicle as a shield between them and any prying eyes. He motions Peter with the gun. "Up against the car."

Peter places his hands on the cool metal surface of the roof, spreading his feet slightly. With one hand keeping the pistol steadily trained on Peter, Ayoub uses the other to briskly pat him down, ensuring he has no weapons or hidden devices.

"I already got rid of the pistol," Peter tells him flatly.

Finding nothing, Ayoub steps back, and with a gesture of the gun, indicates the passenger door of the sedan. "Get in."

Peter hesitates for a moment, his gaze darting to the stolen Toyota and back, wishing he had any other option. But he knows he hasn't. So reluctantly, he moves, opening the door and slipping into the passenger seat. The warm temperature inside of the car is a stark contrast to the outside chill. Yet, Peter finds it stifling.

Ayoub, now back in the driver's seat, grabs a phone from atop the dashboard and shoves it towards Peter. On its screen, a split-screen live feed displays security footage of two concrete cells; Michael in one, Mayu in the other, both appearing disheveled but alive. The CCTV footage is captured in night vision, illuminating their forms in a ghostly light. Their eyes shine with a haunting gleam, indicating the oppressive darkness of their confinements.

A time stamp in the corner of the screen correlates with the current time, confirming the live feed's immediacy. Peter's eyes trace the outlines of Michael and Mayu, both actively searching their dark, isolated enclosures for a means of escape as they move about, the eerie green tint of the night vision capturing every moment of their anguished search.

"See?" Ayoub smirks, satisfaction evident in his eyes. "They're both alive and well. And they'll stay that way so long as you do everything you're told."

———

MICHAEL'S FINGERTIPS trace the harsh surface of the concrete. Every inch is a cruel reminder of their imprisonment. But within the quiet, within the despair, there is an indomitable spirit not yet extinguished.

Every so often, he murmurs the words, "I'll find a way," his voice a resolute whisper. Even confined and surrounded by unyielding concrete, the flame of rebellion, of resistance, burns bright. Musa isn't the only one trained from a boy by a CIA field agent. Michael is the son of Peter Black; adversity is not something he buckles under.

Hours slip by, indistinguishable in the ever-present gloom. Michael, his eyes now accustomed to the oppressive dark, scrutinizes every inch of his cold cell. Desperation fuels determination; where hope is dim, the smallest crack, the faintest light, becomes a lifeline.

Now on his hands and knees, his numb fingers trace the cold, unyielding surface of the floor until they catch on an irregularity—a subtle inconsistency in the suffocating uniformity of his prison. It's buried under a thick layer of dust and crud that he wipes away with his hands. He leans in, his breath misting the cold surface underneath, and his fingers explore the anomaly.

A brass plate about a foot square, slightly loose.

"Mayu," he calls, a renewed vigor lacing his whisper, "I think... I might have found something on the floor."

Silence. Then the faintest hint of movement, the rustling of fabric against concrete as Mayu shifts closer to the wall.

"What is it?" Her voice is a lifeline, a beacon in the dark.

"A metal plate. It's loose. I think... I think it might lead somewhere." The hope in his voice is tangible, a silken thread spiraling through the oppressive dark, binding them together across the chasm of their separate cells.

"Can you remove it?" Mayu's voice is tense, threaded with a fragile hope.

"I'll try," Michael promises.

Minutes morph into hours, each passing second resonating loudly with the relentless tick of an unseen clock. Every scrape, every movement is magnified in the oppressive silence. Michael's fingers, raw and bleeding, work with dogged determination, prying at the edges of the plate.

And then, with a resounding pop that spirals through the silence, it gives way.

"I did it, Mayu," he breathes, triumph and terror intertwining in the tremor of his voice. He peers into the dark void beyond the plate. "God it stinks. I think it's a sewer, or something. I can't see much, but it's something."

"We need to explore it," Mayu responds, a fragile hope making her voice tremble.

"But you're in there, and I'm in here." The realization is a cold slap, an icy hand squeezing his heart.

"No, listen, Michael," Mayu's voice is insistent, piercing the dark. "Whatever it is, explore it. See where it leads. Maybe there's a way to get me out from where you're heading."

Michael hesitates, the thought of leaving Mayu behind, even momentarily, a dagger twisting in his chest. But in the inky blackness of their prison, despair yields to necessity. Every passing second is a drumbeat, a relentless countdown

"Alright," he affirms, his voice laden with the heaviness of the decision. "Stay close to the wall. Stay with me, even if it's just through this concrete."

And with the promise of return echoing in the suffocating silence, Michael ventures into the unyielding dark, the sliver of hope a fragile flame amidst a sea of shadows.

———

Texas.

THE ROAR of the helicopter's blades mows through the still Texas air, the black machine contrasting sharply against the vast expanse of desert below. Bennett's gaze, veiled by dark sunglasses, sweeps across the rolling borderlands that sprawl beneath him, a patchwork of arid terrain and sparse vegetation. The headphones clamped over his ears drown out most of the chopper's noise, and he straightens in his seat when the radio crackles to life: an incoming message from Langley. Instantly, like a hawk locking on to its prey, Bennett's hand shoots to the receiver.

"What have you got?" he demands, his voice a razor-sharp edge of anticipation.

There's a moment of static before a clear voice responds, "We've just received word. The missing Toyota pickup from the truck stop—the one where the explosion was—it's been spotted by local law enforcement. It's been abandoned just outside Hondo."

Bennett's grip tightens. "Any sign of Black?"

"Not confirmed, but it's our best lead so far," the voice replies.

Bennett takes a deep breath, eyes narrowing as he processes the information. "Give me the exact location. Tell law enforcement to meet me there."

"Doing it now. But Paul, there's something else."

"What?"

"About ten minutes ago Aria came back to Langley with Kara Tate."

Bennett's brow pinches together. "Kara Tate?"

"Yeah. She's been helping Black."

"Helping him, how?"

"Well, and this is gonna sound weird, but she was found snooping around your uncle's place."

"My uncle's place?"

"Yeah. She spoke with your mom, I think."

"What about?"

"I'm not sure. But I think it's got something to do with Peter Black shooting Sonya."

"But why would she end up at my uncle's?"

"I don't know. I'll keep you updated."

"Thanks, Alex."

The coordinates come in. The helicopter veers in the new direction, speeding toward Hondo. Bennett's pulse quickens with the machine's acceleration. Every fiber of his being is attuned to the hunt, and Peter's capture is the only thing that will satisfy his thirst.

———

Waco, Texas.

The rugged airstrip emerges ahead, and Ayoub's grip on the wheel tightens. The sedan makes its way over the gravelly terrain, dust billowing behind them in the first light of morning. Ayoub's piercing eyes scan the surroundings, the atmosphere thick with unuttered anticipation.

A small, weather-beaten hangar stands alone amidst the stark landscape of Waco. The sun has just begun its ascent, casting ominous shadows that dance along the edges of the abandoned airstrip. Ayoub steers the car into the hangar, headlights illuminating the desolate space.

Peter's gaze fixes on a Cirrus SR22. The sleek form of the plane looks out of place in this derelict setting. As he steps out of the car, something immediately catches Peter's eye. Drag marks mar the ground, leading to a pair of feet protruding from beneath a tarp sheet. A cold shiver wriggles its way down Peter's spine, the brutal reality of his predicament all too real.

With his focus rooted on the ominous feet, the eerie silence is suddenly fractured by the sharp sound of Ayoub's voice, resonant and cutting. "Turn around," he barks, pulling Peter's attention away from the body beneath the tarp.

Ayoub's cold, efficient movements offer no room for hesitation. He wrenches Peter around.

"Give me your wrists," he orders.

The frigid touch of metal against Peter's skin, the fastening of handcuffs, and he is rendered powerless, wrists bound in front of him.

With Peter restrained, Ayoub maneuvers him towards the Cirrus SR22. Each step is a jarring reminder of Peter's helplessness, his every movement dictated by the captor at his side. Ayoub pulls open the gull-wing door and pushes Peter up onto the wing, forcing him to step into the back of the craft.

Inside the plane, Ayoub secures the handcuffs to a sturdy metal bar that juts out from the seating, ensuring Peter's complete immobilization.

With his prisoner secured, Ayoub takes his place at the helm of the plane. The ignition quivers to life, and the engine's roar adds to the tension building inside of Peter.

"Where are we going?" he asks, his voice strained but defiant.

Ayoub twists around, his eyes glinting with sinister satisfaction. "You'll soon see," he sneers in a cold voice before turning back around.

The plane lurches forward, and the uneven ground beneath jolts and rocks the aircraft as they leave the hangar. In the midst of the glaring sun, amidst a scenery painted with harsh shadows and eerie light, the plane accelerates down the dirt airstrip, and begins ascending.

With the blue sky lurching up in front of them, Peter finds himself adrift in a perilous limbo, the deafening noise of the engine a cruel accompaniment to the thoughts racing through his mind. Yet amidst the cacophony and terror, amidst the unyielding restraint of metal against skin, there's a tiny sanctuary of rebellion.

Feeling the familiar smoothness of the metal strip beneath his tongue, Peter adjusts its position. He's become adept at concealing things in his years undercover, a habit that has saved him more times than he cares to count. When Ayoub patted him down, he didn't check Peter's mouth. He should have.

As the plane ascends into the glaring sky, Peter's perilous predicament is both emphasized and contrasted by the hidden metal strip beneath his tongue—a secret, silent rebellion against his captor. The crossroads between his physical restraint and inner defiance marks the beginning of a silent warfare. In this dance of predator and prey, amidst the roaring engine of the plane and the unyielding skies, an unsettling game of terror and defiance unfolds.

———

HONDO, Texas.

THE ROTOR BLADES of the all-black helicopter send gusts of wind whipping across the dry Texas landscape as Bennett lands near the outskirts of Hondo. The distinct profile of the stolen Toyota stands out against the vast backdrop, like a lone sentinel in a sea of golden grass and blue sky.

As the dust settles, Bennett spots a group of Texas Rangers already gathered around the abandoned Toyota. He strides over, ID in hand. "Operations Officer Bennett. What have we got?"

One of the Rangers, a tall man with a weathered face and a Stetson shading his eyes, extends a hand. "Ranger Calhoun."

Bennett gives a nod of acknowledgment, his gaze fixed on the Toyota. "Any signs of my man?"

Calhoun shakes his head. "No. Looks like he abandoned the car here. There ain't much around, no buildings, no locals."

The only sound, apart from their conversation, is the creaking of an old, rusted windmill that stands sentinel in a nearby field. Its eerie groan seems to punctuate the desolation of the scene.

Calhoun points to the ground near the Toyota. "My bet is he changed vehicles. You see these?" A set of tire tracks is clearly imprinted in the dusty ground. "Definitely a sedan, from the looks of it. But I couldn't tell you the make just from looking."

Snapping a few pictures with his phone, Bennett turns back to Ranger Calhoun. "Any CCTV in the vicinity?"

Calhoun chuckles dryly. "Out here? This is old country, Operations Officer Bennett. That windmill is about as tech-savvy as we get."

Without wasting a moment, Bennett heads back to the helicopter. As he settles into his seat, he grabs the radio and dials Aria Patel. "Aria, it's Bennett," his voice crackles through the connection as the call connects. "We found the

Toyota. But he's switched vehicles. I'm sending you images of the tire tracks now. We need a—"

"Mr. Bennett," the authoritative, yet familiar voice of Director McLean cuts through the line.

"Director," Bennett responds, his tone becoming instantly respectful.

"What's the status with Black?"

"We tracked him near San Antonio. Found his abandoned vehicle and the tire tracks of his new one."

"And local law enforcement?"

"They're on it, Director. An APB is out to every agency in Texas, the FBI included. He won't slip through."

"Good. It sounds like the locals can find him without you. I need you back at Langley."

Bennett's eyes, weary yet determined, narrow. "With respect, Director, I can be of better use here. Black is a top asset turned fugitive. It's critical we contain this before it spirals into a scandal for the agency."

"No," Director McLean says, her voice firm. "Return to Langley. We have another situation."

"You mean Kara Tate?"

"In part. She's making unsettling claims about your uncle."

"Claims? What claims?"

"I'll brief you when you return."

Silence engulfs the line as the call goes dead. Bennett's eyes, veiled with a mix of frustration and curiosity, stare into the distance. The chopper's blades whirr, impatient and restless.

"You heard the woman," he says to the pilot, his voice a

blend of resignation and anticipation. "Take us to San Antonio airport. We'll catch a flight from there."

With Bennett's words still lingering in the air, the chopper shifts direction, veering off into the looming uncertainty ahead.

————

LANGLEY, Virginia.

A GLARING LIGHT illuminates Kara as she paces the cold, sterile holding cell, her reflection bouncing off the stark white walls. Her unease is palpable, every nerve stretched taut, filling the space with her silent anxiety.

In another part of the CIA headquarters, Director Sandy McLean and Aria Patel observe her through the live feed on a CCTV monitor, their eyes tracing her every movement.

"It makes no sense," Aria breaks the silence, her gaze fixed on the screen. "Why would Ben Knight send David Harrison's widow birthday cards and Mother's Day cards?"

Director McLean's fingers drum against the table, a storm of contemplation raging behind her eyes. "And Kara Tate is certain that at least one of the sons is alive and behind the Wolf Pack?" she inquires, her voice carrying the weight of unuttered concerns.

"Yes," Aria confirms.

A pause, charged with unsaid words.

Director McLean's gaze is piercing. "What about Black?"

"She knows nothing about where he is and I'm inclined to believe her."

"Does she know anything about him shooting Sonya Kahn?"

"She claims he and his son's girlfriend are hostages. That the Wolf Pack used them as leverage to make him shoot Sonya and go on the run."

"Have you checked this out?"

"Our team found the son and girlfriend's New York property empty, and both youths are unaccounted for."

A potent silence seizes the room as McLean absorbs the information, her fingers now steepled against her temples.

It's then that the silence is shattered by a cough, sharp and abrupt. It draws both women's attention to the corner of the room, where Kirsty Lang sits, clearly under watch, her presence a reminder of the blurred lines between ally and suspect.

"I asked you earlier, ma'am," Kirsty interjects, the steel in her voice belying the vulnerability of her position. "About what happened that day in Afghanistan. Everything we're witnessing now has to do with back then. In the files, I discovered it was Malik al-Nasri who facilitated the intel on Harrison's location. He was the one who led them to him. The same Malik al-Nasri who was killed along with Ben. As crazy as it all sounds, it all slots into place."

A shadow of unease passes over Director McLean's face. The room, inundated with an oppressive silence, seems to constrict as Aria turns her gaze to the Director, anticipation and accusation mingling in her stare. "What is she talking about, Director?"

Director McLean takes a moment, a swallow betraying

the complexity of the story she is about to unravel, the specters of the past being forced to the surface. "In 2007, I led the mission," she begins, her voice imbued with an unwilling reluctance. "Ben was the field operative, with Peter Black as our trigger man. The initial mission was to terminate David Harrison and retrieve the two sons, bring them back to America. We were hopeful that we could return them to their mother. But as Ben's reports began trickling in, it became evident—Jimmy and Max were lost to us."

Aria's gaze, unyielding and probing, remains fixed on McLean.

"They were meant to be retrieved and treated, assessed for their psychological state," McLean's voice, wavering yet firm, continues to untangle the story. "But their experiences, their indoctrination at the hands of their father—it was irrevocable. There was no turning back."

"No turning back," Kirsty repeats, her voice cutting through the tense silence, a demand for clarity and revelation. "What do you mean by that, ma'am?"

The confession is painful, each word a shard of glass. "We were forced to make the most agonizing decision. Both boys were ordered terminated. Harrison's influence had distorted their humanity," McLean admits, the weight of regret lending a tremble to her voice.

The air grows dense as Kirsty's voice, a knife of accusation, slices through. "Max Harrison was thirteen. Ben Knight executed a child," she asserts, each word sharp and incisive.

McLean's defense is instinctual, borne from a history of unspeakable decisions. "You don't know what those boys did," she retorts. "The oldest, Jimmy, we had videos of him setting fire to American soldiers and laughing with his father while they screamed in agony. The execution we found Max at, that wasn't his first. At thirteen, he had already cut the throat of a farmer who had allowed American soldiers to fill up their water canteens on his property. His father and his men had tied the farmer and his family up. That's when they started recording the initiation of Max Harrison. I can tell, as someone who witnessed the footage, he looked eager to please his father and older brother. Those boys reveled in the suffering of other men. Max, even at his tender age, was an executioner. The boys we sought to save were long gone by the time Malik al-Nasri got us their position."

"So you ordered their deaths?" Kirsty's challenge hangs heavy in the air.

The Director's affirmation is haunting. "Yes."

"How'd they die?" Aria asks.

Director McLean takes a few seconds to steady her voice. "We lost Jimmy to the wilderness," she then tells them. "Max... Ben took on that burden. And don't think he didn't fight me all the way on it."

"I bet he did," Kirsty murmurs.

"But, in the end, Ben always understood duty. He carried out the order and buried Max somewhere in Afghanistan."

Aria's eyes flit between McLean and Kirsty, the complexity of their predicament hanging heavily in the air. Every revelation, each piece of the intricate puzzle, seems to compound the weight of the narrative unfolding before them.

"And now his brother is back," Aria voices the chilling thought, a shudder of realization permeating the room. The specter of Jimmy Harrison lingers ominously. "I looked into some of what Kara Tate was saying. Indeed, Yasin Farid has links to the two Harrison brothers. The FBI had missed it because it came much earlier in Farid's life. He was eleven when David Harrison took the boys. Perhaps eventually they would have gotten to it, but probably without the context of David Harrison and his links to Peter and Ben."

Director McLean absorbs the revelation, her voice a subdued whisper. "You really think it could be Jimmy Harrison behind the Wolf Pack?"

"I do, ma'am," Aria replies.

"And you think he could be framing Black and using him as a pawn in some macabre game of chess?"

"That's what I keep telling you both," Kirsty insists from her corner, her eyes aflame with a mix of vindication and anger.

"Then what is Harrison's next move?" Director McLean muses aloud, the question a ghostly echo, lingering, haunting.

THIRTY-FOUR

In the dim light of the tunnel, both Musa and Umar kneel on their prayer mats, facing Mecca. Their foreheads touch the ground in reverence as they immerse themselves in prayer, the resounding noise of their devotion filling the underground space.

Once their prayers conclude, the men rise, roll up their mats, place them to the side, and begin inspecting their cache. The tunnel is filled with the chilling sight of weapons and explosives. Twenty sixty-gallon barrels, all stuffed with five hundred kilos of ammonium nitrate each, line the deepest part of the tunnel, right beneath their target.

Umar carefully checks over the detonator, ensuring all its connections are secure and the timer is functioning. The device, designed to unleash devastation, lies dormant for now, but it is ready.

Musa, with a practiced hand, picks up an AR-15 semi-automatic assault rifle, inspecting its chamber and magazine meticulously. The cold metal feels familiar, and he nods in satisfaction before moving on. Nearby, Umar does the same with a Benelli M3 tactical shotgun, handling its pistol grip with a chilling familiarity. Both men have combat experience. Among the first foreign fighters to join ISIL, they were involved in some of the fiercest fighting in Raqqa, both when they took the city in 2013 and later on when they lost it in 2017. It was on that initial battlefield that they met, he and Umar.

Beyond the firearms, the men retrieve sets of body armor, making sure every plate is secure and in place. They then move to the gas masks, their large round eyes seeming to stare eerily back at them. Clipping his mask on his body armor for easy access, Musa glances at Umar, who is attaching a tear-gas canister to his own armor.

Umar finally breaks the heavy silence, his voice low and even. "How close are they now?"

Musa pulls out his phone. Swiping a finger across it, the screen illuminates their faces in grim light. On it, they watch a dot hover over a map.

"They should be landing soon," Musa comments.

The weight of anticipation fills the air, as thick and oppressive as the gas inside those canisters. With both men continuing their preparations, Musa walks to a bricked-up entrance farther down the tunnel, Umar following close behind. Leaning against the wall are two sledgehammers, their intentions with the entrance evident.

"Now we wait," Umar says.

Musa takes a slow breath, the gravity of their mission evident in his eyes. "Just two hours," he murmurs. "Two hours until my father is finally avenged."

The tunnel, sensing the impending storm, seems to close

in on them, amplifying the magnitude of their determination.

———

THE ENGINE'S hum fades as Peter is jerked awake by the
plane's abrupt landing. His body is stiff, his mind a storm of
half-remembered dreams. As consciousness stirs within him,
the stark reality of captivity reemerges.

Nevertheless, eight hours in flight has at least granted
him sleep—which is a lethal weapon in the struggle that lies
ahead.

They've landed on another isolated airstrip, a stark,
nondescript expanse. The cold morning light pierces through
the windows, revealing a barren landscape that extends
endlessly; its features a mix of elements that could place their
location anywhere from the Midwest to the Atlantic.

Ayoub is efficient and silent, unlocking Peter from his
seat and marching him out into the crisp morning air, his
gaze as stern and inflexible as the handcuffs binding Peter's
wrists.

Guided by the firm grip of Ayoub, Peter is led to a
nondescript panel van that blends seamlessly into the barren
surroundings. Ayoub forces Peter into the back, chaining his
cuffs to a bench that lines one side.

With Peter secured, Ayoub slams the back doors closed
and jumps into the front. The engine's roar fills the silence as
they pull away, the desolate expanse outside a silent witness
to the latest stage of a journey shrouded in uncertainty. In
the back, Peter is alert and ready. Rest has fortified him, and

in the silence of the moving van, amidst the rattle of chains and the cold whisper of steel, a defiant resolution crystallizes.

Pushing aside any fear he has for where this journey may end, Peter carefully moves the metal strip to the edge of his lips with his tongue, managing to get a grip on it with his teeth. One slip and he'll lose it forever, leaving him trapped and defenseless.

With his mouth lowered to his hands, he nimbly takes the thin strip between his fingers. The metal is perfectly shaped to manipulate the small mechanisms inside the handcuff lock. He begins gingerly probing the lock, trying to find the right angle and pressure to release the cuff.

The going is slow, each careful movement requiring precision and patience. With every passing moment, sweat beads on his forehead, his arms ache from the unnatural position, and his jaws tense with the effort. He hopes the van's noise will keep his efforts concealed.

The thoughts racing through Peter's mind keep him determined: images of Michael, of Mayu, Mother, Magda, of every case he's worked on, and every risk he's taken. He can't let this be the end.

As the van continues to rumble down the road, Peter works doggedly at the lock. Time seems to stretch, and the boundaries between minutes and hours blur. But the stubborn persistence of a man with nothing left to lose can accomplish miracles.

And then, finally, a distinct sensation—the feeling of the lock starting to give. The metal strip is working its magic. Freedom and his predestined meeting with the man behind all of this feels tantalizingly close.

MICHAEL AND MAYU sit on the cold floors of their cells, Michael's gaze fixed on the surveillance camera, its red light a glaring reminder of them currently being observed. That blinking light means the camera is active; they are being watched. But it isn't constant. There are gaps in their captor's vigilance, brief moments of blindness that Michael has observed over the arduous hours of captivity. Times when the light goes off.

Like now.

Anticipation surges through Michael as the camera's red eye fades; it's now or never. With the camera blind, he rushes to uncover the hatch, clawing the crud away that he'd spread back over it after his earlier discovery.

He pries it open; a rush of dank, musty air greets him. There's no ladder, just a dark passage barely wide enough to accommodate his frame. The absence of a clear path isn't a deterrent, though. It is an invitation.

He lowers himself into the abyss; an entry into the bowels of the earth. The space is suffocatingly narrow, each move forward a physical struggle against the oppressive confinement. Darkness is omnipresent, impenetrable and absolute. Yet, within this void, Michael's determination illuminates a path. Every inch forward, every moment of claustrophobic progression, is a triumph against the suffocating silence of his cell above.

The sounds of his movement reverberate, a solitary rebellion in the depth of the earth. The muted tap of dripping water punctuates the silence, a reminder of the world left behind.

After what seems a relentless eternity, a dim light begins to puncture the darkness. It's distant yet assertive, a silent whisper of the outside world, of freedom.

As Michael inches forward, the oppressive confines of the tunnel relent, yielding to a space where breath isn't a luxury but a right. The light, dim yet unyielding, is a testimony to the world beyond—a realm where Michael can turn the tables on his captors.

"Mayu?" he calls behind him.

"Yes?" comes her faint reply.

"I think I might have found a way out of here."

————

CIA Headquarters, Langley.

The monolithic structure of the George Bush Center for Intelligence casts an imposing shadow in the morning light as Paul Bennett steps through its automatic glass doors. Having just arrived from Texas, he's a mixture of exhaustion and alertness; he hasn't slept in over twenty-four hours.

Right after showing his ID at the front desk, he takes the lift to the operations room. Inside, he steps into an expanse where a maze of computer terminals blinks back at him, a silent chorus of vigilance. Digital maps glow on the walls, blinking with dots and moving lines.

At the center of the room, a figure he knows all too well stands anchored—Director Sandy McLean. A tall, imposing woman with a posture as ramrod straight as the building housing them, the streaks of silver in her once-blond hair, pulled back in a tight bun, confer upon her an aura of earned authority.

McLean's piercing blue eyes are fixed intently on Bennett as he enters the room. "Paul," she greets him.

"Director," Bennett responds respectfully.

"You're aware of why you're here, I assume," McLean's question hangs in the air, though it's not really a question but a prelude.

"Partially. But I need to be brought up to speed," Bennett's voice is steady, his gaze unwavering.

They retreat to the corner of the room, the baleful dance of lights and shadows painting a vivid backdrop to their hushed conversation.

"We have a situation," McLean begins, the gravity of her words stark against the hum of activity around them. "Kara Tate brought something to our attention that's far-reaching, with implications that thread back to Ben Knight."

Bennett's jaw tightens at the mention of his uncle.

"She's found a connection we overlooked," McLean goes on. "Something that goes back all the way to our operations in Afghanistan and spans to the present day, and it's bearing its fangs, Paul."

Bennett's focus narrows, every word from Director McLean painting a picture of intrigue and impending confrontation. She tells him about David Harrison, about the mission to retrieve the boys, Max's death, Jimmy going missing, then about now—the birthday and Mother's Day cards, the sinister dance of anonymity leading back to Ben's doorstep.

"And Ben was sending these cards?" Bennett asks, the implausibility of the assertion etching lines of incredulity across his features.

"I don't think so," McLean confirms, her gaze unwavering. "I think someone was doing it from his house. But Ben never installed security cameras in his home."

"Didn't like the idea of being watched," Bennett adds. "Which is ironic."

"Ironic or not, it doesn't end there," McLean continues, "there's a belief, a strong one, that one of Harrison's sons is alive—and that he's seeking retribution."

Bennett absorbs the information, the sinister dance of past actions and present reckonings hanging in the room. Then he asserts, "I need to speak to Kara Tate."

———

ON THE LONELY street of a quiet suburb, the early morning light delicately paints long, intricate shadows between rows of identical, cookie-cutter houses. Birds are just beginning their morning songs, and the world seems to be waking up slowly. Every so often, the rhythmic patter of a jogger's feet punctuates the silence, and farther down the street, the faint jingle of a leash can be heard as a dog walker makes their rounds, their breath misting in the cold morning air.

Against this backdrop of suburban serenity, Ayoub's nondescript panel van sits inconspicuously on the road, its engine silent, its presence blending into the mundane surroundings.

Exhausted from the long journey, he steps out of the van, pausing momentarily to survey the tranquil surroundings. With deliberate movements, he makes his way to the rear, the doors groaning loudly in the otherwise hushed ambiance of the dawn-lit suburb.

Peter's pale face stares back at him, eyes squinting against the sudden intrusion of light.

"Time to move," Ayoub says coldly, climbing into the rear with him. He leans over Peter, unlocking the chain that binds him to the bench.

Peter is acutely aware of his surroundings. Every movement, every sound, is amplified, the adrenaline coursing through his veins heightening his senses. As Ayoub focuses on the locks, his jacket momentarily parts. It is but a fleeting moment, yet in that instance, Peter's gaze is drawn to the sight of the Glock holstered within.

Once the chain is off, Ayoub steps back. "Now get out," he barks.

Stepping onto the road from the van, Peter tries to get his bearings, but signs for Elm Street and Maple Drive offer no real clue. Just another generic American suburb.

Ayoub checks the surroundings, ensuring no prying eyes are on them before he addresses Peter. "It's time to meet Musa," he says, emotionless.

Peter, his hands still handcuffed in front of him, is led toward a manhole cover on the other side of the street. A manhole hook dangles from Ayoub's hand.

"Are we going down there?" Peter's voice wavers slightly as they pause at the edge.

Ayoub shoves the hook at him. "Take it," he orders, but Peter stands his ground, his jaw set with determination.

"What about Michael and Mayu?" Peter insists, his voice resolute. "I need to see them first. Alive."

Ayoub's eyes, cold and piercing, lock onto Peter's, assessing the defiance before him. With a begrudging sneer, he pulls out his phone and swiftly navigates to the live security footage of the cells.

However, as the images load, both men are met with an unexpected sight—Michael's cell is empty. A wave of disbelief and rage washes over Ayoub. Quickly, the phone is flipped around as he goes to dial up his friends and warn them.

He never gets the chance.

Peter seizes the moment. The glint of the discarded handcuffs catches the early morning light as they clatter to the ground. With a burst of unexpected agility, Peter lunges at Ayoub, catching him off guard. In one swift motion, he wrestles Ayoub toward a thicket of bushes where they are shielded from the street. Peter's movements are quick and efficient as he rapidly subdues Ayoub, pinning him on his back. The transformation in Peter is startling; his eyes, previously uncertain, now gleam with a dangerous intent as he whips the Glock 17 from the inside of Ayoub's jacket and presses it into his cheek.

A mixture of fear and realization dawns in the expression of Ayoub as he feels the crushing weight of Peter atop him and the unyielding chill of the gun.

"Where are they?" Peter shouts down at him.

Resistance flashes in Ayoub's eyes. He isn't ready to give in without a fight. His muscles tense, and he tries to buck Peter off. But Peter doesn't waste a moment. He smashes Ayoub with the gun, again and again, pistol whipping him into submission, whilst simultaneously maneuvering his knees so that they trap Ayoub's arms to the ground.

Ending the barrage, Peter snarls, "Where are they?"

Ayoub, bloodied and beaten, his eyes glazed with the early signs of concussion, merely smiles up at him; daring Peter to shoot him. But Peter has another idea. Inside the back of that van he found something. From his back pocket, he produces a crumpled plastic bag, the type you carry your groceries in, and thrusts it over Ayoub's head.

The world becomes a blur for Ayoub as the bag clings to his face. Every inhale is a struggle, the plastic sticking to his mouth and nostrils, each breath shallower than the last. His eyes bulge, and his face turns a shade of deep crimson as the seconds stretch on. Just when the edges of his vision begin to darken and his struggles wane, Peter yanks the bag away, allowing Ayoub to gulp in desperate, ragged breaths.

"Talk!" Peter's demand is sharp, reverberating amidst the thick foliage surrounding them.

Coughing weakly, Ayoub's voice trembles, barely audible. "There isn't much time," he rasps, the strain from the previous suffocation evident in his raw voice. "They won't wait for us."

Peter is unforgiving. His face inches from Ayoub's, eyes blazing, he warns, "You better tell me everything the next time I ask."

But his enemy is filled with the fervent energy of the fighter. "I am always ready to go to paradise," Ayoub murmurs before his split, bloody lips purse into a smile.

Peter acts with methodical precision. The plastic bag is thrust over Ayoub's head again, creating an airless cocoon around him. The suffocating sensation is immediate and overwhelming. The first inhalation is met with a vacuum, the bag collapsing inward, sealing itself to his mouth and nose. Each attempt to breathe grows more frantic, the lack of oxygen and the building carbon dioxide in his blood setting off a primal alarm in his brain that screams in his head for him to BREATHE!

His eyes roll back, only the whites showing, as his body convulses involuntarily. Ayoub's hands claw at the ground beneath him, his fingernails digging into the dirt, searching for some form of release. Muffled screams reverberate within the bag, and beads of sweat form on his forehead, merging with tears of anguish that stream down his face. The world outside becomes distorted, fading in and out as Ayoub teeters on the precipice of unconsciousness.

And just as the shadows begin to engulf his vision, Peter, gauging the critical moment with unsettling precision, yanks the bag off. Air rushes into Ayoub's lungs in a violent, gasping inhale, a lifeline pulling him back from the brink. Coughs and sobs mix together as Ayoub tries to recalibrate, the sharp pain in his chest a testament to the trauma inflicted.

Gasping for each breath, his voice barely more than a broken whisper, Ayoub relents, "Forget your boy... Musa only has eyes for you... Just go down there... He's waiting for you..."

Eyes narrowing, Peter asks again, "Where are Michael and Mayu?"

Frantically, Ayoub replies, "I told you. It doesn't matter. He only wants you. Go meet him."

Peter glances over his shoulder, eyes fixing to the manhole cover in the middle of the road.

CIA Headquarters, Langley.

Kara Tate, despite the whirlwind she finds herself in, sits with a steadfast composure. The interrogation room, with its gray walls and silence, amplifies every breath, every heartbeat.

The door swings open with a controlled precision, and Paul Bennett steps in, the weight of the last days etched across his seasoned features. His eyes lock onto Kara's.

There's no prelude to pleasantries, no courtesies—the gravity of the unfolding narrative leaves no room for the superfluous.

"I want you to tell me everything you know, Ms. Tate," Bennett says, his voice sharp and direct.

A few minutes later, Bennett sits there deep in thought. "That's a hell of a lot of coincidences," he remarks.

"It is."

"And have you ever seen Jimmy Harrison?" Bennett's question is sharp and direct.

"No," Kara responds, her voice steady. "But your uncle might have known where Max is."

Bennett's gaze, piercing and cold, fixes on her. "Max Harrison is dead, Ms. Tate," he reveals, his voice a blend of icy conviction and suppressed emotion. "My uncle did what he had to do. But you could be right about Jimmy. There's every chance he survived and is now out for revenge."

"But why is he trying to frame Peter?" Kara asserts, the conviction in her voice as unwavering as the storm they find themselves adrift upon. "Why not just kill him like al-Nasri and Ben Knight? Why toy with him like this? There has to be someone on the inside. Otherwise, how could they incriminate him like that?"

"I know," Bennett confesses, checking the door before continuing in an undertone. "I've had my suspicions for a while now that someone inside the CIA is working with the Wolf Pack."

The shocking assertion chills the air. Trust, the cornerstone of their clandestine world, is as elusive as the shadowy figure orchestrating the intricate dance of betrayals and confrontations.

"You're in danger," Bennett's voice, laced with an unbreakable conviction, punctures the silence like a knife. "If there's a double agent, they might target you next, Ms. Tate. It means you're not safe inside this building."

Kara's heart rattles in her chest as she absorbs the revelation. In this murky theatre of intelligence and betrayals, every revelation is a step deeper into the rabbit hole.

"I have somewhere safe you can go," Bennett asserts. "But we have to leave now."

MICHAEL PUSHES FORWARD, drawn magnetically towards the dim light. Every inch of progression fuels his hope; the light a silent testament to freedom, a whisper of the world outside this suffocating captivity.

The tunnel, barely wide enough for his shoulders, begins to hint of an end. And then, there it is—a blockage. Bricks and masonry clog the path where part of the sewer tunnel has collapsed. The light barely seeps through the gaps, painting the debris in shadows.

Every breath heavy with the weight of the moment, Michael begins pulling at the bricks. The gap widens; enough for his head, but the victory is short-lived.

His eyes, now accustomed to the darkness, widen as they take in the sight before him. The other side of the tunnel is illuminated by the inviting light, but it's even narrower, constricting, immovable. There's no way through.

Defeat, cold and bitter, clashes against the heat of his desperate hope. Every breath is a mix of dank air and stifled aspirations. He pulls back, retreating to his cell, the victory of the found passage now a haunting fraud of what could have been but isn't.

"Mayu?" Back in his cell, his voice is a broken whisper, a mingling of frustration and undying resolve. The defeat isn't final; it can't be.

"Michael," she replies, her voice muffled by the wall, so close but so far. "What did you find?"

"I couldn't get through," he admits. The dim light from the uncovered hatch casts an eerie glow, painting his cell in gloom. Checking the camera, he finds it still dormant, a silent, unseeing sentinel in this moment of crushing revelation. Turning back to the wall, to Mayu, Michael adds, "But I have another idea."

THE STENCH of the sewer tunnel assaults Peter's senses, a vile blend of decay and refuse that clings to the damp air. The uneven ground beneath his feet is slick with residue, and the murky water rising up his boots ripples with the frenetic movement of rats. In the front of the van he found a flashlight; its feeble beam now cuts through the darkness, casting jittery shadows that dance along the wet walls.

Ayoub trudges ahead of him, his back straight, his own gun now in the hand of Peter and trained on him, a constant reminder of who's in control—at least for now. Dripping water echos eerily through the narrow space, like the seconds of a ticking clock, and the farther they venture, the louder the clock's tick. Peter's every sense is heightened; the dampness in the air, the dripping water, the weight of what's ahead, all of it making his steps heavy and deliberate.

Up ahead, the tunnel wall is broken, a jagged hole beckoning them to step through. Ayoub stops momentarily, glancing over his shoulder, a flicker of doubt crossing his eyes. Peter gestures with the gun, and with a resigned nod, Ayoub steps through the opening.

As Peter follows, the narrow confines of the sewer give way to a vast underground chamber. An old, cobweb covered diesel generator takes up the room's center, and a tunnel leads off from it. When Peter shines the flashlight down the passage, the beam is eaten up by darkness.

"Is that where he is?" he asks, his voice filling the confined space.

"Only one way to find out," is Ayoub's ominous reply.

They move on. Ayoub leading, Peter following, their footsteps repeating in the cramped tunnel. As they progress, Peter notices halogen lamps strung along the ceiling. They look freshly placed there, no cobwebs hanging from them, and he wonders what else he might discover down here.

He doesn't have to wait long. Soon, they come across

something far more sinister. Where the tunnel widens, barrels upon barrels are stacked neatly in rows along the wall. Peter can guess what they contain, and the implications are made clear by the wires connecting each of them together. Peter swallows hard, a heavy dread settling in the pit of his stomach.

It is then, as he eyes the barrels, that the stillness of the tunnel is interrupted by a vibrating sound. Ayoub's phone, inside Peter's pocket, springs to life, its insistent ring bouncing off the walls. The weight of the moment tightens as Peter, the Glock still trained on Ayoub, pulls out the ringing device and eyes it with suspicion.

"Answer it," he instructs, holding it out to Ayoub.

"It'll be for you," Ayoub replies, a smirk evident in his tone.

Peter grips the phone with his free hand, the Glock-17 unwaveringly aimed at Ayoub. With little choice, he answers it.

The voice that greets him, cold and dripping with malevolence, is unmistakably that of Jimmy Harrison. "Do you know what day it is today?" he sneers.

Peter's mind races, but he replies flatly, "No."

"It is the fifteenth anniversary of my father's death at your hands. For fifteen years, I have lived under the hell of that day, with every anniversary filling me with an unmistakable void. I feel myself transform into that boy who was told his father had been murdered by an infidel. His life forever thrown into an abyss." He pauses, possibly to swallow down the bitterness. "But now," his voice comes back stronger, "now I will give this day new meaning. For now, it will be known as the day you DIE!"

Suddenly, the dimness of the tunnel is decimated by an overpowering white brilliance. The powerful halogen lamps flare to life, their glow consuming every crevice and corner of the tight space. Peter's pupils violently constrict, rendered momentarily sightless by the overwhelming luminescence.

As he's still reeling from the sudden illumination, Ayoub, harnessing the element of surprise, lunges at him. Their two bodies clash in a struggle for dominance, made even more claustrophobic by the constraints of the tunnel. In the melee, Peter's flashlight is snatched away, smashing on the ground and dying out completely.

Then Ayoub is gone, leaving Peter to stagger through the incandescence, a hand held across his throbbing eyes. But he's not alone for long. A rush of stomping boots resound through the confined space, growing louder as they approach, and strong hands seize Peter. His grip on the gun weakens amidst the chaos. The Glock-17 is sent skittering across the tunnel's uneven floor, quickly swallowed by the darkness beyond the lamps' reach. Pinned and overwhelmed, Peter's world becomes a dizzying whirlwind, a blend of stark lights and encroaching shadows.

And then, just as he's able to make out the shape of a man, the overpowering lights go out abruptly, plunging the tunnel back into an impenetrable darkness. At that precise moment, the unmistakable glint of a knife's blade looms from the abyss. Peter is blind, his eyes still adjusting from the blinding lights, but his heightened senses, attuned to the immediate danger, propel him sideways, the blade swishing past, narrowly missing its intended target.

In the complete darkness, Peter is now virtually defenseless. He doesn't yet realize that his attacker, Musa, is not hindered by the same handicap. Musa's eyes, aided by a pair of night-vision goggles, are locked onto Peter with predatory precision. Every movement, every breath Peter takes, is watched, anticipated, and countered in the silent duel that unfolds in the depths of the tunnel, where light and dark converge into a dance of brute force and survival.

———

EMERGING from the depths of the tunnel, Ayoub steps into the weaker, flickering light at its end, where Umar awaits.

They immediately embrace, a silent exchange of solidarity and brotherhood flowing between them in the absence of words.

"Time to get changed," Umar whispers, nodding down at a fat holdall stuffed with the paraphernalia of death.

Ayoub begins his transformation into battle-ready warrior. With meticulous precision, he dons body armor, each piece a layer of defense against the impending confrontation, the cold, hard plates a stark contrast to the warm, fleeting touch of human embrace they've just shared.

Umar watches in silent support as Ayoub straps a gas mask over his face; his identity now obscured, he morphs into an ominous figure, both menacing and resolute. Shells, gleaming under the feeble light, are loaded into a Benelli M3 tactical shotgun, each one a harbinger of the violence that awaits.

Fortified and ready, Ayoub stands alongside Umar, two warriors ready for battle. Having taken a few moments of silent communion, Umar murmurs, "It is time, brother."

Picking up one of the sledgehammers from the bricked up entrance, he hands it to Ayoub, before Umar takes ahold of the other. That's when both men turn their attention to the blocked entrance—and the next phase of their terrible plan.

THIRTY-FIVE

CIA HEADQUARTERS, LANGLEY

A THICK AIR OF TENSION CLINGS TO THE WALLS OF Director Sandy McLean's office. Adorned with the accolades and scars of a life dedicated to the covert, they bear silent witness to the unfolding drama.

Director McLean is currently on a call with the man in charge of the FBI field office in Austin. The body of a local Waco pilot has been found in the hangar of the man's own airfield. Nearby was an abandoned sedan—one with tires that match the tracks found in Hondo.

Kirsty Lang sits quietly in a corner by the door, like some cheerleader caught smoking and sent to the principle's office.

"Your man could be anywhere," the special agent's voice, steely yet burdened, travels through the line.

"What about missing planes?" McLean asks.

"One, belonging to the man he killed. We're checking where it is now."

Kirsty, restrained yet defiant, interjects, "I'm telling you, Peter is under their control. They're using Michael as leverage. He didn't kill that guy. They did."

However, before the weight of her words can settle, Aria Patel storms into the room, confusion and urgency etching every feature.

"Kara Tate's gone," she announces. "And when I just checked with security, they told me Paul Bennett signed her out. Why in the hell would..."

The sentence, hanging, incomplete, is swallowed by a pounding bang that suddenly reverberates through the building, shaking the very foundations of the establishment built upon secrets and silent wars. Operatives and analysts get up from their desks, confusion written across their faces. Whether they like it or not, they are now hostages of the unexplained dread gripping the fortress.

As if choreographed, the banging is suddenly joined by the wailing of alarms. The auxiliary lights come on, painting everything red, and at the same time, blast shutters begin falling down the windows and exits, sealing them in—the building becoming a prison.

"Are we under attack?" a voice asks the Director when she steps out of her office.

"I don't know," McLean replies, raising her voice to be heard.

As for the banging, it is incessant, mocking, and offers no respite. McLean, a general amidst her soldiers, picks up the building telephone from a nearby pillar, reaching out to security. "What's going on?" she asks the second it's answered.

"I'm afraid, ma'am," the head of building security

replies, "the systems's been tripped by some sort of computer virus. The whole thing's infected with it."

"How in the hell did someone get a virus into the CIA?" McLean blasts back, every syllable a demand for answers.

"We don't know, ma'am, but we sure intend to find out."

"And what about the banging?"

"I'm not sure," security says. "I just sent two guys down to the basement to check it out."

———

THE TWO SECURITY guards descend into the basement, the ominous banging growing louder with each step they take. The dimly lit corridors, usually so familiar, now morph into an eerie labyrinth of ominous sounds and unsettling shadows. The guards exchange a glance, hands hovering above their holstered pistols.

The unsettling procession of loud thuds is accompanied by the unnerving sounds of crumbling and falling rubble. Each thump sends chills down their spines; the intrusion is real, tangible and closing in. The source of the noise is pinpointed to an old storage room, its door looming in the pale, inadequate light like the entryway to a haunted crypt.

Their breaths become heavy as they near the room. More unsettling sounds of intrusion rattle the usually inert space of the basement, bringing to life a reality the guards can barely fathom.

They find a monstrous crack splitting the wall on the other side of the room, the masonry tearing apart, forming a hole, fracturing the sanctity of CIA headquarters. With pistols drawn, the guards stand their ground as the wall breaks open.

"Hold it there!" Their voices are powerful yet edged with fear.

The banging halts, granting a fleeting respite before a sinister silence heralds a menacing prelude.

A canister thrusts through the widening gap, skittling along the floor towards them. Tear gas, like an unholy mist, engulfs the guards, forcing them into a panicked retreat, their calls for reinforcement choked by convulsive coughs.

As the incapacitating haze of gas surrounds them, the hammering recommences and the barricaded entrance succumbs, breached and yielding to the invaders. Through raspy, gasping breaths and watered eyes, the guards fight to maintain control.

"We're under... attack...! Repeat...! We're under—"

The harrowing blast of a shotgun ends the communication in blood and violence. The second guard, fueled by adrenaline and terror, discharges his pistol with frantic desperation. But the punctuated retort of an AR15 seals his fate, echoing the final notes of resistance.

In the heavy silence that follows, a chilling proclamation has been made. The CIA headquarters, usually a fortress of secrets and power, is now a preyed entity, infiltrated and vulnerable. The invading darkness marks the chilling overture of a new chapter of terror in American history.

———

ABSOLUTE DARKNESS SURROUNDS PETER, swallowing him like the vacuum of space. Every movement, every sound is amplified in the intense silence, making the atmosphere all the more chilling. He's engulfed in a fatal dance where sight is a luxury, and instincts are his only guide through the pitch black.

From this inky void, a blade materializes and a voice, chilling with hatred, pierces the silence. "This has been a long time coming, Azrael." Despite the darkness, recognition takes hold.

This must be Jimmy Harrison, Abu Musa, the leader of the Wolf Pack. The ghost that has been haunting Peter since this all began.

The confrontation unfolds in the oppressive pitch black. Peter, blinded, relies on honed instincts, his senses alert to every movement, every whisper of the blade that seeks him in the dark. Musa, adorned with night-vision goggles, is a wraith, his every strike guided by the sinister green hue of infrared vision.

Musa advances, his training in tantojutsu evident in every calculated movement. The sharp blade of the knife, an extension of his own sinister intent, executes the "Yoko-men"—a horizontal strike aimed at Peter's temple. The blade slices through the air, its chilling whisper telling a tale of imminent danger.

Peter, almost as if guided by some unseen force, tilts his head, narrowly avoiding the sharp edge. He is a product of Krav Maga, a discipline rooted in practical, efficient defenses honed for survival. Instinct and training meld into a seamless dance of defense amidst the abyss of total darkness.

The "Tsuki" follows—a thrust aiming straight for Peter's heart. Musa's movements are fluid, a deadly dance painted with precision and intent. Peter sidesteps, his breath a silent echo of the pulse racing through his veins. Yet, the blade finds its mark, grazing his side, drawing blood that spills into the darkness.

In the impenetrable black, every movement, every breath is amplified, filling the void of Peter's mind. Musa's strikes, guided by the eerie illumination of night vision, are a series of shadowed nightmares. The "Kiri-age"—an upward cut, then the "Kiri-oroshi"—a downward slash, each move a testament to his skill, his intent written in the whispering strokes of the blade.

Peter, veiled in darkness and armed with his instincts, counters. He is a silhouette of defense, each parry and dodge a dance on the precipice of life and death. Even still, the blade finds its mark occasionally, drawing lines of red that testify to the dance of combat unfolding in the silent, haunting blackness.

———

THE TWO MEN have split up.

The grim weight of his mission evident in every step, Ayoub ascends a staircase. His fatigues and body armor give him an almost militaristic bearing. As he emerges at the top of the stairs, the window of an office frames him for a brief second, a soldier stepping from the shadows.

Unclipping a tear gas canister from his body armor, he pulls the pin and tosses it ahead of him, the thing spinning and hissing. Thick, acrid-smelling gas fills the air, stinging the eyes and lungs of anyone hiding close by. A figure emerges from the haze, coughing and gasping for breath, staggering toward Ayoub from an office.

The terrorist raises the Benelli, smirks behind the screen of the gas mask, and turns the woman into pink mist with three rapid, pumped shots, the shells spitting out the side of the shotgun and skittling along the floor. The rush is intense, but he has no time to dwell on it. He must keep moving.

The corridors and offices of the building have become a grotesque tableau. Dead bodies, some in suits, others in civilian clothing, litter the hallways, their final moments of panic and terror forever etched onto their lifeless faces. In the distance, Umar's AR-15 barks away, its rapid shots piercing the heavy air, quickly followed by the slower, but just as deadly, rhythm of Ayoub's pump-action shotgun, the sounds punctuated by haunting screams.

Ayoub, keeping his senses alert, spots a pair of legs protruding from beneath a desk. His approach to them is methodical, predatory. The two women hiding under there freeze in terror when he reaches them.

With cold precision, he points the Benelli at them, the sharp report echoing through the corridors.

———

PETER AND MUSA ARE APART, each man breathing heavily into the pitch black tunnel. "I didn't know what would happen to your brother after I handed him over to Knight," Peter's voice reverberates off the tight walls, a confession thrown into the abyss. "I thought he'd be safe. That they'd take him back to your mom."

"I don't care," Musa sneers. "You are nothing more than a godless machine, Azrael. Programmed in the wilds of

Alaska to kill with the efficiency of one. You only ever have eyes for your mission. There is no—"

Peter uses the brief lapse to his advantage, lunging forward. But he's met with another flash of the blade, feeling it bite into his side, just below the ribs, and he staggers back. This one feels deeper than the others, the sharp edge shearing the flesh.

Pushing the pain into the corners, he hears Musa's voice again, filled with malevolent triumph, coming at him from the darkness itself. "That fat traitor al-Nasri gave up my father," he spits. "Knight took my brother. And you... you took everything!"

He explodes at Peter. The blade slashes through the air, glinting at him as he escapes it by shaping his body and parrying. But Peter can't just be defense, he has to attack.

Now is the time.

With desperation and quick thinking, Peter sees an opportunity. As Musa makes another thrust with the knife, aiming for Peter's heart, Peter boldly and abruptly moves his forearm into the blade's path, feeling it pierce all the way through the flesh and lodge between his ulna and radius bones. The shock of it causes Musa to momentarily freeze, his eyes wide.

Using this split-second pause, Peter, through gritted teeth and surging pain, twists his thick arm violently, leveraging the position of the knife between his bones to rip it away from Musa's stunned grip.

The knife skitters along the floor, and Musa reacts to losing his advantage with fury, his face contorted in rage. Now weaponless, he charges forward, the eerie green light of his night-vision goggles illuminating Peter's form. In this stark, haunting blackness, the dance of death morphs into a ballet of hands and feet.

Musa has trained almost every day for the past fifteen years for this fight. His fists become instruments of war, each swing a note in a deadly symphony. The "teep" kick, a hallmark of Muay Thai, thrusts forward aiming for Peter's chest, Azrael narrowly avoiding it in the darkness.

Nevertheless, in this void, Peter is not defenseless. The veiled world is a canvas where instincts and training paint their own vision. Sensing the movements of his opponent, and seeing their outline at the last second, he melds the fluid movements of Pencak Silat, a dance of defense and offense, with the raw, unyielding strikes of Krav Maga.

Musa, though, is a rabid animal. A flood of lethwei elbow strikes and Muay Thai kicks seek the blind fighter. In the black echo of the tunnel, each hit and miss resonates, a chilling reminder of the peril dancing in the shadows. Musa's "sok ngat", an elbow slash, cuts through the cold air. Peter, a specter of defense, parries, yet amidst this haunting ballet, Musa's follow up kick finds Peter's side, connecting with the knife wound.

A surge of pain ricochets through him. He staggers, before gathering himself, a hand leaned on the cold wall. Shaking himself, he gets back in fighting stance. Because in this dance where death is an ever-present threat, retreat is not an option.

Peter throws himself at his opponent. Blind yet absolutely unyielding, the intricate dance of Pencak Silat intertwines with the visceral, instinctual strikes of Krav Maga. Each blow, each parry, is a stroke painted in the silent, pitch black canvas of the tunnel. In a surge of relentless determination, Peter's fists connect. Seizing his moment, he rains blows, relentless and unforgiving, upon Musa. The haunting green light of the night-vision goggles, now symbols of a faltering predator, is extinguished as Peter rips them from Musa's face, making them both blind, a predator turned prey.

The silent victory hangs in the air. Yet, as triumph courses through Peter's veins, Musa, his hand, swift and potent, finds Peter's wound. Fingers, cold and relentless, thrust into the raw vulnerability of the torn flesh.

Pain, profound and deafening, surges through Peter as he slips to his knees. The darkness, oppressive and victorious, reclaims its prey.

Musa, now free, springs back to life. A powerful kick to the head sends Peter sprawling, his back colliding with the cold, damp floor of the tunnel.

As he lays prone, the silence is pierced by the metallic click of a gun being cocked. Musa, a silhouette painted in the oppressive darkness, stands over him, the pistol's cold barrel staring down at him.

Peter stares right back at it, expecting the end any second now.

But the trigger remains static. Instead of a bullet, Musa's cold voice slices open the silence. "Your time to die is not now, Azrael," he says. "Before then, I want you to see something you love die. I want your soul drenched in pain, eyes haunted by the images of loss. Only then, when despair has consumed you, will this dance reach its finale."

The gun's indifferent gaze remains on Peter as Musa withdraws, leaving Peter on the ground. Then, once he's far enough, he spins around and runs off, his rapid footsteps resonating sharply in the tunnel.

Gritting his teeth, Peter uses the last of his ebbing strength to lift himself up. As he staggers after Musa, his foot hits the knife. Reaching down, the pain in his body tugging at every muscle, he picks it up, the knife becoming his only companion as he stumbles unsteadily past the barrels of explosives towards a faint light.

He has no idea where it leads, where he will emerge, or what he will face. All he has is forwards.

———

THE ONCE GRAND lobby of the building is now a war zone. Debris scatters the floor, and the stench of gunshots hangs in the air. Broken shards of glass shimmer ominously under the flickering red light, casting dancing reflections amidst the chaos.

Director Sandy McLean, Aria Patel, and Kirsty Lang are creeping about in the midst of the disarray. McLean's sharp eyes scan their environment as Aria and Kirsty follow her lead. They discover employees huddled under desks, their eyes wide and filled with terror. Silently, McLean motions them to follow.

"We need to get them to my office," McLean whispers to Aria and Kirsty as they escort several trembling analysts from their hiding places. "The door's blast proof and locks manually, so isn't affected by the virus."

Gunshots continue to reverberate from other parts of the building, a haunting reminder of the lingering threat. Umar and Ayoub's unrestrained firing instills terror, the sounds of their brutality making many of the group shudder as they move along.

As they reach McLean's office, one of the rescued analysts whispers, his voice shaking, "Why isn't the armory open? We need to defend ourselves."

"The virus has locked it down," McLean explains tersely. "Only myself and field agent Patel are armed. We're doing the best we can."

It's true. Both are armed with standard SIG Sauer M18 Compacts, fitted with seventeen round magazines. Meaty prospects as far as pistols go, but no match for the AR15 and Benelli M3, as well as the men's body armor.

With everyone locked inside the office, Aria and Kirsty exchange determined looks before plunging back into the ominous halls, the three women splitting up.

As the growing wail of sirens penetrates the building from outside, McLean's phone vibrates, the screen illuminating with the worried face of the local SWAT team leader.

"We're setting up a perimeter now, Director," he says urgently. "What's the situation inside?"

McLean's voice is a low whisper as she relays the details, her words punctuated by distant gunfire and terrified screams.

———

WHILE DIRECTOR MCLEAN liaises with the help gathering outside, Kirsty Lang has discovered a group of analysts on a lower floor and is now leading them through a large open plan office.

"Watch out!" The whisper is urgent and choked with

terror; an analyst, his face ghostly pale, points toward the far end of the room. Time freezes, every breath suspended, as the menacing silhouette of Umar, AR-15 in hand, comes into stark relief against the haunting red gloom.

Adrenaline courses through Kirsty's veins. The group duck down low, using the desk partitions as cover while Umar turns their way and begins marching towards them.

Every movement meticulously choreographed, Kirsty begins guiding the group skillfully away from Umar's predatory gaze as he scans the desks looking for more victims of this terrible assault. Each step the group take is a delicate weave through the sprawling maze of desks.

Amidst the suffocating silence and chilling proximity of death, they manage to escape him, Umar passing right by them as they practically crawl along on the other side of the room, until they are scampering out the door and down a corridor, their silent exodus a testament to human resilience.

———

Aria Patel descends into the basement looking for survivors who may have taken refuge down there. The M18 Compact in her hand feels both like a tether to safety and a reminder of the pervasive danger. Her steps are cautious, her ears tuned to the sinister concerto of distant gunshots and anguished screams filtering from the floors above.

As she ventures deeper, the harsh, artificial lighting casts elongated shadows, rendering the austere corridor a labyrinth of threatening silhouettes. A chill, as piercing as the screams above, goes through her as she stumbles upon the lifeless bodies of the two security guards. The sight of them fills Aria with sadness; their valor and the tragedy of their deaths on full display as they lie motionless upon the ground.

A sudden movement in the shadowed recesses of the corridor snaps Aria's focus. Adrenaline courses through her veins, her grip tightening on her weapon as she pivots sharply, the M18 aimed at the emerging figure.

The haunting backdrop of chaos above seems to recede into silence as Aria's gaze fixes on the bloodied mess that comes staggering out at her, the man deeply disoriented.

"Don't move!" Every fiber of Aria's being is attuned to the imminent threat, the intoxicating mix of fear and training rendering her senses supernaturally acute.

But as the man's face, pallid and inscribed with lines of agony and confusion, comes into view, Aria's tense posture softens. Realization dawns when she realizes who stands before her.

"Peter," she murmurs.

She holsters her weapon, rushing to his side, the urgency of the moment rendering her movements both frantic and precise. Peter's eyes, a turbulent sea of confusion and realization, attempt to anchor themselves in the present.

"Where am I?" His voice is a fragile whisper.

"Langley," Aria responds.

Recognition dawns, a swift and electrifying realization that strikes Peter like lightning, awakening the dark recesses of his memory. His voice trembles as terror and urgency intertwine.

"There's a bomb underneath the building," he stammers. "You have to get everybody out." His eyes, wide with the dread of his own revelation, mirror the chilling import of his words.

"But the building's locked down," Aria retorts.

"Then bring everybody down here. Through there," Peter urges, his hand trembling as he points back to the darkness from which he emerged. "There's a hole in the wall. It leads to a tunnel that'll take you away from here, away from the bomb. Get everyone out that way."

Aria's heart hammers against her ribcage, each beat mirroring the gravity of Peter's revelation. "Stay here," she commands. Every second is a ticking time bomb, each moment, precious and slipping through their fingers like sand.

As Aria sprints back towards the haunting sounds of distant gunfire, Peter's gaze hardens. In the icy grip of terror and realization, a steely resolve is forged. Peter begins moving again, determined to find Musa, and, ultimately, find his son.

However, as Peter abandons the basement, a menacing shadow emerges from the darkened recesses of a nearby cabinet—Musa. His intense eyes scan the corridor before he makes his way towards the hole, the gateway to the labyrinth beneath.

He doesn't plan on sticking around for what comes next.

———

Director Sandy McLean's stern features are bathed in the red illumination of the emergency lighting as she takes cover near the entrance to her office. Umar has found them and is now holed up at the other end of the corridor, about fifteen meters away, hidden within the cover of a corner.

Every bullet that thunders through the corridor from his AR-15 is a harsh reminder of the imminent threat that looms.

The corner of McLean's office, the walls filled with reinforced concrete, acts as the sole barrier between the resilient Director and the armed assailant at the opposite end of the corridor.

Amidst the break in automatic gunfire, McLean, a mix of nerves and steely resolve, counterattacks with her M18. Each shot fired is precise, measured.

One hits a poking shoulder.

Umar cries out as he stumbles back from the impact of the bullet against his body armor. It'll keep him busy for a moment, the gunman groaning in pain, trying to catch his breath.

In the meantime, the phone clutched in McLean's other hand is still connecting her to the outside world, to the SWAT team desperately trying to infiltrate the building that has become their prison. "How long until you're inside?" she asks, the urgency shaking in her voice.

"They're still working on the virus," the man on the other end informs her. "And we're trying to cut through the blast shields now. But they're not exactly designed to be broken through. It's gonna take some time."

The ominous hum of disc cutters permeates the background, a mechanical chorus to the surreal standoff unfolding within. McLean's heart pounds against her ribcage, each beat resonating with the urgency of the moment.

Silence slams through the corridor, oppressive, haunting. McLean goes to shoot as she senses Umar about to emerge, but all she gets is a click. Every round in the M18 is spent. The director of there CIA now trembles, a vulnerable prey amidst predatory shadows—a cornered rabbit before a snake.

Umar senses the shift, an opportunist thriving amidst chaos. He leaves his cover, AR-15 spewing death as he moves along the corridor, a storm of bullets tearing through the air, relentless, insatiable. The corner McLean and the others hide behind is hit with a barrage. Concrete crumbles and explodes.

They're driven back, and can do nothing except watch as Umar's shadow grows; the bark of rapid gunfire filling them with panic. Director McLean, renowned for unwavering resolve, now teeters on the brink, a heartbeat away from the inevitable.

Yet fate is fickle, untethered to the whims of tyrants and the sinister dance of invaders.

As Umar strides forward, bullets spraying wildly, his perceived invincibility blinds him, and he fails to spot Aria Patel hiding in an adjacent corridor he marches past. She emerges behind him, a specter, unseen, unmarked. Every ounce of training, every shadowed operation in foreign lands, converges into this moment of silent defiance.

Umar advances; victory, so close it pulsates through his veins, blinds him. His footsteps, a relentless march of terror, are deaf to the silent sentinel behind him.

Aria's M18 barks; one shot, piercing, final, to the back of the head. It comes out the other side, shattering the glass of the gas mask.

Umar collapses; the slow march of doom arrested. The terror dissipates, giving way to a silence, profound yet triumphant.

In the debris-laden corridor, beneath the flickering red lights, Aria, McLean, Kirsty and the others stand, unbroken.

Aria's breath is a mix of relief and gravity as she turns to McLean. "Peter's alive," she exclaims amidst the lingering echoes of gunfire.

"Black is here?"

"Yes. But that's not the worst of it. There's a bomb under the building. We need to evacuate, now."

"But the blast shields," McLean puts to her.

Her voice firm, Aria states, "There's another way."

———

PETER'S WORLD is a haze of agony and confusion. Every step is a struggle against the blackness that threatens to engulf him, to pull him under. His blood, dark against the sterile floors of CIA Headquarters, leaves a haunting trail as he staggers forward. The knife in his hand is both a weapon and a lifeline, a tangible anchor in a world that seems to be spiraling out of control.

Memories, fragmented and elusive, flicker through his consciousness. Michael. His son's name, a mantra, resonates in the hollowed corridors of his mind, driving him forward, propelling him through the suffocating darkness that seeks to claim him.

The resounding blast of a shotgun reverberates through the building, a haunting harbinger of violence and dread. To Peter, each echo is a call, a siren song pulling him towards the epicenter of the conflict, towards answers, towards Michael.

A wounded soldier in this clandestine battlefield, Peter is driven by a father's love, an unyielding force that defies the boundaries of physical pain and mental disarray.

As the looming sounds of gunfire and commotion filter through the corridors of the building, getting closer, Peter's steps, though faltering, are unwavering.

———

Kirsty Lang, Director McLean, Aria Patel, and others plunge into the icy silence of the basement corridor, a sanctuary from the chaos upstairs. The red glare of the lights turns the splattered blood of Peter into a menacing display against the cold, gray floor.

"Peter," Aria mutters under her breath. "I left him here," she adds, turning to the others.

McLean's sharp eyes follow the trail of blood towards a stairwell. "Looks like he's gone upstairs."

"We can't leave him behind," Aria says, her voice barely above a whisper.

Turning to her, Director McLean's voice is firm. "Find him, Aria," she commands, each word a mixture of order and desperation.

Giving her a silent nod, Aria turns and walks away, a lone warrior following the blood trail of a fallen comrade.

Kirsty's gaze lingers on her before she, McLean, and the others venture toward the ominous hole in the wall. "Stay sharp," McLean murmurs to Kirsty, her voice a mix of caution and courage.

The group advances, edging closer to a looming store room. The dim illumination from the corridor casts elongated shadows that dance ominously against the stacked boxes and machinery inside. Their footsteps lead them deeper into the room.

"There." Kirsty's hand points towards the looming silhouette of an opening. A broken hole in the wall that McLean and Kirsty begin guiding the others toward.

It is as they step through, that the chilling discovery of the bombs unfolds.

"God, no..." Kirsty's whisper, sharp and haunting, pierces the silence. Twenty barrels of ammonium nitrate, their deadly composition laid bare, connected by a sinister network of wires.

"This is... this is meant to bring down the entire building," McLean says, her voice a haunting whisper that mirrors the chilling revelation.

"The whole area," Kirsty adds.

"I need to warn them," McLean mutters, the realization cold, biting. She pulls out her phone, dials the SWAT team. "We have bombs," she says the second it's answered, "a whole tunnel lined with ammonium nitrate right underneath us. Clear the perimeter now!"

———

PETER'S labored breathing haunts the corridors of the George Bush Center for Intelligence. Ayoub's Benelli and the screams that come with it provide the occasional interlude.

Every corner Peter turns, the eerie sight of slaughter

intensifies, bodies strewn everywhere, the walls covered in blood, every room a silent witness to a chaos that defies understanding.

His side, bleeding and throbbing with pain, serves as a stark reminder of the grim reality of the battlefield he's traversing, a far cry from the sanitised corridors of power and intelligence that they were only minutes ago. In these haunted offices, the clandestine, overseas war against jihad has come home.

A woman, shaking and in shock, holds her knees underneath a desk when the ominous silhouette of Ayoub looms into view. Time contracts for her, every second a stretched eternity where life and death are separated by the thinnest of margins. Ayoub's combat boots come to a stop next to the desk and the shotgun's lethal muzzle is aimed at her, the woman clenching her eyelids shut.

But death is held at bay by the swift and unexpected flight of a knife, its trajectory precise, its impact lethal. The weapon doesn't quite find its intended mark, Ayoub's neck, but it does strike him in the leg, planting itself in his thigh, stopping the shot and temporarily stunning him.

The world spins into havoc as Peter lunges at Ayoub, landing on top of him. The gas mask is ripped away, exposing the vulnerable human beneath the terrifying assailant. Every blow, every hit that rains down, is powered by the searing need to find Michael, to rip away the layers of mystery.

"Where is he? Where's Michael?" The plea, desperate and haunting, echoes the unbearable torment of a father severed from his son amidst a nightmare.

Ayoub, though, is resilient and malevolent. He turns the tables with a savage knee to Peter's wounded side. The pain, white-hot and blinding, is an unsparing reminder of the brutal reality of the battlefield, where mercy and ruthlessness are estranged companions. Before he knows it, Peter is the one on his back and Ayoub now stands over him.

"You know," Ayoub sneers, the cold muzzle of the shotgun pointed at Peter's vulnerable form, "he said we weren't to kill you. Had to leave you to one of them. But they're not here."

Death, imminent, is, however, held at bay by the swift intervention of a solitary gunshot that pierces the chaos. Ayoub, his reign of terror brutally brought to an end, collapses, a hole in the side of his head.

Peter, trembling and gasping, turns to meet the steady gaze of Paul Bennett. In the haunted corridors, amidst the grotesque dance of violence and survival, it is his pistol, smoking and resolute, that decides things. Bennett is a lighthouse amidst a storm.

Reaching Peter, he offers him his hand, lifting Peter from the cold ground that is stained with his blood.

"We need to get out of here," Bennett urges.

"The building's locked down," Peter responds in a ghostly whisper.

"There's another way out," Bennett assures him.

"The tunnel?"

"No. Another."

With Bennett leading the way, they move to a corner of the building, where a sole emergency exit is unblocked, the blast shield open the other side. They burst out of it onto a loading bay at the back of the building, the two men stepping into the tepid embrace of the sunlight. The blaring sirens of emergency responses fill the air as Bennett, with a blend of urgency and precision, ushers Peter into a waiting car, before getting into the driver's side.

As they drive off, the rearview mirror reflects a haunting tableau—the grandeur of the building, such a bastion of the free world, is now a prisoner of an unseen terror.

———

HEAVY BREATHING and hurried footsteps fill the tunnel. Director McLean and Kirsty Lang form a vanguard for the scared, but determined group they lead. Every eye is wide, every breath thick with the mingled taste of fear and the stale air of the underground passage.

The further they get from the grim gallery of meticulously placed explosives, the easier their breathing becomes. Each barrel, silent and menacing, paints a haunting narrative of impending destruction, a sinister countdown to an unfathomable catastrophe.

Passing the inert generator, they emerge through the tear in the sewer wall. Further along, daylight shines down from an open manhole, a ladder leading up to it.

"There," Kirsty says, pointing at the light.

They soon reach it, and with McLean and Kirsty manning the bottom of it, the trembling contingent makes their desperate ascent up the rusted ladder, the cold grip of fear momentarily eased by the tangible nearness of escape.

Rapid footsteps make them turn toward the hole in the

wall. Aria Patel, her face a mix of angst and bewilderment, comes swiftly towards them.

"I couldn't find him," she tells them. "But the other gunman is dead. Shot in the head. It must have been Peter."

Within the concrete confines of the underground, the three women think about it, an eerie silence washing over them.

Then the world erupts.

A roar, devastating and absolute, shatters the morbid silence. The ground quakes, walls shudder, and in the sewer, the unseen explosion is felt as a violent tremor that almost knocks them off their feet. A mile away from the core of the blast, they are rocked, but not shattered; shaken, not obliterated.

Above, the iconic edifice of the George Bush Center for Intelligence, a monolith of espionage and power, faces an apocalyptic demise. Floors collapse, the proud structure implodes, sending a plume of smoke and debris skyward. Windows shatter, sending a rain of glass glittering downwards like a perverse spectacle of glittering fireworks.

The building's hallowed corridors are consumed in the cataclysm. Every corner, every room, surrenders to the unrelenting force of annihilation.

America watches. The nation, bound in a collective gasp, witnesses the chilling spectacle unfold—the very heart of its intelligence apparatus, reduced to smoldering ruins, a cutting betrayal reverberating the vulnerability of even the mightiest bastions.

In the silent aftermath of destruction, amidst the rising smoke and settling dust, Kirsty Lang, Director McLean, Aria

Patel, and the shaken survivors encapsulate the coming reality of the post-apocalyptic dawn. Amidst the rubble and the ruins, in the resounding silence of a sanctuary violated, a new chapter of defiant resilience and haunting vulnerability has been birthed.

THIRTY-SIX

THE DEAFENING BLAST OF THE EXPLOSION ROCKS the car violently. Peter's head snaps around, eyes widening as they lock onto the terrifying spectacle at their rear—a monolithic cloud of smoke ascending angrily, obscuring the skyline.

"I'm sure everyone got out," Bennett says, his voice a low, steady anchor amidst the unsettling chorus of wailing sirens that immediately begin to fill the air outside.

The two men are silent for a moment. Peter's gaze, still locked on the mushrooming smoke, is pulled away as Bennett's voice tears through the silence.

"It's Aria," Bennett confesses sharply. "She's the traitor."

Peter's eyes lock onto Bennett, disbelief and confusion painting his features. "What?"

"Everything, it circles back to her," Bennett continues, his voice laced with a toxic mix of bitterness and revelation. "Ben and I, we had our suspicions from the beginning."

"Aria is the traitor?"

"Aria and Jimmy Harrison, they were involved," Bennett's words slash through the air, every syllable a testimony to an intricate dance of betrayal and revelation. "Kara Tate was beginning to figure it out. That's why I had to get her away."

"Kara?"

"Yes," Bennett replies. "She's here. Waiting for you."

The car comes to an abrupt stop outside a nice house in a nice suburb. Peter instantly recognizes it as Ben Knight's house.

"Come on," Bennett says as he opens the car door. "She's inside."

Peter lifts himself out, his whole body protesting in ripping, burning pain. They reach the front porch. Bennett's fingers wrap tightly around the key as he turns it in the lock, his knuckles white as the door swings open.

"She's in the living room," Bennett says, nodding in its direction.

Peter staggers across the hallway, and when he reaches the doorway, he realizes he's been fooled.

The living room, shrouded in ominous shadows, reveals Kara Tate—her wrists bound, eyes reflecting silent terror. Beside her, equally imprisoned, sits Pamela Bennett.

Peter's voice, trembling yet defiant, cuts through the eerie silence. "But—"

The unfinished sentence hangs in the air, a haunting prelude to the electrifying jolt of Bennett's taser. Electric tendrils snake through Peter's body, each volt erupting in silent screams and unuttered revelations. He collapses, the world spiralling into a haunting dance of shadows and silence, until unconsciousness envelopes him completely.

THE DAY IS SINISTERLY quiet as Musa, pulls up to a nondescript workshop nestled between towering buildings. With a deep breath, he unlocks the door and steps into the silent darkness beyond, his phone in hand displaying the live feed from the cells.

The image on the screen shows Mayu sitting against the cold wall of her cell, her eyes a mix of defiance and despair. And for Michael, he seems to be asleep on his cot, a coat concealing his form.

Musa, equipped with a Taser X26P dart gun, descends the wooden staircase into the basement. The air is chillingly stagnant; it reeks of despair. Reaching the cell doors, he calls out, his voice sharp, "Get up against the back wall!"

A silence, then Mayu's shadow stretches across her cell, but Michael remains still.

"Michael, get up!" Musa commands, one eye on the screen of his phone. "It's time to meet you dad. Time to look him in the eyes as you die."

"He's been really sick," Mayu's voice filters through the oppressive air.

Unswayed, Musa thrusts open the door to Michael's cell, the taser steady in his hand as he shoots the darts into the coat. But in that split second, movement to his left, from beneath the camera's blind spot, catches his peripheral vision.

He whirls around too late.

A figure, swift and brutal, crashes into him. The brick in Michael's hand comes down with the unforgiving force of days of pent-up fury. It makes contact, and Musa is painted in a storm of red dust, slumping to the floor of the cell, unconscious.

Victory and trepidation fuse in the silence. Michael's breath is heavy, the aftershocks of the confrontation pulsating through the silent air. Musa's phone, its screen now a flickering dance of fractured light, lies beside the defeated captor.

Michael snatches it up. He first tries Peter's phone—but the call dissipates into the ether, unanswered. Next, he tries Kirsty Lang's from memory—a bridge, a lifeline in the engulfing chaos.

"Hello?" comes Kirsty's voice, a familiar anchor in the tumultuous storm of captivity and betrayal.

Relief, sharp and profound, courses through Michael. "It's me, Michael."

"Michael?! Oh my God. Are you okay?"

"Yes. But that doesn't matter. I've got one of them. I'm using his phone," his voice is a mix of victory and apprehension.

"Michael?" Kirsty's voice trembles. "Oh, God, it's so good to hear your voice."

"I need to know where Dad is, Kirsty," urgency, raw and unfiltered, colors every syllable.

A pause, heavy with difficult truths. Then, "Michael, your dad... he was last seen inside Langley before... before it blew up. The entire building is gone, Michael."

"No," Michael states firmly. "He's not gone. This guy just said we're going to meet my dad. That means they have him."

"Okay then. Let me think." Kirsty's voice, a mix of

anxiety and revelation, cuts through Michael's resolute denial. "You said you're using his phone now, right?"

"Yeah."

"Then I might be able to do something. It might just help find your dad."

———

PETER'S AWAKENING IS BRUTAL, every sense heightened, every nerve ending on fire. The sensory overload is a harsh accompaniment to the stiff soreness that binds his body. Ropes, biting and unyielding, mark their cruel outline against his flesh. With each attempt to move, their grip tightens, a constant reminder of his newfound captivity.

As his vision swims into focus, the contours of Ben Knight's living room emerge from the haze of pain and disorientation. Kara Tate is beside him. Her eyes, once fiery and untamable, now reflect a mix of dread and resilience. Pamela Bennett, a figure of enigmatic grace even in captivity, completes the haunting trio of prisoners, sitting the other side of Peter in the same, rope bound, status.

Before he can piece together the jarring puzzle of captivity and betrayal, Paul Bennett's voice, a sinister mix of mockery and ominous delight, pierces the unnerving silence.

"Ah, you're awake," he says.

Peter's gaze, piercing and defiant, is met with Bennett's sinister amusement.

Pointing at Pamela, the gesture an ominous prelude to revelation, Bennett asks, "Have you met my mother? Or should I say my adoptive mother. Not that the adoption was legal in any way. I believe that it would violate several human trafficking laws these days."

Pamela, a silhouette of dignified silence amidst the storm of accusation, bears Bennett's piercing gaze with enigmatic calm.

Then his eyes are back on Peter.

"You don't even recognize me as the boy you picked up from the ground that day?" Bennett's voice is a chilling blend of mockery and sinister delight. "Ben and I were afraid you'd recognize me."

Frowning, Peter murmurs, "Max Harrison?"

"Got it in one," Bennett retorts, the sinister symphony of unveiled truths reaching a crescendo.

A wave of confusion crashes through Peter. "You're Max Harrison?"

"Ah, recognition at last," Bennett retorts, his voice laced with sardonic pleasure. "But let me make it clearer for you, Peter."

The room, thick with tension, listens as Bennett weaves his tale, every word, every sentence, a horrifying piece of a jigsaw puzzle none had expected.

"Back in 2007," Bennett begins, his voice steady, each word measured, "Ben Knight was supposed to kill me. But he couldn't. He saw a child, not the son of the terrorist you were all hunting."

Peter's breath hitches, everyone's gaze riveted on Bennett —this new entity before them. A boy turned specter, a child turned enemy, an ally turned traitor.

"He and his sister here, a child psychologist, they spirited me away," Bennett continues, his voice as cold as his eyes, devoid of warmth, of humanity. "Fake papers, a new identity, Max Harrison becomes Paul Bennett. Raised in the obscurity of Montana. I was their dirty little secret," Bennett's voice lowers, the menace in his tone palatable. His eyes, cold orbs of hatred, bore into Peter. "Hidden away. But I never forgot. Never forgot what you people did to me. What you took from me."

The room, though silent, vibrates with the unspoken horrors, the unsung victims of wars fought in shadows.

"Eight years ago, at college, Jimmy found me," Bennett divulges, his eyes gleaming with the sinister revelation. "Ever since then, we've been plotting, waiting for the right moment."

It is then that the sinister melody of Bennett's phone breaks the chilling silence, an ominous prelude to the unfolding storm of unveiled truths. "Ah, that'll be Jimmy now," he says as he answers the call.

The voice on the other end, however, is not that of his brother. It is chilling and unfamiliar, and it escalates the everything. "No, not brother," Michael Black's voice fills the line. "Retribution."

Right on cue, sirens wail in the distance, their shrill crescendo piercing the tense atmosphere of the room. Panic flashes in Bennett's eyes. Each wailing siren a harbinger of his impending doom.

Realizing he has no time, Bennett turns the aim of his SIG Sauer on Peter.

Peter's muscles tense, every fiber of his being screaming in silent rebellion. Bennett's gun, cold and ominous, hovers inches from his face, the scent of oil and metal invading Peter's nostrils.

He's not done fighting; not yet.

Peter lunges, his body still attached to the chair, yet his spirit as untethered as a storm. His elbow, a weapon forged from pain and betrayal, slams into Bennett's wrist. The gunshot meant for his skull embeds into the ceiling, the echoing bang a testament to Peter's untamed defiance. Bennett howls, the gun clattering impotently to the floor.

With the chair as an extension of his body, Peter hurls himself at Bennett. Bound, but a soul unbroken, every head-butt, every collision of bone against bone, a symphony of retribution and pain.

Bennett, caught in the storm, grunts, his face a canvas upon which Peter paints his vengeance. The room, once silent and ominous, resonates with a visceral orchestra of impacts.

The door crashes open. Aria Patel, McLean, SWAT police officers—they flood the room, their weapons an unspoken threat against the backdrop of the confrontation.

Bennett's eyes, wild and frantic, dart between Peter and the officers. The impending end, undeniable and nigh, seeps into his bones. Yet, Peter's onslaught does not yield.

With the chair clattering against the floor with each movement, Peter's assault is the pounding rhythm of unsung pain and betrayal reverberating in the silent room. Aria and McLean, their grips firm yet urgent, attempt to pull him from the storm's epicenter. But Peter is lost to the tempest, each blow, each impact an echo of the storm raging within.

As they finally pull him away with the help of the police officers, Bennett's bloody, beaten face is the last image before darkness claims him. Michael's name, a whispered plea, resonates in his head, and then, nothing as he passes into an exhausted unconsciousness.

EPILOGUE

PETER'S EYES FLUTTER OPEN TO A STARK WHITE ceiling, a sharp contrast to the shadowed danger of his recent ordeal. The beeping of the heart monitor punctuates the silence, each beep an affirmation of life. He tries to move but finds his body unresponsive, every muscle aching, a painful reminder of the trauma he has endured.

Michael's voice, steady yet tinged with relief, breaks through the silence. "Dad, you're awake."

Peter's gaze shifts, meeting the relieved eyes of his son. Beside Michael, Mayu hovers, her eyes shimmering with unsung tears.

"You gave us a scare, Peter." Mayu's voice is soft, yet carries the weight of a storm of emotions she's barely containing.

Peter tries to speak but his voice is a ragged whisper, the words struggling to escape. "What happened?"

"You lost almost a liter of blood," Michael informs him, his voice thick with unsaid emotions.

Before Peter can process the weight of his son's words, the door opens and Kara Tate steps into the room. Her eyes, carrying the visible effects of the silent war they've just traversed, meet Peter's. A mutual, unspoken acknowledgment of the journey through shadows they've both endured passes between them.

Michael and Mayu exchange a glance before stepping out of the room, leaving Peter and Kara in a silence broken only by the steady beeping of the heart monitor.

"I should thank you, Kara." Peter's voice is soft, but each word is laden with profound gratitude.

"For what?" Kara asks, the stoicism in her voice failing to mask the undercurrent of emotions.

"If you hadn't dug so deep, hadn't found out about David Harrison... we'd never have connected it all back to Bennett." Peter's eyes hold hers.

Kara's gaze doesn't waver. In the silence, amidst the beeping monitors and the stark hospital surroundings, she leans forward and the two lock in a firm embrace, the silent room reverberating with the unsung narrative of warriors traversing the ominous dance of betrayal and alliance.

———

ONE WEEK LATER.

THE SECURE CONFERENCE room inside the 'temporary' CIA headquarters buzzes with low murmurs. Officials, agents, and analysts fill the seats around a massive polished oak table, the room's dim lighting giving everything a serious, almost spectral ambiance. On the screen at the front, a series of images and classified documents shift in a continuous slide, showcasing the events that led to the shooting of Sonya Kahn.

Peter sits rigidly, hands clasped on the table, his face a mask of stoicism. Each slide is a reminder of one of the most challenging chapters of his life, where choices were made in mere milliseconds, and every action had consequences.

An analyst stands up, adjusting his glasses. "As you can all see from the presented evidence and various eyewitness testimonies, Officer Black acted under extreme duress and within the bounds of the protocol when he neutralized Sonya Kahn."

Director Sandy McLean interrupts, "And may I remind everyone that Kahn was heavily involved in several covert operations against our own, directly leading to the loss of both American lives and the lives of our allies."

Murmurs of agreement echo through the room. A senior official speaks up. "While it's regrettable that protocol was broken and that a life was lost, in the larger context, Officer Black's actions likely saved countless others."

There's a pause, the gravity of the situation weighing heavily. Then another official adds, "Not to mention the heroism of Officer Black's subsequent actions. His contribution on the fateful day of the attack likely saved the lives of many of our colleagues."

The room goes silent, every eye now turned to Director McLean. She scans the room, her gaze finally settling on Peter. "In light of all the presented evidence and the unanimous consensus of this board, Officer Black is officially exonerated for the shooting of Sonya Kahn."

A collective sigh of relief ripples through the room. Some pat Peter on the back, congratulating him, while others exchange nods of approval. One of those to nod is Aria Patel.

Once the room clears, only Director McLean and Peter remain. She approaches him, her stern demeanor softening just slightly. "Peter, you've been through hell and back," she begins, her voice soft yet firm. "Not just with the Sonya Kahn incident, but everything that followed. And losing Ben... that was a blow we all felt deeply." She pauses, giving the weight of Ben Knight's loss its moment. "You've shown remarkable resilience and dedication."

Peter's eyes momentarily fill with the pain of loss. "Ben was a good man. He showed that with saving Max Harrison. It's a shame it never worked out."

"He should have shared the information," McLean interjects.

"But he went against orders. In Ben's mind, he was protecting the boy, then the man. He was protecting Paul. It's why they killed him early. Only Ben would have been able to make the connections once we got to New York. I'll miss him."

McLean offers Peter a rare smile. "You've done well, Peter. Exceptionally well."

"Thank you for your words, Director."

And with that, Peter leaves the conference room, the weight of the past and the sorrow of losing a friend and comrade finally lifting, making the path ahead clearer than ever.

———

ONE MONTH LATER.

THE GRAND BALLROOM of the Waldorf Astoria is a blend of twinkling lights, shimmering dresses, and bubbling champagne. Journalists, editors, and media magnates from all over New York have come together to honor the year's best in journalism. The most awaited moment of the evening is just about to happen: the award for the "Story of the Year."

"And the award goes to..."—the presenter's voice elongates the pause, thickening the air with suspense—" Kara Tate for her unforgettable piece on 'Running with the Wolf Pack.'"

A round of applause breaks out, the clapping so thunderous it's almost overwhelming. Kara, elegant in a deep blue gown, gracefully walks to the stage. As she takes the award, her heart beats fast, not from the weight of the trophy, a gold pen on a plinth, but from the weight of the memories associated with the story.

"Thank you," she starts, her voice steady, eyes glistening with unshed tears. "This story was the hardest I've ever had to write, not just because of the danger involved but because it was deeply personal. It's an honor to share it with the world."

She thanks her editor and colleagues and takes a moment to remember those lost along the way. As she walks off the stage, holding the award, the applause continues to ring in her ears.

———

THE AFTER-PARTY IS in full swing when Kara's editor, Heidi, approaches her. "That was a powerful speech," she says, clinking her champagne flute with Kara's.

"Thanks, Heidi. Couldn't have done it without you," she replies, her mind seemingly elsewhere.

Seeing her distant gaze, Heidi asks, "You okay?"

Kara smiles. "Just a lot on my mind."

It's then that her phone vibrates with a text. When she spots who it is and reads the message, the smile increases. She looks around the room, filled with laughter and chatter, and then back at her editor. "Heidi, I think I need to go."

She nods, understanding. "Take the night, Kara. You deserve it."

Exiting the hotel, the cool New York breeze greets her. As she steps away from the entrance, a familiar figure approaches from the shadows. Peter, looking dapper in a suit, walks up to her, a hint of a smile playing on his lips.

Without a word, Kara steps into his embrace, and they share a tender kiss, a moment of peace in the chaotic tapestry of their lives.

Hailing a cab, they slip into the back seat, leaving the glitz and glamor of the award night behind. The taxi pulls away, the city lights reflecting on its glossy surface.

The streets of New York pass by in a blur as the two of them, hand in hand, head into the unknown night—their futures uncertain but their bond unbreakable.

Don't miss GHOST OPERATIVE. The riveting sequel in the Peter Black Thriller series.

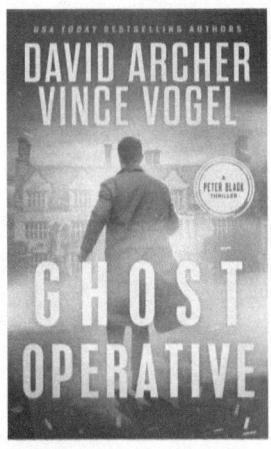

Scan the QR code below to purchase GHOST OPERATIVE.

Or go to: righthouse.com/ghost-operative

NOTE: flip to the very end to read an exclusive sneak peak...

DON'T MISS ANYTHING!

If you want to stay up to date on all new releases in this series, with these authors, or with any of our new deals, you can do so by joining our newsletters below.

In addition, you will immediately gain access to our entire *Right House VIP Library,* which includes many riveting Mystery and Thriller novels for your enjoyment.

righthouse.com/email

(Easy to unsubscribe. No spam. Ever.)

ALSO BY DAVID ARCHER

Up to date books can be found at:
www.righthouse.com/david-archer

ROGUE THRILLERS
Gates of Hell (Book 1)
Hell's Fury (Book 2)

JACOB HUNTER THRILLERS
The Kyiv File (Book 1)
The Bogota File (Book 2)

PETER BLACK THRILLERS
Burden of the Assassin (Book 1)
The Man Without A Face (Book 2)
Unpunished Deeds (Book 3)
Hunter Killer (Book 4)
Silent Shadows (Book 5)
The Last Run (Book 6)
Dark Corners (Book 7)
Ghost Operative (Book 8)

ALEX MASON THRILLERS
Odin (Book 1)
Ice Cold Spy (Book 2)
Mason's Law (Book 3)
Assets and Liabilities (Book 4)
Russian Roulette (Book 5)

Executive Order (Book 6)
Dead Man Talking (Book 7)
All The King's Men (Book 8)
Flashpoint (Book 9)
Brotherhood of the Goat (Book 10)
Dead Hot (Book 11)
Blood on Megiddo (Book 12)
Son of Hell (Book 13)

NOAH WOLF THRILLERS
Code Name Camelot (Book 1)
Lone Wolf (Book 2)
In Sheep's Clothing (Book 3)
Hit for Hire (Book 4)
The Wolf's Bite (Book 5)
Black Sheep (Book 6)
Balance of Power (Book 7)
Time to Hunt (Book 8)
Red Square (Book 9)
Highest Order (Book 10)
Edge of Anarchy (Book 11)
Unknown Evil (Book 12)
Black Harvest (Book 13)
World Order (Book 14)
Caged Animal (Book 15)
Deep Allegiance (Book 16)
Pack Leader (Book 17)
High Treason (Book 18)
A Wolf Among Men (Book 19)
Rogue Intelligence (Book 20)
Alpha (Book 21)

Rogue Wolf (Book 22)
Shadows of Allegiance (Book 23)
In the Grip of Darkness (Book 24)

SAM PRICHARD MYSTERIES
The Grave Man (Book 1)
Death Sung Softly (Book 2)
Love and War (Book 3)
Framed (Book 4)
The Kill List (Book 5)
Drifter: Part One (Book 6)
Drifter: Part Two (Book 7)
Drifter: Part Three (Book 8)
The Last Song (Book 9)
Ghost (Book 10)
Hidden Agenda (Book 11)

SAM AND INDIE MYSTERIES
Aces and Eights (Book 1)
Fact or Fiction (Book 2)
Close to Home (Book 3)
Brave New World (Book 4)
Innocent Conspiracy (Book 5)
Unfinished Business (Book 6)
Live Bait (Book 7)
Alter Ego (Book 8)
More Than It Seems (Book 9)
Moving On (Book 10)
Worst Nightmare (Book 11)
Chasing Ghosts (Book 12)
Serial Superstition (Book 13)

CHANCE REDDICK THRILLERS
Innocent Injustice (Book 1)
Angel of Justice (Book 2)
High Stakes Hunting (Book 3)
Personal Asset (Book 4)

CASSIE MCGRAW MYSTERIES
What Lies Beneath (Book 1)
Can't Fight Fate (Book 2)
One Last Game (Book 3)
Never Really Gone (Book 4)

ALSO BY VINCE VOGEL

Up to date books can be found at:

www.righthouse.com/vince-vogel

PETER BLACK THRILLERS

Burden of the Assassin (Book 1)

The Man Without A Face (Book 2)

Unpunished Deeds (Book 3)

Hunter Killer (Book 4)

Silent Shadows (Book 5)

The Last Run (Book 6)

Dark Corners (Book 7)

Ghost Operative (Book 8)

JACK SHERIDAN MYSTERIES

A Cross to Bear (Book 1)

The Clay House (Book 2)

Into The Woods (Book 3)

The End is Nigh (Book 4)

A Step Into The Dark (Book 5)

Holier Than Thou (Book 6)

Streetlight City (Book 7)

An Offering for Sin (Book 8)

A Lark on the Wind (Book 9)

A Glass Darkly (Book 10)

Never Came Home (Book 11)

ALEX DORRING THRILLER

Agent 192 (Book 1)

The Hitman's Death (Book 2)

The Wrong Man (Book 3)

Who Dares Wins (Book 4)

The Highwaymen (Book 5)

The Ring (Book 6)

ABOUT US

Right House is an independent publisher created by authors for readers. We specialize in Action, Thriller, Mystery, and Crime novels.

If you enjoyed this novel, then there is a good chance you will like what else we have to offer! Please stay up to date by using any of the links below.

Join our mailing lists to stay up to date -->
righthouse.com/email
Visit our website --> righthouse.com
Contact us --> contact@righthouse.com

 facebook.com/righthousebooks

x.com/righthousebooks

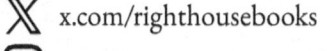 instagram.com/righthousebooks

EXCLUSIVE SNEAK PEAK OF...

GHOST OPERATIVE

PROLOGUE

CHRISSIE JACKSON, EIGHT, HUDDLES IN THE corner of her mom and dad's ensuite bathroom, knees pulled tight to her chest. The tiles are cold against her back as her wide eyes fixate on the locked door. Mom's voice resonates in her head, a stern command laced with fear: "Stay here, honey, no matter what."

Outside the door—men's grunts, the shuffle of feet, and the sounds of things breaking apart paint a scene she can't see but imagines.

A sudden thud against the door sends a jolt of fear through Chrissie's tiny body. Her hand flies to her mouth, muffling the scream that threatens to escape. Her breath comes in short, sharp gasps. *Bang!* The door rattles again, its hinges groaning under the weight of another impact. Chrissie flinches, squeezing her eyes shut. Each sound from outside—the thud of bodies hitting the wall, the muffled cries of struggle—tightens the knot of panic in her stomach. In this small, tiled room, Chrissie Jackson is alone with her fear, the sounds of the unseen fight just a terrifying sound-track to her imagination.

Then silence falls, like a suffocating blanket, the chaos of struggle abruptly cut off. Chrissie's heart thunders in her ears. It is the only sound she can hear. Then, footsteps—a slow, deliberate approach that freezes her blood stone cold in her veins.

The feet stop just outside the door, and time hangs still. Chrissie's tiny body trembles uncontrollably, fear clutching her throat so tightly she can barely breathe.

Then, a voice, soft, firm, slices through the thick air of dread. "It's okay, honey. You can unlock it." Relief crashes over Chrissie as she recognizes her mother's voice, yet the fear doesn't completely recede. With shaking hands, she fumbles with the lock, retreating as the door swings slowly open.

Catherine Jackson stands in the doorway, her soft eyes and friendly smile marred by the spray of blood that dots her face and clothing. Chrissie's eyes widen. "Mommy, you're bleeding."

Her mother's gaze drops to the red on her shirt. "It's okay, honey. It isn't Mommy's blood." Her voice is steady, but her hands tremble just slightly, betraying the effort behind her calm exterior. Catherine Jackson, once known by the CIA codename Ibliss, hasn't faced such a test in years—taking down three men single-handedly. It is a reminder of the life she thought she'd left behind.

Together, mother and daughter wash away the blood from Catherine's hands and face. Then, as Catherine changes into a hooded sweater she takes from the airing cupboard, she locks eyes with her daughter, her expression serious. "Now I need you to promise me something."

"What, Mommy?"

"I need you to keep your eyes closed as we walk out of the apartment."

Hand in hand, Chrissie obeys, her eyes squeezed shut, trusting her mother to guide her safely past whatever carnage lines the walls. "No peeping." Catherine's voice is gentle yet firm as they navigate the silent apartment, stepping around the smashed furniture and dead bodies.

As they pass the doorway to the kitchen, Catherine can't help glancing inside. Her heart aches as she spots the loafers of a man protruding from behind the breakfast bar—where he had been sitting when the first gunman had opened fire with his suppressed Beretta.

Outside, the cool air greets them, Catherine finally allowing her daughter to open her eyes. "Where's Daddy?" Chrissie's voice is hopeful, innocent.

"Daddy's gonna meet us there, honey." The lie tastes bitter on Catherine's tongue but is necessary for the time being.

Survival now dictates their every move. A painful journey is ahead of them, with only the fleeting promise of safety—a promise Catherine is determined to keep at any cost.

CHAPTER 1

BANGKOK PULSES WITH LIFE. THE STREETS TEEM with vendors selling street food, motorbikes weaving boldly through traffic, and towering skyscrapers casting long shadows over centuries-old temples. In the business district of Sukhumvit, suits and ties brush past saffron-robed Buddhist monks in a dance of life as old as the city itself.

Amid this vibrant chaos operates TransAtlantic Logistics (TAL), a front for the covert operations of the Central Intelligence Agency. From the outside, TAL fits seamlessly into the bustling business ecosystem of Bangkok, a multinational freight and logistics company specializing in the intricacies of international trade. Its office, nestled in the heart of Sukhumvit, buzzes with the mundane activities of logistics and supply chain management, a perfect cover for running a secret station in the heart of Southeast Asia.

It is here in Bangkok that Peter Black has spent the last six months as David James, international freight expert. He currently sits at his desk, poring over financial spreadsheets that tell a story only a select few can read—money laundering for a vast web of illicit traffickers that use Bangkok as a key transit point. Weapons, drugs, human organs, human beings—anything money can buy.

This is one of the perks of the job—that he gets to go after real scumbags. The types that trade people like cattle.

All around Peter, the Bangkok office is alive with the sounds of the seven other employees who conduct the cover work of TAL—logistics and freight. Only three of the ten people working there are actual CIA: Peter, Kirsty Lang, and the big boss, station commander Mark Deacon. It is they who conduct the real work of TAL under the guise of market research and business expansion.

Peter feels the look before he sees it. Glancing up from his desk, he spots Deacon staring at him from the doorway of his office.

"Hey, David," he calls the instant their eyes meet. "A moment, please."

The inside of Deacon's office mirrors the man himself—efficient, devoid of personal touch, yet not without a certain intimidation. The walls are bare save for a few framed photographs of Deacon in various international locales, props that add to his cover as an international logistics expert.

"Sit," Deacon commands, not looking up from the file spread before him.

Peter does so, taking a seat in the chair in front of Deacon's desk.

Now Deacon looks up, his gaze sharp. "Catherine Jackson, codename Ibliss," he starts, the name hanging between them like a live wire. "She was part of the Fallen Angel program with you, wasn't she?"

"Yes, we were in the program together." Memories, brief and violent, flicker in the back of his mind.

"What contact have you had with her recently?"

"None. We don't talk."

"Do you know what she was doing at least?"

"Living the life of a civilian with her husband and little girl, working in technology and finance."

"Except when she was doing a little freelance for us at the agency," Deacon adds.

"That was helping Ben Knight out. Hardly freelance."

Deacon continues, "Well, her husband and three other men were found dead in her apartment yesterday. None of the three men have been identified, but they're believed to be ex-Special Forces, probably working freelance as mercenaries. It's believe that they shot the husband and there followed some type of attack in which all three were killed. She and her daughter are now missing."

The news hits Peter like a punch. "Missing?" he repeats, trying to mask his reaction, to keep his professional façade intact.

Deacon's tone leaves no room for argument. "If she contacts you, you let me know."

Peter frowns. The likelihood of Catherine reaching out to him seems remote at best. "I wouldn't think she'd contact me. That is if she's gone underground."

Deacon snuffs, a dismissive gesture that irks Peter more than he cares to admit. "I guess not. You Fallen Angels never really knew each other. Not exactly colleagues. Most of you were no more than psychopaths let loose in the world with no other orders than to kill."

The words are meant to provoke, and they do, pissing Peter off more than he cares to admit. Yet his expression remains stoic, a skill honed from years of operating in the shadows. They stare at each other, a silent battle of wills unfolding in the space between them, the past six months having seen a lot of these little moments of attrition.

"Is that all?" Peter's voice is cool, detached.

"That's all," Deacon confirms, his tone final.

However, that isn't all. As Peter opens the door, preparing to exit the stifling atmosphere of Deacon's office, an interruption comes. The office receptionist stands at the threshold, a fist raised to knock. "There's a young man here asking for David," she informs them, her voice carrying an undercurrent of uncertainty.

"Where is he?" Peter asks.

She points toward the lobby, where, amidst the hustle of the office, stands Michael, Peter's twenty-two-year-old son. Though initially pleased to see him for the first time in almost half a year, Peter is mortified. He feels a rush of emotions, not least of which is a profound embarrassment as his cheeks flush a deep shade of red.

"Is that your son?" Deacon asks in an undertone as he stands up from his desk.

"Oh, God no," Peter mutters under his breath, striding from the office toward Michael.

"Hey, Dad!" Michael's voice booms across the space, holding his arms out wide. "Surprise!"

Peter embraces him, pulling him in tighter than you'd

expect and seething into his ear, "David James doesn't have any children, numb nuts."

"I'm sure it won't matter," Michael whispers back.

"How'd you find me?"

"My girlfriend's a computer genius, remember?" Michael's reply is nonchalant, as if tracking down a CIA operative in Bangkok is nothing out of the ordinary.

In the background, Deacon watches, his expression hardening into a grim mask.

CHAPTER 2

EMERGING ONTO THE STREETS OF BANGKOK, THE heat wraps around Peter and Michael like a thick, sticky blanket. "Christ, Mikey!" Peter can't help but exclaim. "You could have warned me."

"I haven't seen you in six months. I thought it would be a surprise," Michael responds, the grin on his face wide and unapologetic.

"It's certainly that," Peter concedes, shaking his head. "You do know what that was, right? That office?"

"Oh yeah," Michael says, his grin never faltering.

"Right, and still you thought you'd drop right in?"

"I had to."

"You had to?"

"Mayu could only track down where you were working," Michael replies, still grinning. "Not where you lived."

"And you thought it—"

They are suddenly interrupted when someone leaps at Peter from behind. Decades of training kick in—Peter spins around, his hand reaching for the knife hidden in his waist-band, ready to confront the threat, heart racing, prepared for anything. That is until he sees the smiling face of Mayu, Michael's girlfriend, her arms thrown wide in a gesture of greeting. "Peter?!" she exclaims, joy overtaking her features.

"David," he corrects gently, even as he pulls her in for a big old hug.

Minutes later, they find themselves seated in a quaint eatery nestled by the Chao Phraya River, the bustling noise of the city a distant backdrop to the intimate setting. The table is a colorful array of Thai cuisine—Khao Soy, a rich, creamy curry, the tangy zest of Pad Thai noodles, and the rich, light brown sauce of chicken Panang.

"The food here is awesome," Michael says, his eyes bright, taking in the feast before them.

"Yeah. These little local eateries are always the best," Peter agrees.

After a moment of indulging in the food, Peter's expression grows serious. "There's something I need to tell you, Mikey. It's about Catherine... Ibliss."

Michael pauses eating. "What about her? Is she okay?"

Peter shakes his head. "Her husband and three other men were found dead in her apartment. Catherine and her little girl... they're missing."

Mayu's fork halts midway to her mouth. "Missing? But how? Michael told me she's one of the best assassins he ever saw."

"She is," Peter says. "So if she's gone underground, whatever is after her must be deadly serious."

"What are you going to do?" Michael asks.

"Not much I can. My boss made it pretty clear—if she contacts me, I'm to let him know immediately."

"But you're going to look for her, right? We can help."

Peter gives his son a stern look. "Mikey, whatever Catherine's into, it's extremely dangerous. I don't want either of you caught up in this."

Michael's frown deepens. "But she's our friend, Dad. We can't just sit by doing nothing."

Peter takes a deep breath. "Listen, if Ibliss doesn't want to be found, no one will find her. Not you, not me, not anyone. Catherine is... she's exceptionally gifted at vanishing. If she truly does need our help, she'll find *us*."

Mayu nods slowly. "Peter's right, Michael. If anyone can handle this, it's Catherine Jackson."

Michael leans back, the tension easing from his shoulders. "Okay," he finally concedes, albeit reluctantly. "We'll wait. But if she reaches out—"

"We'll be ready," Peter assures him.

CHAPTER 3

PETER STEPS BACK INTO THE OFFICE, ONLY TO FIND Deacon waiting for him in the doorway to his office.

"David," he calls out, "my office."

Deacon is already closing the blinds when Peter enters. "Lock the door," he tells Peter.

Once he has, the office now drenched in shadow, the two men move to the back of the room, where an ornate dress mirror commands attention. With a precise push to its top right corner, a subtle click breaks the silence, and the mirror swings noiselessly outward on a hinge. On the other side is a hidden chamber, very different from the office's façade of normalcy.

They move inside, Deacon shutting the mirrored door behind them. Within, the walls are alive with illuminated maps and screens, all of them painting a vivid picture of the illicit trade routes they're surveying.

This room they call the Bunker.

"What the hell were you thinking, Black? Letting your son waltz into our operation like that?"

Peter remains a picture of calm. "He surprised me. It wasn't planned and definitely won't happen again. Michael's... resourceful."

"Resourceful?" Deacon repeats. "This isn't a family reunion, Black. It's an undercover operation. Years of work, six months in Bangkok, all could be blown because you couldn't keep your personal life separate. Give me one good reason why I shouldn't write you up for this."

With a measured tone, Peter attempts to reason with him. "I absolutely understand the risks. And, trust me, it won't happen again. But writing a report, escalating this— it's not going to fix anything. It'll only draw more attention to a situation we've already contained."

"Contained?" Deacon rounds on him. "You call this contained? I have half a mind to pull you out of here myself. You know what's at stake! The networks we're after, the lives on the line!"

For the innumerable time, their eyes lock in a silent clash of wills. "I know exactly what's at stake," Peter asserts, his voice firm, resonant. "Better than most."

A heavy sigh escapes Deacon. "You're lucky I believe in the work more than I care for protocol. A report doesn't just go against you, it goes against all of us. But consider this your final warning, Black. Any more surprises, and it's not just a report you'll be worrying about."

Peter nods, understanding both the concession and the thinly veiled threat that accompanies it. "Understood. There won't be any more surprises."

The following silence is heavy but quickly broken into

by the shrill ring of the Bunker's telephone—hardwired to the station's secret line.

Both men freeze. This is only the third time anyone has called it in the six months they've been here. They exchange a glance before Deacon takes a seat and prepares to answer. The outside world, with all its heat and chaos, feels miles away as he braces for whatever comes next.

"Hello?" Deacon answers, his voice laced with caution, the receiver tight against his ear.

A voice, anxious yet determined, crackles through from the other end, "I don't have much time, so I will get straight to my point. I am a scientist with the Chinese government. The information I possess... it will stop chaos."

Deacon's skepticism is obvious. "Who am I speaking to? How did you get this number?"

Ignoring the questions, the caller presses on. "Names are irrelevant. What matters is the information I have. I'm coming to Thailand soon with my family for a vacation, and I don't want to return to China. Not myself—and not my family."

"What kind of information are we talking about?" Deacon cuts to the heart of the matter.

"It's not just what, but who. There are people on your own side who you think are friends, but they're not. They are working against you. In two days, I arrive in Thailand. I will be watched by members of the Chinese security services posing as my bodyguards, but there's a moment I can slip away from them—on Ko Pha Ngan, at the market. My watchers stay with my family... use my wife and son as leverage to ensure my compliance. I will have to..."

"How can we verify your claims?" Deacon cuts in, leaning forward.

"Verification will come. When we meet, I will provide evidence, a glimpse of what I hold. But full disclosure, the entirety of what I know and have, comes only after my family is safe. Safe in America."

"And if we decide to help you, what then? You're asking for a lot without much to go on."

A hint of desperation creeps into the scientist's voice. "I'm asking for sanctuary. In return, you gain an advantage that could tip the scales on a global level. I know the risks, but my family... their safety is my priority."

"If what you say holds truth, we'll find a way to meet on Ko Pha Ngan. But understand this: if this is a trap, there will be nowhere on this planet you can hide." Deacon's tone is deadly serious, leaving no room for misunderstanding.

There's a brief silence, then softly, "I understand. I will call you again on this number in two days when we arrive. That's when I will tell you when and where to meet in Ko Pha Ngan."

"We'll be there. Ensure your 'evidence' is compelling," Deacon replies with a nod to Peter.

"Thank you. This... it's more than just defection. It's about correcting a path that should never have been taken in the first place."

The second the scientist is done saying this, the line goes dead.

Peter and Deacon share a look that speaks volumes. This could be the break they've been waiting for—a major defection.

Deacon calls Kirsty Lang into the Bunker, and she soon enters. As they settle into their seats, the shock of bright pink in her otherwise jet-black hair glows under the strip lighting.

Deacon doesn't waste time. "We just got a call. A Chinese scientist claiming to hold world-changing information wants to defect. Says he's coming to Thailand with his family for a vacation in two days. Says he's gonna be with bodyguards."

Kirsty leans forward. "Sounds like it could be big. Only those critical to the CCP are afforded that kind of attention when they're abroad. But it also sounds exactly like the kind of bait someone would use if they wanted to draw us out."

Peter nods. "She's right. If this is a setup and we bite, we're not just blowing our cover; we're walking into a trap with our eyes wide open."

Deacon casts a dismissive glance at Peter. "And since when did you become an expert in operational security, Black? We need actionable intelligence, not paranoia."

Kirsty, ever the voice of reason, calmly interjects, "Actually, Peter has a point. We've managed to stay under the radar for six months. Rushing into this without considering the risks would be reckless."

"But let's not forget the reason we're here," Deacon says. "To gather intelligence. If there's even a chance this scientist is legitimate, we owe it to ourselves—and potentially countless others—to check it out." Exhaling a heavy sigh, he then adds, "That said, we will be proceeding with caution. Ko Pha Ngan is touristy enough to provide us some cover, but we'll need a solid exit strategy if things go south."

Kirsty, already steps ahead, nods in agreement. "I'll start working on the logistics. We can use tourist drones for aerial recon without drawing too much attention."

Deacon nods. "All right. Let's get to work. This might be the break we've been waiting for... or the trouble we've been dreading."

CHAPTER 4

THE DAY OF THE MEET, KO PHA NGAN THRUMS with the life of tourists and locals. Kirsty takes point on a Kawasaki Ninja ZX-6R, the hum of the engine a soft rumble in the late morning buzz. Waiting at the side of a busy road, she's vigilant, eyes scanning the flow of traffic, the casual lean of her body disguising the tension that grips her. A discreet earpiece keeps her connected to Peter and Deacon.

Setting off, she blends seamlessly into the traffic, all while keeping a protective watch over the car behind her, the one that ferries Peter and Deacon.

Unseen above, a drone glides silently, a ghostly sentinel on autopilot. Programmed to lock on to Kirsty's GPS signal, it hovers discreetly over them, high enough to escape notice yet omniscient.

Inside the air-conditioned car, Peter and Deacon sit in a bubble of cool silence as they move steadily along a narrow street lined with venders. The Phangnan Food Court looms ahead, a bustling hive of people, all writhing about under the harsh glare of the midday sun. Its sheet metal roof shelters a world unto itself—rows of stalls flanked by barbecues and woks, bursts of fire punctuating the air.

The team parks their vehicles at opposite ends of the market. Peter and Deacon, now on foot, have Kirsty shadowing them discreetly through the crowds. The smells are intoxicating, a heady mix of coconut milk, sizzling meats, and the tang of spices dancing through the air. The hustle and bustle of people moving around the plastic furniture creates a cacophony of voices, laughter, and the clatter of dishes. Above, fans dangle from the rafters, whirring futilely against the hot, thick air, doing little more than stirring the scents of a hundred meals into a fragrant whirlwind.

To Peter, Deacon and Kirsty, the setting is anything but casual. Their trained senses, wound tight, are attuned to the slightest anomaly; every burst of laughter or sudden movement is scrutinized and cataloged. The food court becomes a chessboard. Each person is a potential pawn, every shadow a place to hide. As they navigate toward the rendezvous point, their eyes search for the man who claims to hold the keys to averting a global catastrophe.

Last night, the scientist had called again. "I'll be at Phangan Food Court at one p.m., unless something goes wrong. The tables are numbered. I'll be on table one twenty-three. It's to the left of Joy's Kitchen. One o'clock, okay?"

He was very exact. And no, nothing had gone wrong. Because as Peter and Deacon walk through the food market, they spot a tall man in his thirties with neat hair and glasses occupying table 123, to the left of Joy's Kitchen. The clock hanging from the ceiling in the middle of the court has just chimed 13:00.

Kirsty has positioned herself to oversee table 123 and its approaches without being obvious. With practiced ease, she slips her phone from her pocket and activates the drone's feed, her eyes flicking across the screen to scan for any external surveillance. Confident, for the moment, that no unseen eyes are upon them—or at least none that she has detected—she slips the phone away. Her attention, razor-sharp, then returns to table 123, where the meeting is about to begin.

As Peter and Deacon take their seats opposite him, the man's anxiety is obvious. Sweat beads on his forehead, and his leg moves under the table in a constant, jittery rhythm. Around them, the food court lives and breathes the chaos of everyday life—dishes crash, arguments flare up, children's laughter pierces the air, and the fire from the woks leaps up as if trying to escape.

The scientist looks like he wants to leap up and escape too. His gaze flits nervously around, his pale complexion clear evidence of the risk he's taking in just being here with them. The boxed food on the table, meant for his family and their bodyguards, stands steaming in front of him.

He starts to speak, his voice barely rising above the ambient noise of the market. "I don't have much time," he begins, his eyes darting to the boxed food. "The information I have... it's critical to America, to the West, to everyone. But my family's safety comes first. They must be safe in America before I can share what I have to tell you... No, not tell. To *warn* you about."

"We can't move forward without knowing who we're dealing with," Deacon asserts, his gaze locked on the scientist. "Firstly, what's your name?"

The scientist hesitates, before eventually relenting. "Zhao Hang," he says quietly.

"And who is Zhao Hang?"

"I specialize in AI within a top-secret government program. But understand this—my full cooperation comes only after my family's safety is guaranteed in America."

"America needs to know what we're protecting you from, Zhao. We need proof of your claims about critical information," Deacon pushes.

Zhao's resolve hardens under the weight of Deacon's insistence. He reaches into his wallet, retrieving something concealed within a secret compartment. With deliberate care, he unfolds the paper, revealing a photograph that catches the sunlight drifting into the food court.

It shows Zhao alongside several other individuals, all clad in hard hats, standing within an immense underground chamber. The vast space, carved directly from the bedrock by machines, is illuminated by harsh, artificial lamps that cast long shadows behind each figure. The sheer size of the cavernous room suggests an endeavor of significant ambition and secrecy.

"This," Zhao begins, "is located ten miles beneath the earth's surface."

Deacon leans in. "What is it?" he asks, his eyes scanning the details of the image.

"A chamber large enough to accommodate the Eiffel Tower," Zhao states, allowing a brief moment of pride to color his tone. "That is where they have placed it."

"Placed what?"

"Cyclone."

The word hangs in the air.

"What is Cyclone?" Deacon inquires.

Zhao's expression empties, his gaze turning distant as if he's witnessing the unfolding of an apocalypse only he can see. "The end," he whispers, the words barely audible over the surrounding din of the food court.

"The end?"

"Yes, the end."

"And what does Cyclone do? How does it bring about the end?"

Zhao's reply is foreboding in its simplicity. "It does what a cyclone always does. It turns things upside down. What was once one way is now another."

A chill runs through the air, unnoticed by the bustling crowd but deeply felt by Peter and Deacon.

Zhao shakes himself and checks his watch. "I don't have much time," he says. "Only once my family and I are safe will I give you everything."

"On Cyclone?"

"Yes. And not just that. I will give you the keys to destroying it."

Understanding dawns on Deacon's features. He nods. "If what you say is true, then I have no other choice but to take you and your family in."

Relief floods the features of Zhao Hung, his tightly coiled body loosening, the jogging foot not so frantic. "Oh, thank you."

Deacon continues, "But we need a plan for your family's extraction. It's not going to be easy with those bodyguards."

Zhao, as it turns out, has already formulated a plan. "We're spending a day at Thong Nai Pan beach in three days' time. The two bodyguards will be driving myself, my wife, and my son in a minivan. The coastal route is long and secluded, enough for you to... intervene."

He scribbles down the details on a napkin, the route, the van, the address of the place they're staying, everything Deacon and the others need to know about the bodyguards.

"And if we pull this off, you're giving us 'the keys to destroying' whatever China has planned, as you put it?" Deacon asks.

"Yes, everything. My knowledge can save the world from disaster."

Their meeting is abruptly drawn to a close by the beep of Zhao's watch, a preset alarm. Zhao stands, casting a nervous glance around the crowded food court. "That's my cue. Remember, Thong Nai Pan beach, three days' time. Survey our villa so that you're right there when we leave. Ensure my family's safety, and I'll deliver what I promise."

With that, Zhao walks off, disappearing into the throng of people, leaving Deacon and Peter to reflect on the weight of their next actions.

Scan the QR code below to purchase GHOST OPERATIVE.
Or go to: righthouse.com/ghost-operative